Last Light Falling

The Covenant

Book I

By

J. E. PLEMONS

Published by Blarney Stone
Publishing 2860 183A Toll Road
Suit 21305
Leander, TX 78641

BLARNEY STONE
PUBLISHING

ISBN: 978-1-7356623-9-8

This book is printed on acid-free paper.

Printed in the United States of America

Library of Congress Cataloging-in-Publications Data
Plemons, J.E.
The Covenant / J.E. Plemons. — 1st ed.
p. cm. — (Last Light Falling series ; bk 1)

Summary: The prophecy of the end is near and it's up to Gabriel and Arena to help prepare the world's demise by the wrath of God. Souls will rest in the providence of these ordinary twins put in an extraordinary situation, but when fate chooses them, they will have to accept their destiny changing their lives forever.

I.Title.
[Fic] — dc22
First edition, March 2014

Dedication

To Melanie, Gabriel, and Mikaela, my loving family, for their encouraging and unyielding support. Thank you for bearing with my relentless and sometimes intolerable labor over this series.

And so it began...

When the Lamb opened the fourth seal, I heard the voice of the fourth living creature say, "Come!" I looked, and there before me was a pale horse! Its rider was named Death, and Hades was following close behind him. They were given power over a fourth of the earth to kill by sword, famine and plague, and by the wild beasts of the earth.

— Revelation 6:7-8

Part I

The Gift

CHAPTER 1

I wake up startled yet again, sweating and horrified by the recurring nightmare that haunts me in my sleep. I've suffered too long to accept this, and unless God Himself reaches down with His hand and changes my fortunes, I'm afraid the nightmares are here to stay.

My bedroom door slowly cracks open, and before I can fix my squinting eyes on it, the sunlight creeps through the dusty curtains and blinds me.

"Wake up, Arena," says a tired but anxiously optimistic voice. "I believe someone has a special day to enjoy."

"Thank you, Myra," I gratefully respond, still half-asleep. "Is Gabe awake?"

"I think he's still in the bathroom. He's been in there for quite some time now." My brother has been spending an inordinate amount of time in the bathroom lately for reasons I would rather not know.

Yes, this is a special day, because it's my fifteenth birthday, but I don't really feel all that special. Not only is my birthday shared with my twin brother, Gabriel, but it's also the same day as the accident—another year, another reminder.

"I made something very special for you this morning. Also, don't forget that you and your brother will be spending the day with Daniel," Myra says enthusiastically.

"Great," I say half-heartedly, trying to be excited about the idea. If it were legal for me to drive, I would, but since I'm only fifteen, I guess being chauffeured around is better than the alternative.

I was born Arena Danielle Power, and to my mother's delight she was graced by the presence of my twin brother,

Gabriel William Power, four minutes later. Technically I'm older since I was introduced to this world before my brother, though I don't think he finds it to be too amusing whenever I mention it. I wouldn't trade Gabe in for anybody in the world. He's all the family I have left, and I love him dearly.

Myra and Daniel Merryman are our foster parents. Even though they can be annoyingly protective sometimes, I really do believe they care for us, and I truly respect them for taking us in. They feed, clothe, and love us. What more can you ask for from what some may call "strangers"? Biological or not, they are loving parents. The two-story house we live in is modest at best, and their financial resources are quite limited, but for the last three years, they have provided us with more than what we had growing up.

Every birthday that comes and goes leaves me more depressed and bitter. I can't tell if it's the idea of living one more year without our parents, or that I start high school in two days. The idea makes me break out in hives. My fifteenth birthday, a milestone in a young woman's life, is the one day I should be excited about, but all I can think about is how I'm going to cope with another school year filled with half-witted socialites.

I slowly get out of bed and dawdle my way to the bathroom, knowing my twin brother is still in there. I delay as much as I possibly can before I knock. There are just some things I don't want to know about boys, especially my brother. I'm sure there is a good explanation as to why he stays in the bathroom for so long. Whether or not it's my obligation to restrain myself from the curiosity as a sister, I can no longer stand here waiting to relieve my bladder.

Enough is enough. I turn the doorknob just enough to feel whether it's locked. Surprisingly, it's not, which leads me to believe nothing shameful is going on in there.

As I open the door, I'm shocked. My brother is standing in front of the mirror, vainly staring at his reflection, making sure every gel-soaked piece of hair has been evenly placed, as if he were doing surgery on a Rogaine client. Gabe is not one to groom himself in the hopes that someone will notice him. He spends more time observing others than worrying about himself, which is why I respect my brother's astute behavior.

Gabe engulfs himself in advanced encryption algorithms, mathematical principles, laws, and theories. Wow, I'm bored just saying that. But if anything, it's the mundane observations and normal teenage experiences that really keep my brother's brain under duress. If there's a problem, then he'll surely find a solution, but not without the common hormonal stress that comes with being a teenage boy. He's never had a girlfriend, unless you count the imaginary Anime characters in the books he frequently drools over at night. Let's face it, my brother is a geek, but I love him just the same. He is family, and I would protect him at all costs.

Gabe is extremely smart, caring, sincere, giving, and selfless. He always wants to do the right thing and would sacrifice his own agenda to help others. I, on the other hand, couldn't be any more the opposite. I'm moody, blunt, selfish, and have no fear. Gabe turns the other cheek when someone knocks him on his ass, whereas I will put my foot up theirs, but I'm trying hard to be more like him.

"Gabe," I say, "what are you doing?"

Gabe looks at me, startled, responding rather shakily, "I . . . uh, just thought I would do something different since, you know, I'm one year closer to manhood."

"Manhood?" I snicker. "Judging by the nicks on your face, I see a careless boy with a razor he shouldn't be using yet." I could have saved him the trouble by plucking that rogue chin hair with my tweezers, but I can see now why he nicked himself—he's using my razor, the one I run up and down my hairy legs every two weeks. If it weren't so socially unpopular I would never shave my legs.

"Deride if you must, but when it comes time, I'll be the one playing the field while you wallow in sadness with your boyish looks."

"Wow, did you really just say *playing the field*?" I say with a churlish eye roll. Gabe knows no more about the play-ing field than he knows how to be a player. I pinch his arm.

"Ow! What did you do that for?"

"Just making sure you're real and not some android pretending to be my brother."

There must be something in the air causing these delusions of his, because I've never known my brother to go to such great lengths to groom for the opposite sex. He's a shy wee lad with the girls, but I guess I should be happy that he's making a concerted effort to change that, even though I'm not too delighted about the *boyish looks* comment. Big deal, so I don't paint my face up like a clown, masking the truth underneath. Who am I hiding from, anyway?

After I wait patiently for Gabe to leave his vain state of mind, I take advantage of the little hot water he so kindly left for me. I quickly bathe the important parts before the cold water forces me to scamper from the shower and into a warm T-shirt and a pair of shorts—my normal attire. I'm not much for fashion, nor do I usually wear makeup—unless it's a special occasion, of course. Although today may be special, it's too damn early in the morning to get all dolled-up.

When I head to my room to brush my hair, I gaze upon a small locket lying on top of a wooden music box. I pick it up and open it as I often do, staring sadly at the picture of my mother inside. As I look at myself in the mirror, I notice some of the same traits I share with her. I sigh. It's all I can do to keep the tears from rolling down my cheeks.

My hair is the color of midnight, and my milky-white skin has turned a light olive from the summer sun. I have my mother's pouty bottom lip and hazel eyes that soften under dim lighting in a continuous spectrum of caramel and green shades. The only feature I don't share with my mother are my thick, dark eyebrows. I really get tired of plucking these hairy caterpillars. I would pluck them for hours, as tears roll down my face from the pain, just so I would fit in with the other girls—but they grow back so fast, it just wasn't worth the pain. I figure it makes me unique, at least that's what I often tell myself. Some days it just doesn't seem too convincing.

I place the locket around my neck and hurry downstairs to meet the other family members. I call them *family* even though we are not related in any way. Our foster parents really have done a lot for us. Since no one has yet adopted us, I feel as though this has been our chosen home. When I reach the living room, I'm surprised to see Niki sitting at the table. She is Myra and Daniel's biological daughter, who has been a special comfort to me. I'm so excited to see her, especially since we've shared a close bond over the last couple of years. I love my brother, but I really needed a big sister in my life to help me through my awkward pre-teen years. I usually hang out with her when she is home, but she is five years older, and work and college have taken much of her time away from the family. Maybe things would be different if she still lived at home.

I wrap my arms around Niki. Whatever bitterness I had this morning has quickly dissipated.

"So, tell me, how does it feel to be fifteen?" Niki asks.

Normally I don't care about my birthday (since the accident), but for some reason, today feels quite special, as if something in my life is about to change. "Feels like I can't wait to turn sixteen so I can get my driver's license," I say, wide-eyed.

As I take a seat at the kitchen table, I fix my eyes on the beautifully decorated strawberry cake topped with fifteen silver sparklers and frosted in red, white, and blue. It looks like Myra went to a lot of trouble to make this for Gabe and me. I have to admit, something does feel different about this morning. This is the first birthday cake we've had since we were nine years old. But I don't much care for cake anymore—not since our parents died on our ninth birthday. Even when Myra and Daniel took us in three years ago, we never celebrated our birthday with a cake. Maybe Myra knew that it would conjure up bad memories because we always started the morning with a birthday breakfast and ended the day with a birthday dinner, but never a cake, which was perfectly fine with me. Why we have one now is puzzling, but I'm not about to ruin the festivities that Myra has so graciously prepared.

When she cuts into the cake, the aroma of fresh strawberries fills the air. As much as I want to eat, I let the slice sit on my plate for a minute, while Gabe devours his. Gazing into that strawberry cream-filled confectionery display extinguishes any thoughts of hunger I had; instead, it conjures up haunting memories I wish I could erase. These recurring nightmares have haunted me for the last six years.

Our ninth birthday couldn't have been more depressing. We had no grandparents to go see that year. My dad lost his job, my mother's sister, Angela, revealed her recent miscarriage, and my parents' lives were taken from us in a car crash. The only thing remotely memorable about that day was the sweet chocolate frosting on the cake. The only present I got to open was a locket that my mother passed down to me from her mother. Gabe and I never had a chance to open any of the remaining presents, and from that point on, my life completely changed.

I don't remember uttering a single word for an entire year. We stayed with our Aunt Angela until I was eleven, but she had a nervous breakdown and became incapacitated, from what I can only assume was a deep depression. Her husband was killed overseas during an undisclosed military training accident, and she hadn't been able to bear any children since her miscarriage. Couple that with the burden of raising two young kids who lost their parents, and I can understand why her life was unsettling. The courts ruled that she was unfit to care for us, so we were sent to a foster home. After a year in the system, we were taken in by Myra and Daniel, our new, and hopefully our last, foster parents. I don't know how Gabe responds, but when I'm asked about my parents, I just hastily say they died. I keep it short and simple. I try to erase the details in my head, but sometimes it's just impossible. Gabe and I were in the car with my parents when it happened. I can recall every detail of that moment. It replays in my head over and over.

That day, the hospital called to tell my father that his mother had a heart attack and was in critical condition. At that moment—when your eyes are open, but you don't see anything except what's rolling through your mind—I had a premonition of a man dressed in black standing in front of a blood-red flag with seven black stripes. Nothing has ever been so tattooed on my mind. My heart suddenly sunk to the floor. I had no idea what it meant or where it came from. That vision was quickly derailed by the scampering of my parents panicking about our grandmother's condition. They insisted we stay at home, but we desperately convinced them otherwise. I couldn't bear the thought of staying at home and waiting impatiently to find out if my only living grandparent was okay.

We quickly ran out the door and raced to the hospital. Imagine what five seconds can do to alter the course of your life. That is all it would have taken to avoid the unthinkable.

My father never ran the old, battered stop sign across the railroad tracks on Wright Street. It was an on-going joke about his Boy-Scout nature when it came to traffic laws. But that day, he raced as fast as he could past the rusted sign. And out of nowhere, we were plowed on the driver's side by a fully packed cement truck. In that one instant, time stopped.

My mother and father turned almost completely around from the sheer brutal impact. My dad's glasses stuck to the ceiling of the car, and I could almost see every bead of broken glass suspended in the air. The car flipped over and over, tossing us like rag dolls. Fortunately, for Gabe and me, our seatbelts secured us tightly.

The impact of the truck was too great for our vehicle to protect my father from his fatal injuries. The airbags failed to deploy, and my father's head smashed into the steering wheel, breaking his neck, and killing him almost instantly. I turned to see if Gabe was hurt; he was disoriented by the crash, but he seemed to be intact, without any visible injuries.

As adrenalin pumped through my veins, I crawled out the shattered window to get to my mother. The ceiling was caved in, and I couldn't reach her in the front seat. As I opened the smashed-in passenger door, I saw her eyes fighting to stay open, as blood dripped down from the side of her head and ear. She was almost unrecognizable. I knew right away she sustained severe internal injuries by the way she was grimacing and holding her side. I knew she was dying.

My insides shriveled as my mother gasped for one last breath of life. I tightly held her face, sobbing until my tear ducts ran dry and irritated. The adrenaline was quickly wearing off, and so was my will to sit up. My body couldn't stabilize me anymore, so I collapsed to the ground and stayed there until the ambulance came.

The choices we make decide the fate of our destiny. Today is the beginning of mine, and it's all too depressing to try and understand the significance, if there is any.

As I continue to gaze intently at the colorful festive cake on the table, it dawns on me. I remember what Niki told me last summer during the Fourth of July festival.

Myra had another daughter named Grace, Niki's younger sister. Grace was the perfect student and model citizen. She was the most caring and giving individual in her community. She gave up every bit of her spare time, helping others even when she didn't have to and asking for nothing in return. She had the fervor and vigor to take on the world with compassion, and she didn't care what it took to do it. She sacrificed every ounce of her life to change people with her kindness, even if it meant changing only one person. I truly believe she was chosen for a much-needed cause in this world that many of us so seemingly avoid—selflessness.

On the early evening of July fourth, Grace's fifteenth birthday, she finished a long day of volunteering at the homeless shelter and couldn't wait to go home for her family's annual firework festivities. On her way back to the car where Niki was waiting, Grace fell lifeless on the pavement. A gunshot to the head killed her instantly. It was a useless act of bloodshed that had nothing to do with her—

it was collateral damage resulting from a gang dispute. An innocent victim plagued by yet another string of street violence.

Myra never mentioned anything about Grace's death, nor did I feel the need to ask. I feel somewhat cold and hardened inside every time I think about it, and it's all I can do to muster up a quick smile before anyone notices. While I try to enjoy the rest of the morning birthday celebration, I can't help but notice Myra's glassy eyes as she smiles. Could this specially baked gesture actually be a broken memory from the death of her daughter? As I stare at her right now, it saddens me to imagine what's going on in her mind. I too have that broken-heartedness. Ever since Niki told me about Grace, I prayed deep inside that Gabe and I could stay forever with Myra and Daniel. Regardless of how Gabe may feel about wanting to be adopted, I allow my selfishness to terminate any of those hopes because of the kinship of brokenness I share with Myra. She loves me just as much as my real mother loved me.

As I stare motionless at the rest of the uncut cake, covered in red, white and blue frosting, I realize now the emotional attachment that I share with Myra will not easily be broken. Aside from our last name scripted in black icing, I wonder if this is what Grace's cake may have looked like on her fifteenth birthday. Suddenly, I don't feel like eating, yet I feel compelled for Myra's sake. As strange as it may seem to be eating birthday cake at 8:00 in the morning, it's worth it to see Myra's face light up like my mother's.

CHAPTER 2

The meaning of our last name—Power—never sparked any interest until this morning, but somehow our last name that's scripted on the cake has roused a curiosity. I know that both my mother and father were born in Ireland before moving to the States, so we obviously have Irish blood, but *Power* just doesn't seem to speak "Irish surname." It sounds more like the last name of a superhero.

The curiosity begins to eat at me as I enjoy my slice of sugary decadence. I look up at Myra and smile with approval. "You've outdone yourself, Myra. I don't think I've ever eaten anything quite like this. It's pure, sugary heaven."

"Yes," agrees Gabe with his mouth stuffed.

"Thank you for all the trouble you went through to make this for us," I kindly acknowledge. I know she must be thinking about Grace when she smiles at our every indulgence.

"You are both very welcome. Fifteen is a very special year," says Myra.

I imagine she's thinking of her fifteen-year-old daughter. Maybe that's why she made the cake—to enjoy the thought of remembering Grace in me. I get up from the table and hug Myra, and out of nowhere, I whisper in her ear, "I love you, Mom." She squeezes me with acceptance, not saying a word, as if those three words didn't shock her. This is the first time I called her anything but Myra. I don't know why I said it, but it felt good to say.

The curiosity of our last name is still killing me, so I quickly excuse myself and go back upstairs to my room. I search the Internet, and I'm shocked to find what my last name means. Not what I was thinking at all—in fact, it suits us just fine. "The Poor Man," I say with a slight eye roll. It's evident that we were perfectly chosen for this name.

We were born to Abigail and William Power. Growing up, we had little to nothing in the way of clothing and food. My dad worked at a cement plant day and night, and barely made enough for us to eat well. My mother educated and nurtured us and did what she could for our family, but her health prohibited her from working. It hurt her so dearly not being able to help with the income. She did, however, prove extremely valuable to our education.

We were homeschooled before we started the second grade at public school. My mother was a brilliant woman. Before she could finish her PhD in linguistics, her health deteriorated quickly, keeping her bedridden for quite some time. The summer before my seventh birthday, she was diagnosed with Multiple Sclerosis. Every year that withered away, so did a little of my mother, who I deeply adored. When my mom left this earth, a part of me went with her, and I haven't been the same since.

She was determined to teach us multiple languages when we were young. I think it made her feel better, teaching us as a continuation of her education. Her well-trained, educated tongue taught us how to fluently speak Russian and French. It became second nature to Gabe and me, especially Gabe. There wasn't anything he couldn't absorb in that swollen brain of his. I never thought much about learning a different language at the time because we were so young, and I don't know of what value it serves for us now, except for the little joking chit-chat Gabe and I share when we don't want anyone to know what we are saying. It's sort of our secret language.

Other than a little Italian, Irish Gaelic is the only other language that Gabe and I speak to one another. This is a sacred language our Uncle Finnegan taught us when he was home from Iraq, waiting to be deployed again. For three years, my Uncle Finnegan, my mother's brother, stayed with us during his retreat. He loved my mother so much that when her health was diminishing, he promised to care for her whenever he was sent home. He never married, but he always kept family a priority.

We lived in a house that was short of sub-standard living conditions. I owned three outfits and one pair of shoes that had been glued, taped, and stapled more than once in their long, miserable, pathetic existence. My mother couldn't work because of her condition, and my father's income was just enough to supply us with the basic needs. I never knew what poor was until I went to school. Comparing myself to others around me was absolutely depressing. Kids could be cruel, with their contemptuous remarks at my expense. I loathed every moment I had to walk the uninviting halls to my classes.

Ironically enough, the first school I ever attended gave a poverty-stricken impression, which reflected nothing of the kids who went there. The sunken ceiling was spattered with water stains that cast certain artistic figures if seen at the right angle, just as the ones we used to see in the clouds when we were younger and more imaginative. Unfortunately, social popularity replaces that when you get older.

The dingy walls looked as if they hadn't been washed in decades. Most of the dirt was plastered with eroded tape that once held educational posters from years past, only to be replaced by new ones peppered throughout the halls. Yet none of this seemed to distract my presence from the banter that would ensue. As much as the name-calling, vicious taunting, and snarls contributed to my vulnerable insecurities, the disgusted stares from girls frightened me the most— as if I had the plague. I knew right then I was going to be their designated target for the rest of the school year. Though I tried painfully hard not to let them see that it bothered me, inside I was broken, even angry at times with my parents, because they didn't make any effort to clothe us better. It wasn't their fault, though, and my anger toward them was unjust.

I didn't have many clothes, but I always seemed to have a dress for special occasions, which I would begrudg- ingly wear to please my mother. I absolutely hate wearing dresses. I find it cumbersome to pose like a statuette for others, restraining myself from getting dirty, or, God forbid, sitting with my legs uncrossed.

One time, when I was eight, I was invited to Shelly Baskins's birthday party. I was among girls whose social status was indicative of their behavior. They all seemed so comfortable in their lavishly extravagant dresses, while I awkwardly wore my homemade attire.

Before opening presents, we all gathered outside, where the backyard resembled more of an enchanted forest than your typical half-maintained lawn. I had to restrain myself from naturally wanting to squat and pee behind a bush like I did when I was out hunting. Now, I normally use indoor plumbing when convenient, but when I'm in the woods, nothing feels quite as natural as relieving yourself among nature. I restrained myself from doing that, of course, for the courtesy of others.

Shelly Baskins—I really hated that girl. Okay, hate is a strong word, but I badly wanted to spit in her food, if not on her smug face. She was the rich girl at my school who would undoubtedly let you know it. If you weren't part of her circle of friends, you were teased, taunted, and ridiculed unmercifully. I was invited only because my mother and Shelly's mom knew each other, and Shelly had a crush on Gabe, but I know it tore her up inside to have to invite me just to see Gabe. Really, eight years old and having a crush on a boy. I thought boys were disgusting at that age. What made her so special?

This was the same person who purposefully spilled grape juice on my white blouse at the Christmas pageant, the one who deceitfully dripped candle wax in my hair, leaving it virtually unmanageable for a week. Oh, I absolutely detested Shelly, with her insufferable childish pranks, but I felt sorry for her at the same time. Six months later, her mother was diagnosed with terminal cancer. As angry as I was about her menacing hatred toward me, seeing her cry uncontrollably at school over her mother's fate changed my heart for her. I knew what it was like to have someone very dear to you become ill and helpless. In that instant, I forgave her for all that she had done to me. After that day, we never spoke again.

I'm usually fishing, hunting, practicing martial arts, or playing sports while other girls worship their nails with fancy polish, or prancing around like Disney princesses until someone notices them. I try hard to hide my figure, not flaunt it in a constricted dress.

I may be a little rough around the edges, but I'm not oblivious to the fact that I'm still a girl. In fact, I've unfortunately developed physically much faster than the other girls my age. Some call it a blessing, while I see it as a curse. I don't need boys gawking at me for approval, nor do I see them as equals, intellectually speaking, of course.

I don't hate guys—in fact, if the right one does exist, I'll snatch him up in a heartbeat. I just don't see the need to drool over knuckle-dragging Neanderthals who want to pry into more than just my thoughts. My body is sacred, and it should be treated as so. I'm not at all afraid of guys; I can handle them just fine. It's the catty girls I detest, and they don't seem to mind teasing you and giving you a complex until you develop an eating disorder. Girls can be absolutely cruel to one another. I can only imagine what my brother must have gone through with his personal bullies.

My brother is frail and meek. He is the kind of person who will help you out when you least expect it and never expect anything in return. When he is being picked on, he retracts quickly and recoils with kindness out of defense. He's a bit delusional about his peers. He tries hard to see the good in them and somehow change their ill will toward him without dispute. Even though I agree with him, it doesn't come as natural to me. I guess people like him and Grace are badly needed in this world if it's to survive.

He is one of the smartest fourteen-year-old kids I know, excuse me, now fifteen. He will never admit it because of his humble nature, but his gift is surely that of intelligence. He tested off the charts during an IQ test when he was ten years old. Periodically, my brother saw a specialist to monitor his mental and behavioral growth when he was younger.

Gabe had a condition when he was born. The swelling on his brain was considered life threatening, and the doctors told my parents that he would unlikely survive the first year of his life. I don't know why, but my mother never told us until his motor skills and general IQ were first tested. His level of intelligence at that time clearly enticed doctors and specialists to evaluate him daily. It wasn't until my mother insisted that he was left alone after a month of prodding.

Gabe often felt sick and depressed every time he was taken to the specialists. I think deep inside he pretended to be sick and non-responsive during that month just so he could be back at home. He would purposefully fail tests to avoid being a lab rat for the rest of his young years. Smart as he is, he is still a boy at heart.

I, on the other hand, have deep-seated anger toward anyone who pushes my brother around. I'm not as forgiving as Gabe, though the humbling experiences in my life have greatly changed that. I know revenge is something we were taught to avoid, but I'm strong enough to defend myself and do whatever is necessary to protect my family, especially my bullied brother. Though we're twins, I still feel like a big sister.

I was taught by the best in combat training from Uncle Finnegan, who was a former Special Ops leader, but martial arts has changed the way I defend myself.

When Finnegan stayed with us those three years before our parents died, he taught me and Gabe the essentials of survival. Though it may have seemed a bit nonsensical for our age, I never once questioned our time together.

I think Gabe was actually more helpful to Finnegan than Finnegan was to him. Finnegan always had a knack for encouraging our gifts, and Gabe's certainly never went unnoticed. Finnegan was always impressed by some of the technological advances in Gabe's inventions, and he would almost demand that Gabe show off some of his gadgets to his special teams' coordinator. But Gabe was extremely protective of his inventions, and because he didn't have a patent on any of them, he kept them to himself.

He still invents today, but not with the same passion he had before. I believe it's his way of coping with the loss of our parents.

I've seen what Gabe can do. It's not only impressive; it's a joy watching someone practice what they were gifted to do. Talent shouldn't be wasted, and if I could just figure out what mine is, I'd be more than happy to pursue it. I do recognize some of my gifts, but I don't necessarily know how I would ever use them for a career. I'm excellent with knives, archery, hand-to-hand combat, and just about any kind of hand gun, most of which I learned from Finnegan. Not that I'm trying to boast about my skills, I just feel quite confident about them and it comes natural to me, just like physics comes naturally to Gabe.

An eight year old playing with throwing knives probably isn't ideal, but it was the childhood I had come to know. I know my parents wouldn't have approved of Finnegan teaching me such things, but it's what I was good at. I would practice every day out in the woods, far enough away so my mother wouldn't suspect anything. Finnegan and I kept it our little secret. That's just how he bonded with me. Parental guidance wasn't his strong suit, but I guess being in the military most of your life and having no kids blinds you to common sense.

Although my mother didn't have a clue about all the weapons Finnegan exposed me to at an early age, she was very grateful for his presence while my father was away most of the time working. Regardless of the paternal detachment I may have had growing up, it was Finnegan who taught me the fundamentals of self-sufficiency. I don't begrudge my father for not being around. I realized how hard he worked to keep our family surviving, but it would have been nice to be around him more while I was young.

Finnegan taught me very well about the art of warfare, how to be invisible to my enemies, and sly enough to be virtually unseen to the deadliest killer. This is probably why I didn't play with dolls all that much as a kid, or have tea parties with the neighborhood girls, because of Finnegan's nonsensical way of living vicariously through me, as if I was the son he always wanted. I guess he noticed right away that I had the potential to be an efficient and effective hunter. He taught me how to hunt for food and not sport. I'm absolutely opposed to sport hunting. The idea carries no sensible purpose, and I detest the very thought of it. I knew of several hunters in town who took pleasure in killing for the fun of it, and I was all too eager to let Finnegan know about it. When I was eight years old, Finnegan showed me and Gabe how to counter such scum.

We would set trip wires along the tree line of the back bank where most of the deer would stroll. This was the only creek in the area that wasn't dry. Finnegan knew exactly where the poachers would set up for the best line of sight to the deer. He was always one step ahead of them.

We set up decoys in that line of sight, just across the creek. They looked incredibly real, and no one would ever know the difference. When the hunters came to the spot that Finnegan said they would, it was all too easy to deceive those rednecks. After shots were fired, striking the decoys down, the idiots quickly ran toward their kill, half-drunk of course, tripping the lines we set. From there it was too hilarious not to laugh, yet I restrained myself by covering my mouth with my shirt so we weren't heard.

The tripped wires gave way to a large, rotting branch as our counter weight that was slightly supported by a steel rod. When the lines were pulled by the hunters' feet, the steel flung out like a cannon shot, leaving the half-ton branch falling with force and pulling a net, camouflaged with leaves, up in the air with our prey. The hunters became the hunted, and I reveled in every minute of it. My sides delightfully hurt from the laughter, seeing beards and butt cracks pressed tightly against the hanging mesh. That was probably the last time I ever laughed that hard with enjoyment.

Before Finnegan was deployed, he left me with his mentor and good friend, Henry Matsuda, to make sure I continued with my martial arts training. I guess he knew something I didn't, but nevertheless, I greatly enjoyed it, and I have been training ever since three to four times a week. Henry is a very understanding teacher when it comes to managing time, but when we are training, he unremittingly pushes me to the point of exhaustion. While it wears me out, I crave enough of it to come back for more—it's an addiction. Not only does it make me stronger, it keeps me from drowning further into depression after the death of my parents. I train, while Gabe invents. Mask or not, this is how we cope from the madness inside.

It's been nearly five years since we've seen Finnegan. Apparently, he was needed for a highly classified special ops arrangement, but we never heard from him again. Not a sin- gle letter, call, or visit. No one knew where he was, and the government never shed any light on the subject. I could only conclude one of two things: his location and status was top secret and kept hidden from kin, or he was dead. As much as I wanted to believe the former, I heavily considered the later as reality. That's about the time when the unrest started here in America.

It's 2053 in the year of our Lord, and much has changed in our nation's capital in the last six years. The providence of our democracy has diminished, and yet they glean it to be well preserved. Our precious government has weakened our country, empowering other nations to take strong measures in changing the very foundation it was built on. The freedom that we as a people who have shed our blood for, struggled to maintain, and even waged war in an effort to keep its exis- tence no longer stands strong.

The deep roots holding this country together have been poisoned by greed, power, and the governing evil that prevents us from making civil choices. We have become a nation that heavily depends on others to stay afloat in this economical downfall. Ever since the great quakes shook the Earth four years ago, killing hundreds of millions across the world, including our very own nation, it has destroyed any selfless desire to recoup. With the San Andreas Fault collapse leaving most of California completely under water, killing nearly seventeen million people, and the New Madrid fault line scarring the central part of the country, killing more than eleven million, America has experienced a catastrophic economic collapse.

Cash no longer exists and has been replaced by credits, a government-designed monetary system that allows us to earn points based on the contributions we provide to the federal government. The CCD, Central Credits Distribution, which is networked throughout the entire nation, automatically deposits funds to your identification card based on salary or hourly pay from your job. Much in that aspect works the same as it had before—you work and you get paid, except with credit points. When these points are added to our identification cards, the government evaluates each individual, knowing what each person is worth to them.

They keep close tabs on anyone they feel is suspicious for what they are buying, or, more importantly, where they buy it. The freedom we thought we had has vanished. Unfortunately, many people are still convinced, naïve, delusional, or just plain brainwashed that the government is looking out for our every need. I guess the only freedom we have left is whether or not we blindly accept it.

Social security no longer exists. The money that was invested was needed for the loss of bank funds during the economic collapse. High-debt credit cards were pardoned by the government in an attempt to help save the economy. After the economy dipped too low for the country to maintain its value, other nations surprisingly aided us, but for a heavy price. That was when our country turned from its own principles we worked so hard for, changing our ideology forever.

Other nations strongly suggested that we were better off working in unity than divided if we were to preserve the world's economy. We were one of the few nations left to commit to the credit-point system.

The middle class is all but gone, and America has dwindled down to class wars. The social order has labeled our worth into four categories: politically rich, wealthy, poor, or a Watcher.

The politically rich are those who either contribute to or work for the federal government. They are treated quite well for their contributions. Wealthy exists as it always has— those who inherited riches. And then there's us—the poor, a term I should be used to, but despite the negative connotations it has had in the past, it's not even on the same level as the poverty-stricken towns that exist today. These are filled with "Watchers," a derogatory term for someone who takes up space, contributing nothing for the better of the nation, only to sit and watch as onlookers pass by.

"Watchers" is an expression we have unfortunately infused in the vernacular today. Some people still refer to them as "homeless," as was the term in the past. Those are the people I have more compassion for. Most are unable to work or can't even function among the public because of mental, physical, or emotional illness and depression. The government holds no loyalty or concern for those who don't contribute to their gluttonous ways.

Just like Gabe, I have a heart for these people. I ask myself every day how any person has the right to judge someone before they even know them, but more than that, my brother will always remind me that we shouldn't judge anyone at all.

During the early years of the newly founded government, many Watchers were killed for just existing. This was the government's way of intimidating people into thinking that if they worked hard, they would reap the rewards, and if they failed to contribute to society, they would be exterminated. It was also a message to those who questioned the philosophies of the nation's new direction. America is no longer a great nation—it has become a mockery governed by spineless, godless, self-absorbed creatures.

Poor or not, I'm proud of the name that was given to us and the heritage it derives from. I just lie quietly on the bed and soak up the silence for a minute. It's so quiet and peaceful right now, I can hear the second hand clicking on the clock hanging above me, and every few seconds a robin perched outside by my window sings a tune. The silence almost immediately evaporates as my brother's clogging feet rumble up the stairs. I never have to worry about Gabe trying to sneak up on me. I can hear his heavy shuffling a hundred feet away.

There is a surprising knock at my door, yet I know it can't be Gabe because manners isn't necessarily a quality trait he subscribes to. "Come in," I say softly.

"Hey, Scrapes," Niki calls with a smile.

Scrapes was a nickname my father gave me when I was a kid. Judging by the name, apparently I skinned my knees quite often. I had no fear of getting cut, bruised, or scraped. It was one of the first things I ever shared with Niki. I was shy when we were taken in, and it was her presence and gentleness that bonded us. I knew whenever she called me by that name she had something important to share with me.

"I have something I want to give you," she says. She walks over to the bed and sits next to me just like my mother did when she comforted me after I had a bad day at school.

"Here, I want you to have this," Niki says. "It's a friendship bracelet my sister, Grace, wore. I have one just like it. We got these a year before she died, and it was our special way of knowing we had each other's back."

Speechless, I hesitate a little from accepting the gift because of what it means to Niki.

"Thank you, I shall never take this off my wrist," I say as a tear tries to escape from my eye.

"I know we are not biological sisters, but it doesn't matter to me. You're my little sister no matter what, and I will always love you."

I know how much Grace meant to her. I know deep inside she somehow blames herself for letting Grace go alone to the shelter that day. The tear that was hanging on for dear life scurries down my cheek. I hug Niki and don't want to let go. I want to feel like this for eternity.

"Hey, you're fifteen now. I'm not going to let you go to your first day of high school without something unique to wear," says Niki joyfully. She pulls out a colored sack from behind her back, and I excitedly look through its contents. It's a brand-new black skirt and shirt lined with tiny diamond sequins, and a pair of black boots with laces and buckles. These boots were made for me. They look like something I would hunt in, and yet they have a girlish appeal. This must have set her points back a little, because the boots alone must have cost her 100 credits.

"I have to go to work now, but I will be back tonight," Niki says.

"I don't know what to say . . . you have done so much for me. Thank you, sister." As I hug her once more before she leaves, I know right then that God placed Gabe and me here with this family for a reason.

"Arena," calls Daniel, coming up the stairs, "we are leaving for the library in about ten minutes; I'll go tell your brother. Oh, and, uh, I almost forgot, this came in the mail for you yesterday."

He hands me a padded envelope addressed to me, but with no return address. I'm a little apprehensive about opening mail that doesn't have a return address. I've read too many horror stories about letters being sent out to random people and exploding upon opening. I'm too paranoid to open it, but the curiosity is killing me. I let it sit there on my bed for a minute, still hesitant to look inside, while I put on my shoes and wait for Daniel to leave the room.

"Well, I'm not going to know if I don't open it," I say to myself. I look inside the envelope and find a letter that has been folded twice. It's covered in some sort of thin black material that shimmers. It's anx-lead mesh, a material that was created to shield plant workers from radiation in the nuclear factories in Russia. Finnegan told Gabe and I about the discovery of anx-lead in the Russian mines. I remember because he wore a jacket lined with it when he first came back from Iraq, and I kept inquiring about the material, annoying him to the point that he had no choice but to tell us what it was.

It feels so smooth, but why is it wrapped around this letter? And better yet, why is it in an envelope marked to me with no return address? There's something hard in the folded letter, an impression of what feels like a key. As I unfold the letter, a silver key drops out, and the blood rushes out of my body as if someone is draining my soul. I sit there on the bed stunned, as if every muscle in my body has contracted all at once.

Three words are written on the letter: *I'm still alive.*

CHAPTER 3

I stare at the letter, wondering where it came from and who sent it to me. Maybe I'm a bit delusional from the mass exodus of blood from my head, but could this have come from Finnegan? Whoever sent this wanted to make sure the key was masked with the anx-lead mesh. This is possibly the only way the key could be virtually undetected by the x-ray machines during the mailing inspections. The government has reduced the amount of material that can be shipped or mailed due to heavy speculation of possible terrorist activity. Anything slightly unusual and it's normally destroyed and traced back for some outrageous interrogation.

There's a cluster of numbers at the bottom of the paper separated by peculiar dashes. Puzzled, I try to convince myself that this letter was mistakenly sent to me, but how conceivable is it for parcel service to switch mailing labels? And if they did, whose package do I have and where is the package I was supposed to receive? The shock has worn off a little, and I've acknowledged the fact that there is no mistake. This was purposefully sent to me, but why?

I hear the rumbling of feet again, and Gabe comes rushing through my door. "Are you ready to go or what?" he badgers.

As I turn to him, I nonchalantly hide the letter underneath my thigh, hoping he won't notice.

"What did you get in the mail, a birthday package?" he inquires. I respond only with a confused look on my face. "The opened envelope is on the floor, and the letter is sticking out of your shorts."

I love my brother to death, but he can be a meddling little ass. But, I got to hand it to him, he has a keen eye even compared to the most observant of people. He's beyond observant; in fact, his intuitive nature has given him a strength I wish I had. He can sense when something bad is going to happen. Though sometimes eerie, his gift has benefited us more often than not.

I remember the first time he saved my life. Two years ago, we were walking home from school and decided to take a shortcut through the back street of Devine's Rock and Fence Company. Gabe's instinctive senses stopped us in our tracks, turned us in a different direction, altering our course and saving us from being crushed. Five seconds later, an overloaded forklift lost its balance and dropped two tons of limestone where we would have been walking. He hasn't been able to explain how he sees things before they happen. And it's never at a time you want it to happen, but at a time that is unexpected, yet purposefully necessary.

"Can you please keep this between you and me? I don't want Myra or Daniel to know about this. I don't know what to make of it, and I'm a little freaked out," I say quietly, wrinkling my brow.

Gabe studies the letter intently and without hesitation, he immediately notices the groups of numbers. "These numbers are coordinates. The first set of numbers is most likely latitude, and the second set of numbers is longitude," he says without doubt. "But I have no idea who is supposed to still be alive and why."

"You don't suppose this is from Finnegan, do you?

"Finnegan? Even if he is alive, why would he send you this. Besides, it's not like Finnegan to be so cryptic."

"Who else could it be?"

"I don't know, but it's obvious they want you to find out."

"What do you suppose these coordinates have to do with this key? Do you think the key could open up whatever is at those coordinates?" I wonder.

"Possibly, I say we check it out," says Gabe anxiously.

"Whoa, wait a minute." I stand up. "We're still speculating it's someone we know. What if it's just bait from some child molester? I'm curious about what this key may open, but I'm still a little uneasy about the situation," I retort.

"Arena! Gabriel! It's time to go!" shouts Daniel from downstairs.

"Take the letter with you, and we'll figure out the coordinates at the library," says Gabe.

I grab the letter, fold it back up with the key inside, and stick it in my pocket. I quickly run downstairs and out the door, but before I can get into the car, my feet stop in their tracks. The corner of my eye is suddenly occupied by a shadow standing beside a tree.

A man dressed in a long, black robe is staring in my direction. For just a slight moment, I hesitate to get in the car. It's a priest, but he notices I'm fixed on him now, so he walks away.

"Arena, get in," says Daniel.

Almost hypnotized by what I see, I quickly come to and get in the car. A priest walking in our neighborhood, staking out our house, is odd, but there's something very familiar about that man. I'm having a case of déjà vu.

"What's up with you? You still freaked out about the letter?" whispers Gabe.

"You didn't see that priest by the tree staring at us?"

"No, what priest?"

Okay, now I'm more than a little freaked out, because the most observant person I know didn't even notice the random priest standing near the bushes. Did I imagine it? I can only think about one thing right now, and that's trying to figure out what the hell this letter means.

Gabe and I are always at the library every Saturday. Every chance we have, that is where we want to be. Since there really is no place around here in the city to hunt, nor is there any need to, reading has become the next best thing in my life. I made a pact with Myra and Daniel; as long as I maintain good grades, I can train with Henry as much as I want. And the library is just the place to exercise my brain.

Carrington, a small northeast Texas city, looks old and depressing, but it's vibrant during the daytime. At night, though, it becomes a ghost town due to the government's nationwide curfew—another one of the major changes this country has had to suffer through. Everyone plans their time carefully, choosing to do most of their shopping during mid-morning. Federal officers are spread out like ants, monitoring civilians' behaviors. If you are caught in public past the 9:00 curfew, you are subject to a minor violation if it's your first offense, but you will be arrested and sentenced to farm labor if it's your second.

I've heard stories of farm laborers being deprived of food and water and even submitted to public beatings. Of course, government officials deny any abuse and explain that those who are punished are hardened criminals. Contrary to public opinions of our patriotic protection, I've seen with my own eyes a man being pounded unmercifully by clubs in a restaurant alley for taking food from the dumpster. Beaten unrelentingly for simply surviving is repulsive and absolutely unwarranted.

I know I was taught to reserve judgment, but to witness this act of cruelty is unjust. Our government uses these types of tactics to intimidate and nothing else. To extract its own people in order to advance the nation's image is an abomination that I will not conform to. I have no respect for our new government's direction, nor do I put any faith into the people they chose to perpetuate it.

The anxiety of revealing the location of these coordinates is stirring in my stomach even more. As we pull up to the library, Gabe cautiously places his hand on mine and squeezes with mild force. "I feel something unnerving," Gabe says with a look of concern on his face.

"Like what?" I say.

"I don't really know, I . . . I can't see it, but feel as if someone—"

"Someone is following us," I quickly finish his thought.

"Yes, how did you know?"

"I've had that same feeling ever since we left the house." I feel uneasy. The imaginary priest that Gabe didn't see behind the tree has been gnawing at me.

As we get out of the car, Daniel's phone rings. He seems a bit upset and is pacing back and forth. When he hangs up the phone, he turns to us, a look of disgust written on his face. "I've been called in to work," he gruffs. "There has been some kind of emergency, and apparently I'm needed. I'm truly sorry, guys; I hope you can forgive me."

I chime in with confidence, as if I have a brilliant solution to the quandary, "Gabe and I can take the bus back home when we are done. It's no problem, we've done this before. We know our way around this place. It's not like we're kids anymore." Gabe nods in agreement, and Daniel hesitates for a moment, looking at the few federal officers to our right.

"Okay, you promise me you will be back before curfew? I'll let Myra know just in case of an emergency," Daniel says.

When Daniel drives away, I smile and suddenly realize how much he respects and trusts us. With what happened to Grace, I imagine how hard it would be to allow us to be on our own. This is truly the first step we've taken to prove our responsibility to our overly protective but caring foster parents. I quickly turn to Gabe with my brow furrowed, "Don't screw this up."

The town's library is vast and ornately decorated. It dwarfs other buildings next to it and makes the dilapidated courthouse even less appealing. The detailed granite fixtures that protrude from the upper ledge of the library tell a story of the ancient Greek culture. Every recessed panel of stone is engraved with a depiction of a Greek god. As fascinating as it is on the outside, it's additionally grand on the inside, where the stately halls are extensive and the ceiling towers over you majestically. Portraits of kings line the hallways, and almost every floor tile is hand painted with images representing the ages of humanity and the wars that forever changed them.

Gabe and I quietly walk up to the second floor where the computers are located. I secretly hand the letter to Gabe so he can look up the GPS coordinates that hopefully will answer some questions.

I'm so nervous; I get out of my chair and pace the aisle of books. I weave my way down the religion aisle and press my head against the shelf until I see a book that catches my eye—*The Book of Solomon*. I take it off the shelf, but before I can open it, I gasp. The same priest, who was standing outside our house, is pacing back and forth across the aisle.

I quickly retreat behind the other books. Just so I know I'm not imaging this, I creep my head up to take a second look. I can see him from the side, placing a book back on the shelf, and it just hit me like a ton of bricks. I remember this man from before—I saw him years ago at the Foster Care Center.

I remember him talking to one of the administrators with an elevated voice. He seemed very concerned about something, and I remember the director of the Care Center coming over to calm him down. I don't remember anything after that, but I know this is the same man. I gather my thoughts and walk quickly over to where Gabe is looking up the coordinates.

"Did you find anything?" I say, panting.

"Yes . . . what's wrong with you? You look like just saw a ghost."

"It's nothing, I'll tell you later. Did you get any information?" I ask again.

Gabe's forehead quickly crinkles. "Yes, it's printing right now, but—"

"No buts. Let's go right now, come on."
I shove the letter in my pocket, grab Gabe by the arm, and snatch the printed directions from the printer. We carefully scurry downstairs without anyone noticing we are in a hurry. We reach the basement floor, where all the periodicals are kept, making sure to look behind us every so often to ensure that no one is following us.

"Okay, what's going on? Tell me now," says Gabe intrusively.

"I saw that priest upstairs, the same one I told you about in the car on the way over here," I say, flustered.

"Okay, okay, I believe you, but what makes you think he is following . . ." Gabe pauses and remembers what he said earlier, before we got out of the car.

"Exactly. You knew this. It's what you were feeling," I concur.

"Look, let's just stay down here for a little while and figure out this map before we make too much out of this," Gabe calmly says.

We sit down at one of the unoccupied tables to decipher the coordinates. It's so drab and dark down here, we have to turn on one of the table lamps. As we look at the directions, we notice that these coordinates are less than fifteen miles from here. The aerial view reveals an old, white building covered by trees. A gravel road connects the building to a small county road where it's fenced off. It's hard to tell from the picture, but it appears that most of the road has been covered up.

"So what's the plan?" asks Gabe.

"I think we need to lay low for a little while. I don't want Myra or Daniel getting suspicious, especially with the trust we've finally established with them. I need a while to think about this. We have no way of getting there except on foot, and I'm not about to walk fifteen miles there and back, risking getting caught past curfew," I suggest.

We stay in the basement a little while longer until I feel it's safe for us to go back upstairs. I'm still a little suspicious of the priest who I think is following us, and I won't hesitate to do whatever is necessary to protect my brother. Maybe he is or maybe he isn't following us, but it just seems too much of a coincidence that the same priest who was at the Care Center arguing with our foster coordinator was near our house and now at the library. Servant to deity or not, I feel a responsibility to defend my family against all walks of life. If there was anything I was taught of value from Finnegan, it was to have an innate awareness of deceptions. Evil prowls on the tempted, and what may seem impossible most certainly can be.

With no signs of the priest wandering around the aisles, we spend most of our time in the library reading. I could spend my whole life in here and never become bored. There are so many things I want to learn about, so I just dive into the first book off the shelf that interests me. I'm reading Paleo-Hebrew inscriptions from Jonathan Bell's *The Ancient Hebrew Culture*, while Gabe loses himself in a Dan Bricklin technology book.

While I'm reading, I glimpse over and notice three girls coming toward us. Two of them recognize Gabe and snicker back and forth to each other. They are dressed in what one could only call trendy to the point of begging for attention. Anything else would fetch the fashion police or may otherwise tarnish their prestige. I think I may vomit now.

The leader of the group appears more confident, distinguishing herself from the other two girls, flaunting her double-slutting attire, a term I picked up from Niki. Apparently, it means to expose two sexy areas, like your chest and legs at the same time. "Dear God, kill me now," I say under my breath.

My first impression is that they have never seen a library before, much less a book, and stopped here only to get directions to the nearest mall. As judgmental as that sounds, I quickly try to erase any negative impression I had and offer a friendly gesture of hospitality.

"Hi, I'm Arena, and this is my brother, Gabe," I say in a friendly manner. I spoke for Gabe's sake, because I know he's shy around girls, especially attractive ones. Before I'm able to welcome them to join us, I get a crooked snarl from the leader followed by eye rolls from her entourage. I take it my generosity has gone unnoticed.

They walk past me as if I don't exist, and stand next to Gabe by the computer consoles. "Hi, sweetie, you mind if we just slip by here and use this computer?" the leader seductively says to Gabe. I don't think I've ever seen Gabe's jawbone retract that far. His catatonic state is almost unbecoming, as his eyes are strenuously transfixed on her ridiculously exposed cleavage.

I do believe if this girl wasn't such an attention-seeking slut, any other girl would have slapped Gabe's eyes from his sockets already. "Sure," Gabe spits out.

"He's cute in a nerdy kind of way," one of the girls says, as the other girl shares her sentiment with an agreeable nod. Gabe may have the attributes of a geek, but he's still an attractive-looking guy, even if he is my brother. It's only fitting for these half-witted snobs to use the library for social networking instead of its original intention.

"Come on, Gabe, it's getting late, we better go," I say, trying to avoid eye contact with the girls.

"Now, I don't think that's your decision. Gabe can think for himself," chimes in the leader firmly.

Okay, now I'm just pissed. I have the ability to crack this bitch's neck in half if I truly wanted to, but I'm really working hard at turning the other cheek like Gabe has taught me.

I turn to Gabe and speak in Russian. He knows I'm mad if I'm speaking in another language, and Russian isn't exactly a dialectal tongue I use to express kind words with. "If you don't get up now and leave with me, I'm going to put my foot up that girl's ass and use it for a slipper," I coarsely say.

Gabe immediately gets up from the chair, nearly falling over, and apologizes to the girls. "I'm sorry; you'll have to forgive us. It's been a long day, and we really have to get back home."

The leader smiles at Gabe and turns to me with a scowled brow, giving me a half-cocked smile of disapproval. Oh, how I want to slap those waxed brows off her face. I pick up my book and walk over to Gabe, but I just can't help myself as I lean closer and hover over the computer screen. "Aw, interesting," I say with a surprised look on my face.

"What?" the girls say with revulsion.

"Gabe, they do have opposable thumbs, I was beginning to wonder," I say, trying hard not to crack a smile. I gesture with my head to Gabe that it's time to leave.

As we walk downstairs to the lobby, I suddenly realize that we will be going to the same high school as these presumptuous imbeciles. What have I just done?

"Well, I hope you're happy now, because you get to endure the discomfort of those girls at school all year. I think you really gave them a great first impression," Gabe chides sarcastically.

"Yeah, well you didn't seem to make it any easier with your gawking. Oh, and by the way, girls don't really appreciate you staring at their tits while they're talking to you, well . . . most girls."

I don't know how guys are, but girls can be downright mean and hold grudges for life. The ability to shrewdly manipulate your peers into giving you a higher ranking in the pecking order is hazardous. When girls master this, all is lost in our schools, and the social hierarchies these girls have pervasively developed will be convincing. I check out my book, *Ancient Hebrew Cultures*, and we wait outside for the bus to arrive.

When we get home, all I can think about is food. The smell of roast and potatoes coming from the kitchen is like an aromatic punch in the face. Saliva is literally dripping from my mouth. Myra is an exceptional cook, and tonight is no exception, because this is our birthday meal. Gabe and I both have the same favorite dish, and we almost always ask for this dish on our birthday. But when we walk into the kitchen to get a better view of what our stomachs are about to receive, we see a spread of food on the table fit for a royal feast—you would think we were having company over tonight.

There's a moist and tender roast smothered in gravy, surrounded by roasted red potatoes and carrots accompanied with slices of caramelized onions, steamed asparagus drizzled with a butter sauce and lemon curry zest, freshly baked garlic bread, poached pears with silky smooth chocolate mousse inside, and homemade apple pie with whipped cream.

Daniel comes in the door, and I ready myself for this royal feast. I patiently wait for Niki, Myra, Daniel, and even

Gabe to get their plates before I devour my first helping. Three plates later, and my appetite has surrendered. I almost feel guilty for eating so much food. I excuse myself from the table and leisurely ascend upstairs to what feels like my deathbed. I haven't eaten like that in years. If I was carb rationing, I failed miserably.

I lie on the bed relaxing for a while, reading my new library book when Gabe walks in. "Have you given much thought about the key and the coordinates?" asks Gabe.

"I don't really feel like thinking about it right now."

"Maybe I can change that," says Gabe confidently. "Come to my room. I need to show you something."

I'm reaping my gluttonous indulgence for good food while I lie on the bed unwilling to move, but I somehow manage to rouse myself from my overstuffed stupor. I curiously walk to Gabe's room to see what he's up to.

"I mistakenly put in the longitude coordinates. This is where the coordinates are supposed to show," Gabe says, pointing to the laptop screen.

"That's only a mile away," I say.

"Yeah, and it's just two blocks from the school. You can barely make it out, but it looks like an abandoned gas station with an attached garage," Gabe says. "We can do this, you know—after school."

"I'm not going to be a lab rat in a baited building. What if some sick, twisted pervert sent out these random envelopes with the same letter and key, and he is there just waiting for the first person to show up so he can torture or rape them? I'm not going anywhere near there until I have thoroughly staked out the place," I say.

"Well, then I'll go alone," says Gabe.

"Fine, don't come calling me when you wake up with a rag in your mouth and find your testicles hooked up to a car battery."

"Look, I don't need your help, and I don't need you to baby me every step I take," Gabe objects, his voice now elevated.

"Baby you! Seriously, that's what you think? I'm here to protect you," I shout back.

"Protect me from what . . . curiosity?"

"It's curiosity that will get you into trouble if you're careless," I retort.

"You can't stop me," he says defiantly.

I want to desperately throw this key out the window and never have any mention of this letter again. The thought of burning it occurred to me, but in the heat of the moment, I throw the key on the floor out of frustration. I toss the half-folded letter at Gabe's head, but it misses and floats down to the side of his fish tank. All I can do is stand there in silence, mesmerized by the fish, until I notice a purplish glow emitting from the back of the letter.

I walk over to the tank to take a closer look at the letter and observe a startling discovery. There is writing on the letter, glowing from the black light on Gabe's fish tank. As if this was the discovery of the year, Gabe swiftly removes the black light from the tank and brings it closer to the letter. As I unfold the paper, we expose a hidden mes- sage.

Gabe reads the message aloud, "I need your help. Use the key to unlock the basement. Father Joseph will guide you both for further instructions. Love you both . . . Finnegan."

CHAPTER 4

The anxiety I've just recently developed is assisting my stomach in depositing my dinner. Before I lose my meal, I sit and calm myself, swallowing every few seconds to keep the food down. Gabe is rendered speechless, and we both just sit in silence for a few moments. We haven't spoken to or heard from Finnegan since he was last deployed six years ago. I just assumed he was dead when we were living with our Aunt Angela, because he never once wrote to her, yet the government never gave us any indication that he was dead either. It all seemed too strange at the time, but the death of my parents overcame any delusions I had of his whereabouts.

This changes everything now. Whatever I considered doing with that key earlier has been completely withdrawn. I pick it up off the floor and feel a sense of hope. I'm suddenly embarrassed that I ridiculed Gabe's ambitious effort to find the coordinates of the place. But he's right, and I know now what we must do.

We spend the next hour devising a plan on how we are going to get to the abandoned building without anyone knowing. We both agree that skipping class on the first day is not an option, so we are forced to persuade Myra and Daniel that we will be coming home late because of an after-school program that Gabe and I are interested in. To keep them less suspicious, we will wait until the end of the week to let them know. I've never had to lie to Myra and Daniel, nor have I ever wanted to deceive them, but this is something I know they wouldn't understand.

Because the country has been on high alert recently, there will be an unusual amount of federal officers surrounding the school. Less than two weeks ago, a few anti-government groups formed a small militia and tried to take out a federal facility near the Capitol. The revolt failed miserably and all were shot to death except the leader, who was brutally beaten and sentenced to a public hanging that was nationally televised. We'll have to have a very keen eye if we are to sneak into the building. Trespassing is punishable by jail time. It's ridiculous what our country has turned into, and since there is no longer state government or state rights, the federal government's regulations have depleted our basic freedoms and ideals.

Not only does the government regulate the amount of fuel we consume, but they also influence our eating habits by rewarding credit points to those who purchase food from federally aided food companies.

Because of the arrogance of our leaders, oil supplies from other nations have been completely shut off, the United Nations has been abandoned, and Israel is no longer our ally. Israel, the one nation that our country could not afford to lose its support, is now independently struggling with war against the Muslim nations.

Since the fall of the Dome on the Rock, the surrounding regions have stopped waging war against Israel out of Holy terror. Four years ago, two misguided missiles fired from border adversaries, slamming into the Dome on the Rock, and leaving it in complete ruins, as along with the peace keeping between the Jews and Muslims. Many felt that God was punishing them for all the small wars that were waged. Before the destruction of the Dome, many religious groups during the faith movement almost came to an agreement to relocate the Dome to Mecca, but such actions would inevitably lead to violence, and the Israelis were too ambivalent about the Movement. Since then, no one has seen the site of the destruction, but there have been rumors that a new structure was being built, yet no one has seen it.

Because our government has turned its back on Israel, it has in essence turned its back against God. Unfortunately, the people seem to accept the nation's social philosophies regardless of its lack of moral principles. The leader of our nation is still voted into office by the people, which may be the only democracy left in this country. Although I believe political influence and federal manipulation of votes is spreading like cancer, I will still try to reserve judgment.

I'm so anxious to understand what all this means that I just can't sleep. All I can do is impatiently wait, knowing that one key could possibly shed some light on my future. I just lie in my bed and gaze at the ceiling, trying to remember what it was like before our parents died. I can almost feel my mom's hand stroke my hair. I close my eyes and place my hand on my cheek as I try to summon one of the many memories of my mom wrapping her arms around me.

I continue to embrace the reminiscences as long as I can until my heart becomes numb. I turn over and grab an old family photo from my bedside and stare deep into the memories it holds. I squeeze my pillow tight until my knuckles turn white, and it's all I can do to keep from crying, but it's no use. My heart still aches, and because I can hear Gabe through the thin walls crying just the same, I surrender to my pain. I turn my head over so the pillow can soak up any tears that trail down my cheek as I fall asleep.

CHAPTER 5

The first day of school is perpetually the same, with the exception of this year. My first high school experience is about to begin, and I'm too nauseous to think about it. The consensus in this country is that high school is just another unsuccessful experiment that fails to prepare young people for the adult world. Do I really want to subject myself to this for four years?

When our mom educated us at a young age, we were way ahead of the curve when we started school, but Gabe shouldn't even be here at all. With his intellect, he already surpassed college-level education at the age of eleven, but because of his fear of being separated from me, he continues to pretend otherwise. It makes me somewhat sad that he's wasting his potential, but I'm glad he's around. I've always felt like we were meant to stick together.

The first day is always tough—new faces, new teachers, and a new school. The only thing worse is having new ene-mies. I just remember what awaits me in those bleak halls—the three half-wits in the library who were ostensibly taking advantage of my brother's kindness and the callous rejec-tions I received. "Lord, give me strength and wisdom," I say to myself before I go downstairs to eat breakfast.

It's hard to wait when patience is your enemy; the clock seems to tick slower than normal, and I feel like my body is aging while I sit.

"Okay, you guys ready?" says Myra.

Gabe nudges my elbow and gives me an almost half-stern look. "No matter what people may say, can you please promise me you will at least try to guard your heart and ignore their remarks?" I'm apprehensive at first, but I eventually nod in agreement.

When we arrive at school, I'm in awe at how many students are walking around the school grounds. The school may not be big, but it dwarfs the small middle school we were attending. As we walk to the entrance, I can already feel the eyes glued to me. What's attracting all the stares? Is my skirt tucked into my underwear? I gradually slide my hand toward the back of my skirt just to make sure. Maybe it's because we are new faces to most of these people—either that, or a bird just crapped in my hair.

I just look forward and try to avoid any eye contact, when out of the corner of my eye, I see her—the leader of the half-wits. I really need to come up with a better pet name. From a slight distance away, someone cheerfully and annoyingly shouts, "McKenzie!" As the leader turns and responds, I now no longer need a pet name. McKenzie: friend or foe, hopefully neither.

I grab onto Gabe and hurry up the steps before McKenzie notices us. I swing open the door as hard as I can, but it hits something on the other side with a deep thud. "Holy crap, are you okay?" I say with deep concern. I just knocked out an innocent boy standing behind the door.

"I think so," he says.

"I'm so sorry. Do you want me to get the nurse?" I ask.

"I'll be fine," he answers while holding his head. This isn't exactly how I wanted to introduce myself on the first day of school, but I try to make the best of the unfortunate greeting nonetheless. I carefully grab his hand in an attempt to forgive my clumsy introduction.

I help him to his feet. "By the way, I'm Arena and this is my brother, Gabe."

"My name is Jacob," he shyly introduces. He has shaggy brown hair, glassy blue eyes, and walks timidly with his head down, as if he is avoiding someone.

"Would you mind showing us where the administrative office is so we can pick up our class schedule?" I ask, smiling.

"You sure you want me to show you?" he says with a confused look on his face.

"Uh, sure, why not? We're new to this school."

"It's just that most people around here don't normally acknowledge me. My peculiarity isn't exactly inviting," Jacob explains.

"You seem perfectly normal to me, and even if you weren't, I would still ask for your assistance," I comfort.

He just smiles and keeps his head down as we walk. I can tell he doesn't have much by the clothes on his back. He probably hasn't eaten a decent meal in a long while either, judging by his malnourished frame. Behind the dirty clothes and shaggy hair is an innocent, young man who desires not to be invisible. Oddly enough, I'm smitten by his presence for reasons I can't explain. Maybe it's his honesty that's genuinely cloaked behind his . . . *peculiarity,* as he says.

The halls are colorful and covered with an assortment of flyers, streamers, and signup sheets. When we come to the administrative office, I thank Jacob for walking us, and despite the awkwardness, I ask him if he wants to sit with us during lunch.

"Sure, maybe, I'll look out for you both," he says, unsure of himself. I can tell he probably doesn't frequent the lunchroom much, most likely because of the crowd of people there. He seems like the kind of person who prefers being alone.

We walk into the office to pick up our class schedule when we promptly notice we are in the same classes together. Gabe sighs in relief. While we walk down the wide, blanched halls, I hear an obnoxious chanting coming from the south wing. Out of sheer curiosity, I ask Gabe to come with me to check it out.

The noise grows louder as we make our way around the corner. To no avail, it's just a bunch of dumb jocks encouraging one another to leap from what appears to be a ten-foot metal ladder into a baby pool filled with water balloons. There is writing in black marker on the balloons: Squash the Beavers. Wow, really? They couldn't come up with anything wittier like Damn the Beavers, or how about a classic Freudian innuendo: Trim the Beavers, since we are, after all, home of the mighty Scissortails. What makes a Scissortail mighty anyway?

As the mantra continues in unison—Jump! Jump! Jump! Jump!—the jock proudly leaps from the ladder, missing ever so slightly and crashing onto the hard, tiled floor. As he grabs his knee in anguish, rocking back and forth on the floor grimacing, I try hard to hold back a chuckle. All I can do is shake my head and remember a quote I once read: "Only two things are infinite, the universe and human stupidity, and I'm not sure about the former." I guess Albert Einstein was right.

As much as Gabe probably wants to laugh, he quickly runs to the aid of the injured football player. Gabe has always been fascinated with medical journals, medical books, and just about anything to do with the human body. He may not know exactly what to do for someone medically, but his intentions are of far more value. He just wants to help in any way he can.

Gabe kneels beside the poor boy's foot, but before he can help him sit upright, he is forcefully pushed back by a much larger guy. It's Derrick Maitland, a tall, stout, broad-shouldered ox, who happens to be the captain of the football team. He may have the gladiator physique and the counterfeiting charm that only the naïve would fall for, but it's the air blowing from his ears that leads me to believe his pea-sized brain rolled out. Judging by the stature of his fellow teammates, he appears to be the strongest in the crowd. I recognize him right away from all the local commercials he does with his dad.

His father, Gerry Maitland, owns Maitland Financial Services and one of the largest federal car dealerships. He's known for being a very astute businessman, but crooked as well. Judging by Derrick's reaction, I'm pretty sure the apple doesn't fall far from the tree.

"Don't touch him, you freak! This doesn't concern you!" shouts Derrick.

I push my way through the crowd to come to the defense of my brother "Hey! He was just trying to help your friend," I growl.

"Who the hell are you?" says Derrick.

Now it has become so quiet, the only background noise is the wincing from the fallen idiot. "I'm his sister," I say, as I point toward Gabe. By the look on Gabe's face, I know I've just made it worse for him from here on out. I didn't mean to embarrass him in front of everyone, but I'm not going to stand there and let him be stepped on like that, even if a little dignity is stripped.

"Do you know who this is? This is our starting quarterback. I don't need some geek pretending to be a doctor and messing up his knee even more," says Derrick.

This country is sinking deeper into debt, freedoms have all but been banished, and the nation's poverty is heavier than it ever has been, but God forbid if football were to ever be outlawed, an uprising would tear this nation apart.

"Look, I don't give a damn if he's your gay lover. Gabe's intentions were to help and not harm him," I say defiantly.

Okay, at this point, I probably stepped over that line Gabe constantly reminds me about. The faces among us collapse with shock, and the circle that surrounded the injured boy is now widening back a little. Derrick rises to his feet, puffing out his chest like a threatening rooster. He walks toward me, but I do not move. My feet are planted in cement. Finnegan always told me that no matter what, never let your enemy see your fear. Sometimes just your appearance and demeanor can make your opponent respect you, even before combat has taken place.

I don't think that's the case here, but I stand my ground nonetheless. His face flourishes so red, I'm waiting for fire to somehow come spewing from his mouth. Through grinding teeth, he snarls, "I don't think I made myself clear. You and your nerdy brother better leave right now before—"

"Before what?"

"You think this is a game? Look around you, sweetheart, because what you see are the players that control your game. You've been given fair warning this time, but whatever happens next will be by your choice," says Derrick.

"If there are any malicious actions, it will be by your hand, not mine," I retort. Right then, a nurse and two school administrators come racing down the hall, breaking up the scene, and saving us from any more discomfort.

"Come on, Arena," Gabe says, tugging my arm. As we walk down the hall and the crowd begins to dissipate, I feel my forward movement ceasing.

Derrick grabs Gabe's shoulder and says in a soft, but demonic voice, "Hey, you little shit, you're going to wish you had gone down a different hall, and don't expect Sis here to fight your battles for you either."

As he turns to walk away, he follows my steady but livid eyes staring him down. "Girl or not, I will break you," he adds with vigor. I just roll my eyes and walk away. He may be strong, but he's dumb, and I'm confident I have the skills to take him down if the time ever presents itself.

Gabe walks a little faster ahead of me, as if he doesn't want anything to do with me. "Gabe, Gabe! I'm sorry," I say sincerely.

"You're always doing this. You think you're helping me, but you're just making it worse. Why can't you just leave things alone? I was fine. I would have just walked away and nobody would have remembered any of this. Now I fear for my life walking down these halls, nervously wondering where, when, and how those guys are going to dismantle me," Gabe retracts.

"I truly am sorry. You do know my intentions were good. You're my brother, you're all the family I have left, and I'm here to look after you no matter what," I say.

He pats my shoulder, his way of showing that he forgives me, but not without disappointment. I don't think he would ever deny that if push comes to shove, I would be there to protect him. "Come on, let's just go to our first class," Gabe says, as he strains to smile.

We get through all of our classes without a hitch and gratefully encounter no more altercations for the day. Because I was too nervous to eat in the cafeteria today, like every first day of school, all I can think about is going home and pigging out. I guess some things never change.

I feel terrible about not going to lunch and looking for Jacob, but he probably never showed up. When the last bell rings, Gabe and I exit the school and wait outside by the street for Myra to come pick us up. We are outside a little early, but it's only because we are trying to avoid Derrick or any of his jockstrap henchmen.

As I'm looking around, making sure no one can spot us behind the tall hedges by the sidewalk, I see him—the same priest who has been following us, standing behind a stop sign by a park bench. Enough is enough. I'm prepared to get to the bottom of all this. Though he's reluctant at first to consent to my request, I eventually persuade Gabe to gesture the priest to come over while I look for a place to hide. The priest readily acknowledges Gabe's gesturing attempt, and thoroughly examines the federal officers' positions before he walks across the street. I sneak behind the bushes and patiently wait until he's standing next to Gabe. As the priest approaches my brother, I pick up a stick on the ground and sidle up behind him.

"Hello, son, you must be Ga—"

I swiftly poke the jagged stick into the priest's right side, digging just enough to convince him I have a knife and I'm ready to use it if necessary. With his robe blocking the officers on the other side of the street, I hide behind his black cloak. "Who the hell are you, and why have you been following us?" I sternly say.

"Arena, stop! He's a priest, for God's sake," Gabe interjects.

"Okay, your holiness, start talking, I'm bloody good with a blade," I say.

"I'm Father Joseph, a good friend of your Uncle Finnegan," he says in a thick Irish accent, as sweat drips down his forehead.

Without hesitation, I pull the stick from his side and let his arm go. "I'm sorry, Father, but you can never be sure of things these days," I say.

"You're uncle has taught you very well, Arena. And you must be Gabriel," Father Joseph says. "I know Myra is probably coming soon to pick you up, but we have much to talk about and very little time to waste."

"How do you know Myra?" I ask.

"In time, my child, we'll speak more, but it's imperative we keep this our little secret, okay?"

"Yeah, okay."

"I take it you received the letter and uncovered the hidden message your uncle sent you?"

With wide eyes open, Gabe responds, "Yes, but finding the message—"

"Was quite easy," I interrupt. I really don't need Father Joseph to know our struggles with the letter. It may show a sign of weakness. After all, he needs our help, and I want his confidence in us assured.

Right then, as I look at Gabe, I know that our plans this week have just been expedited. We decide to meet after school tomorrow at the old, abandoned gas station.

Before Father Joseph walks away, he digs into his pocket, pulls out an object, and places it in Gabe's hands. "I almost forgot. Finnegan told me to give this to you when you turned fifteen."

It's a pocket watch. The inscription on the back of the watch says "William C. McManus." This watch belonged to our grandfather, Connor McManus, a man of devout faith. I read somewhere that a pocket watch was a common object that's passed down through the generations to the male as a customary token of honor. I believe that token has been passed down to a well-deserved young man. Father Joseph puts his hand on Gabe's shoulder as a proud father would do to his son. Gabe's lips are quivering, and I desperately want to console him, but I know this is not a moment.

"Remember to bring the key with you; it's time to uncover your fate," he says as he walks away.

CHAPTER 6

My room seems so quiet right now that all I can hear are the thoughts racing through my head and a constant ringing in my ears. Butterflies flutter in my stomach in anticipation of our meeting with Father Joseph. I don't know what to expect. Regardless of the so-called ties he has with Finnegan, I'm still a bit suspect of our engagement. I don't know how I'm going to get any sleep tonight, but I do know one thing for sure: tomorrow is anew beginning for Gabe and me.

I hear footsteps lightly tapping up the stairs and know right away that it must be Niki. I've lived here long enough to recognize the patterns of everyone's footsteps as they ascend the stairs. I walk over to the door to open it before she can knock, and greet her with open arms.

"Hey, girl, how was your first day at school?" she says, hugging me.

"Well, I–uh," I stutter, then pause for a few seconds. "I think I may have put Gabe in an extraordinary situation that he'd rather not applaud me for."

"What did you do?" Niki asks. I explain to her the unfortunate circumstance and my intentions for Gabe, and by the look on her face I notice the immediate concern she has for him. I now feel even guiltier about what I did, but somehow she makes me feel better about what happened today. She has a knack for making the most negative situation seem better than what it appears to be. This isn't exactly my area of expertise. I'm afraid my tough words may come a bit hard to chew with my brother.

"I know Gabe could probably use some encouragement. It may sound better coming from you, and who knows, he's probably forgotten about the whole thing," I say.

"Your brother is obsessive-compulsive, I doubt it," says Niki.

We knock on his door, and as the door creaks open, all I can see is Gabe pacing back and forth and talking to himself. Lying on his bed is an inside-out shirt, with black tape and hard plastic pieces attached to the chest and shoulder areas. His pants appear to be stuffed with something.

"Gabe?" I ask puzzled. I know he desperately could use some comforting words right now, but all I can think about is what we will find in that basement with Father Joseph. It's quite clear what Gabe is thinking about.

"Gabe, slow down, what are you doing? Arena explained to me what happen today," Niki says.

"I'm just taking a few precautions for tomorrow's uncertainties, a small amount of body armor if you will," says Gabe.

"Body armor, really? Okay, look, this is absurd. I know you were worried earlier about getting dismantled, but if you walk around school in this ridiculous outfit, it's almost a guarantee you'll get your ass kicked," I say.

"Easy for you to stand there and lecture me on the rules of engagement. I don't have the luxury to defend myself with the skills you possess. I have to be a little more creative," Gabe says.

Niki sits quietly on the bed and reaches out to take Gabe's hand. "I greatly understand and value your position about turning the other cheek, but there will come a time when you will need you sister the most to help you. Your intentions for seeing the good in people is valued by your heart, not by a law, and even if you wanted to change someone's heart, you can't. That is the choice they will have to make. That's in God's hands, not yours. Instead of striving to follow every little rule, try leading with your fist. Who knows, it may save you one day? Arena won't always be there, ya know. I couldn't be there for Grace."

Niki's advice leaves Gabe nearly motionless. His face flattens a bit. Whether it was what she said, or just the presence of an older, wiser sister consoling her little brother, it's enough to trigger calmness in Gabe. As we leave the room, I look back and see Gabe sitting on the bed with his eyes closed in tranquil peace. When he prays, burdens are lifted. I'm a true believer in prayer; in fact, I try to pray before unwanted circumstances happen. Sooner or later they will, it's inevitable.

*   *   *

Morning comes and it's a new day, and I'm much too anxious to get out the door instead of eating breakfast. Gabe and I walk to one of the side areas of the school just to avoid any unwanted presence of Derrick. Gabe looks a little nervous, but not nearly as edgy as he was yesterday, so I propose we stay here as long as needed before the bell rings.

It feels so peaceful sitting underneath one of the largest pecan trees on campus. The birds chirping beautiful songs brings back memories of being on my granddaddy's farm, lying on the haystacks, looking up at the clouds with no worries. Behind us, nestled between the tall bushes that nearly cover the school windows, emits the most glorious scent of honeysuckle. I can hear the faint buzzing of the bees transporting its nectar. Everything seems almost perfect as I close my eyes to the rays of the morning sun peeking through the branches.

As the light dims on my eyes, I feel a coldness wrap around me, as if the clouds have blocked the warmth of the rays. Unfortunately, the sun is being blocked by McKenzie Woods's disproportionate head. Great, the perfect morning is being shadowed by Lucifer's daughter. Is it me, or do all girls with attitude stand with their weight shifted forward on one leg and their hands resting on their hips?

"I heard your little stupid stunt yesterday nearly cost your brother's life," she says.

"The only stupidity I witnessed yesterday was someone taking a leap of faith into concrete," I say.

"Look, bitch . . ." she barks ruthlessly.

"Excuse me?" I say, standing to my feet. Gabe has clutched onto my arm.

"You're nothing special here, so don't try to pretend you can fit in. We don't need your kind here. That's right—everyone knows you live at one of the foster homes. You're just another problem child that the government should have trashed along with all the other Watchers. I'm actually surprised you're wearing something that's not stitched from burlap."

I'm just speechless. Gabe, still clutching onto my arm, constrains me, but I don't budge an inch. I'm finding this change of attitude to be more like Gabe is proving to be difficult.

"Hi, sweetie," McKenzie charms with a wink at Gabe. She looks me up and down in disgust, rolls her eyes, and walks away, nearly tripping on the large roots beneath the pecan tree.

"Wow, way to restrain yourself, Arena. Hell, even I thought she was a bitch," Gabe says surprisingly.

Before my anger consumes me, I struggle to give him an acknowledging smile. "Thanks."

As I walk out a little from underneath the tree, I can see McKenzie around the corner, laughing it up with her friends and mocking me. I look up at the eaves of the school, then down at the ground around me. Whether or not my vengeance is unjust, this brief, but objectionable engagement has pissed me off beyond my control.

"What are you doing?" asks Gabe hesitantly.

"Nothing, just a little pest control," I smirk under a sinister grin.

A yellow jacket's nest is loosely attached underneath the low-hanging eave. It also happens to be right above McKenzie and the girls. I pick up a decent-sized rock just big enough to disturb the nest and possibly knock it right off the eave.

"Whatever you are thinking about doing, please don't, Arena, and reconsider," advises Gabe.

"Hey, I'm doing better. I restrained myself from plucking those ridiculously bleached follicles atop her swollen head. Besides, this is very therapeutic for me."

Gabe quickly hides behind the tree as I release the stone with accuracy, resulting in a direct hit. The nest floats down on top of the bushes, scrambling the bees like fighter jets right in the girls' direction. The girls are screaming, running in circles, and flinging their arms about like mad orang-utans. It's a sight to behold.

I realize what I've done is probably morally wrong, but it did put a smile back on my face nonetheless. I try to redeem myself and save them from being stung since they are too stupid to just run into the school. I notice a water hose connected to the side of the building. I turn on the water and spray the bees away along with a good soaking of the girls. The bees vanish, and all three girls stand there soaking wet, looking at me with utter hatred.

"You're welcome," I beam. McKenzie lets out a bellow and grits her teeth, staring me down. "Hey, I just saved you from being severely stung. An allergic reaction to bee stings isn't something to whiff about. I think an appreciation is in order—don't thank me all at once now."

If these girls had lasers beaming from their eyes, I would be charcoal right now. I actually think they halfheart-edly believe me, because the other two girls wave their hands in the air as a gesture of thanks, except McKenzie, of course. Jacob, who I suddenly notice leaning beside a nearby tree, is laughing at my not-so-nice antics. I indulge in his charming support and return the amusement with a smile.

The school bell rings with a chilling reminder that this day has just begun, but before we leave for our first class, Gabe surprisingly gives McKenzie a small wave good-bye. I don't know if he's doing this out of his commonly nice nature, or he somehow really believes McKenzie likes him. In his most apologetic voice, he still feels the need to smooth out the worst of conditions just to reassure that this was an accident. "You know, you really don't look all that bad . . . in fact, your hair looks really good when it's wet."

"Gabe," I say.

"What?" he asks.

"Shut up."

It will be all too good if I don't have to see McKenzie for the rest of the day. I can only imagine what lies she'll be spreading around about me.

We're studying cells in biology class. I already know this stuff from reading in the library, so I can afford to close my eyes for a few minutes.

This must be pure boredom for Gabe, yet he still looks giddy from the lecture. With his passion and knowledge for science and enthusiastic personality, he really should be the one teaching this class. The timbre of Mr. Jennings's voice has put everyone, with the exception of Gabe, in a hypnotic state. Drool drips from the boy's mouth who's sitting in front of me. The only thing keeping me from totally conking out are tiny voices whispering behind and to the right of me.

In the corner desks near the window, four girls are gossiping like a bunch of cackling hens about someone. Then they glance in my direction, smile, and give me a thumbs up. I look at the clock and notice that the bell, thankfully, is about to ring. As much as I want to hurry to get in line first for lunch, I'm much too interested in why those girls were gesturing at me. I tell Gabe to wait for me before he leaves, and I eagerly go over to the girls to see what all the fuss is about.

"So what's going on?" I pry.

"We heard what you did to McKenzie, Brittney, and Lorie this morning. I'm Jade, by the way," the girl says.

"Brittney and Lorie? I guess I don't have to worry about a formal introduction," I sarcastically say.

"Brittney is the one with the short, blonde hair," says one of the girls.

"I guess you already know McKenzie," Jade says.

"Yes, we've met before," I smirk.

"We just want to personally thank you for that little piece of entertainment. They have deserved that for a long time," says another girl.

As funny as it may have been, I really start to feel badly for what I did, and these girls just reiterated why I'd rather be alone. Listening to girls gab in dramatic fashion about someone else's misfortunes is no different than when I had been made fun of. Right then I understood why Gabe reacts the way he does toward others. Regardless of whether someone deserves something or not is not for me to judge.

These girls are really beginning to annoy me now. "Really, I was just trying to keep them from being stung," I say sincerely. They seem a little stunned by my response, and so does Gabe. If there was a smile on my face, it has disappeared. All I want to do is go to lunch, so I promptly turn and walk out the door.

To my surprise, Jacob is standing outside the cafeteria with his hair pulled back away from his beautiful eyes and his head held up high, smiling. This is really the first time I've seen his face underneath all that hair.

The cafeteria is packed today. By the amount of extra teachers, administrators, and security guards, something important must be going on. I grab my food tray and look for a place to sit. Since we got here later than I wanted, Gabe, Jacob, and I have to search hard for a place to sit.

There appears to be several seats in the back unoccupied that will do. Gabe starts to sit at the end of the table, but I gesture for him to sit toward the middle next to a girl who seems to be alone. Since we haven't made many friends yet, I think it will be a good idea for us to start now.

"May we sit here?" I ask politely.

"Sure," she says.

"I'm Arena, and this is my brother, Gabe."

"It's Gabriel, but most everyone calls me Gabe," he retorts.

"And this is our friend Jacob," I continue.

"I'm Juliana. I've seen you before," she notices.

"Really?"

"I think I may have seen you at the retirement center."

"Oh, yeah, Gabe and I worked there part-time during the summer. Our foster mom got us that job. She knows the staff administrator there."

"So you have foster parents too? I visit my grand-mother at the center; she's the only living family I have left. I used to live with her, but her health got worse over the last two years, so she wasn't able to care for me. I was put in foster care this past year," Juliana explains.

I feel a genuine sense of empathy for Juliana, as I remember the first time we were taken into foster care. The conversation with Juliana feels so comfortable, and not once do I have to think about what I'm going to say that's usually accompanied with uneasy, awkward pauses. It's as if we are meant to sit here. The similarities we share with each other are therapeutic for Gabe and me. This is something we've needed all these years.

Juliana's frail, tiny body makes her look vulnerable and insecure, but when she speaks in her humble and innocent voice, she becomes visible. Her hair is dark as coal, and her beautiful olive skin is purposefully covered up with long sleeves. She was badly burned on her left arm when she was ten in a house fire that killed her mom. Her dad abandoned her when she was born, leaving her mom to raise her. She lived with her grandmother up until a year ago, and now she's like us. I don't think there is a better person we could have befriended at this school than Juliana.

Since we don't have classes together, we promise to meet here at lunch from now on. Hopefully, the four of us can keep this bond strong, because we are probably going to need each other throughout the school year.

Jacob excuses himself from the table before the lunch period ends. "I'm sorry, guys, but I have to be somewhere early for the next class. We'll catch up tomorrow, okay?" When he leaves, Juliana and Gabe both look at me as if they are waiting for me to say something.

"So, you going to ask this guy out or not, because apparently he's too shy to do it," Gabe goads.

"You might want to keep your mouth shut when you eat, dear brother." I point my fork in his direction. His smirk has amazingly vanished as he stuffs his face.

I'm inclined to admit I may have somewhat of a small crush on Jacob, but I refuse let my emotions carry this conversation about it any further. I'm not about to let Gabe's comment get to me. I'm not embarrassed about it as much as I'm a little annoyed about Gabe trying to perpetuate something he knows nothing about. I admit I'm attracted to Jacob, but that's my business. I don't know quite what it is, but there's something about him that makes him more attractive than the rest of the boys in this school.

Of course this day wouldn't be complete without another McKenzie sighting. Coming from the side of our table, I feel her green eyes gunning for me.

"Well, looks as though you took my advice this morning. Nice to see that you're sticking to your own kind. Let's try to keep it they from now on," she provokes.

That's it. I've had enough; she's going down right here, right now. I push my chair out has hard as I can, but Gabe grabs me and reminds me of more important things. "Arena, stop. If you do this, you risk getting expelled, muddling our plans this afternoon. Remember?" he reminds with his eyebrows arched.

I almost forgot about Finnegan and Father Joseph. I sit back in my chair and try to calm myself.

"That's right, listen to your brother, he seems to be the smart one," McKenzie continues to rib.

"It's not worth it, Arena, not now anyway," Juliana calmly diffuses.

"I promise you before the end of the school year, you and I are going to have more than words," I warn with my eyes fixed on hers.

"Is that a threat?"

"Bitch, you wouldn't know the difference."

"Well, let me make this plainly clear. If you think you don't have much now, I'll make positively sure my dad sees that your family never will." Her crooked mouth bends a fake smile before she saunters away.

And it just hit me, Woods. McKenzie is the daughter of Mayor Allen Woods. Mayors really have no power to persuade or the authority to regulate, punish, or judge since there are no state or city governments in place anymore. But if you are appointed by the federal government as magistrate, then those powers which flow from the top can be just as dangerous. Supremacy in this nation has been reduced to intimidation, and the totalitarianism it reflects has been a masquerade for years. The extremists believe it to be run by foreign nations, which isn't all that unbelievable.

"She is just jealous of you, Arena," says Juliana.

Really? Jealous of what? There is nothing about me that's all that special. Why would anyone want to be like me?

"You are very beautiful, and she knows it. Do you not see that?" Juliana sincerely remarks. "All the guys gawk at you, and you don't even recognize it. McKenzie has to make great efforts to dramatically get the attention she thinks she deserves to turn heads, but they all are attracted to you."

I tilt my head down because I'm really too embarrassed to accept the compliment. No one has ever said anything so kind to me before. It just seems all too strange to me, and maybe because I've been so caught up in my own world that I haven't ever subconsciously noticed my "beauty."

"Thank you for your kindness," I say. When Gabe gets up to dump his tray, I lean in closer to Juliana. "Just so you know, your beauty has not been unnoticed. I can tell by the look on my brother's face when he looks at you, and he has great taste in girls," I softly say. Juliana smiles and looks in Gabe's direction.

The bell rings.

CHAPTER 7

Well, I've managed to have two unpleasant encounters, and there is still half a day to go. For the rest of the day, we avoid any hesitation in-between classes just so we can evade any presence of Derrick. Since he is older, his classes are on the other side of the hall, but sometimes upperclassmen have to pass the freshman halls to get to their classes.

We have made it to the last class of the day: French. Everyone is required to have two credits of foreign language, and since Gabe and I already know the language very well, it makes an already uncomfortable day less stressful.

Before I sit in my assigned seat, I glance over in the corner and see Juliana. I don't remember noticing her on the first day of class. I wave to her and by her surprise, she apparently didn't realize it either. "At least we have one class together," I say.

"I'm glad, I was hoping lunch wasn't the only time we could meet up," she agrees.

"Hey, did you know Gabe is assigned a seat right next to you?"

"Funny how you don't know your surroundings when you feel invisible to the world."

"Well, you're visible to Gabe and me, especially Gabe," I say cheerfully.

I know this class is supposed to be easy, but the absolute boredom I have to endure right now is painfully killing me. Everything is moving in slow motion, and when I think it's about to come to a complete stop, an air-raid siren suddenly starts screaming.

The teacher looks panicked, as if this isn't a drill. Maybe this is a surprise drill and she just seems caught off guard.

I've only heard a siren going off once while I was in school, and that was for a tornado, but the weather is sunny and pleasant outside today. People are running in the hall, passing our door in a blur. We all quickly get up as the teacher preps us to go to our designated area.

That hellish squeal pulsates louder and louder when we exit the hall. Students panic for no good reason as they run to their areas. Teachers are hurriedly talking on their phones, and security guards racing down the halls. There are so many students trying to pass each other in the tightly packed halls, I lose sight of Gabe and Juliana. I push my way through the crowd, calling out Gabe's name, but the siren is too loud. I can't find him anywhere.

I find a chair outside one of the classroom doors and stand on it to see if I can get a better look in the crowd, but I see no sign of Gabe or Juliana. Students are running and screaming, and I become worried, not so much from the panic, but because I lost Gabe in all this mess. Why is everyone running in a panic if this is just a surprise drill? As I turn in the direction where most of the commotion is coming from, I notice three soldiers with full body armor wearing gasmasks coming toward us.

If there is truly something to warrant this type of engagement, I'm not leaving here without Gabe or Juliana. I hurry down the hallway and side step my way through the hall, hugging the lockers with my back to avoid the lunacy of people scampering over one another.

I veer past the administrative offices and notice that it's empty, so I dash down to the next intersection of hallways. To the right is the gymnasium, and to the left is a back door that leads to the parking lot, where two federal officers stand. I'm forced to either backtrack or go toward the gymnasium. It's evident by the sheer panic that no one followed the rules about dismissing to their designated areas. Everyone is supposed to be sitting down by their lockers, but that's not happening. If I know Gabe, he would have gone to a place that has more than one exit. I taught him to always leave his options open if there ever came a time he were to encounter a dangerous crisis—I guess this would be considered one.

I run to the gym as fast as I can, but it's empty. I hustle over to the double doors that lead to the back of the men's locker rooms where I hear a small noise. It sounds like heavy panting near the back corner of the bleachers, but I can't make out who it is. I go behind the metal stands to get a better look and find Juliana. She's curled up in a fetal position on the floor behind the bleachers, crying.

I rush over by her side. "Juliana, are you hurt? Was Gabe with you?" She looks like she is in shock. The only thing she can do is point to the double doors where Gabe must be. She doesn't seem to be injured, just scared.

"Okay, stay here and don't move, I promise I'll be right back," I assure her. I slowly open the doors and peek in both directions. Small drops of blood dot the floor around the corner.

I hurry around the corner and find Gabe sitting up against the wall with his hands on his face. I kneel down so I can get a better look at his face. His cheek is swollen, blood is dripping from his nose, and his clothes are soaking wet. "Gabe, are you all right? What the hell happened here?".

"I got lost in the crowd when everyone started to run. I couldn't find you, so I took Juliana toward the gym, thinking that maybe everyone would be gathering there, not to mention there are at least three exits that gave us options if something bad were to happen," Gabe says with exhaustion.

"I knew you would come here, I taught you well, young Padawan," I say, smiling.

"Yeah, well don't flatter yourself, Obi Wan, I still got the shit beat out of me," he says.

"Let me guess, Derrick?"

"Juliana and I were coming through the gym, and when we noticed no one else was here, we decided to go through the locker-room exits. I pushed the doors open right when Derrick was coming out. He fell backward and just stared at me. I tried to apologize, but that obviously failed. He recognized me, and he and two other guys dragged me into the showers, hosed me down, dragged me back into the hall, and punched me twice in the face. I didn't really feel anything. My swollen head felt numb. The siren was so loud—no one could have heard anything going on in here even if there was somebody around to help. When the sirens started to wind back down, two gunshots fired, and the guys just took off and left me here," Gabe says.

"Are you sure you heard gunshots?" I ask.

"I'm almost positive, but then again, I could have imagined it too since I was hit pretty hard in the face. Not sure why they felt the need to throw me in the shower. Was a beating not enough?" Gabe says.

"That would explain your soaked clothes," I say, examining him. "Let me see your face. Yep, we're going to have a hard time explaining this one to Myra."

"Where is Juliana?" he says, concerned.

I almost forgot I left her behind the bleachers. "Come on, she's in here," I say as I lift him up.

When we walk back into the gym, the ear-bleeding sirens stop. Juliana is still there, crouched down under the bleachers. When she sees Gabe, she immediately gets up to help him, and I can tell there's a special relationship building between these two.

She carefully leads him to the bathroom and begins nursing his wounds. A faint noise is coming from outside the gym that sounds like some kind of commotion, but because my ears are still ringing from that damn siren, it could be a flock of blackbirds chattering in the trees for all I know.

I peek out the back door while Gabe is being nursed. Teachers, administrators, and about a half-dozen guards and federal officers are conversing over one another. Students start to pour back into the school as the disorder dies down. My phone suddenly rings. I pull out my phone. Eight missed calls, and Myra is calling right now.

The sound of her voice is almost inaudible because she is yelling so loudly in a panic. Apparently, I never heard the phone ring with all the frenzy and noise. I explain to her that everything is okay, and that everyone is being led back into the school. I reassure her that it was probably a false alarm. The only kind of crisis that would prompt a siren to go off around the city is an attack from some overzealous anti-government group causing sheer panic and widespread looting. If this was a false alarm, someone is sure to get fired.

When I notice Juliana picking up Gabe's pocket watch, I quickly remember to remind Myra that we will be coming home late and that we will have a ride home. I can tell by her voice that she's not too thrilled about the idea, but I convince her anyway.

We head back to our classroom like everyone else and listen to the teachers explain that a false alarm was issued and that nothing bad has happened. I can tell by the teacher's explanation that not even she's convinced.

A speaker suddenly comes on and a deep voice addresses the entire school: "We sincerely apologize for this unnecessary panic. There is no real threat to worry about. This was only a false alarm. If there is any medical attention needed, we will have nursing stations set up outside the main office. We have taken the appropriate measures to ensure that this mishap will not happen in the future. Again, we apologize for any anxiety this may have caused you. Your parents will be immediately notified that everything is okay and back to normal. Thank you."

If this was a false alarm, then why were there full body-armored soldiers with gasmasks storming the halls? These kinds of precautions make you wonder what we are preparing for.

The last bell rings, and we are finally dismissed from school. I hurry to grab Gabe out the door, but he's too busy talking with Juliana, so I just leave them alone for a few moments. I overhear Gabe asking Juliana if she would like to come over and have dinner with us sometime. Not that I'm eavesdropping, but by the size of Juliana's grin and batting eyes, it appears my baby brother is starting to grow into a man.

"I hope you feel better in the morning," Juliana says to him, as she plants a small kiss on his forehead before she leaves.

"Wow, that was fast. She thinks you're the cat's meow," I joke.

"Yeah, I guess getting beaten up has its perks," he grins.

After being closed up in a dark, stuffy school all day, the sun seems so bright when we go outside. I notice an unusual amount of federal officers scattered across the school grounds, roaming back and forth across the street. I guess the wailing sirens this afternoon provoked them just enough to be a little more alert, like a disturbed hornet's nest.

We cautiously walk down the street two blocks where the old, abandoned gas station is rusting away. There are too many stations like this withering away that stretch across the nation. Oil, a once-precious commodity, has dried up because of the indifference of our political leaders. The only foreign policy that hasn't been spoiled is our waiver of debt from China and the ever-growing relationship with Russian leaders.

Our political leaders are attempting to gain back our country's world power and dominance through illegal arms trade with untrustworthy nations, even if it means sacrificing the needs of our very own people. It's evil no matter how you slice it. Like my uncle used to say, *You can't put syrup on dog shit and call it pancakes.*

I'm beginning to feel a little nervous with all these vigilant officers pacing the area. Gabe shudders anxiously while we walk toward the wrecked garage. Suddenly, he stops and grabs my hand. Out of some innate suspicion, he quickly steers me to the right of the garage, behind some tall bushes growing up next to an old billboard. I'm a bit apprehensive at first, but my brother's intuitions aren't something to circumvent. I crouch down, peering through the cluster of leaves, wondering what it could be this time.

Within seconds, an armored car races around the corner, followed by a dozen federal officers dressed in black with gray sleeves. I've never seen uniforms like these before—must be a special unit, because they are each equipped with a Beretta XM37, a very lethal, light, and extremely accurate weapon at long ranges. If it's a gun, I know it like the back of my hand, thanks to Finnegan.

As soon as they pass, we sneak around the fence to the back of the station. I peek through the broken window and thoroughly inspect the inside just to make sure we're not going to be ambushed by vagrants.

We carefully climb through the window. The gas station looks as if it hasn't been touched since the day it was shut down. Years of dust covers every inch of this place.

Into the next small area that leads to the garage, a dark figure moves against the blackness of the windowless room. I stop in my tracks and stay as still as I can. The figure moves toward us, then Father Joseph steps into the light.

"You made it, good," he says, as he bows his head. "Thank you Lord for Your protection, in His righteous and holy name, Amen."

When he looks up, his eyes grow wide. "What happened to you?" Father Joseph asks, referring to Gabe's swollen face.

"I was a human punching bag for someone's fist. It's a long story," Gabe says.

"Come, children, this way," he says, as he guides us to the garage area. "Did you bring the key?"

"Yes, it's right here," I say, pulling it out of my pocket.

"Gabriel, help me with this, please," he says.

Gabe and Father Joseph struggle to push back an old, broken deep freezer against the wall, revealing a large, black-rubber mat exposed beneath it. Father Joseph pulls back the mat to uncover a flat, metal-gray door imbedded into the concrete floor.

There is a lock on the door, which can mean only one thing: this is the basement Finnegan wrote about in his letter, and this is the key that opens it. Without hesitation, I put the key in and turn. My face brightens, and goose bumps run through my body when I hear a click; it's like opening up a present on Christmas morning. The door is extremely heavy, and the darkness below doesn't seem too inviting.

I use the light on my phone to see if there are any stairs that lead down this deep dwelling. Underneath the opening, I slide my hand across and locate a light switch. As I click the switch, a trail of illumination unveils a set of steep stairs leading down through a long lit corridor.

As we descend underground, Father Joseph closes the heavy, well-insulated door behind us. I feel like I'm in some kind of post-apocalyptic bunker, waiting for zombies to come pouring out from behind the end of the hall.

While we quietly walk through the long, narrow tunnel, I'm too inquisitive to tolerate this awkward stillness, so I speak up to break the silence. "Did you know about this place?" I ask Father Joseph.

"I have never been down here through this part, but yes, I've known about this from your uncle. This was built years ago, about the time of the first rebellion. There are many tunnels underground connecting government buildings, but this I have never seen," he says.

Gabe keeps to himself and stays silent while we are walking. I'm not sure what's going through his mind, but there's an uneasy expression on his face. I want to say something, but I keep to myself and let him be.

We walk through the concrete tunnel about another hundred yards and come to another gray metal door with yet another lock. I use the same key to unlock the door, but before I open it, I take a deep breath and pause as I look at Gabe. When the door opens, all three of us just stand there in complete shock. I can't believe what I'm seeing—I'm absolutely numb.

Have you ever wondered what's in those top-secret government facilities that are supposedly hidden beneath the earth, the ones that create a special kind of fear and excitement from fabricated stories written by conspiracy theorists? What's impossible has become possible, because I think we just stepped into one.

This underground dwelling holds the most sophisticated testing lab for high-tech weaponry you can imagine. It houses an arsenal fit for an army, and its precision machinery is unmatched by even the best government facility. Three of the ten-foot walls hold every kind of gun imaginable: semi-automatic pistols, revolvers, shotguns, rifles and carbines, assault rifles, submachine guns, and weapons I have never seen before. Just being in this room would get Father Joseph shot. Because Gabe and I are under the age of eighteen, we would be sentenced to slave labor.

Up until about five years ago, gun control was a problem in America. Because too many guns were being put into the wrong hands, provoking fear and widespread shedding of innocent blood, the new regime made it clear that all guns would be banned and that those supplying these weapons would be severely punished; some were imprisoned, but most were executed.

Guns being smuggled in from Mexico stopped the day the border was completely shut off by a specialized group of federal soldiers spanning the entire Mexican-American border, killing anything that threatened to infiltrate the country. The "death fence," as they called it, was used to separate this border. This electrified fence was charged with enough voltage to kill on contact. Not exactly an ethical means of disconnection, but the government deemed it to be proactively efficient. It was erected from one end of the border of Texas all the way to the other end in California about ten years ago, before soldiers were deployed to the border.

In the beginning, guns were being confiscated from door to door all over the United States, and those who refused to give up their arms were beaten and sent to labor camps. This heinous course of action propelled the first nationwide rebellion against the new government.

As the insurgence escalated, so did severity of the government's punishments. Those still with guns were no longer prosecuted or sent to labor camps; instead, they were executed on the spot. Because the death toll was so incomprehensible, the few remaining riots that were left quickly died down, and the final revolt by the American people ceased.

Those left who pledged to keep the right to bear arms relinquished their weapons and accepted the new era. Those who surrendered their guns but refused to submit their loyalty gained no favor from the new regime and were immediately executed. The only firing weapons around are used by federal officers.

On the far wall to the back is a target range, set back about thirty yards. In the middle of the room are metal tables designed to take a beating. Tools of just about every kind lay beneath them. Electronic devices, circuit boards, wiring, and some special kinds of metals are scattered on top of the tables.

There are several bulletproof vests sitting in the corner right below what appears to be a roll of anx-lead mesh. Just as Gabe starts to drool over the tools, a plasma cutter in the other corner catches his eye. With these tools, Gabe's brain, and these resources, there is no telling what he can create. Just when I think we are done gasping and gawking at this weapons facility haven, I press a button on the far left wall next to the bulletproof vests and part of the wall creaks   to the side, revealing another room.

I walk in the room and my knees begin to buckle. I clutch onto the side of the wall to brace myself. "Guys, I think I'm going to stay in here for a while. You can stay out there, but I need some time alone with my new friends," I say as if I've been hypnotized.

I don't think I've truly been in love before, but if I have, I didn't know it. They say it's the most spectacular, indescribable, deep-euphoric sensation that warms your heart and leaves you overcome by a feeling of serenity. When I look upon the walls, that's just how I feel at this very moment.

Boldly displayed on the walls are pounds of sharpened steel waiting to be thrown, swung, and wielded by a master swordsman. Every knife, blade, and sword gracefully hanging here is handmade with masterful precision and perfectly balanced for my hands. But the most eye-popping of them all are the two authentic Japanese katana Samurai swords, signed by Yoshihara Kuniie Saku. If it is fate that we are here, then I was born to wield them.

I carefully take one off display and hold it in a *jodan-gamae* stance, pretending to devour my enemy, striking down in *kesa-giri*. Still pretending, I kneel down to my opponent and pray for mercy upon my dead enemy. While other girls pretend to role-play as fairy princesses or delight in a fanciful soiree of dolls during imaginary tea parties for social enlightenment, I am busy pretending to wield my bloody sword into the belly of my foe, conquering the feats of evil and freeing the slaves. Who says I didn't have an enlightening childhood?

When I'm done with my imaginary fight, I turn around and see Father Joseph and Gabe staring at me with a frightened look on their faces. As I start to get up, they both back up from the door.

"Go ahead, you take all the time you need in here. We'll just be right outside the door," says Gabe with a disturbed stare. I place the sword back on the wall, then grab a nice Ka-bar knife with a black sheath, and stuff it into my pocket.

I walk over to the tables next to Father Joseph and Gabe to share my enthusiasm about the swords, but they just look at me like I'm crazy. "What?" I ask. They are staring down at the protruding bulge of the knife.

"I'm not stealing this. It was here for us, right?" I say. "It wants to be used."

"I do believe she's got the right idea," Father Joseph agrees. "Come and sit, Arena, I have much to tell you both." I can tell by the determined look in his eyes that what he is about to share with us is of great importance.

"About sixteen years ago, I was devoting my time to the seminary, discerning the Lord's call. There was a day when we were supposed to give witness to our conviction that God had brought us here. Before our time had come, I met a young man in the community who helped me when I was struggling to understand my faith. That man became a life-long friend who I have trusted to this day. That man was your Uncle Finnegan," explains Father Joseph.

"Wait, Finnegan was called to be a priest?" I ask, a little distraught.

"No, but he was called to do other things to serve our Lord and advance the Kingdom. Before the Lord called me to further my participation in the priesthood, your uncle had left the seminary and became a deacon in the military. He has since changed his profession, as you know, but his faith has never changed."

"Did you know our father?" Gabe asks.

"I did, through Finnegan's relationship with your mother. Every so often, I would visit Finnegan and his sister, your mother, and that's when I met your father. I first met him on the day your mother went into labor.

"I was there at the hospital when you two were born. I remember that day very well, pacing the halls, praying over your mother. She was having severe complications during labor. Later that evening after you two were delivered, your mother asked me to pray over you both. She looked very distraught and so transfixed upon you two. I didn't think anything about it and just assumed she was weary from the delivery, but there was something else that was on her mind, something that almost seemed to frighten her.

"Several days went by before I got a call from your father. He told me that your mother was crying ever since she left the hospital and that she wanted to speak with me. When I went to see her, she had a glow about her; her eyes were piercing through me as if I was invisible. She sat up and asked me if I ever had a vision from God before, and if I could interpret the one she had after the two of you were born.

"At that time, I'd never had a vision, much less the ability to interpret someone else's. I've spoken to and heard from the Lord on many occasions, but what she shared with me that day even took me by surprise," says Father Joseph, as he gazes deep into our eyes.

Now I'm a little frightened, but too curious not to ask. "So what did her vision reveal?"

Father Joseph is trying hard to hold back tears, but he recovers quickly and places his hands on our shoulders.

"Your mother was very strong in her convictions, and she always accepted what life arranged for her. She kept a secured covenant with the Heavenly Father to do His will and that she would be blessed beyond the realms of this Earth. She stopped crying and peacefully looked into my eyes with solace, as if God Himself was looking upon me as a father would do with his dying son, and she said to me, *I see a man standing next to my children who are grown. Two angels descend from the clouds. One covers the children with a shield, while the other stands next to them with a flaming sword. The man is dressed in black with markings on his shoulder, seven black stripes covering a blood-red stain. People are covered with fire, and children lay silently on the ground, starving to death.*

"She stopped and couldn't say any more. It seemed too much of a burden for her to carry on with her vision, and I never received any more than that from her, nor did I feel the need to. God had revealed enough. She did, however, tell me one more thing before I left, and to this day I still have a hard time understanding it. She told me that she would never get to see her children grow old and that—"

I put my hand on his arm and shake my head. "Please . . . don't, I can't . . ." My lips shake and my cheeks wet from tears. Gabe looks down, and hides any pain he has been suppressing for the last six years while I walk over to the target range. I stand there for what seems like an eternity until my knees give way, and my will to rest on my feet breaks. I fall to my knees, burying my head into the ground, and cry uncontrollably.

Has my time to grieve ended? It's been six long years, and I have yet to find the strength to stop mourning the loss of my parents.

I have not lost my convictions, but I'm beginning to lose interest in my fate. Devout or not, I'm still human, and I just can't seem to find reason in my parents' death. My mother and father were deeply rooted in the idea of finding hope in suffering, but I just can't come to accept it yet. Not right now. I understand we are to face struggles in our lives, but sometimes it's just too hard to keep a level perspective when your heart is hardened. I just pray I'm given the strength to endure this pain, and that peace will soon follow.

Father Joseph lets us have our time of grievance. After a moment, I pick myself up, walk over to Gabe, and put my arms around him. "I'm sorry." I say, my lips quivering

Father Joseph grabs our hands and hovers over us "There is no shame in weeping, my child. It is your weakness that shows your strength. We must be reminded to surrender to the strength that God provides, for His strength is made perfect in our weakness."

"Your mother was a very remarkable woman, so much that God gave her two remarkable offspring. I knew there was something extraordinary about the two of you that day at the hospital. The glow in your mother's eyes, your father kneeling down and praying over you both for hours that night, and one of the most unusual traits that the doctors had ever seen from twins—two identical birthmarks. But it wasn't necessarily that you both had identical birthmarks in the same place, as extremely rare and special as that is, it was the silhouette of them—perfectly shaped crucifixes, as if God Himself had drawn them and placed them there on the back of your necks, marking you for something yet to come."

Gabe and I glance at each other and feel the back of our necks even though we are fully aware of our markings.

"You both have been special to me from the moment you were born, and I have focused and devoted my life to protect you and make sure you would never be separated," he says.

"It was you," I say, "you were at the Foster Care Center that day. I remember you arguing with the director, but I had no idea who you were."

"Since you had not been adopted in over a year, the foster-care coordinators were about to make a very hasty decision, separating you two. There was a couple who eagerly wanted to adopt Gabe. They had no intentions of adopting two children, and I wasn't going to allow that to happen," he says.

Father Joseph leans against the table. "I fervently prayed all day for that paperwork to fall through, but even still, I knew I had to convince them to terminate the adoption at all costs."

"I'm indebted to you for your gracious determination. I wouldn't have been able to survive without Gabe in my life," A hint of sadness drifts from my voice. I stare at the ground, then look over at Gabe. I can't even begin to think that we could have been separated. "I don't mean to be ungrateful, Father, but why were you sent to keep us together?"

"Because God had other plans for you, and that is why I'm here with both of you today," he says.

Now I find myself sitting attentively upright, curious behind the real reason why we are here. I can barely control my nerves.

"After the revelation your mother had shared, it was clear to me at that moment that I was chosen by God to guide and protect the two of you," Father Joseph says.

"So why didn't we ever see you during our childhood?" I ask.

"As you know already, religion has been in a constant state of flux in this Godless nation since the regulation of the church tax that was created ten years ago by the federal government. Those tax burdens caused an uprising from the church and believers began to rebel against the government," says Father Joseph.

"How?" asks Gabe.

"A percentage of the money that was given to the church by the people was transferred to the government as a subsidized payment. In return, the government would only allow those churches that contributed to assemble in a place of believers. People stopped giving and boycotted federally owned companies. Church assemblies were banned, leaving vacant buildings to wither. Those who directly rebelled were convicted of sedition because of their disloyalty and hatred for the government, and for that, they were sentenced to labor farms to rehabilitate, or in this case, brainwashed." His face begins to deepen behind a solace pause.

"Being of the clergy, we were no longer of value unless we were directly appointed by the federal government, and our presence among the youth was forbidden. The government was afraid that we might be persuasive enough to change your ideology, causing a new rebellion. I had to stay hidden, yet close enough to protect you.

"This is no longer a free America; it has become a restricted nation that will soon plummet to its demise. Freedom of religion died the day most of this country put their trust in the government and its economical endeavors. No longer can people go to church to worship, so as our Father has taught us many times, I take the church to the people," says Father Joseph.

"So, you have been watching over us all these years like . . . some bird of prey, and we've been clueless of your existence? So why come to us now and reveal yourself?" I ask. I feel a slight sense of rejection in my heart toward Father Joseph, yet I feel compelled to restrain my emotions because he kept Gabe and me together. I know it sounds absolutely absurd to think he could have somehow changed the fate of my parents' death if he was there, the day of the crash. Maybe it could have altered the unfortunate event, but it really doesn't matter anymore, and I can blame no one for their death. I can't justify my hasty reaction. My heart slowly succumbs to God's grace and this ridiculous notion that I feel resentful disappears.

"On the very day of the car crash, God had spoken to me. I felt so numb after what had happened, especially knowing what your mother had predicted. I could barely hold myself together to believe it, much less understand it. The only thing I remember clinging to that day was the taste of whiskey . . . and then it happened."

"What?" I dare to ask.

"That very evening, an angel came to me in my dreams and revealed the very purpose of your existence in this world. I was chosen to help fulfill that existence. I was given complete and clear instructions to make sure that you two were not to be separated at any time at all costs, and that on your fifteenth birthday, I would come and deliver the message that God had shared with me to give to you. This vision was meant for your eyes to see," Father Joseph says with conviction.

At this point, my anticipation is wearing thin, and patience has become my enemy, and it's all I can do to keep from screaming.

Father Joseph looks directly into our eyes with authoritative intentions, and says to us slowly and clearly, "You two were chosen by God."

CHAPTER 8

Gabe has lifted his hands from his face and looks across the room at me. "Chosen to do what?" I attentively ask.

"Chosen to do His will, to expose the wickedness of this nation and of this world by exterminating the very evil that tempts your heart. You will seek out the one who starves His children from Him and lead those who accept His name as their Father. You were born into this world to help lead the children of God away from evil. Many will follow, but most will deny His existence and die unmercifully.

"They will be free to make their own choices, but it's up to you to lead them when they do. He has extended His grace far more than we deserve . . . and now we must answer. May God have mercy on us all," Father Joseph mightily states.

With my back to the wall, I slide down to my bottom and grab my knees tightly. I just stare at Gabe with disbelief. I've become numb and speechless to the idea that I'm supposed to do what Father Joseph asks. How can I be chosen for something so inherently pure when I battle my sins on a daily basis? I feel sick to my stomach, and I want to just crawl in a hole and die. After a few minutes of being disconnected to the world, I slowly get up and try to contemplate this lunacy. I'm not sure what's real anymore, and I'm growing ever-more eager to dismiss this madness. I've become less reticent and slightly pissed.

"I'm not saying I don't believe you or that my mother had these visions, but listen to the lunacy spewing from your lips. This is absolutely ridiculous. We're fifteen years old. I know nothing about killing a man, much less thousands. What the hell do we have to offer?" I ask.

"We're all born into this world with uncertainty, but each one of us has a fate, and it's up to you to blindly accept it or not. You two were chosen to do His will, and I have been chosen to make sure you carry out His wrath," he asserts.

There is nothing but silence in the air as his words hang heavy. My body is numb, and all I can feel are the little hairs on my arms standing up. I just stand there and wait until my mind stops racing and slows down enough to comprehend what just happened. Just when I think everything in my life begins to settle, I'm pulled into another season of uncertainty. I suddenly feel so void of anything that's real that I start to subconsciously giggle inside.

Gabe speaks up. "Assuming you are correct and this vision was purely from God and not your subconscious, why, of all the people in the world, would He choose two ordinary people who can barely get through a day of school without being pushed, punched, ridiculed, snickered at, or made to feel totally invisible?"

"Why indeed would God choose to do His bidding by empowering common, ordinary, everyday people with supernatural gifts and abilities? Because He is God and everyone has value to Him. It's what people least expect."

"You're clearly insane, you know," I simply say, frustrated with this ridiculous conversation.

"If your mother was here today, would you question her sanity?"

Now I'm irritated. "My mother is not the issue here."

"From what I know of her, I believe she's more than that."

"Then you've clearly misinterpreted the message."

"I didn't ask for any of this any more than you did, but I hold true to your mother's faith. She's the true reason why you're here . . . and deep inside I believe you know that."

I move away from his cold stare and briefly disengage from the conversation. I stand there wondering what my mother would say to me right now, as I painfully search for a moment of clarity.

The truth is, I only came here because of his ties with Finnegan. Anything else is a departure of my better judgment to come here whether or not I dismiss his prophetic claims.

"I'm only fifteen years old," I whisper.

"And David was just a boy, but his courage did not go unnoticed when he challenged Goliath. Why should you be any different?"

"Maybe because this senseless debate is absolute madness, and you've subjected yourself to believe it. The only thing I can take from this conversation is that your sanity is now in question, or maybe you're not just fucking drunk?"

"I wasn't expecting you to just simply accept this without a hint of incredulity, but I know your mother taught you better than that, especially to hold that acid tongue of yours."

"Has she? And what would you know of that? Were you ever around to see it?" I ask, aggravated now.

"I didn't have to, but I knew your mother well enough to know that she stood by her convictions without a hint of hostility. I see so much of her in you, and in that respect, I at least deserve a civil tone from you."

I feel dejected. "I, didn't mean to—"
"I know," he says softly. "Arena, I'm not here to hinder you."

"Then don't."

"Look, I understand the burdens that you and your brother have had to carry all these years, but eventually you're going to have to let faith decide your choice to believe or not . . . your mother had to."

"And if I choose not to?"

"Then humility will decide for you."

I suddenly feel a slight sense of guilt shower over me while I muse over the selfless nature of my mother's faith. I may have been out of line with Father Joseph, but I just can't entertain the idea of this conversation . . . not right now, anyway. "Suppose what you are saying is all true, in a relative sense. How are we to know who is evil, who to forgive, who to lead?" I ask.

"Call on Him and He will guide you. Listen to Him and He will show you. You will know your enemy, and the time will come when you will have to slaughter him. Those who listen will follow, and God will forgive all who ask."

"Did the sixth commandment suddenly divorce your moral conscience? You know, Thou Shalt Not Kill?"

"There's no escaping death."

"So what the hell are you suggesting—that Gabe and I just pick up a gun and go on some killing spree? Have we not been taught to love one another?" I ask.

"Indeed. But you two are extraordinary children in extraordinary times, and God Himself has called you to do both," he says as he clings to his rosary.

"Children, in the past two years, I've seen things so wickedly frightening—the kind of things you only read about in books—that would make your skin crawl from your bones. Believe me, this is very real, and you will soon know it. The world is a wicked place now, and the enemy is out there waiting to devour you like a lion ready to pounce on his prey," he says.

"And just how in the hell are we supposed to survive this?" I ask, still unconvinced of this insanity.

"No man shall kill but by the hand of God, and He has His hand wrapped around yours. Keep your mind clear, meditate on Him, and you shall see for yourself," he proclaims. His face softens as I stand there and wonder how much validity there is in his words, or if he's truly crazy. Whether or not I'm privy to his thoughts, my mind struggles to believe any of what he's saying.

"If you're so assured of our safety, then why were you sent here to protect us?" I ask.

"My part in this is not finished."

"So, are we here to save the world or something?" I say with a hint of sarcasm.

"No, you cannot save it. You are here to prepare it for its end." He carefully places a tattered scroll onto the table. Okay, at this point I'm no longer bitter or angry, but simply frightened. The idea of some strange priest, determined to plan out my future that will supposedly end sooner than I would like, isn't comforting at all. I'm very aware of the words in the book of Revelation and the Hell of which it speaks, but I damn well know I don't want to be on this earth when it's actually unleashed. I walk over to examine the parchment with Gabe and notice that the words around the top portion are in Hebrew. I can only translate some of the words but can't completely understand what it says. "What does it mean?" I ask.

Father Joseph speaks in Hebrew, "The prince who is to come will enter into the temple and declare Himself God, and on the dawn of the third day, blood will spill." His eyes stare into ours, possessed with his thoughts, and repeats the words in English.

"For the last four years I've been in contact with two of the world's most exceptional archeologists who have been searching for some of the last remains of the Dead Sea Scrolls. They have had a daunting task retrieving the artifacts, especially with the insurgence of extremists fighting over the territory where the first scrolls were found. No one has seen this particular scroll, except for the archeologists who discovered it a month ago near the West Bank on the Jordanian border, and us three. These two men sacrificed to get this to me, and if the Israeli government knew I had this, I would be dead."

I've grown tired of trying to reject Father Joseph's message, and I'm just too overwhelmed with all of this. My mother told me that people fear what they don't understand. Well, I'm scared, and I don't understand any of this. Yet the only thing clinging to my conscious that may persuade my assurance of my fate is my mother's vision. But something appears to be missing from all of this. Why haven't we discussed Finnegan's dilemma? After all, he is the one who sent the letter to us.

"So where does Finnegan fit into all of this?" I ask. Father Joseph just silently stares at us with no expression on his face. "I haven't heard from Finnegan in over five years. I was the one who sent this letter. I knew you two would not agree to come here if I didn't include Finnegan in all of this, nor did Finnegan.

"He told me that no matter what it takes, convince them to come here, even if it means deceiving you. Believe me, it was not my intention to lie to you. I was apprehensive about sending this letter to you at first, but I knew I had been called by the Lord to carry out His message and that I would die doing so. For years I have prayed for Finnegan, not knowing if he was still alive, until I received this . . . " Father Joseph places a photo on the table. "This was sent to me seven days ago by your uncle."

I look up in surprise, my eyes wide. "I convinced myself he was dead all these years."

"I'm sorry, Arena, but I don't exactly know where he may be, or if he wants us to know," says Father Joseph.

"Apparently, he's safe enough to send this to you," chimes in Gabe. The photo looks like it was taken from high ground. I notice that part of the area resembles Israel from the photos I've seen in my library book. I take a closer look and recognize that the picture is concentrated on the large structure that looks like a shrine.

"What is this?" I ask.

"That's where the Dome on the Rock stood years ago," says Father Joseph. His face is transfixed in a mysterious gaze as he draws deeply toward the photo.

"And now?" asks Gabe.

"And now . . . the Third Temple stands."

"I thought the Third Temple referred to Jesus and we were the stones that built it," I say.

"Whether figuratively or literally, it doesn't really matter now. The end of history is nigh, regardless," says Father Joseph.

I look at the picture more closely. This is without a doubt the most volatile piece of territory on the entire planet. With my body slightly trembling, I avoid looking at anyone, for I have no other words to speak. Have we truly been chosen by His Divine hand? As much as I have a difficult time believing all of this, I don't know if I'm able to reject the idea just yet. I feel like I've been deliberately deceived all these years, but deep inside I strangely accept it. There is no doubt now that our lives are about to change forever. I feel a heavy burden suddenly lift off me, as if our mother is standing behind us, with her arms wrapped around us, comforting our spirits.

I glance at the clock on the wall. I don't want to let go of this feeling right now, but we were due back home ten minutes ago. "Gabe, we've got to go, we're late," I say.

"Yes, that's good, because I think that's enough heavy-burdened information for today. Let's meet here again tomorrow," says father Joseph.

Before Father Joseph drops us off at the corner of our street, I put my hand on his shoulder, demonstrating my loyalty and thanks. I'm reluctant to say anything because I'm still a little bitter from being emotionally drained, but I feel the need to anyway. "Thank you, Father . . . for your protection, and all you have done for my family."

As we walk the rest of the block, I can't stop thinking about what our future may hold, but I'm also inclined to rid myself from the entirety of it all. I can understand Father Joseph's stance in all of this, but the idea seems a bit far-fetched and slightly ludicrous. Maybe he's right, but until I'm assuredly convinced of his irrational debate about my destiny, I'll just pretend to accept it and humor his good will. It may not be what's asked of me, but it's all I can really offer at this moment.

Before we get to the door, I suddenly remember what Derrick did to Gabe's face and quickly contemplate what we are going to tell Myra and Daniel. While I'm trying to conjure up a tall tale for Gabe's misfortune, the door opens and there stands Myra, smiling. "Hey, glad to see you two make it back home. I've got dinner ready," she says in her usual cheery voice.

I'm a little startled and confused by the response. Does she not see Gabe's face? Has she suddenly developed a form of blindness? Still nervous about the response, I just blurt out the first excuse that pops into my head regardless if she noticed Gabe's face or not. "He ran into a flagpole!"

"What?" she says, perplexed.

Her vision must be hindered, so I casually walk through the door as if nothing happened at all. It's not until I get through the foyer when she notices. "Dear God! Gabe, are you okay? That looks terrible." Concerned as she is, I'm pretty sure she isn't boosting Gabe's self-confidence at the moment.

"It was an accident. I'll be fine, most of the major swelling has gone down," says Gabe, unconcerned. His response to Myra's reaction certainly shows a change in his demeanor since the first day of school. If he was lacking any self-confidence or struggling with insecurities, he's been cured. I guess after today, both of us have changed.

I'm so tired, I just want to go upstairs, take a shower, and collapse on my bed, but talking with Niki always seems to alleviate my weariness. She's sitting in the living room, so I detour from the stairs to see her.

"Hey, Sis, come sit down and tell me about school," Niki says. Before I sit down, I can't help but to give her a hug like I always do. "You seem a little different today. Anything interesting you want to share with me?" she asks.

I think to myself for a moment before answering, because somewhere dwelling deep within my conscience, I feel the need to share the discomforting conversation we had with Father Joseph, but I can't. Whether or not she would understand as my sister, none of what transpired this after- noon must ever be mentioned. Even if she is loyal to my secrets, only Gabe and I can be privy to such matters, at least for now. It's in my best interest to just keep the conversation to the normal small chit-chat before I reveal something I'm not even sure is true. "I've made some friends at school," I say instead.

"Well, that's good. What are their names?"

"Juliana, who I think has a thing for Gabe, but don't mention that to him," I say, "and Jacob, but he's just a friend," I quickly add. Niki smiles, as if she knows I may have a slight crush on Jacob, but she doesn't push the conversation any more than that.

I guess he's the first boy I've been attracted to who hasn't acted like an ass, but I still try to convince myself that he's just a friend.

"Don't worry, I won't mention anything," says Niki with a wink.

After a nice meal, I like to lie down in bed and read into the late hours until I fall asleep. But tonight is different. I try to fall asleep, but it's useless, so I get out a book of poems my mother wrote when she was young. They always comfort me when I'm depressed, but tonight I just want a little of my mother to speak to me when I read the verses. All of her poems were about her experiences growing up. I find a passage in the back of the book that I remember my mother telling me about when she read it to me for the first time.

Someone has left this earth and didn't even say good-bye, what a waste, did somebody really have to die? His whispers remain in silence, yet his spirit has departed, I don't really know how to feel, but our hearts have all been hardened.
A wife and child now left behind, I just cannot explain, the words I say, I just can't find, there is nothing here to gain. We stand in silence to hear His call, as we mourn for another day,
and when my knees break down and fall, I speak to my Father and pray.

The poem was about a young man who killed himself because he had no money to feed his family and no job to support them. One of his legs was torn off from a farming accident out in the fields that left him disabled, depressed, and jobless. The only thing he knew how to do was farm, and when that was gone, so was his will to live.

I remember my mother being angry with this man for what he did to his family, and many times she prayed to God to have mercy on him. My mom always thought suicide was a selfish and cowardly act regardless of the situation, but at the same time, no one really stepped up to encourage, help, or give simple comfort to the man during his depression. She said they were both wrong—wrong for killing himself, and wrong for not helping their fellow neighbor.

I put the book away and kneel by my window, then pray as I do every night. I meditate and speak to my Heavenly Father for what seems like an hour, and the only thing that keeps me from continuing is the deep roar of thunder in the distance. It's almost as if God is moaning from the sky.

I slip back into the bed underneath the shroud of blankets and try to fall asleep. While I turn my head and look out the window, lightning fills the sky and thunder rumbles, putting on a dazzling show as rain showers down, accompanying the two in a trio of nature's wonders. After a few minutes, the rain begins to gradually calm my thoughts. My eyes grow heavy, and I fall asleep.

Suddenly, a clap of thunder booms like a cannon right outside my window, disrupting my dream. I awaken to the darkness as sweat runs down my spine, but not from a nightmare this time, from the word of God.

I pull the sheets back, sit up, and clasp my fingers together, holding up my knees, when my door creaks open. It's Gabe with sweat on his face and a look of terror in his eyes.

"Are you okay?" I ask.

"Yeah, I think so. It's just . . ." he says, then pauses.

"Just what?" I ask.

"I had a dream, a vision, or whatever. I believe God spoke to me, or to us. You were there in the dream kneeling next to me on a stone next to a—"

"A tree with white blooms that appeared to be alive. I believe it was a cherry blossom," I finish his thought.

"Yes! And the two angels next to it. You had the same dream?" Gabe asks.

My tongue suddenly rests in silent, so I nod instead.

CHAPTER 9

As long as I've known my brother, I've never had the slightest indication of what he's thinking, much less finishing his thought. Regardless if we are twins, it's not like we share the same brain. This is becoming a little spooky. We both try to calmly discuss the dream. What might be confusing to others seems perfectly clear to us, and it's only because it was meant for us and no other. The dream was beautiful; it was like no place I'd ever seen. I can only describe it as a breathtaking view of vibrant color teaming with lively wonder surrounded by celestial creations. I'm completely without words that describe the place where we sat.

God stood before us, but He was not physically seen, and yet we knew He was there all around us—in the flowers, trees, the vast sky and space, and in the very air we breathe. His voice was like a father talking to his children, preparing them for a long journey, and His instructions were clear:

Trust no man who serves another god or idol. Two men will help guide you through your journey — one will leave this earth before your time is finished. Nation by nation, the world's messages will be overcome by a mass of blackness and into a dead of silence. By nightfall your nation will have started what can't be stopped in a string of horrifying events. On the seventh day of the new moon, your journey will begin. As the sky grows dark in the east, many lives will perish. Blackness will devour the Earth, covering the light of the sun. Your nation will soon succumb to another. Blood will rain from the clouds causing famine like no other. When the moon turns as red as blood, you will know the time is near. Do not fear your enemy. Do not worry, my children, trust in Me. Don't boast in victory, but pray for your enemy. Do not seek revenge for the death you meet, for it will be by My wrath that is just. Go and fulfill your destiny. So it has been written, so it shall be done.

*   *   *

Another morning has come, but it's unlike the others I've awoken to. I feel less engaged to entertain the new day after last night's dream, but I guess I have no choice. I feel somewhat lost, and the only thing somewhat calming my racing thoughts is the welcome chance to see Jacob's face again.

Whether or not what Father Joseph told us was true, it's my choice to believe it or not. It's becoming painfully apparent that my faith is lacking, but I'm beginning to see now.

I descend the stairs, less excited about today's venture, as I'm disinclined to convince Myra again about our afterschool rendezvous. Surprisingly, she's very understanding about us coming home a little late from school, and she has no quarrels about any afterschool programs. I feel somewhat guilty lying to her like this, but I have no choice. This is the way it has to be.

Before we leave for school, I embrace her longer than normal. I even give Daniel a hug, clasping onto the back of his jacket as if this is the last time I will see him. Gabe follows suit. You can tell Myra knows something is up, but she doesn't make too much over the exchange of long good-byes.

"Okay, what are you two up to? You need something?" she asks with a half-crooked smile.

"No, we just appreciate all you have done for us over the years. We can't really say enough to thank you, and sometimes it feels much better to just show you," I say.

Myra looks a little choked up, so she just smiles and gives us one more squeeze of gratitude.

"So, we were thinking about inviting some friends we met at school over for dinner tomorrow if that's okay," I say.

"Of course, I will prepare us a nice meal," says Myra.

As we get out of the car, I spot Juliana waving at us. We meet under the large tree, the same one where McKenzie insulted me on the second day of school. I guess this is sort of our new morning meeting place, but it would only be complete if Jacob were here.

Just as I start thinking about him, two hands cover my face from behind. "Guess wh—" says a husky voice. I thrust my elbow back into the stranger's sternum. Down they go, tumbling to the pavement, nearly breathless.

My stomach completely sinks and my cheeks blush abash. I'm mortified.

"I'm so sorry, Jacob! I didn't know it was you. I'm so, so sorry," I plead, trying to help him up.

Okay, now that's Arena: 2 and Jacob: 0.

"Wow, Arena, a door to the head and a punch to the gut. You sure know how to treat a guy," Gabe says, laughing.

"Not funny," I snap, staring down Gabe.

Jacob laughs a little and adds to the joy of Gabe's comments, but I sense he does it just to make me feel better. "Looks like you can take care of yourself. I like that in a girl," Jacob flirts, struggling to lift a grin.

I think he's made me smile more this morning than I have in the past year.

"Gabe, your eye looks much better and it looks like most of the swelling on your nose has subsided," says Juliana, as she examines Gabe's injuries like a well-trained nurse.

The bewilderment on Jacob's face obliges me to explain Gabe's misfortunes with Derrick's fist. "Well, I give you credit for not running from him," says Jacob.

"Who said I wasn't trying?" Gabe retorts.

"So, I thought it would be nice if you guys could come over to our house for dinner tomorrow," I say.

"Sure," says Juliana, as she looks at Gabe, not necessarily addressing me.

"I could use a good meal," says Jacob like any typical male would say referring to food. When the bell rings for class, we all agree to meet for lunch at our normal table.

I'm feeling very good today, and there seems to be very little right now that can sour my mood. That feeling doesn't last long though when I approach my locker and see it covered in honey. Seriously, who takes pleasure in making someone suffer for no reason at all? I can think of nothing that I have done to anyone that would warrant such a shameful act of juvenile mischief. I suddenly remember the soaking of three unpleasant girls and retract that thought. So maybe I do deserve this. I try to delay my accusations, but that lasts as long as it takes my eyes to blink.

I'm assuming this is the work of McKenzie and her two chimpanzees. Let me retract the last part of that statement— two baboons. I don't want to insult the intellect of a chimpanzee. Who else have I intentionally rubbed the wrong way? I was going to reserve judgment for these three cretins, but I can hear them trying to hold in their laughter, waiting for my reaction around the corner.

It would be all too easy to just snap their little necks, but I'm going to ride this out for the rest of the day and see how much grace I'm willing to extend. I can't let them see that it bothers me, so I just pretend I don't even notice it.

As Gabe and I walk around the corner to our class, I address the baboons with a smile. "Hi, nice morning isn't it? You all have a blessed day," I say cheerfully, as we pass six stunned eyes and one crooked lip.

"Are you feeling okay?" Gabe asks, perplexed.

"Aye, I'm feeling just fine, my dear brother."

"Well, stop it because you're freaking me out."

*　　*　　*

At lunchtime, the four of us sit down at our usual spot and discuss the particulars about where and when to meet at our place for dinner. "I can text everyone our address," says Gabe.

"I don't have a phone," says Jacob.

"Okay, I can send you an e-mail then," says Gabe.

"I don't have a computer either," Jacob says.

"Really, how do you communicate with everyone?" Gabe asks.

"I talk to them in person," retorts Jacob, making Gabe look silly, "but if I need to do some research, I just go to the library. I'm not much of a socialite on the Internet."

"Are you done?" I harshly ask Gabe. He just looks at me with his crinkled nose. "Well, I think it's a shame we have to depend on technology to communicate. What would we do if everything went down, just sit and twiddle our thumbs?" I try to mask any embarrassment Gabe has unintentionally caused at Jacob's expense.

"Here, give me your hand," I say to Jacob. I carefully grab his slightly callused hand and write down my address in permanent marker. I pause for a moment before I add my name, just in case he falls victim to immediate short-term memory loss. Amnesia can be a bitch.

Today's lunch is less than stellar, but because I'm in a good mood, I clean my tray except for the genetically engineered glob of chocolate gel resting in my bowl. The only resemblance to chocolate pudding I see is the dark skin that's formed on top, keeping any germs from penetrating the surface.

I excuse myself and take my tray to the wash line. On the way I see McKenzie making a mockery of some poor kid's clothes at the adjacent table. As much as I want to stuff this chocolate mud in her face, I just concentrate on looking forward, hoping to avoid her unwanted company.

Right before I pass her, two guys bump into my tray, it flies upward and sends the paper bowl of pudding onto McKenzie's chair. I quickly observe to see if anyone saw the flying pudding, but it goes unnoticed. Plus, McKenzie is still taunting the poor guy across the way. I find myself having a battle with my ego—should I do the right thing and say something, or do I pass up an opportunity of what goes around comes around? It is McKenzie after all.

This is quite the conundrum, I reject the latter, but before I can even take a step, it's too late. McKenzie sits down on the congealed chocolate custard. She quickly stands up, belting out a cry in disgust as the pudding hangs onto the back of her jeans for dear life.

If I hadn't been pontificating about my dilemma, I could have saved her from the embarrassment. Oh well, such is life. All I hear is a roar of laughter and a very angry McKenzie while I drop my tray off. I don't look back; I just keep walking, hoping she hasn't spotted me and making a link to the incident. I can only smile.

Lunch is over and it's back to another stimulating hour of educational apathy. I know the teachers do all they can to share their knowledge without stepping on the philosophical egos of the administration, but because they are told exactly how to teach, it really cheapens the instruction kids get.

The educational system in this country lacks a sense of encouragement, and has delineated our intellect based on our weaknesses instead of our strengths. It has failed miserably at giving students the skills and tools they need that would have otherwise shaped us for a world that is less appealing now than it was ten years ago. Students are no longer able to foster creativity, distinguishing their gifts from others, but are merely forced by the government into vocations they were not meant for. And from what I now know about my fate in this life, I truly believe that's exactly what our leaders had intended.

We walk back to our lockers before class begins and just out of sight by the water fountain, I spot Derrick. I grab Gabe, warning him that we should take a small detour. He takes my hand off his arm out of defiance. "No! It's my right to walk these halls just like anyone else. I'm not afraid." His hands shake uncontrollably.

"You sure about that?" I ask, looking at his trembling fingers. "Okay then, I got your back, bro." We walk down the halls with Jacob trailing behind, and, as expected, Derrick spots us like an owl, stalking a mouse.

He lunges forward and pushes Gabe's head into the lockers, giving him a small cut from the sharp sides. Gabe tries to stand up, but he slips back down from the force of Derrick's shoe.

"I think I really need to reevaluate that turning-the-other-cheek thing," Gabe says as I hold his head up.

"This isn't the freshman hall. What makes you think you can pass by our hall?" Derrick asks while hovering over Gabe. Derrick couldn't care less about freshmen walking these halls, but because it's Gabe and me, he feels the need to display his egotistical manhood to the whole school. Of course Derrick is no more of a man than I'm a royal princess with etiquette. He's a small-minded, shit-smelling, roid-raging prick, and I'm being nice.

I spring to my feet and sweep Derrick's legs out, bringing him down hard to the floor. Before he can get up, I've already strategically planted my foot on the side of his face and my thumb firmly embedded into the nerve near the back of his spine.

He lays there unable to move, like an opossum waiting for his enemy to leave. I let go after a few seconds, hoping he will understand I'm not here to back down. He struggles to get up, but immediately tries to brush off the embarrassment of being taken down by a girl in front of a crowded hall.

"Is that all you got? You think catching me off guard like that is going to stop me from breaking you in two?" Derrick lunges toward me, but I stand my ground knowing he is too easy to defeat. Gabe tries to get between us, but Jacob pulls Derrick's shoulder.

"Leave her alone!" Jacob shouts.

Derrick turns and swings his arm toward Jacob's face, throwing him off balance and falling to the floor.

"What, is this your girlfriend? You honestly think she wants to go out with trash like you? Does she know you're going to end up like your father? You don't belong here, Jacob. Go back and stay with the other Watchers," says Derrick.

My heart suddenly sinks into my stomach as I look down at Jacob's face. His head tilts downward as if he shamefully accepts Derrick's comments. I'm saddened by the turn of events and it's all my fault. I couldn't care less where Jacob came from. His father's past matters nothing to me, nor do I feel any different about my relationship with Jacob. I'm more pissed now at Derrick's comments than I am at what he did to Gabe.

There is nothing but silence now until the second bell rings for class to start.

"This isn't over. The next time we meet like this you'll wish you had transferred," says Derrick, pointing at us. When he leaves, the crowd immediately dissolves.

I walk over to Jacob, but he doesn't look like he's in the mood to be helped up; instead, he rejects my hand and pulls himself up, trying to erase the possible embarrassment that he just encountered with Derrick.

While we walk to our class, I waver over the idea of talking to Jacob about Derrick's cruel intentions. What he said about his father being a Watcher stirs my nerves to the point where I can't let this awkward silence linger. I hate prying, but I can't help not knowing, so I just ask anyway. "What did Derrick mean back there?" I say softly. Jacob doesn't answer; he just looks down without any emotion, and I know I shouldn't have said anything.

I move my hand toward his, then interlace my fingers in-between his and hope he doesn't reject me. His warm hand grasps mine, and I can just barely recognize the corner of his mouth raise as if he wants to smile. This is the first time either one of us has shown any kind of affection toward one another, and it's the first time I've held a boy's hand like this since Jimmy Larkin in the second grade.

Before we go to class, we pass one of the many televisions that hang in the corners of the hallways and in each classroom. I stop and stare at the news playing in the background, when suddenly, it hits me. Like a villain, I forge a sinister grin. "I think I know how we can calm Derrick's ego."

CHAPTER 10

Before the last bell rings, the television hanging in the corner of the classroom suddenly comes on. The TVs are normally for educational purposes, but when there is pertinent weather information or some national news coverage of importance, class can be interrupted at any time.

The government controls just about everything, but the media still has some slight advantages in pursuing and displaying stories to the people that the government would probably much rather have filtered. This has sparked much of the recent debate going on in what's left of our administration.

The government has a tight lid on global information filtered through the media, especially via the Internet, which has recently been heavily regulated, but today's sudden news coverage is not without a hint of irony—it's about our very own nation. At the bottom of the screen is a scrolling ticker that reads: *Breaking news – A possible class movement on the rise.*

The newscaster comes on the camera and says, "*The ongoing class wars have created a deterrent in policy during a special congressional hearing today that included special guests, Gennadi Gorshkov of Russia, and Delun Yeung of China. The nation's relationship with these two leaders has led to extensive cultural adaption policies. During this international diplomacy, the two leaders have recently exercised their voice about similar changes that have been put into place in their respective countries. Talks between the political parties may have reached an agreement to remove all Watchers from a twenty-mile radius of every city. This restructured policy goes on to include a possible relocation of poverty-stricken families to designated poor regions, which according to leadership is deemed necessary and is less likely to disturb a future international economic policy. Though these talks have not been confirmed as resolute, Russian and Chinese leadership have vowed to see these policies successfully determined by the end of the week. The president says he doesn't . . ."*

The broadcast suddenly turns to black followed by an eerie silence, and the television shuts off a minute later, leaving us wondering what was going to be said next. This information was obviously not supposed to leak out, and the government has now forcefully stepped in, controlling the media's outlet of information, but too much has already been said. The events that have been prophetically broadcast are now in motion and can't be stopped. It has begun.

For a moment, nobody says a word; they just look down at their desks, wondering if they will be the ones relocated. Our teacher looks a little stunned, but doesn't hesitate to stand up and try to make everyone feel at ease. "It's the same old mantra we hear from our government and nothing ever happens. I wouldn't worry too much over this. Information can always be misleading."

Misleading, really? Do you honestly think we're not smart enough to determine what this administration is capable of doing after what this country has gone through the past ten years? I understand the teacher's intentions, but at least give us a little credit.

Before anyone can say a word, the final bell rings, leaving everyone hanging on with a little more uncertainty now. After this troubling news, I find the little time I spend with Jacob outside a bit unsettling before Gabe and I meet with Father Joseph in the den. That's what we call the fortified concrete structure. Like clockwork, we find ourselves sneaking into the back window of the gas station and through the side room where Father Joseph waits.

"Have you heard the news lately?" Father Joseph asks with an unearthly stare. His question is directed toward me, as if he's trying to drive home his point from yesterday.

"Yes, or at least most of it before it was shut off," I say.

Father Joseph takes a key from his pocket and hands it to Gabe. "Here, take this, just in case we somehow get separated from here on out. I made a spare copy."

We walk into the den, and it's the same as it was yesterday, but it still feels absolutely incredible to walk into a room with this much hi-tech weaponry. I don't know if I'll ever get used to it.

"Come and sit, there is someone waiting to meet with you," says Father Joseph. Out from the hidden room where all the knives are located pops out Henry Matsuda, my martial arts instructor.

"Henry!" I run to him with open arms. "I'm so glad to see you," I say, hugging him.

"Gabriel, it's always great to see you. Any new inventions you've been working on?" Henry asks.

"No, been too busy trying not to worry about getting my head kicked in at school, but with all this equipment at my fingertips, I may be able to find a cure," says Gabe.

I haven't seen Henry in three months, since the beginning of summer. He usually gives me the summers off to work my craft at a pace I'm normally more comfortable with, but I still try to emulate my exercises as if I'm back in the dojo with him.

"Have you been disciplined in the arts? Has your practice continued or suffered since we last met?" Henry asks.

"You can be the judge of that," I say with poise. I hope I haven't overstepped my bounds, any arrogance aside, but I'm feeling rather confident today.

"You might want to step back, Gabe, I think God's work is on display," Father Joseph says softly, pulling Gabe back by his shirt.

"Don't let your overconfidence expose your weakness. Respect can go a long way, my young student. Why don't you go ahead and take off your backpack and let's just see what you have learned," Henry says.

"I think I'll just leave it on for now," I say.

"Don't get too cocky," he says.

Henry takes his position as I take mine, but I stay on the defense at first, blocking everything he gives me. After about two minutes of blocking his punches and kicks, he steps it up a notch.

"That's a good warm-up, Arena, but that's child's play for you. Let's test your other skills," he says.

Henry runs toward me, and with his arm raised to the right of my shoulder, he swings a phantom punch with his back turned to me. He then slides down to sweep my legs, but to his surprise, my instincts have matured. I jump and turn with a back kick to his head. He seems to stop playing around with me now and becomes more serious.

I dodge every kick and counter with a knee to his chest. If he only knew I was just playing with him too. Ad-libbing in dramatic fashion, he grabs a wooden stick from the table to intimidate me.

He comes at me at every angle he can think of, and it becomes too easy for me to either block or dodge, and I finally pin him down with the stick to his throat with a simple *Sambo* move. "Nice move," he says.

"This is where I slit your throat, of course," I respond playfully.

He gets up, perspiring and panting, yet I've failed to find one bead of sweat resting on my skin. "Kung Fu," Henry says loudly. This is where I should excel because it's my favorite of all the martial arts.

I stand in a firm horse stance as Henry comes at me, attacking with strong center punches, and quick, short-burst kicks. He swings his elbows and fires a right punch as I counter with a left grabbing block and a right dragon claw to the throat. I follow by a sweep to his front leg and finish with a right knife-edge kick to his other leg. Henry lies on the floor and his face is in total shock. My eyes pierce through him like daggers.

He gets up and opens with a right-left punch combination. I block the first shot with a left tiger-claw parry and follow with a right tiger-claw parry. I take control of Henry's left arm and apply a tiger claw to the face and groin. I look into Henry's eyes and say, "If I wanted to, I could just end it here and rip your testicles off right now, but like you said, respect goes a long way."

I pull down his head with his left arm and strike the back of his neck with a right swinging forearm. He gets up quickly, playing right into my next move. He swings upward with his elbow to my jaw, but I turn around, taking my backpack off and sliding his right arm through the loop. He tries to counter by ducking under to release his arm, but I slip the other loop from the backpack onto his left arm and turn once more, leaving his useless limbs tied to a Hello Kitty backpack and his knees on the ground.

"Looks like you're ready for school. Shall I pack you a lunch?" I arrogantly banter.

He sits there briefly, looking defeated, but quickly smiles. "Well played," Henry resigns. I help him up and give him a competitors hug.

"You taught me well, and I want to thank you for all you have done. Really, you've been like a father to me, Henry. It means a lot" I thank him.

I can't help but glance at Gabe and Father Joseph, both staring in silence with their mouths wide open.

"God have mercy on the boy who tries to take advantage of her," says Father Joseph to Gabe.

"Come and sit down, Arena," says Henry, trying to catch his breath. "You've obviously proven your skills to master such techniques, but will it be enough when you actually have to use them?" My face suddenly flattens.

"No doubt you're gifted, but you lack one thing that takes most people a lifetime to understand," he continues.

"Yeah, and what's that?" I deflect.

He pauses, looks into my eyes, and says, "Humility. This I cannot teach you, and I'm afraid your respect is deprived from it."

I just sit there and ponder the complexity of Henry's wisdom, and realize the only thing complex about it is my will to accept it or not. How much more of my life will unravel before I see the simplicity of its very nature? Humility is the sharpest weapon of a warrior—it's unscathed under God's grace.

"I know what's in your heart, Arena. I've seen the pain on your face throughout the years, but you and your brother were chosen whether you accept it or not," Henry says.

I gape upon his face, puzzled and slightly stunned, and now realize Father Joseph must have filled him in about why we are here. Either that, or he has already known for reasons I can't explain.

"There is obviously something very special about the two of you. I know you acknowledge it, but now you must embrace it and never let go. I came here today just as Finnegan had instructed me, to help prepare you both for the hell you will witness from this day forward. I promise you won't be able to run from this, but if you lead, I will certainly follow," says Henry.

I gaze down at the floor with troubling thoughts that are less musing than the fate at hand. Henry's solemn face is pierced with an uncertainty I have not seen before, which makes this engaging moment even more unsettling.

"I will not allow you to go down a path you're not ready for," Henry says. His words share a small comfort that briefly lures me away from my disturbing gaze, but the reality of all this is beginning to consume me with fear.

The disquieting silence leaves Father Joseph kneeling down on the ground to pray. "Before we begin, let's acknowledge God's mercy and grace, and give thanks to our Lord," he says.

After Father Joseph prays over us, Gabe takes over the tools on the far right table and begins soldering right away on some circuit boards he finds in a plastic box, while Henry takes me into the knife room to train me with the swords.

Just a few days ago, I was preparing for high school, trying to avoid new enemies, and now I'm training and preparing to kill my enemies.

A couple of hours go by as we lose track of time. I leave the knife room and try to pry my brother away from his gadgets. "We need to go, Gabe. Remember, we have dinner plans tonight." He ignores me, so I'm forced to interject. "Hey, Casanova! Juliana is waiting for you!"

He abruptly drops his tools and says, "So what are we waiting on?"

Before we take off, I glance at Gabe's handiwork and notice a box of hi-tech gadgets sitting on the table next to him. I spot a couple of wireless pinhole cameras inside the box near the bottom. "Gabe, can these cameras transmit a signal from any source?" I ask.

"Of course, as long as the source is no further than two miles away. You just need to dial in the signal code and match the frequency of the camera to the frequency of the coded source. It's quite simple really. Why?" Gabe asks.

"No reason, just curious," I say, as I carefully slip the small cameras into my pocket without anyone noticing before we leave the den.

We walk into the house, and the aroma of roasted duck is so overwhelming, my saliva is trying to escape my mouth. I quickly go upstairs to shower and change into something more appealing than I normally would wear. I'm a jeans and T-shirt kind of girl, but tonight must be special if I want to get Jacob's attention. I put on a tight black skirt and a low-cut, delicate-knit black top that fits snugly around my girlish curves—but not exceeding to the naughty exposure that would otherwise make me a whore . . . unless that's the idea, *shit*.

I try on a pair of Niki's black high-heels and wonder how in the hell any girl would want to subject their feet to this unnecessary pain. I take two steps and nearly fall flat on my face as my ankle rolls to the side. Guys have no idea how much time and trouble we go through to make them smile. I should get an award tonight if I make it through the evening without tripping.

As I finish putting the last touches of light makeup on my face, I stare into the mirror and see a young woman before me. All dressed up, I can really see my mother's reflection now. Gabe spends the next thirty minutes making sure that every hair on his head is evenly placed.

"Hey, Gabe, you've spent enough time on your hair. You think it's worth thirty minutes for her to notice it? You do look very nice though." I pause and poke my head back in the bathroom. "So don't screw it up by acting like an animal at the dinner table. You better bring your big-boy manners tonight."

The doorbell rings and I can only assume it's either Juliana or Jacob standing outside, so I run downstairs to greet them. I open the door where they are both shyly standing in their well-dressed attire. I eagerly greet them, butnot without gawking at Jacob first. I can't believe this is the same guy I see at school hiding underneath those baggy clothes. "Hey guys, come on in," I say.

"Where's Gabe?" Juliana anxiously asks.

"He should be coming down any minute. You look very nice Jacob," I say sweetly.

Jacob just stands there and stares, and any words he's trying to spit out are suppressed by distraction. Juliana nudges her elbow into Jacob's ribs to break his hypnotic state. "You look very nice yourself," he stutters. Juliana rolls her eyes and shakes her head.

Gabe comes racing downstairs with the largest grin I've ever seen on his face. He looks at Juliana like she's a piece of meat and the only thing he can muster is, "Hey."

"I like what you did with your hair," Juliana admires as she runs her thin fingers across the side of hishead.

Gabe turns to me, smiles, and mouths, "Yes, it was worth it." I watch my baby brother escorting Juliana into the dining room with all smiles and realize he's finally embraced a state of happiness after enduring so many years of depression. Jacob stares at me, making for an awkward moment, until he gestures his elbow out for me to hold on to.

"Wow, what a gentleman. I haven't seen one of those in a . . . well, I haven't seen one until now," I say while he gallantly escorts me into the dining room.

After a pleasant meal, Gabe and Juliana go into the living room along with Niki and Myra, looking through photos while Jacob and I go outside and sit on the porch swing. We just sit there without talking, gazing across the horizon, waiting for the awkward silence to break.

"I'm really sorry about yesterday. I didn't mean to step into your personal space. What Derrick said was really none of my business," I say. He remains silent, so I hold his hand to comfort him. I struggle to change the subject and wonder if I'm really capable of making this a pleasant moment. His large hand caressing mine feels comforting, but as he nudges closer to my body, the sensation in my heart grows warm with delight. I almost forget about the awkward silence.

After a few minutes of the quiet intimate moment, Jacob finally speaks up. "My mother killed herself when I was young, and my father never recovered from the loss. His mind began to deteriorate and depression manifested from a combination of the loss of his job, wife, and the motivation to raise his son. He left when I was twelve, scrounging about among the other Watchers. I tried to get him to come back home, but his mental state was too far gone—he didn't even recognize his own son, and I didn't have the heart to have him brought in to the mental ward," Jacob says with a stone-cold face. I feel overwhelmingly speechless right now. I don't know how to respond to what he just told me. I'm sad, depressed, but glad he trusted in me to tell me his past.

Those who are mentally incapacitated are sent to the ward and given a full lobotomy, an archaic convention of weeding out the sick. Most patients die within months. After yesterday, I'm absolutely stunned he said a word at all, much less this. I have no words to say that will console him, so I just lean my head on his chest as he puts his arm around me.

"Where do you live?" I bravely ask.

"I live alone in a room right above the Jensen's Cleaners building. My father was good friends with the owners, and I begged them to let me stay there to avoid being taken into child custody."

I want more than anything to help him find a home; I even come up with this crazy idea in my head of sharing his predicament to Myra, hoping she would take him in to our home, but I quickly erase the idea and just hold on to him tightly before the night ends.

"Jacob," I say softly.

"Yes?" he whispers.

"Do you believe that God has a plan for every human being on this earth?" I ask.

"Why, you not happy with yours?"

"Well, no, but—"

"If there's no plan, then what's the point? Stray from it or not, we all have a destiny," Jacob wisely says.

For some reason, a feeling of comfort covers me. I sit up momentarily and turn to Jacob and do what I have never done with any boy—I steadily lean into his lips and caress my mouth softly against his. My heart grows ever brighter, dispersing a radiant burn throughout my body. When our lips finally disengage from the intimate moment, we sit on the swing together and hold each other tightly until the evening ends.

Before the 9:00 curfew draws near, Myra asks Niki to take Jacob and Juliana home. All I can think about is the last and only kiss I may ever have, because you never know what uncertainty tomorrow may bring. Before he leaves, he unhooks his cross necklace and places it around my neck. I don't say anything, but just smile as he touches the back of my neck ever so slightly, making the tiny hairs stand up and creating the most dazzling sensation I have ever felt. "It looks much better on you," he says as he walks toward to the car.

I'm smitten with a feeling I can only assume is love— something I've never really felt toward a boy before. I'm so engrossed in this feeling that I completely forget about the world around me, or realizing I'm sitting in the living room, until I recognize Derrick's father in one of his obnoxious commercials on TV. Suddenly, the commercial is abruptly interrupted. Myra, Daniel, and Gabe's eyes are glued to the breaking newscast. The news anchor explains the recent explosions that occurred tonight in downtown Chicago, killing thousands of people.

"There has been mayhem ever since the two explosions took place near the John Hancock building downtown. This footage shows what happened just before the first explosion. As you can see, it appears what we can make out are close to two hundred federal officers searching for select individuals and detaining them. Many of the detainees are being shuttled onto large federal vehicles. If you look to the far right side, you can see a fifty-vehicle convoy leaving the city. It's unknown whether or not if the explosions were retaliation from those being detained or a brutal force of action from the federal officers. This chaotic and cruel upheaval is disturbingly reminiscent of the gun riots five years ago that caused our nation to experience one of the darkest hours in its history. Although the president's reorganization policy has come under sever scrutiny, causing a growing resistance among much of the nation, there has been no official word from government officials of Martial Law being declared. We ask viewers to be advised that the footage we are about to reveal is extremely graphic and may not be suitable for children to see . . ."

It doesn't take more than ten seconds to roll, when the screen turns blue followed by a series of beeps and a scrolling message at the bottom of the screen that reads: *Technical difficulty, please stand by*. It's obvious now that the feds shut down the broadcast and were most likely responsible for the explosions. All I can think about is when the next city will be hit.

"What's happening to this country?" Myra asks as she covers her mouth with her hands in distress. I haven't the heart to tell her that it will soon be extinct.

I understand the nation's tragic direction, but I'm still a teenager trying to survive high school at the moment. I grab Gabe's shirtsleeve and gesture for him to go upstairs.

"What's so important you need to drag me into your room?" says Gabe, perturbed. I get out the pinhole cameras from my top dresser drawer and toss them onto my bed. "You took those from the box?" he says, surprised.

"Yes, now what you said earlier back in the den about getting these cameras to broadcast on any source . . . you can still do that, right?" I ask.

"Of course, but why?" he says.

"What do you say about getting Derrick back without physically hurting him," I say.

"Look, I don't condone revenge, Arena," says Gabe, as he rubs the back of his bruised head.

"Just this one time, Gabe. I promise I won't ask you again."

"I'll need to take my laptop tomorrow, and a code receiver attachment," he reluctantly says. The distress drawn on his face makes this plan less enticing now.

"What . . . is it Derrick? Are you afraid of the consequences? Gabe, he beat the hell out of you for no reason other than just being a prick" I say.

"Derrick is the least of our worries."

"What do you mean?"

"You sure you're ready for this?"

"Look, Derrick will never know, I can assu—"

"No, not that. Are you sure you're willing to accept your fate? I mean, when the time comes, will you do it?"

"Do what, run?" I ask, perplexed.

"Pull the trigger. Will you have it in you to take another man's life when it counts?"

I sit there, pondering what he's getting at, and as much as I want to be confident in my answer, I have no response to give. I honestly don't know how I will feel. I know it's inevitable, but I've been avoiding the idea of it since the dream. I give him the only answer I know.

"I guess in this life, I will have no choice." There is a lingering silence before Gabe drops the conversation and continues with Derrick's payback plan.

"So, I think I have an idea how to pull this off, but I'm still not too thrilled about this, Arena." Gabe uneasily says.

I put my arm around him and squeeze. "Thanks, little brother."

Unamused, he parts my embrace. "You do realize we're twins."

"Is that what Mom told you?" I sarcastically jest before I walk to the bathroom.

"You can keep telling yourself you are older just because you came out first, but I was in the womb four minutes longer, which makes me seasoned," he contests.

*　*　*

Morning has arrived, and I can already feel the clouds growing darker as a storm slowly approaches from the west. I see Jacob and Juliana waiting for us underneath the old tree. I feel a little chill in the air as we pass the side of the school building. Behind us, next to a crowd of people, stands Derrick and his cult followers. Gabe fretfully picks up his pace toward the tree and meets Juliana with a half-excited hug. His sporadic and jumpy reaction to every person passing by within twenty feet exposes the fact that he's on edge.

"Why are you so nervous, Gabe?" asks Juliana.

"Is it that obvious? All right, I change my mind, Arena, this isn't going to work. I can't do this," says Gabe.

"Can't do what?" asks Jacob.

The bell rings before Gabe can explain. "I'll tell you later."

We hurry around the building to the front doors to avoid any altercations, but a large crowd of people moves toward us and Derrick is among the pack.

It's too late. Derrick spots us, stops, and waits for the crowd to move through the door before another ridiculing moment begins. Derrick signals for us to walk ahead, as if he is exercising a rare kindness with his nice gesture, but I know all too well there is no humanity hiding in that demon seed.

While we all walk by Derrick, Gabe, the last to pass, is purposefully tripped at the top of the stairs by Derrick's Neanderthal foot. A security guard approaches the door as Derrick bolts, leaving Gabe crumpled on the steps. Blood drips from Gabe's head, but not bad enough to send him to the hospital. Juliana quickly pulls out a tissue and wipes the blood from the front of his scalp.

Gabe's eyes pierce mine, his nostrils flaring. "Okay, Arena, we do it your way. I'm in."

I don't need to say anything to agree fully with his request.

"Do what?" Jacob asks again.

"You guys go ahead to class, while I take Gabe to the nurse's office. We'll meet up at lunch. I just want to make sure this isn't too deep for stitches," I say to deter them from any suspicion of our true intentions.

While they walk off to class, Gabe and I take a shortcut down the other side of the halls and through the gymnasium. Since no one has gym class until later, this is our chance to implement my plan.

I ask Gabe to watch out for anyone coming while I go into the janitor's closet next to the boy's locker room. I climb up a folded ladder, push the tiles back from the ceiling, and pull myself up into the rafters. Like a cat, I quietly patter across the pipes just above the shower area while holding on to cables to balance myself.

I use a small knife I took from the den and cut a nice tiny hole in the sheetrock for the pinhole camera to peek through. I set up another camera in a different location to capture every angle of the showers we may miss with the first camera. I swiftly climb back down to the janitor's closet, replacing the ceiling tiles as if they hadn't been disturbed.

"We're good to go. It's all you now," I say to Gabe.

"Seriously, this is your plan? How do you even know when Derrick showers?" Gabe asks.

"Because two little annoying volleyball players in our French class are always giggling and going on about how Derrick stays to watch the girls' volleyball team practice while the other football players are showering from football practice. They talk about waiting on him to finish showering everyday outside the locker room, as if somehow they might get a chance to see him in a towel. Well, today they are going to get a lot more than that."

"You're a twisted, little girl, you know that?" he says, incredulous.

Gabe still has to set up the coded receiver adapter on the main receiver box that sends out the signal to all the televisions in school. Since the main box is set up in the administration office, we have to be a little craftier. I take the lead on this and concoct some story about rescheduling one of my classes to one of the administrators. While she is pulling my file, leaving the box unattended, Gabe hurries and attaches the adapter.

"We're good to go," he says. I quickly dismiss the rescheduling request to the administrator and eagerly walk out the door. While I'm walking back to class with Gabe, my mind nervously begins to recant this devious prank. I'm not sure what we are about to reveal is any different than Derrick's deceitful behavior, but I can't seem to make myself deviate from the plan either.

I watch the clock tick away on the wall and anxiously wait all day for this moment. The bell rings, and I hurry Gabe to the lunchroom before Jacob and Juliana get there. Gabe sets his laptop that's hiding in his bag to the same channel as the cameras and configures the remote control settings. We now have a visual of the showers on the laptop. The only thing left is to switch to the television view remotely and let the show begin.

Gabe monitors the laptop in his bag throughout the lunch period, waiting to see when the other football players have finished showering. I start to get cold feet on this whole operation, having a conflicting battle with my conscience, and I realize I can't seek revenge on him, not like this.

This predicament rides me all through lunch until Gabe gives me the go ahead on the switch view. I look at the yellowing around Gabe's eyes from where Derrick's first punch landed, followed by the lump on the back of his head from the locker, and finally gazing at today's recent injury to the forehead. I whisper to Gabe right as the bell rings, "Do it."

CHAPTER 11

While people are walking back to their classrooms, the televisions all around the school turn on to Derrick's backside. Jaws drop in total shock, and a herd of people stop in the middle of the halls like a cattle round-up. Not until about thirty seconds pass do they finally realize that it's Derrick, and a roar of laughter follows.

People are shoving and prodding to get a glimpse of Derrick's manhood on the screen, mostly the girls. I unexpectedly spot a few teachers taking a furtive peek instead of running to the administration office or at least turning off the television.

It's absolute pandemonium, and the only thing I have on my mind is moving as far away from this mayhem as I can. I grab Jacob's hand and lead him through the crowded spectacle to my next classroom, while Gabe and Juliana briefly follow. Jacob holds my hand tight, unwilling to let me go in an attempt to interrogate me about the incident. He says but one word, "You," and by the shrug of my shoulder and grin on my face, he finally cracks a smile, kisses me on the cheek, and walks off.

After five minutes of a bare-naked man fidgeting with his junk and singing a poorly written rendition of the school song, the televisions turn off and the damage has been done, and somehow, I feel worse than before.

Students begin to file in after the bedlam calms, and all I can do is hope we get through the rest of the day without being connected to this prank. I'm watching the clock, counting the seconds before the bell rings, when suddenly a voice on the speaker comes on, *Arena and Gabriel Power, please come to the administration office.*

My heart immediately drops into my stomach, and my face pales. Everyone in the classroom turns to one another, whispering and snickering in a failing attempt to be unnoticed. I'm sure they are all wondering just like me if we are being called to the office in connection to the shower event.

As we walk to the office, I can see Derrick's wet hair through the administration window and immediately recognize our doom. There's a small amount of sympathy straining to escape my conscience, but the last two days of Derrick's vicious torment is killing the part of me that cares. I know what we did was wrong and we deserve to be punished, but to see Derrick's face as we walk through the doors is priceless, and I realize it was worth it.

Principal Karnes swiftly exits her office and gets right to the point, "It appears that there may be some misunderstanding between you two and Mr. Maitland. He claims that you had something to do with this . . . unfortunate prank," she states, trying very hard to hold back a smile.

Principal Karnes was almost forced to resign last year because of Derrick's father, Gerry, who happens to be the president of the school board. As the rumor goes, Derrick's father was rebuffed by Principal Karnes when he attempted to make a pass at her sexually. Principal Karnes tried to file a sexual harassment lawsuit, but was denied because of the monetary connection Derrick's father has with the school. The only thing that kept Principal Karnes from resigning was her contract through the end of next year, which could not be terminated. So if there is any kind of lenience we may receive, it will only be because this prank happened to Gerry Maitland's obnoxious, shit-stained son.

With his lips pressed tightly together and brows furrowed, Derrick stares me down, as if I were wild game ready to be shot. I just give him a look of dismay as if I feel sorry for him even though I can't stop laughing inside.

"I know these are strong accusations, but it's my job to ask, and I want you to be honest with us. Can you tell us anything you know about what was televised on the screens earlier?" Principal Karnes says.

I pause for a bit, and everything that Gabe, my mom, and dad taught me about dishonesty is wearing on my conscience. And just as I start to spill my guts, the most surprising thing occurs. Gabe, the one person who's never lied, shakes his head from side to side, as if to warn me not to say anything that would cause our expulsion and ultimately jeopardize our plans with Father Joseph. I quickly play dumb and answer the question that was directly asked of me, which brings me to my next thought.

It's as if Principal Karnes knew exactly how to word her question so it couldn't possibly force us to confess. Somehow, I get the feeling that she wants Derrick to squirm, whether or not that's an ethical measure a principal should take. She's on our side, and I will take what I can get.

So I replay the question over in my head before answering, *Can you tell us anything you know about what was televised on the screens earlier?* What I want to say is that I'm sorry this happened to this gentleman, but after glancing over at Derrick's hand-slitting-throat gesture, I quickly change my response.

I look up at Principal Karnes and say embarrassingly, "His penis is smaller than I imagined."

Principal Karnes's face turns bright red, and her head tilts downward enough to hide her smile. I feel a release of tightness in my side now and know we are in the clear.

She's having such a hard time recovering from my response that she just dismisses any accusations Derrick had. "Okay, you two can go back to class," she says with a smile.

"Hey! Wait, this is total bullshit!" Derrick responds.

Principal Karnes quickly interrupts, "Watch it. We have no proof that these two did this to you, regardless of what kind of conflict lies between you. This meeting is over."

I can feel the heat from Derrick's anger and his piercing eyes stab me in the back as we walk away.

The final bell rings for the day.

I stroll the bleak halls back to my locker and suddenly think about our journey with Henry and Father Joseph. I try to stay grounded and keep a rational mind about the whole thing, but there's a part of me that can't help but wonder if there really is any truth to it all. But to be honest, I've felt slightly disengaged from the absurdity of it because of our new friendships with Juliana and Jacob. I try hard to avoid any dark thoughts about our future with them, knowing what Gabe and I may be enduring. I just don't know what to believe anymore. I just try to focus on today and make every second count with the ones we love.

I tell Gabe not to wait on me and that I will meet up with him outside under our meeting tree. I want to spend a little private time with Jacob before shoving off to the den. The intimate moment we shared last night is still lingering, and my heart has not stopped glowing. After a few moments of alone time, I say goodbye to Jacob and give him one last kiss before I leave.

I walk outside by the meeting tree, but Gabe isn't there, which is very unlike him because of his extreme punctuality. I wait a few moments until twenty minutes have passed, but when he doesn't show up, I begin to worry. I quickly run back in the school, down the hall by the gym, with my heart racing and my thoughts conjuring up images of Derrick's fist in Gabe's face again.

I turn down the adjacent hall and run into a crying Juliana. "What's the matter, is it Gabe?" I say. She nods her head and points to the back of the gym where the fitness room is located.

I race over to the room; the door is open, but the lights are off. I peek inside without being heard and see Derrick and two of his henchmen surrounding Gabe, who is backed up in a corner. I sidle in and get low to the floor without them noticing me. I observe my surroundings so I can strategically see the most efficient way to take these guys down.

It suddenly comes to me; I will take the enemy by surprise, and I'm not holding back this time. Derrick kicks his foot up to Gabe's face, but Gabe blocks his kick just like I taught him in the den the other day.

"What is this? The Jesus freak is fighting back. I thought you were a turn-the-cheek kind of guy?" asks Derrick with a sinister look. Suddenly, Derrick silently tilts his head down and recognizes my tiger claw firmly wrapped around his testicles from behind, and I squeeze harder and harder while my other hand is pinching the sciatic nerve in Derrick's neck, rendering him immobile and useless.

The two other morons have no idea what is going on because it's so dark and I'm hidden behind Derrick's large frame. I whisper in Derrick ear, "Gabe is that kind of guy, but I, on the other hand, well . . . I'm still working on it." I squeeze just hard enough on the back of Derrick's neck to drop him unconscious, but not hard enough to kill him.

When Derrick hits the floor, the other two boys stare in shock. "Who's next?" I ask. One of the boys picks up a weight bar and lunges the semi-heavy unbalanced pole toward me. I swiftly slide to the left, grab the bar, and push it back up into his head, knocking him out cold.

At this point, the other boy just wants to leave because he's too embarrassed or nervous to apologize. I give him a few steps before swinging a pulley bar at his feet, and trip him onto a bench press. For good measure, I sling my throwing knife between his legs just below his crotch to make my point clear. He's terrified and pleads his forgiveness.

I pull the knife out, just close enough to his groin, and hold it up to his throat. "Today, this shit ends," I say, pointing over to Gabe and Derrick's limp body. He shakes his head with a terrifying but agreeable gesture.

"Arena, that's enough!" shouts Gabe. I struggle momentarily with an anger I have not come to know until now.

"Arena, let him go," Gabe continues.

I angrily hesitate before I pull the knife away from his bulbous Adams apple. I give him one last piercing glare before I let him run off. My mind is becoming dangerously unpredictable, teetering on the edge of hatred. Whatever distractions Gabe and I had at school before, they cease to exist now.

An uninviting sting grows inside my stomach, and a sudden darkness hovers over me.

It's here.

Part II

The Fallen

CHAPTER 12

The sun melts into the dusty air and the clouds grow darker in the west. Gabe and I begin our usual trek to the den when out of nowhere two dozen birds flying above us in a V-shape formation drop right out of the sky and onto the ground below us.

I grab Gabe's shoulder, drawing him back away from the falling birds. It was like they just hit a wall and fell to their demise. Gabe and I both pause in shock and look around for something that may have caused them to just drop like that.

The backside of one of the birds is completely missing, and another has its upper cavity blown out, but not a single bird has any gunshot to show for its death. It's just too bizarre to understand. Just then, we feel a wave of air pushing through the leaves on the tree in front of us. I hear, and feel, a low-pitch rumbling sound with a constant frequency moving through my body.

From a distance above the clouds, we see a passenger jet veering at an unusual downward angle like it's out of control. The extremely low-roaring noise in the background gradually grows louder and louder, until it blasts the sky so furiously the trees begin to tremble. More and birds fly erratically above us in strange circular patterns before they plummet to the ground around us.

I can't tell where the noise is coming from, and it's beginning to make me nauseous. I look over to the school and see one of the teachers covering his ears while his nose spontaneously bleeds like a fountain.

"Run!" I shout to Gabe, grabbing his arm as we dash for shelter toward the den. My heart beats faster and faster, and my eardrums pop as we sprint across the street. It's not until we reach the other side that I'm suddenly stopped by an excruciating wailing of screams behind us.

When I turn around to the awful shrieking in the distance, I see hundreds of students vomiting and lying on the ground, shaking uncontrollably. Some have blood running from their noses, while others just lie there, lifeless. People on the streets are dropping to their knees, holding their stomachs and ears in pain. I nearly lose it when I see a man's chest explode and watch his insides pour out onto the ground.

We run as fast as we can and make it inside the gas station when an abrupt explosion ripples through the air, shaking the integrity of the structure, and knocking us down. Through the dingy window, fiery-red ash cascades to the ground, and a plume of black smoke trails from the north side of the school. The sky bellows again a deep roar, rumbling and crashing to the earth with a great blast of fire.

We watch in horror as the chaos unfolds into screams. Helpless people lie unconscious. "I can't stand here and do nothing, Gabe. We need to help these people. Come on!" I lift the window, adrenaline coursing through my veins, when suddenly, the door on the floor to the tunnel unexpectedly swings open. Father Joseph's head pops up.

"Children, come now. Hurry, it's not safe out here," he asserts.

"We need to help these people," I say desperately.

"We can't help them, it's too late. Come on now. I can't risk you two getting killed."

Walking through the tunnel gives me a tremendous headache, and my ear passages have suddenly closed. I can't tell if it's from being closed in this semi-pressurized passage, or from that low, excruciating roar that sent everyone to the ground, puking up their insides. I ask Father Joseph if he saw people lying on the ground or if he heard any low humming noise, but he's too busy praying to answer me. By the time we get to the doors, my ear canals finally open up and my nausea retreats. Henry is sitting at the table, intently glued to a laptop screen.

"You will be safe in here," Father Joseph assures.

Gabe's face pales, "what the hell is going on?"

"We don't know yet, but downtown is flooded with federal officers, and riots broke out when Henry and I left. We had to walk on foot because the entire interior of the city is blocked off, and we wanted to avoid being detained. We fled to the old church, trying to wait out the chaos."

"So, how did you get here?" Gabe asks.

"Henry and I found another metal door like the one to the den in the basement of the church. Through that door were a slew of underground tunnels, one of which led us to what looked like an underground cathedral about hundred yards from here to there," says Father Joseph, pointing to the back wall. He moves over to a small crevice in the concrete and pushes a button. The wall moves back and reveals the tunnel they came through.

I walk over to the opening and peer in, but all I can think about are the tragic events that are taking place outside the school—seeing my own classmates lying lifeless on the ground. I place my hand on the cold concrete wall, stroking my raven hair and brood over the absence of our friends. And it dawns on me.

I turn to face Gabe. "Jacob and Juliana, did you see them before we left?" I ask, panicking.

Gabe's eyes grow big, then his face gradually turns red with anger. He curls his fist and pounds it into the table. "Dammit, we shouldn't have left them!" he shouts.

"I'm sure they're fine," says Father Joseph.
I resent the fact that we left them, but there's nothing I can do to change it now. "We'll find them. Don't worry, they're smart enough to take shelter," I try to reas- ure Gabe, but mostly trying to reassure myself.

"We need to get home to Myra; I'm sure she is worried sick right now," I say to Father Joseph.

"In time, Arena. We need to make sure it's safe before going back out there," he says.

Henry pounds the table. "What is going on here?" He glares at the laptop.

"What is it?" asks Gabe.

Henry looks confused. "Our network connection is completely gone."

"It's probably from the explosion earlier, or maybe there was damage to the cables during all the chaos," says Father Joseph.

"You don't understand. This is not a LAN line or a wireless access point connection. This is a government signal that is utilized by the feds, which is directly uplinked to an orbiting military satellite. These signals never go down unless the satellite has been decommissioned—or worse, destroyed," says Henry with his hands on his head.

It has been about an hour since the explosion now, and I can't stop pacing back and forth, wondering about the status of Jacob and Juliana, what awaits us aboveground, and if my family is still waiting for us safely in the house. "Okay, we've waited long enough. We need to move now," I hastily say.

Father Joseph walks over to one of the tables and grabs a flashlight. "As much as I don't want to separate the two of you—"

"Then don't!" I interrupt.

"We really need one of you here in case one of us gets caught. Remember, we have to trek on foot now," says Father Joseph.

Gabe runs over to one of the boxes under the table and digs around until he pulls out something small and shiny. "Here! We can use these."

"What are those?" I ask.

"These are tracking devices that link to each other with this coded cell satellite. This device has its own coded frequency for these tracking devices only, so no Internet connection is needed. They have about a twenty-mile radius, but we will still need to attach it to something outside," explains Gabe.

"Your house is about two miles from here. We may be able to make most of the trip through some of these tunnels," says Father Joseph.

"The question is, who goes and who stays?" I ask.

Henry stands up and says, "I recommend Gabriel to go with Father Joseph and Arena to stay here with me. Arena and I have some unfinished training that is necessary."

I'm hesitant to agree to anything at this point, but because Gabe is more intuitive than me, he will more likely avoid any danger he foresees, therefore, this is probably the best decision. "Fine," I say.

I pick out a nice gun for Gabe and make sure it has a full clip. "Here, take this one, it's accurate and powerful. Just make sure you have the safety off."

After Gabe turns on the tracking devices to make sure they work, he looks at me as if I won't see him again. Since our cell phones are no longer useful with communications shut down, we agree that I will follow an hour later. With only two miles to travel, that should give them more than enough time to get to the house safely. After Father Joseph prays over both of us, I give them both one last hug before they leave through the tunnels.

After I get back from deploying the cell satellite outside, I come back to the den, curious as to what Henry has planned for me. "So, what is this unfinished training all about?" I ask.

"I have nothing left to teach you. You have the strength, speed, accuracy, and confidence that is required of any cunning warrior going into battle, but it's your faith that you wield that will serve you best."

I pause briefly over his concern before I reset the chamber of the Beretta 92FS I took off the wall earlier. Henry quickly grabs my hand.

"Guns can only go so far, but what good is it when you run out of bullets? If you want to survive, then it is imperative to understand the means of a silent killer, Arena. A gun will eventually fail you, but a blade will remain your friend," he says with a stony stare.

Henry pulls out the two swords that I drooled over the first day I laid eyes on them. There is nothing quite like holding cold steel in your hands and waiting to slay your enemy with the swinging grace of one stroke. Henry is right: These may be my weapons of choice when the time comes; after all, it's what I'm most comfortable with. Henry watches as I go through my progressions with the blades, striking in every position I know, and some that I came up with on my own.

I practice throwing knives at wall targets and two human-like mannequins to make the time pass without worrying. With extreme accuracy and little effort, I crouch on a chair, flinging daggers that gash into their eyes and necks.

"Here you go, Arena, I think this will fit you," Henry says as he hands me a black jacket knitted from a material I've never seen before. It's very lightweight, but strong enough for a knife not to cut through without extreme pressure. I put it on and tie it together, and it feels as though it was tailored perfectly for me. The back is designed to hold two Samurai swords, coincidentally the two that I hold in my hands.

Henry made this for his daughter years ago, hoping she would become interested in the arts, only to be disappointed by her rejection of them. I guess it's not meant for everyone.

"Well, it fits perfectly. I guess it was meant for me after all," I say. As I take off the jacket and pull the sleeve from my arm, my face flushes with anxiety as I notice the red flashing dot on the tracker has now disappeared.

"Gabe! Something has happened; his tracking device has stopped. We have to go now," I demand. I dash out of the room, grab two commander-sized M1911 pistols with sound suppressors, four full clips, three stealth-throwing knives, and my favorite scorpion dagger, or jugular ripper, as they call it.

Before me and Henry leave, I quickly turn on the television in the backroom just to see if there is any live local coverage of what we may run into. Surprisingly, a few stations are working, but the signal is weak. The only station that comes in clear enough is the national news with a recent story being developed…

"It's being reported that tens of thousands are being detained and shipped off to various classified locations. Many citizens have been killed in the past few days, and an outcry from the people has gone unnoticed, yet this impasse has fostered a brutal retaliation by federal government officials of every city in the nation. The ongoing riots and rebellion has desisted, leaving no hope for the fallen. A national Internet blackout has stopped all digital communication for most of the nation's population and it is yet known if the event that has been initiated by our very government has had any global effects tied to foreign trade, or if any outside threats have deterred any international relations with our allies. The leadership has tried to portray this nation as . . ." The television feed shuts off and the screen turns blue. No other channels are working, and now all communications or information has ceased to exist.

As dangerous as it may seem, going outside may be our best hope. Gabe's a smart kid, but I'm better suited for combat in these situations thanks to Finnegan. Wow, how I miss him right now. Besides, I know my way from here outside rather than fighting to find the right tunnel that leads home.

Like a prowling alley cat, I saunter on the balls of my feet in front of Henry, behind a line of bushes. The streets are completely dead, and not a soul in sight for the last mile we've walked—probably due to the curfew. Since I've never been out past curfew, the silence in the air makes me shiver a bit. Just about two hundred yards away, we spot about fifty federal soldiers, half of which are wearing gasmasks, and marching, or rather, goose-stepping, like German soldiers. It's quite an unusual sight.

We finally make it to the house with no signs of any federal officers in the vicinity. The lights are still on, so that's a good sign. An unfamiliar car is parked in the driveway as we walk to the front porch. I quietly open the door, making sure I don't make a sound. Standing inside the living room, an old man with a disheveled face is holding his hat. I move closer and see everyone: Gabe, Juliana, Myra, Daniel, Niki, and Father Joseph. I'm so excited that I rush into the living room with Henry trailing behind me. The smile on my face gradually flattens when I notice everyone's morose expression. I'm so confused to what I'm witnessing; Myra and Niki are crying, and Juliana is hiding her face, burying it into Gabe's chest, while Daniel holds his glasses in his hands. Daniel always has his glasses, and to see Niki crying like that is starting to frighten me. It's an oddity I'm not sure I want revealed. Shouldn't they be happy to see me?

"What?" I manage to whisper.

Gabe finally speaks up with his trembling lips. "Arena . . ." He pauses, then says, "They didn't even give him a warning, they . . ."

"They what, who?" I ask, anxiously.

"It's Jacob," says Gabe softly.

I have no words, and my eyes fill with tears. "Where is he?" I ask, barely getting out the words.

Gabe looks at me as a tear trickles down his cheek. "Arena, he's dead."

CHAPTER 13

If I had a choice of living out this pain for the rest of my life, or being shot dead at this very moment, I think I would prefer the latter.

"Jacob was just trying to help me find my watch. I accidentally threw it away in the dumpster behind the store," says the old man.

I realize now that the man is the owner of the cleaners who allowed Jacob to stay in the bedroom above the store. "They tried to arrest him for rummaging through the garbage on private property, but I tried to tell them that he was with me. They didn't want to listen, and when Jacob jumped out of the dumpster, they just shot him without any warning," the man continues.

I'm so paralyzed from the shock; words can't flow from my lips, so I just stare through the void of empty silence and sink into oblivion for a few seconds. And then suddenly, every fruitless event of my entire life races through my brain in a single flash just as my eyes refocus back to reality, and the blood comes rushing back to my face like an ocean wave. My knees buckle, and I fall to the ground, as if my soul has just left my body. I cry uncontrollably, releasing all the pent-up emotions bursting from my spirit, followed by screams of rage.

I therapeutically rock myself back and forth into a stupor, trying to erase the pain or at least mask it temporarily. I run upstairs to avoid the sad, consoling faces or any empathy that may follow. I just want to weep alone right now, cling to my dagger, and drown in my own mourning.

I walk over to my window and gaze up at the few stars I can see through the muddy sky and wonder what my mother would say to me right now. What kind of advice might she offer, or would she just gently hold me in her arms without an answer?

I look down at the black street and wonder why I was born into this world. Every bit of anger and rage I'm harboring is battling my will to forgive, and unexpectedly, I'm reminded by the poem my mother wrote that I read earlier. I drop to my knees, cover my face, and attempt to pray through this chaos swimming in my head.

I feel emotionally overwhelmed and completely lost, but it suddenly comes to a complete halt. A distant gunshot fires outside. I immediately get up and peer out the window to see officers running down the street about four blocks away. A family is being forced out of their house and put onto a bus, but the father appears to resist and is quickly shot in the head.

Children are screaming and running to their dead father as two more officers pull them off and fling them to the ground. They eventually get one of the kids onto the bus with their mother, but the other one tries to run and is promptly shot in the back. My heart sinks, I gasp for air, and I shiver with anger.

I grab what I can from my room, stuff it into my backpack, and race downstairs. "We have to go, now! Everybody get up!" I yell.

"We heard gunshots," says Daniel.

"Officers down the street, they're here to come take us. It's started. We need to go now!" I say, running toward the door.

I look around the room and notice Juliana and the old man are gone. "Where's Juliana?" I ask Gabe.

"I had the old man take her back home. I thought her family might be worried."

"Dammit! We have to get her, it's not safe!" I shout.

"What do you mean? What the hell is going on?" Gabe panics.

"Wait, let me get some things before we leave," says Myra.

"No! Forget about it, there isn't enough time, let's go!" I insist.

We run to the back door, but there are already officers waiting there. The front street is flooded with about dozen, and now there is nowhere to go.

"Come, hide down here until they leave," says Myra, pointing toward the basement.

We race downstairs and the basement door shuts. I do a head count: Gabe, Henry, and Father Joseph. Myra, Daniel, and Niki are not here. I climb back up to see what happened to them, but it's too late. The cracking sound of the front door breaks open, and the muffling voices from Myra and Daniel plead with the officers. I snug my ear against the basement door and listen.

"Is there anybody else residing in this household?" one of the officers asks.

"No, it's just the wife and I," says Daniel. Foot-steps scuffle right outside the basement door. I remove my ear and carefully turn the lock without making any noise. My heart thumps deep inside my chest.

"Take 'em to the bus with the others. Gibbs and Johnson, search the second floor, I'll comb the rest of the area," the officer says.

After a few minutes, I hear the bus drive off and the two officers coming down the stairs with their heavy boots.

"Sir, the rooms are clear, but there appears to be more than just the two dwelling in this house, two more kids possibly," says one of the officers.

"How old?" asks the lead officer.

"Most likely teens, sir."

I quietly walk down the steps, and my insides churn. "They're looking for us, we need to find a way out now," I shudder.

Henry looks over by an old dryer and behind it are steps leading to the cellar doors outside. "Hurry, this is our way out," says Henry.

The basement doorknob rattles, struggling to turn upstairs, followed by a commotion. Henry opens the cellar doors when it's clear and looks around outside before we make a run for it. As I ascend up the steps, I hear a scream coming from upstairs. My blood curdles. It's Niki.

"Go! That's Niki, and I'm not leaving her behind. Father, take Henry through the tunnels where it's safer. Gabe and I will catch up," I urge.

"I'll stay here with you, Gabe can go," says Henry. "No, I need Gabe here with me to get back through the tunnels. Now go, I promise we will make it back, trust me," I assure Henry as I stare at the basement door. They make a run for it behind the back fence into the alley, and by the time I turn back around to see if they left, there is nothing but darkness.

"So how are we going to do this?" Gabe asks nervously.

"I don't know, maybe we—"

Suddenly, the door atop the stairs shudders as someone on the other side tussles with the knob.

I panic for a brief moment, then look down by the corner of the stairs and notice a spool of copper wire on in a ragged box. I grab the small spool and wrap the wire around the bottom of the stair rail near the top of the basement. I quickly stretch the other end around the other side of the stair railing, making a simple trip wire.

As the door shakes louder and louder, I nervously look down at Gabe, who's shivering with fright. I walk down the stairs and make sure Gabe has his gun's safety off and ready to fire. "All you have to do is squeeze."

We can now hear the door being kicked by the officer's boot as we prepare for the door to come swinging open any moment. "Aim for the head, Gabe." I climb up on top of the railing beside the door. I want to position myself where the side of the door swinging out hides me, while giving me the higher ground to strike down on the officer with my knife.

The jarred door nearly rattles off its hinges and aggressively swings open, giving me a clear shot to the back of the officer's neck with my dagger. While I reach up, ready to come down with the point of my blade, he effortlessly trips over the copper wire down to the bottom of the stairs and lies motionless. By the sound of the crack of his neck, it appears he has saved us the trouble of killing him. With the door open, I now hear Niki screaming even louder, letting me know she is still in the house.

Suddenly, two officers wearing gasmasks descend down the steps from the cellar doors. "Gabe, look out!"

I quickly pull out my suppressed M1911 and drill both soldiers with ease directly to the head. I stand on the steps distraught for a minute before Gabe shakes me back to coherence. "What's wrong?" Gabe asks.

"Nothing," I respond. I slowly pull the gun down to my side and just stare at the two officers on the floor and realize it's the first time I've killed a human being. I feel empty inside as I gaze at the blood running down the officer's head. This is not how I thought it would feel. As soon as the guilt wears on my weary heart, I feel somewhat cold, but then I soon remember what they did to Jacob, and any regret I had comes to a complete halt. I suddenly feel a fire breath- ing from my soul and anger quickly replaces the guilt. *I'm glad the officers are dead.*

We hurry upstairs into the living room and see no one around until we hear screams coming from the kitchen. Through the kitchen door, I catch a flashing glimpse of someone on the table as the door swings back and forth. I put my foot near the bottom of the swinging door, stopping it enough to where I can see who it is.

Rage pumps through my veins. One officer holds a gun to Niki's head while the other takes advantage, raping her. Without hesitation or an ounce of fear, I charge through the kitchen door and lunge with my dagger toward the officer, holding the gun. It pierces through the bottom of his skinny neck and deep into his throat. I draw my gun quickly to the rapist scum and shove him to the ground.

"Don't shoot, I'm unarmed!" he pleads.

I hover the barrel of my gun over his crotch, and shoot off his cock. "No, now you're unarmed," I correct him. "Gabe, take his gun."

"Are you okay? Can you walk?" I ask Niki, as I help her get up and dressed. She doesn't respond. The shock of being held down and brutally taken advantage of has kept her silent. She just clings to me, hugging and crying.

I pull out my dagger from the officer's neck, wiping off the blood and meaty flesh on his uniform. Niki spits in her attacker's face as he writhes on the floor in pain, moaning and wailing, cursing me for his blood-soaked crotch.

"What are we going to do with him, Arena? He's just going to leave here and tell everyone about this. They will be everywhere hunting us down," says Gabe.

"I guess we'll have to make it harder for him to leave then," I say as I shoot both his kneecaps off. I could have put this man out of his misery with a bullet to his head, but I leave him to suffer instead.

I crouch down next to the man. "You may be in pain here for a long time, but it will be nothing compared to the hell that awaits you on the other side. May God have mercy on your soul," I say through gritted teeth.

"Damn you, fucking whore, and your God," he responds.

"So be it," I say as we leave him.

We quickly run out the back door toward the fence, and Gabe leads us to one of the tunnels, where he and Father Joseph walked earlier. Whether the government figures out who executed their officers or not, we have left our first of many marks to come.

As we race through the underground channels, we are suddenly halted by an explosion aboveground that rocks the interior of the tunnel, causing the passage ahead of us to collapse. We are now forced to either go back or find another opening in the tunnel. "This way," says Gabe. We are led to a dead end, but right above us is a large sewer grate.

I climb the ladder on the wall up to the top and slide the surprisingly heavy grate back. I pop my head out to make sure it's clear before gesturing to the others to follow. We get out and run across an alley and into a wooded area, along the fence line. We cautiously walk through the trees, keeping our distance from the street, and a sharp eye out for federal officers roaming the grounds.

Just past the fence line, we turn into the next alley where I can see our school, which is about four blocks away from the den. I can hear heavy boot steps on the other side of the fence where we are headed, but we are too far ahead and have nowhere to hide.

I stop in the middle of the alley as three officers pull their guns on us, yelling for us to put our hands up. They are heavily armed, but with my hands up, I'm unable to reach for my gun. One of the officers lays down his weapon to the side, pulls out a flashlight, and shines it in our direction. "They're just kids, sir," he says.

"What are you doing out this late in this area?" asks one of the officers.

"Our ride left us at the school, and we had no way home but on foot. Please forgive us, sir, we just want to get home," I say.

"Take them in. We'll put them on the bus with the others," he says to the other officer who's holding a gun. "Let's see some identification first," the officer says. I wait until the officer gets close enough so I can get a good position on the other two. I have a perfect view of all three officers now, and they are arranged in a way that I can take them all out.

"Here," I say, pulling out my identification. Gabe's eyes grow wide, because he knows exactly what is about to happen. I pull out one of the stealth-throwing knives and sling it directly into the officer's eye to my right, then I quickly grab the gun from the officer in front of me and knee him in the side of the ribs. I whip his wrist around and push the barrel to the bottom of his chin. With his hand still attached to the gun, I squeeze his index finger on the trigger, blowing the side of his face clean off.

I draw my gun toward the officer who is struggling with the flashlight and trying to grip his gun at the same time. I don't hesitate to squeeze the trigger as I shoot him square in the head. In a span of about four seconds, three more officers lie dead on the ground. I get a disturbed look from Gabe as I wipe some of the officer's blood from my face. Because of the officer's loud gunshots, more are sure to come. We quickly make a run for it, staying out of the alleys and along the backside of the fence near the trees, but before we make it to the other side, an officer grabs Gabe by the collar and brings him down. I jump on the fence, using the side railing as leverage, and throw myself at the officer's back. With one quick snap, I break his neck, severing his spinal cord.

A shadow dances toward Niki, and I yell for her to duck. With my gun drawn, I eliminate another officer, striking him between the eyes. "Run!" I shout.

We sprint two more blocks closer to the den, weaving in and out between the trees, until we are immediately stopped by the sound of two hundred soldiers marching around the corner from the old gas station. We silently crouch down behind some bushes.

Suddenly, a hand covers my mouth and pulls me and Gabe backward to the ground.

I reach for my dagger and turn to plunge it into whoever is grabbing us, but before my hand can go forward, I stop myself. My eyes widen and glow of relief fills my face.

I withdraw my dagger and wrap my arms around a most familiar embrace. "Finnegan!" I say with jubilation.

CHAPTER 14

I'm shaking with a fear I cannot contain, until a jubilant fever suddenly overcomes my emotional exhaustion.

"Shhh, keep it down," Finnegan whispers.

"I'm so glad to see you."

"Are you hurt?" he asks, examining my blood-soaked face.

I wipe the red from my cheek. "No, this is someone else's blood," I say, trembling with adrenaline.

I stare down at my crimson-stained hands, transfixed for a brief moment before I turn back to Finnegan's eyes. "I killed them," I say as if I just revealed some terrible sin.

"Yes, and it won't be the last."

"Where the hell have you been all these years?" I ask.

Sudden gunfire in the background immediately breaks up our conversation.

"I'll tell you when we are safe, come this way," Finnegan says, as he leads us toward the back of the gas station.

While there's fueled anxiety and trembling fear coming from the others, all I can think about right now is wiping this sticky, congealed blood from my face. The blood on my hands is turning brown and already starting to smell like iron.

We crawl through the back window one by one until we are safely inside. In the next room over, Father Joseph and Henry are waiting as expected.

"Finnegan!" shouts Father Joseph, "it's so good to see you, my friend. How are you?"

"Tired, hungry, and desiring some much-needed rest." Finnegan walks over to Henry, shakes his hand, and puts his hand on his shoulder. "Thanks for taking care of her, she has the blood of a survivor no doubt," he says.

"Finnegan, dear friend, she's more than a survivor. She is absolutely lethal, but without an ounce of control I'm afraid, that may lead her down a dark path." Henry cautions slightly out of earshot.

"I'm sorry we haven't formally met. I hope you can forgive me under the circumstances," Finnegan says to Niki. She is shivering and completely discombobulated by what has happened in the last few hours, so she just stands there, shaking her head.

"This is my . . ." I pause, thinking how Niki has been more than a foster sister in my life. She is the one I leaned on the most when my life seemed to fall apart. "This is my sister, Niki," I proudly say.

Suddenly, gun fire right outside the building forces us to shorten our introductions, so we quickly descend down into the tunnel below.

Upon entering the den, we all sit down as Finnegan shares with us the last two years of his personal hell, up until the recent events that have occurred regarding the last wave of governmental attacks on its people.

"Our administration has been sleeping with the enemy the past six years, battling out international policy, global economics, and worse, a one-world government that feeds off the people it controls. This country as you know is no longer free; it's but a mirage of lies and false hope, masking what it truly has become—a slave nation. And if you are not contributors to this malevolent regime, then you are expendable. They know this. That's why they can control what you buy, what you eat, how and where you live. They even control who has the right to bear children," he says.

"What?" I ask in shock.

"If you haven't noticed lately, not many people in the poorer regions, or even the less-wealthy districts, are having many children. That's because they have been polluting the water you drink and the products you buy with a chemical used to prevent pregnancy that effectively makes women sterile. It's also been proven powerful enough to abort a fetus if one should ever get past the system unscathed.

"China has been doing this for the last twenty years in trying to reduce the population to one they can control economically. Even with the earthquakes killing forty-five million of its people, leaders still plan to reduce the population. Many other nations are following suit in this global plan, and our very own nation has initiated this *New World Order,* as they call it," Finnegan fumes with disgust.

This is no longer the nation that was birthed; it is a withering, old tree that has been poisoned by the blood of evil and it has become our own enemy.

Finnegan continues, "I've seen with my own eyes the very documents and reports that prove these actions have been carried out. I worked on a mission with a special ops team several years ago detailing the movement of a new terrorist threat, and during that mission we captured six Saudi militants who happened to have these documents in their possession.

"Apparently, our administration had been working with the Saudi government in attempts to occupy territories in their region so they could set up massive military bases, and in return, they will grant the nation full immunity as well as protection from neighboring states. This classified international reorder has now seeped into the hands of the Chinese and Russian governments, and your president, dictator, king, whatever the hell you want to call him, now leads this plan with the help of a new military.

"Those like me, who refused to surrender our loyalty to the new order, were imprisoned. Many of us were killed, but those left to live were of value to them for different reasons. I was kept alive because of my knowledge of enemy territories and hidden underground camps. So for the last two years, I've been rotting in a military prison in Iraq because of my skills and my knowledge of their future plans."

"How did you escape?" Gabe asks.

"With the help of what I can only assume was by God's own hands, I managed to persuade them to remove me from my cell to a more reasonable location where I was able to determine more accurately which terrorist camps had moved and which ones were still underground. They drove me to a nearby site outside of Habbaniyah where I could better examine the region and give them better knowledge.

"During the night, the two guards got lazy and drank themselves into a stupor while I manage to escape. God must have been protecting me, because I managed to hitch rides and caravans through a 450-mile journey across enemy boarders to Jerusalem. Believe me, with America's rejection of Israeli political policies, it can be quite difficult finding refuge there. I had no idea what to expect, being an American on what is now perceived by our nation as enemy soil.

"Because I explained to the Israeli leaders what happened in the West and the future of the New World Government, they allowed me to see what the last six years of their nation has gone through. Since the Messianic movement, Jews have been converting and a new culture of Israel has been forming, springing up new leadership devoting to keep God's land protected.

"Ananiah Shemer, an American-born engineer, who has emerged recently to become the new militant leader, has built an army that has been preparing for a stand against a war of biblical proportions, and I've been indoctrinated into this mission, representing counter intelligence for them. Believe me, optimism isn't their strength; it is their faith that binds them together, but when I told them about the visions and how you two fit into all of this, something changed them. Everyone devoted to the faith has been on their knees praying for you both night and day, yet they haven't seen a trace of your future—it's only by faith they choose to believe.

"In the cities, you two are referred to as *mal'achhamavet*, and are well known to the people now," says Finnegan.

"What does it mean?" I ask.

"It's Hebrew for 'angel of death,'" says Father Joseph.

"The photo that I sent to Father Joseph is very real," Finnegan says.

"The temple, you have seen this up close?" asks Gabe.

Finnegan's rugged face deadens, "yes."

"Then it has truly begun," I respond.

"This is about more than just greed—this is about power and pure control, but most of all, this is about the defiance of one nation who stands deeply rooted with a fierce faith not to crumble before these horrific genocides. They are a nation devoted to God and the very place they rest as His promised land.

"Israel stands alone in this fight, and you two were chosen to protect and guard her and her people, and it starts right here in our very own nation—a nation that was once an ally to Israel has now become the enemy," Finnegan says with piercing eyes.

Niki throws her fists down on the table, pushes her chair back forcefully, and stands to her feet. "Are you're all fucking mad!"

"Niki, wait—" I say calmly.

"No! Do you not see what's happening out there?"

"I know exactly what's happening," says Finnegan.

"Then you understand how ridiculous it is for these two to be a part of it."

"It may seem absurd to you now, but believe me, this is very real. They have been chosen," says Father Joseph.

"This is insane," she says hysterically.

"We didn't ask for this," I say to her.

"And I didn't asked to be raped either, but I had no choice."

"The choice of my fate has already been decided . . . I can't change it now."

"So, what, you expect me to be okay with this? I'm not gonna just stand around and watch you die."

An argument ensues over the strategy among everyone at the table blasting at each other on what should or shouldn't be done and why. I'm completely overwhelmed by the childish banter, so I secretly walk into the bathroom to wash off the blood that has now crusted over.

I look in the mirror and see my mom's reflection behind me, stroking my hair as I reminisce about when I was a little girl. I can hear her saying, *You're a very special girl, you know. Regardless of what you become when you grow up, never forget where you came from, stay rooted in your faith, and never back down from what you believe in. Stay close to your brother. You will need each other.*

The image of my mother's face quickly fades away and a new one takes its place, but this time it's Jacob's voice screaming my name as a gunshot pierces his chest. The image quickly vanishes, and tears run down my face. I drop to the floor and weep.

My grief is shortly interrupted by the bickering that's still ensuing outside. I wipe my face, walk out the door, and slam my dagger down on the table, silencing the room.

"Stop it! Listen to yourselves. Have you so lost hope that it has come to this?"

Everyone just looks down in silence before Father Joseph speaks. "Our faith has not been broken."

"Then why do you argue over such petty things? Evil lurks around and thrives on your incessant bickering, waiting for you to give in. I need your minds clear now because I can't do this alone."

"So what are you suggesting?" asks Finnegan.

"We will start here and find out where they have taken the people who have been removed from their homes," I say.

"And then what? This battle crosses the entire nation," says Finnegan.

"We shall prepare ourselves to kill whatever evil lies before us as we make our trek toward the east. If we are to make a change in this war, it will be to cut off the source that feeds it. Our journey leads us to the Capitol, where the enemy sleeps, and I don't intend for mercy to be a part of this plan. Dead or alive, President Kriel will have to answer for the pain he has caused this country to endure, and I will be there to see that he does."

If we can encourage a following to spread like wildfire, we can fight this cancer with a revolution. A rebellion is what this country has needed, and a rebellion it will get.

CHAPTER 15

It's a hard sell, but I convince Niki to stay behind with Father Joseph in the den. I can't afford our journey to be slowed down, much less live with myself if she is killed.

"We have two days left to prepare before the seventh day of the new moon. I don't suspect coming back anytime soon, so take what you can," I say privately to Gabe. He avoids my eyes; I can tell he's disengaged and almost dejected knowing Juliana isn't here with us. "Hey, I need you focused here, okay? You have all the resources you need at your fingertips. This isn't a time to hold back." His stony eyes fix me in an unworried gaze, but his face paints quite a different picture.

"I'm scared," he mutters.

"So am I," I admit, "but we to have to trust each other more than ever, okay? We don't leave each other's side."

He makes a feeble attempt at smiling. "I've already been working on something special for you. I started on it the first day we arrived here in the den. Come and take a look, I think you're going to like this."

He uncovers a box with a small blanket, and inside I find the boots that Niki gave me on my birthday. "You had them here the whole time? Dammit, Gabe, I've been looking for those. I thought I was going crazy when I couldn't find them," I snap.

"I made some minor adjustments to them. They should be effective when you're in a pinch. Go ahead, try them on. They should still be comfortable," he says.

I put them on and I'm wondering what kind of adjustments he made to them, because they feel much the same as they did before.

"Here, push this button," Gabe points.

I press the button and in a blink of an eye, a six-inch blade pops out of the front of the boot. "Whoa! Now this could be useful. I think I'm going to enjoy my new boots." I grin.

"The blade is hidden between the soles, and I also added a titanium-plated barrier near the bottom of the sole for added protection. Just remember: this is a remote button, so you can place it anywhere on your clothing," says Gabe.

My excitement is quickly overshadowed when I glance over at Niki. Her swollen eyes hide behind a veil of tangled blonde hair.

"How are you holding up?" I console.

"I wish I had something to offer, but you seem to have everything under control," Niki says.

"Hardly. You remember the time you consoled me when Lenzie Tullworth kissed Justin Leer, crushing my hopes of asking him to the seventh-grade dance, or the time you kept me from embarrassing myself before I got on the bus when I had a huge rip on my shorts, exposing my purple underwear? Those are the things that sisters offer that can never be replaced" I say, nudging her on the arm.

She breaks into a smile, hugs me, and whispers into my ear, "I love you so much, sister." My heart hovers over a pit of uncertainty when she embraces me. I hold her, wondering if I'll ever see her again. I search her pallid face for some comforting words to add, but I find only sorrow instead. She musters a grin, but a lie hides behind those deserted eyes. She needs a distraction.

"You know, I believe there is something you can offer. Come here," I say, taking her over to Henry. I ask Henry to help her customize my jacket that will be conducive to holding a multitude of weapons. Since Niki is a pretty good seamstress, she can create something tailored for me to wear. I explain to Niki in great detail what weapons it should hold. This should keep her mind busy for awhile or at least until I'm forced to say my good-byes.

While everyone is busy working their craft, I diligently browse the walls for something that I can hone my skills with. After five minutes of shamefully worshipping the arsenal dressing the walls, a less technical and more traditional weapon catches my eye.

I remove a titanium flex Recurve retractable bow from the wall and practice with simple field arrows near the target range. I take aim with my first arrow about thirty yards back, flinging it near dead center. I hear a couple of claps behind me as I turn around to retrieve another arrow from my quiver.

Finnegan inspects my stance like a haughty drill-sergeant. "Not bad for a first shot. Now next time don't release the arrow so quickly. Breathe in deeply and concentrate on your instincts rather than the center of the target, exhale and release," he instructs."

This time I pull a razor-tipped arrow back, turn my head to Finnegan, and smile. "You should be looking at the target, Arena. If I'm the enemy, then I'm a distraction and your target is already gone."

I look in his eyes, wink, and release the arrow. I quickly pull out another arrow, dropping down low and turning behind Finnegan's back while I swing the arrow up toward his neck, with my other hand clutching his hair. "Then I remove the distraction from the equation," I say softly in his ear.

Everyone's busywork suddenly comes to a halt as splintering eyes are planted on Finnegan's flushed face and the target in the distance. I quickly release his hair and pull the arrow away from his neck to end any further embarrassment. He walks over by the others to examine the second arrow. Befuddled with amazement, they cogitate over its razor-sharp fins piercing the butt of the first arrow, splitting it down the middle four inches into the aluminum shaft.

"Or you could just do that," says Father Joseph, pointing toward the split shaft.

Finnegan turns and smiles at Henry. "Lethal, huh?"

"Told you," says Henry, grinning.

I grow emotionally exhausted thinking about Jacob, slinging arrow after arrow until my fingers begin to blister between the chaffing leather guard and my sweat. I feel my body slouching, worn and weak.

"Perhaps you should get some sleep now, Arena. The days will grow long enough without rest" Father Joseph advises.

I agree, so I tend to the incommodious backroom quarters and lie down on one of the scratchy mattresses. This fortified bunker was obviously built as a place of refuge to withstand a surge of atomic detonations and not necessarily as a hotel with accommodating luxuries, but I'm too tired to care, so it will have to do.

I fall into a deep sleep while everyone works into the night. I replay the entire last day of school in my dreams, reliving the horrible events followed by a string of disturbing images. I vividly watch students being forcefully lined up along the gymnasium walls and sprayed with bullets to their death. I see officers with masks shooting canisters of mustard gas across the campus and watching teachers fall to the ground convulsing and spewing their insides out.

Niki is screaming for help as she is being raped by that brutal, spineless prick, but Jacob being shot dead over and over again is the one image that I can't seem to make vanish throughout this devilish nightmare. And then finally, to end this hellish terror, I'm mocked by a serpent's head spewing venomous accusations as he rises from his scaled belly to the feet of a man. It's him again—the man who briefly haunted my thoughts before my parents died. He's dressed in black, wearing a red armband with seven black stripes, standing with glowing malice, hovering over Gabe and me in dark shadow.

He raises himself up on a cross where people flock and kneel before him. Books are open beneath the cross, flowing with red, and another book is opened above the cross, shining with lightning. Bloody flowers rain down as the faceless man slits the neck of a white dove spewing fire and water.

Ash cascades below the bird, while the clear water extinguishes the glowing fire. The dove flies away, and the man is left burning on the cross, as his shrill scream pierces into the vast blackness. Amid his wretched wailing, the unholy ground from where he burns is consumed with ashes to the bellowing abyss below.

With my fists clinging to the sides of the mattress, I'm suddenly jolted awake in horror, sweating. The door swings open and I see Niki standing there. "Are you okay, Arena? We heard you screaming," she pants.

"I'm fine, just another nightmare." I get out of bed and walk into the other room where everybody is eating breakfast. "Where did the food come from?" I ask.

"There's another hidden room over by the bathroom that is stockpiled with food," says Gabe as he stuffs his face with peaches from a can.

"Would you like something to eat, Arena?" asks Father Joseph.

"No, thank you," I reply. After that nightmare, hunger is the last thing on my mind. I suddenly find myself wanting some peace alone where I can pray.

I inquire about the old underground church that Father Joseph and Henry came upon yesterday. I just need some time away from here so I can clear my head and retrain my thoughts. That nightmare has done nothing but put me in a less-than-stellar mood this morning. I leave everyone to eat their breakfast while I grab a lantern and take my morning walk through the tunnel.

About a hundred yards through the dingy passage, I stumble upon the cathedral that Father Joseph described, and I instantly notice a large statue of Christ stretching out over to the left behind some broken pews. I raise the lantern up against the wall and find a light switch. Low lighting hovers over the floor, giving off just enough illumination to recognize my surroundings.

A gorgeous stained-glass mural of angels descending from Heaven accentuates the back wall behind a dilapidated lectern. The ground is covered in dust, showing no signs of passing tracks, but a Bible left sitting open on one of the broken pews looks as though it has been recently used. Oddly enough, it appears to still be in decent condition, except for a few water stains. Dripping from the ceiling and onto the open pages, water causes the ink to blur out most of the words except one spot on the page. I read the only part of the passage on the page that has not been damaged. It's from the book of Luke:

Then he said to them: "Nation will rise against nation, and kingdom against kingdom. There will be great earthquakes, famines, and pestilences in various places, and fearful events and great signs from heaven. "But before all this, they will seize you and persecute you. They will hand you over to synagogues and put you in prison, and you will be brought before kings and governors, and all on account of my name.

I feel a tingling in my body as I close the book, my hands shaking in fear. I walk over to the statue, kneel down, and pray for hours on end until the feeling in my knees go numb. I finally rise to my feet, drenched with an uncertainty that I may one day be all alone on this journey. I struggle to walk back to the den and pause at the door. I gaze upon them all, wondering who will be left when this is all over.

"Look, I know we aren't going to be near the den for long and what we have is great, but how are we supposed to carry all this ammunition with us?" Gabe asks Finnegan.

"We carry what our bodies will allow us and stash the rest in the Black Knight," says Finnegan. Everyone looks at him like he's crazy.

Father Joseph just shrugs his shoulders.

"Is this some kind of cryptic special-ops thing you failed to remind us about?" says Niki.

"You didn't show them?" Finnegan looks to Father Joseph.

"I saw nothing, and just assumed it was long gone," says Father Joseph.

"Okay, what the hell is a Black Knight?" Gabe asks.

Finnegan walks over to the entrance that goes through the tunnel up to the old gas station and presses a button above the door. Another wall opens, with stairs leading up to a dark room. Everyone's curiosity delights in anxiousness as they climb the stairs. Finnegan turns on a switch, and a large full-sized garage lights up with glorious wonder.

"Before you is the classic 1969 Chevy Camaro RS/SS, with a NRE Billet Blackout series twin-turbo intercooled 572-cubic-inch Big Block crate engine pulsating 2000 horses, Fat Man front suspension with Air Ride Technologies, bullet-proof windows and body, double-lined fifteen-by-twelve front tires and 345/35/18 drag radials out back, dual side barrel .50 caliber automatic guns, two front double-barrel shotguns, a hidden rocket launcher underneath the rear bumper, murdered-out two-toned midnight matte black with gloss black racing stripes, oh, and one hell of a stereo system," Finnegan says.

Everyone is speechless and drools over the car for a few minutes until Gabe crouches down by the personalized license plate. "Ah, Black Knight, got it," he says. "So what kind of fuel do you feed this beast?"

"That's the best part about this armored vehicle. It runs on water, pure H_2O, technically hydrogen, but the source comes straight out of the tap. Water is filtered through a series of electrolytic cells, which produces electricity from a chemical redox reaction. These very accurately tuned electric frequencies split the hydrogen and oxygen molecules," explaines Finnegan.

Gabe is absolutely mesmerized. "No way! Well, I'm officially impressed.

"This is absolutely beautiful," says Henry.

"It even has a cup holder," Gabe facetiously adds. Finnegan furrows his brow and bites his lip.

"Nice ride," I say, standing behind everyone. They all turn their heads in unison. "When you're finished drooling, there's something you might want to see down here," I say as I walk back down to the den.

I turn the television on as everyone gathers around to watch. "Out of curiosity, I just wanted to see if there might be some kind of signal left and I came across this," I say.

There's footage of reporters running around trying to take cover while a news anchor in the background tries to describe what's going on. Finally, a new piece of footage shows the sky growing black with smoke and ash, and as the camera pans out, there's an enormous eruption of fire and lava ejecting from a volcano. As the camera pans back to reveal the scale of this event, the anchorwoman begins to voice over the madness in Italian . . .

"What you are witnessing is an absolutely catastrophic piece of history. This volcano, which has been dormant for over a hundred years, has not erupted since March of 1944, but what we are experiencing right now probably feels more like the famous eruption in 79AD, when Mount Vesuvius blew its top, spewing tons of molten ash, pumice, and sulfuric gas miles into the atmosphere, burning communities, cities, and killing thousands."

Just when she finishes, a massive explosion from the mountain shakes the camera violently, and a firestorm comes raining down. The camera falls and the screen turns black. This is just one of many disastrous events that I'm privy to conceal between Gabe and me. I can only imagine how many people will perish from this disaster.

While everyone solemnly returns to their work, I retreat to the bathroom to clean up. I haven't had a nice, warm shower in two days, and I'm beginning to think everyone else has noticed as well. After washing the layers of dirt and filth from my hair and body, I feel new again.

I walk over to bask in adoration at Niki's craftsmanship as she meticulously examines her work. I'm absolutely astonished at the finishing touches she's added to the jacket. It's snug, but breathable, and will hold more weapons than I could have ever imagined. I have her sew the remote Gabe made for my new dagger boots into the jacket sleeves.

Looking at the table where Gabe is working is overwhelming. Gadgets cover the entire length of the tables, scattered about in an unorganized manner, but to see him doing something he loves pleases my soul.

The day begins to break, and I prepare myself for one last night of real sleep. My head falls heavy on the flattened pillow wile my eyes gloss over the others, retreating to their makeshift beds.

*   *   *

A sudden thunderous roar of explosions surges through the ground, waking us from our slumber. While the lights dim on and off from the quake-like rumble, a sudden increase of adrenaline promptly moves everyone to dress. After a few minutes, the rumbling secedes to a small tremble, and calmly settles back down.

Everyone finishes up what they were working on the previous day and prepares to deploy. Gabe's in the knife room, sitting in the corner facing the wall with his head buried in his knees. I can tell he's been crying what I assume can only be about Juliana, but I stay silent; Instead, I sit down next to him and put my arms around his shoulders, and give him a few minutes to grieve over losing her.

I muster some comforting words, "we'll find her."
Truth is I don't know if we will, but it at least gives us hope.

"Arena, its time," Niki says quietly at the door.

"You ready for this, dear brother?" I say to him quietly. He looks at me placidly and nods his head with uncertainty. I load a full mag into his gun and hand it to him before I slip into the other room to gear up.

The jacket that Niki modified fits perfectly and is ready to be married with weapons. I first place four Beretta 92FS pistols in my front jacket where Niki has so elegantly sewn perfect sheaths for these guns followed by six fully loaded clips. Next, I tuck six stealth and six black-widow throwing knives in the sides of my securely knit jacket. Two daggers rest tightly against the sides of my hips, and my favorite scorpion dagger is nestled in a special sheath that has been perfectly fashioned near the small of my back.

I put on an extremely lightweight quiver of titanium arrows, some with razor-tipped edging, and some with heat-seeking explosive tips designed by Gabe. Lastly, my go-to weapons of choice: the two Yoshihara Kuniie Saku katana Samurai swords crossing perfectly into the well-designed sheathes on the back of my jacket. Surprisingly, the weapons attached to my body do not feel heavy at all. In fact, with the tightly knitted fabric in the jacket, I feel comfortable and amazingly mobile.

I feel a little nauseous as I watch Henry and Finnegan getting ready, knowing that I may lead one of those two men to their deaths. I go back into the bathroom and splash water on my face to calm my nerves.

While everyone waits for me outside, I muse over the previous events that have led up this point, and wonder if my life will truly end today. I'm struggling to understand all of this, but I'm finally realizing the truths behind my fate now.

I walk out of the bathroom to be greeted by silence. Not a sound or word is said; they just sit there waiting for some instruction or a speech of some kind, which I'm not good at. I really have no words to say. I look down and notice the Bible that I found in the cathedral is sitting on the table in front of me. I suddenly remember a passage that stuck out to me when I was younger and read aloud from the book of Ecclesiastes:

There is a time for everything, and a season for every activity under the heavens; A time to be born and a time to die, a time to plant and a time to uproot, a time to kill and a time to heal, a time to tear down and a time to build, a time to weep and a time to laugh, a time to mourn and a time to dance, a time to scatter stones and a time to gather them, a time to embrace and a time to refrain from embracing, a time to search and a time to give up, a time to keep and a time to throw away, a time to tear and a time to mend, a time to be silent and a time to speak, a time to love and a time to hate, a time for war and a time for peace.

"Today is a new season, and it is our time to unleash His fury. Whatever vengeance you seek, do not let it be by your own will, for it is by the hand of God that His wrath will be done, and we who have been chosen to do His will have kept a covenant to deliver that wrath. Remember where you came from and who you are. You stand firm in your conviction because it will be the only thing that will save you now," I say with passion. There is a moment of silence as everyone ponders what I said.

"Let us pray," says Father Joseph, "Dear Father, forgive us for what we have done and what we are prepared to do. You have freed us from our sins, but our hearts still keep us in bondage. Change and humble our hearts, dear Lord. Protect your children and give them the strength and accuracy to do thy will. Grant us peace to help the broken-hearted and weakened spirits. Have mercy on those who turn and fall from your grace. Let us not pass what is undone, so we can fulfill your will. *In nomine Patris, et Filii, et Spirit s Sancti, Amen.*"

CHAPTER 16

With the Camaro fully packed with ammunition, I say my last farewell to Father Joseph and Niki before getting in the car. I feel less anxious now about our journey to the Capitol, but still determined to stop the president's warmongering over the people of this dying nation. While his time will come to rectify what he has done, my only sense of urgency right now is to find out where Myra, Daniel, and the rest of the innocent people have been taken.

We make our way around the city to the east so we are not totally exposed. We search the entire day from a distance for signs of rebellion, but there is absolutely nothing indicating any kind of activity, so we decide to move in closer to the city. While we drive downtown, there is a dead calm in the air. There's not one living soul that welcomes our arrival, nor a single federal officer who awaits us.

Thousands of body bags lie scattered outside of buildings, and the only sign of life that remains here is the death of a thousand screams still lingering in the humid air. It's a bloody massacre.

There is so much death that surrounds us that not enough body bags can cover the remaining carnage that lies rotting in the sun. Gabe tightens his fists and looks out the window, worriedly wondering if one of those bags is occupied by Juliana. I can only assume that the dead are from those who refused to cooperate or defied authority and revolted, but you can be sure of one thing—the rules of engagement do not apply here.

We exit the car and search for clues that may help us find where they have relocated those who have been detained. I cautiously open the doors to a small department store, preparing myself for an ambush, but all I see is a deserted place that has been ransacked. Gabe notices a set of heavy tire tracks that trail off around the corner, which can only mean that these were either made from large military vehicles or from a loaded-down bus.

We follow the tracks around the corner, and like a punch in the face, the smell of rotting flesh blows through the air. Hundreds of decaying corpses, including women and children, cover the front lawn of the library and scatter down the street. Their bloated bodies are an overwhelming and disturbing sight. A malevolent anger fills inside me. The wretched stench makes me so nauseous, I'm forced to cover my mouth and nose with my hand.

"This is not a town, it's a fucking grave-site," I seethe with disgust. This is genocide. I can't at all understand why the American government would do something so atrocious. Relocating citizens is one thing, but slaughtering your own people. For what? What could they possibly gain from this? There has to be some kind of political deterrent forced on us by another government.

Seeing this much carnage of innocence nearly destroys my heart as I walk through ravaged streets. As I turn over one of the bodies of the children on the grass, I almost lose control of my emotions. The young boy couldn't be older than six years old, still clutching his stuffed bear. I examine his body a little closer and surprisingly notice that no gunshot wounds are present. His mouth, bluish in color, stands out against his ashen face, and his veins protrude just underneath the skin like a spider web on his neck.

These innocent people were not revolting or struggling to escape from authorities in any manner whatsoever, nor do I see evidence that they were armed to do so; they were trying to flee for their lives when they became asphyxiated by something.

I immediately rise to my feet and turn to the others. "These people were poisoned," I say with certainty.

"What?" Finnegan curiously asks. He and Henry examine more of the bodies that surround us, and it is revealed that none have been taken down by gunshots or any sharp objects that shows any physical wounds. It's evident that the only weapon that could have done this is an invisible one; these people were gassed.

"Arena!" Gabe calls from a distance. "These tire tracks lead across 7th Street and toward the highway."

As I walk closer toward Gabe, I suddenly spot someone darting across a window in the supermarket. I quickly draw one my guns, and everyone stops in their tracks and stares at me.

"What is it?" Henry asks.

"Right there!"

"Where?"

"Did you see that?" I shout in a panic. "There's someone alive in there." I point at the supermarket. Everyone loads a weapon and readies themselves for anything as we walk closer. I ask Henry and Finnegan to position themselves in the front of the store while Gabe and I take the back entrance.

We slowly open the back door and enter the premise with caution. The lights are still on, but not a soul exists as we walk down each empty aisle. I ask Gabe to go down one end of the store as I go around the other side to hopefully trap whoever is running around in here. Another image flashes past my left side, and I quickly turn in that direction of the aisle. Obviously, whoever is in here is frightened and not smart enough to stay still and hide.

I hug the side of the aisle and look out of the corner of my eye. I can see the back of a shoe about three aisles down, poking out just enough to get a clean shot and immobilize the person. I look up and notice one of the ceiling mirrors just above my right side. Gabe is one aisle away from the runner, so I cross the main aisle over to where I can sneak up from the back.

I hold my position, knowing that one more step from Gabe will cause the man to take off around the corner right into my gun. Gabe decides to go the opposite way, making the runner back up from his position and into the main aisle where I have him trapped. He steadily walks back while I quietly and carefully raise my gun. I wait patiently for a few more steps before I make my move. I quickly lean in and grab his neck, and point the gun pointed at his head. He doesn't hesitate to throw up his hands and quickly kneels to the floor. I push his neck downward, while Gabe moves in front of him with his gun drawn on his chest.

The man is dressed like a soldier, with a full gasmask on, but because the loosely fit clothes appear to be several sizes larger than his physique, I can only assume he's not a federal officer. "Take off the mask," I say aggressively.

He slowly removes off the mask and holds his breath, as if he is desperately trying not to breathe the same air that ultimately killed the others outside. I wait for him to let out a breath of air just as a parent would do to their child who refuses to breath out of defiance.

After about fifteen seconds of waiting, Gabe spots a fruit pie on an end cap next to him, and he and I have a debate over which apple pie brand is better, Mrs. Bairds or Hostess. I really have no favorite in the matter—my intention is to irritate this man until he is forced to talk. His brows furrow, and he crosses his arms like a small child who is angry over not receiving any attention.

He finally lets out a much-needed breath of air. "Seriously, you're going to argue over some damn fruit filling from an assorted brand of snacks, which by the way contains a large amount of high fructose corn syrup—"

"Shut it!" I shout, waving my gun close to his disheveled face.

"You threaten a very hungry man at gunpoint? You should be ashamed of yourself. Not exactly a nice way greet someone. I bet you're very unpleasant at home too—".

"Shut the fuck up!"

"Such nasty words from a sweet, little girl. Try nicely."

"*Please* . . . shut the fuck up!" I say.

"Well, aren't you a delight."

By his scraggly beard and dirty face, I can tell he is just a vagrant who happened to wander about in the store and is no threat to us, so I toss him one of the fruit pies on the display. He pauses as he catches the pie and looks at me with his eyebrows raised. "I'm not really a fruit-filled pastry kind of guy, perhaps you have a Twinkie on the shelf," he says as he smiles. I just roll my eyes and lower my gun. This homeless man is obviously just trying to survive, but not without some obnoxious ornery behavior at my expense. He may be of no harm, but he's annoying as hell.

"Where did you get these clothes?" Gabe asks.

"Off a dead officer, of course. Any other brilliant questions?" It's like I'm dealing with a child here.

"Did you see them put anyone on buses?" I ask, irritated by his smart-ass response.

"Maybe."

"Maybe you'd like a Twinkie shoved up your ass." I aim my gun at his crotch.

"Okay, okay, easy. No reason to defile a perfectly good snack. When the officers came, I was in the library on the fourth floor. That's where I like to do my occupational reading, if you know what I mean," he says with a wink.

I grow disgusted hearing about his particular habits, as I can only assume he is referring to his daily bowel movement.

"I heard them talking about the buses while I was hiding underneath a desk. They were combing the floors, searching for every last person, and that's when I heard a gunshot fired outside in the main hall. I looked out and saw an officer lying dead on the floor. One of the detainees must have been struggling with the officer and killed him. I was too scared to stay where I was, so I ran into one of the janitor closets and climbed up into the ceiling. I worked my way over the rafters to a vent, where I could see them loading people onto about six buses. That's when the first convoy left," he says.

"What do you mean first convoy?" asks Gabe.

"After the buses drove off, everyone was waiting in groups for the next buses to arrive when all of the sudden people just started falling to the ground. Even a few of the officers who didn't have their masks on fell. That's when I realized there was something in the air polluting their lungs, so I quickly crawled back down and ripped this gasmask off the dead officer," he says.

"How long ago did the buses deploy?" I ask.

"About two days ago," he says.

"Great, we're about two days behind. How are we going to track those buses from here?" Gabe asks.

"Easy, they're being bused to Angola," the man says, as he smells his fruit pie.

"As in, Louisiana State Penitentiary," says Gabe, looking at me.

"How do you know this?" I ask.

"I overheard the officers talking about it when I was hiding underneath the desk."

"Thanks. Oh, and enjoy your fruit pies," I say.

"What, no Twinkies then?"

"They're all gone," says Gabe.

"What's this world come to when a man can't get a simple Twinkie," whines the man.

I explain to the others where we are going as we get in the car and head east.

The Louisiana State Penitentiary hasn't been used for decades, since most criminals have either expired from old age or they were executed during the first rebellion, when all prisons were ordered to be completely exterminated. Almost all the prisons in the US have been abandoned, with the exception of a few that still stand to serve as exercising training camps for federal officers.

Trials no longer exist to protect the rights of people; those decisions are made within the administration. Because the judicial branch has been severed from the balance of governmental power, there are no courts to prove citizens guilty or innocent. One man can decide the fate of your life, and nine times out of ten you are either sent to a labor farm or immediately sentenced to a public execution, and depending on your crime, you are either decapitated for a quick death, hung, drowned—or for the most vicious criminals, quartered and burned.

We drive through the night to the next city outside the Texas border and keep our distance before entering too deep into town. An old cemetery that sits atop a large hill overlooks the town below, and from our vantage point, we are able to see every activity that goes on. With Finnegan's high-powered scope, he is able to determine how many federal officers are in the city.

"I estimate a few hundred officers occupying the downtown area and about fifty of them are securing the perimeter," says Finnegan.

"I think it's time to draw some deer into the woods," I say.

We walk our way down the hill through the trees until we are about one hundred yards away from the perimeter. I have Finnegan and Henry run some trip wires in the open areas, attaching one end to a tree and the other to a high-powered dart gun that Gabe has created. One trip of the wire and the launcher will release fifty poisonous darts at 300 feet per second, penetrating the skin, and injecting lethal toxins that will render the person immobile within seconds.

While they are setting up the other launchers, I climb up in a tree with a perfect view of the officers. From this viewpoint, I should be able to pick them off with ease and still go unnoticed in the dark trees set against the black sky. "It's time to stir up the hornets' nest," I say, as I pull a razor-tipped arrow from my quiver.

I sit up with my back resting against the tree for support and pull back on the bow with the arrow resting on the shelf. I take a deep breath, aim at one of the officers between the trees, and exhale as I release the arrow. Without anyone noticing, the arrow pierces the skull with deadly silence. The officer's muscles contract all at once, keeping him standing for a few seconds before they relax, and he collapses to the ground. Only then do the other officers take notice, and in sheer panic, they look around to see where the arrow came from. Before I release another arrow, I wait until they all move in closer to the woods.

The officers spread out carefully, moving toward us and combing the area. I spot one with a radio who attempts to call for help, but before he can get out a word on the airwaves, I split his forehead with an arrow. While I wait for the next victim, I sit between forked branches that conceal my entire body when I'm not drawing my bow back. Suddenly, one of the wires is tripped, and within seconds, the darts whistle through the air, killing about twenty officers.

I load my bow with another arrow when the officers that are flanked to the left run toward the tree Gabe is hiding behind. Just before I release an arrow, another wire is tripped, sending darts scattering like flies, and taking twenty-five more officers down. I look over to see where Finnegan and Henry are positioned just to make sure their cover hasn't been blown. They are spread out about fifteen yards apart on the ground, covered in leaves, and they are slowly crawling toward the middle of the field where the first wire was tripped.

There are three officers left standing in the middle of the field looking aimlessly around in all directions, waiting for the next attack. Two officers take off running back to town, while the other crouches down and walks in Gabe's direction. Because Henry and Finnegan have not attached their sound suppressors to their guns, they don't risk the chance of firing shots that may be heard in town, so they quickly run after the two officers fleeing for help.

I load an arrow, preparing to take down the fleeing officers, but before I can exhale, I'm distracted out of the corner of my eye by the officer close to Gabe's position. Gabe is fighting with the safety button on his gun. The officer is now behind the tree where Gabe is hiding and walks around with his gun pointed toward Gabe's head. I know I can't draw my bow back fast enough to kill this man, so out of panic I yell at Gabe.

The officer quickly notices me and fires into the tree. Shots whiz past as I hide behind the branches, dodging the bullets, but I lose my footing and slip downward a couple of feet. I grab onto one branch, but my bow has lodged between me and the trunk. I try to swing out enough to unhinge the bow, but my footing slips again, and I lose com- plete balance, sliding all the way down the trunk and onto the ground with the arrow still in my hand. The bow falls soon after and knocks me in the head, adding to my pain.

Gabe races around the large tree in the opposite direc- tion trying to avoid the officer, but the officer switches direc- tions and heads toward Gabe. I don't have enough time to stand up, so with my butt on the ground, I pull back the arrow as fast as I can, and, without any concentration, I let the arrow fly from the string just like when I first shot in front of Finnegan in the den. In an instant, the arrow impales the upper part of the officer's neck and out through his mouth, merely an inch from Gabe's eye. The sheer dead weight of the man falls on Gabe, knocking him on the ground.

I run over to pull the officer off Gabe. "Thank you," he says, panting as he sits up against the tree.

"Arena!" Finnegan yells from a distance.

The two men racing out of the woods have almost cleared the tree line and back to the grassy perimeter of town. I draw an arrow and aim for the officer who has fallen down since a still target is much easier from a distance. As I release the arrow, the officer falls dead, but the one ahead of him is almost too far out of my range.

I draw one more arrow, aiming just a little higher to compensate for the distance. I stand firm, concentrate on my breathing, and exhale as I fling the arrow through the air at nearly a hundred yards away. As the aluminum shaft travels toward the officer, he dips down over a small hill and out of sight. I close my eyes and wince at my failure to take him down while Henry and Finnegan rest their hands on their knees, their heads down, panting from sprinting after the two officers.

Just then, the officer walks up the other side of the hill with the arrow stuck in his back. He stands there for a few seconds before falling on the ground to his death. An absolutely impossible shot that only divine intervention could have helped make.

"Nice shooting," says Gabe.

Henry picks up an old bird feather from the ground, walks over to me, and smiles. "Here, you can put that in your hat now, you've earned it."

"We better hurry because this moment isn't going to last," I say.

I ask Gabe to carefully unhook the trip wire on the third dart gun and bring it with us. "Finnegan, you and Henry find a uniform that fits—I want to draw some of these officers out of town," I say. "Gabe, I need to know which one of these tipped arrows will give me the biggest bang."

"I think I know where you're going with this. Use the red arrows with the titanium shafts—it should be more than enough to pierce through heavy armor."

"When I give you the signal, try to lure them out toward you in front of the dart gun," I say to Finnegan.

"Here, use this remote to launch the darts. The signal should reach up to about forty yards," Gabe says to Henry.

"This is about being efficient. There are four of us and about two hundred of them, so let's take advantage of what we have and terminate what we can in the first pass," I say.

Henry and Finnegan stand in the alley near one of the town buildings, dressed in a full officer's uniform with an issued helmet and gun, while Gabe and I climb up a ladder on the backside of a bank building to the roof. Gabe kneels at one corner of the roof and sets up some contraption inside his backpack, while I wait for the right time to send the signal to Henry and Finnegan.

I adjust the string suppressor on my bow and take out the red arrow from the quiver that Gabe suggested. I carefully balance the heavy explosive tip on the shelf of the bow. I nod to Gabe so he can signal Henry and Finnegan to get ready.

I pull back the tight string, resting the knuckle of my thumb on the side of my cheek, aim for the armored tank in the middle of the street, and release the titanium shaft of destruction. The arrow sails just beneath the turret on the tank, and a flash of fire instantly lights up the sky, followed by a thunderous roar, sending pieces of metal from the tank flying through the air.

Finnegan and Henry run out in the open, signaling for other officers to come. "The rebels went that way, come on," Finnegan says to one of the leading officers. About thirty-five men are lured into the alley and out into the grassy opening where the darts are deployed, killing almost all the soldiers. The few officers who escaped the darts are shot down with precision by Henry and Finnegan.

I pull a second red arrow from my quiver and strike down another heavily armed vehicle trying to flee. Because the blast is so great from all the weapons the vehicle is carrying, about two dozen officers near the vehicle are killed instantly. With all the officers running in a panic in all different directions, the townspeople begin to fight back. Two armored trucks pull up from the north side and release about a hundred more soldiers to diffuse the small revolt, but their vision becomes quickly hindered by a ball of black smoke from a secondary explosion.

Gabe stands up, turns his palms up, and two coated barrels extend outward from his sleeves. When he squeezes the two triggers below the barrels, dozens of small metal square nets about five inches fling forth, cascading down on the remaining officers who are impaired by the black smoke. Hundreds of these copper metal nets stick to their skin, and fry their bodies with a fatal shock. Their convulsing muscles leave them disabled until they succumb to brain death.

Since the high ground will always have the advantage, I save my ammo and pick off twenty more officers with my bow from the rooftop. The officers left are either shot by Henry and Finnegan, or they have surrendered to the people who have fought back in a first of many revolutions to come. What has started now cannot be changed.

Gabe and I climb back down the ladder and join Henry and Finnegan, who have discarded their uniforms so they are not mistaken for officers by the people. As the smoke from the explosions dissipates from the ground and into the sky, the people gather up all the remaining officers and put them in the center of town square with their hands shackled.

While they are being tied down, I take a moment to walk around the encircled officers, looking them in their eyes, and wondering how many here will ask for forgiveness. All I think about are all those women and children who suffered a senseless death back in our town. I look out toward the crowd gathering around and see that Finnegan is gesturing for me to go.

I walk away with Henry, Finnegan, and Gabe, but I stop just as the crowd turns into complete silence and one voice speaks out.

"Who are you to come here and save us?" asks a woman in the back.

I turn to address the crowd. "I'm no different than you, and I didn't come here to save you from this evil. I came here to give you hope that the choices you make may save your life."

"So what are we supposed to do, just give in and die?" someone shouts.

"We're all going to die, my friend, in some way or another. Death is just the beginning of a new life. There is but one choice you will have to face before the Day of Judgment, and it will undoubtedly decide your fate. You people will not be immune to the darkest of days that will come, nor will you be in such favor the hour of your death. Many of you will be deceived by your own flesh. If you surrender to this," I say, pointing toward the officers, "then you will have dug your own eternal grave."

Right then, a small boy about seven, limps toward me. His face is covered in dirt, and he looks as if he hasn't had a decent meal in weeks. As he gets closer, I see he's wearing a metal prosthetic leg. He hands me a fistful of arrows he fetched from the dead officers. "Thank you," he kindly says.

I kneel down and place my hand on his shoulder, holding back the tears as much as I can. "God has a special place in His heart for you. You will be protected by His hand from now on," I promise as I hug him.

"Are you an angel?" he asks. "Because you glow like one," he says.

"Is that what you see?" I ask. He shakes his head up and down and grins. I stand up and wipe the tears from my eyes as he slowly walks back to his mother.

Before I leave and head back up to the car, I turn and address one last message to these poor people. "You will tell the world of our existence and know that God's wrath will not go undone here. There will be no limitations nor boundary until it is finished."

I walk away, not knowing how many of these people will actually survive. Before we drive off, I kneel down at a large stone in the cemetery. While the others reload weapons and prepare themselves for the next wave of attacks, I suppress any hatred within me and put my head to the ground and pray.

CHAPTER 17

We drive east and stop in a remote area to rest for the remainder of the night before moving on. By mid-morning, we arrive at the next city, approaching cautiously from a distance, but when Finnegan takes a quick scan of the downtown area through his scope, he notices something quite different than what we've already seen. It appears to be normal. Of course, that's all relative when you're defining *normal* in this country. Regardless, there doesn't seem to be any threatening signs from federal officers in the vicinity.

We drive in for a closer look and examine the city's potential grounds for attack. I put on a black cloak with a hood that I got from Father Joseph back at the den to conceal my weapons. What may seem safe from a distance can be an alarming illusion as we approach closer. I certainly don't want to pose as a threat to these people with the sight of my weapons, but I go in assuming everyone is an enemy regardless—I trust no one now.

The streets are filled with people going about their business as if nothing has happened. People are shopping and eating with absolutely no federal officers in sight. By their contented behavior and elegant appearance, it's evident that this is a wealthier district; in fact, I see no signs of poverty. The population appears to be dense, around 250,000, which is considered to be very large these days.

Since the new administration has taken control, the population of America has dwindled by thirty percent in the last ten years due mostly to harsh laws restricting unwanted and non-contributing citizens access to food credits, which slowly caused many Americans to die from starvation. But with the recent news from Finnegan about the birth-control-laced water, I'm shocked that the percentage isn't lower. Prior to this administration, the population was nearly cut in half from an extremely deadly flu epidemic that began in 2035 and wasn't contained until two years later, when a new vaccine was developed. But the long wait for a cure proved to be detrimental, as the deadly disease swiftly swept around the globe, killing nearly four and a half billion. No other age in history has witnessed such atrocities.

Because this town appears to be nonthreatening, we take advantage of the city's amenities and find a place to rest in one of the downtown hotels. I never thought I would be this excited to take a shower in the middle of the afternoon. The warm water running over my skin and cascading down my back like a tepid waterfall never felt so good, and I have it all to myself.

Before the day breaks, we scout out the city, trying to determine why it's so different from the others that have been destroyed and are nearly desolate. While we walk downtown, Gabe and I immediately notice the city library, which is much larger than the one in our town back home. Whether it's false hope or not, we decide to explore the inside, expecting to find it empty, and hoping to discover Internet services, but to our surprise it's filled with readers on every floor.

We wander around until we locate the computer lab on the third floor. The computer screens are lit up, but instead of the solid blue screen we have back home, these have a welcoming city homepage. Gabe browses outside of the homepage, but the search tool is disabled; in fact, there is no other browser to use. The Internet appears to be gated to this community only, creating an intranet network that is obviously monitored with high security.

Gabe tries to hack into a backdoor allowing him to override the internal network, but it's sealed shut without a trace of possible networking avenues outside of this city. As we browse through sites that are allowed, it is clear that the government has restricted any outside access and has contrived an intranet community that makes the new administration appealing. The sites are dictated by what they want you to believe is true. The absolute fallacy of this virtual world they have created is a manifestation of lies and only serves to brainwash the people to believe the world outside of this city has the same comfort as it does inside.

A woman in her fifties, hopelessly trying to look twenty, sits next to me at another computer. I can't help to stare, but I notice a tiny barcode tattooed on her right wrist. As we get up, I notice barcodes tattooed on everyone's wrists. I wouldn't have noticed it before, but now that I'm curiously looking for them, they are everywhere and easy to spot, like dangling earrings. The people are dressed very well and look sparkling clean. Every woman who walks by is wearing makeup, and every man is cleanly shaven. Now that I have become more perceptive of my surroundings, the peculiarity of this strange city provokes a convivial curiosity that drives me to continue exploring it. We decide to wander further in the city, hoping to figure out the meaning behind its cultural abnormalities, at least compared to what we have already experienced.

We meet back outside with Henry and Finnegan, explaining to them the oddity of the barcodes. "Let's split up so we can gather clues more efficiently. I want to explore more of this strange town. We'll meet back at the hotel at ten," I say to everyone.

While Henry and Finnegan drift off in one direction, Gabe and I stay together in another. After an hour of walking down street after street, we find ourselves moving further away from the city and into a residential area. Before we start to go back toward another part of the city, I look over beyond the trees that separate the back of the houses and notice a metal fence.

"Do you see that, behind the trees?" I ask.

Gabe squints his eyes and says, "It looks like a security fence, why?"

"Exactly. Why is a security fence needed in a city like this, especially behind a residential area?"

We take a closer look to examine the stature of the fence. The fence runs in both directions as far as we can see, and stands nearly twenty feet high into the trees. Gabe moves closer to the barrier with his arm stretched. "Wait, stop!" I shout. I pull back his arm before his hands touches the fence. "How do you know this fence isn't electrified?" I ask.

"Because the hairs on my arm are not standing up, and I would be able to hear the flow of electricity humming through the metal veins of the fence," Gabe explains, as he grabs a hold of the fence without a shock. I wonder why they would spend all this time putting up a security fence around the city, but leave the main road u nguarded.

We head back into the city to explore more on the east side of town, where the streets are less even and the buildings are not as pristine. Still, the same cheerful people walk by with barcodes on their wrists, oblivious to the dingy and uninviting dwellings. A palette of illuminating colors splash across the walls on the side of buildings in the alleys, where lesser traffic of people roam.

A bright eyesore of a building pops out down the street as we walk around the corner. It's an old movie theater, with a brilliantly lit marquee flashing the words: *All Day and All Night*. What appears to be a theater front is most likely a pornographic movie house behind the doors, but upon closer examination, it truly is a theater that shows old black-and-white films and television shows from the past. We watch intently as people walk in and out of the theater while having their wrists scanned when entering.

As we walk a little further down the street, people begin to stop and stare, avoiding passing in front of me. I can feel their frightened eyes glued to me as I walk down the sidewalk. Before I know it, Gabe nudges me in the side of my ribs and whispers, "Hey, your knives are showing. So are your guns."

Apparently, my cloak has come open and exposed my weapons, startling everyone around me. I quickly pull my robe closed and continue walking as if no one has noticed, but unfortunately it's too late, because people are whispering about my attire. The whispers get louder, spreading like a cancer down the street, and before we can get through the next block, I feel like an outsider even though my cloak is tightly concealing my weapons.

Gabe steers me to the right, down a back street behind a dumpster, where we crouch down and hide. Less than a minute later, two federal officers walk past the back street toward the movie theater. Whatever clairvoyant thoughts are swimming around that swollen head of his, I'm thankful for yet another one of his intuitive moments of saving us from an unnecessary altercation.

Down toward the end of the back street are what appear to be a couple of prostitutes, but I can't be for sure, and I would like to reserve judgment before assuming. We walk in that direction just so we can avoid any federal entanglements before the day is over, and turn down another street where the smells of barbeque and Italian food fill the air.

To our left are manicure and massage parlors, and to the right are a pawnshop and an old tavern that reeks of bad alcohol. The pungent odor of skunky beer breath coming from an inhibited old man staggering out of the bar is enough to make me gag. When the pub door opens, I get a tiny glimpse of a federal officer sitting at the bar, so we abandon the bar idea and enter the pawnshop instead.

While we look around the store, watching the front window for more officers, we notice an inordinate amount of men being checked before going through a back door of the establishment. Something just doesn't add up, and it's making me a little suspicious seeing credit change hands in private.

I go into the bathroom and climb up into the ceiling tile and onto the rafter bars to investigate what's going on behind those doors. I walk about ten yards and peer into one of the air vents and witness the most horrific sights of bondage. Men are forcing women and children into rooms that are less appealing than a dog cage, and forcing them onto filthy onlookers bidding for their bodies in a commercially sexual exploitation of reproductive slavery.

This place is no more than a front for facilitating human trafficking. The inside of my soul violently shakes, and my stomach tightens. I grit my teeth, my jaws protruding, and boil. It's absolutely abhorrent and demeaning what these men have allowed to go on. The demoralizing atrocities behind these doors is a wretched abomination, and I will not stand for it. While an anger and rage that I can't contain burns inside of me, I quickly descend from the ceiling and back out of the bathroom to explain to Gabe the sickening situation. This city is redolent of filth that suggests a rise of a new Sodom and Gomorrah, and I will crush it before any more children are coerced into any kind of sexual slavery.

I look at Gabe with fury as we walk back outside to consider taking action against this insufferable sight. I pull back the hood of my cloak, untying it, and hand it to him. "You better tame your guilty emotions because mercy isn't an option today," I fume as I draw a sword from my back. If I previously had any guilt-ridden thoughts about killing another human being, they have now completely ceased to exist.

Gabe follows me in as I swing open the door and lunge forward at the man behind the counter with my sword, pointing it toward his neck. "Time to lock up the shop, you grizzly bastard, you're closed for the day," I say.

His eyes intermittently look down at the counter as Gabe searches for the keys to the store. "Where are the keys?" I ask.

"There right here," he says as he cunningly reaches underneath the counter.

He stares at the keys, but reaches for an old Colt Python pistol instead. Before he cocks the trigger, I swing my sword swiftly down and cut off his hand with the gun still attached. The man violently writhes and falls to the floor, holding his severed wrist.

"Since when do keys look like guns?" says Gabe.

"If you wish to keep your other limbs, tell me where the keys are!" I demand.

He points over to the back of the counter beside some leaflets hanging on the wall, where the keys are located. Gabe grabs them, locks the door, and pulls down the shades.

"Now, I'm going to give you a chance to redeem yourself if you so desire," I offer. He nods his head. "Do you believe in God?" I ask.

He struggles to contain the pain from his severed hand. "I don't know," he whimpers.

"For the sake of argument, let's say you do believe in God. Do you believe you deserve to live?" I ask.

"Yes!" he yells, trembling and backing up against the shelf.

"Do you think He would forgive you of the evil pandering you have partaken in?" I ask, pacing back and forth behind the counter.

"Probably not," he answers.

"So, you believe you deserve to live regardless of your sadistic and twisted existence, yet you feel guilty about your behavior because you believe forgiveness isn't an option. You see, if you simply believed in God's existence, you might not be in this predicament, because He forgives all who genuinely asks, and because you believe you deserve to be in this world, you will never find the opportunity to accept His grace to replace your guilt. And here you sit, bleeding to death, avoiding a chance to be forgiven and accept Him into your heart because of the pride that binds you," I say.

I pry the gun from his severed hand and unload all the bullets except one. I spin the cylinder and lock it without knowing where the bullet rests in the chamber, and I place the gun in his good hand, then point it to his head.

"Now, if you're right and God doesn't exist, then neither one of us will ever know it, but if you're wrong, you will know for an eternity. Do you really want to risk that? If you truly believe in your heart that He is your Heavenly Father, then I suggest you ask for forgiveness now before you pull that trigger, otherwise you can hang on to that pride that bellows inside until you are met by the pits of Hell."

Complete silence dominates his conundrum as he thinks about his situation for a minute, then suddenly he turns the gun on me and pulls the trigger, but the only thing exiting the barrel is a clicking noise, resulting in the sound of an empty chamber. Panicking, he pulls the trigger five more times, resulting in the same ominous sound. "What?" he asks, stuttering.

"Looking for this?" I ask, holding the bullet. "You're like too many other sheep on this earth—very predictable." I pull out my Beretta and shoot him in the head. Something inside of me has deeply changed now, because the remorse I once felt has gone. I feel lost in a sea of hatred, and I fear it will only deepen as long as this journey continues.

"The evil we face behind these doors will extend you no grace. Show no mercy here; that will be for God to decide," I say with a rage I cannot contain. "Gabe?"

"Yes?"

"Not one of these motherfuckers leave here alive," I say with a venomous distaste before we go on a killing spree.

When I kick in the back doors, hell is unleashed as I hold back nothing. Through these doors is the image of pure bondage of sadistic torment. There are women being beaten into submission, paying back a debt to their owner, children about the age of fourteen with dog collars strapped tightly around their necks, tied down by chains, and forced into sexual favors. Hundreds of men of all colors and cultures who are bidding, buying, and breeding, roam the halls. Many are engaged in this sick, twisted act of sexual violence in this sinful warehouse.

I waste no time as I strike down the first victim in front of me and slice downward on his chest, spilling blood and intestines onto the floor. Within just minutes, I clear the first hallway—stabbing, chopping, dismembering, even decapitating every wicked and immoral man standing in my way. Gabe takes out those in the first rooms of the hallway with his Desert Eagle firearm, while I make a bloody path for the next hall. Just around the corner, I see federal officers taking advantage of an innocent teen girl tied to a wooden post.

I quickly throw one of my black-widow knives at the back of one of the officer's heads, splitting his spinal cord. The other officer tries to draw his gun, but I pull one of the daggers from the side of my hip and thrust it up in his thorax, twisting the dagger as I pull it out. The dirty floor turns red within seconds as the officer falls to the ground. I untie the girl and tell her to run as fast as she can.

I hear Gabe screaming my name, so I hurry back over to the first rooms where we came in and quickly notice federal officers trying to escape through the store. I run back into the store and shoot the first two officers in the head, then slash through the remaining three with the swords.

I hear gunshots in the hall and immediately race to see if Gabe is in trouble, but to my surprise no one is there. At the end of the hall, three men run to an adjacent room, but the door is locked. One holds a gun while the others carry an ax and a bent metal pipe. I throw a dagger in the neck of the man holding the gun, which drops him to the floor, gasping. The other two men quickly turn around and rush forward with their weapons in hand, ready to pound me over the head. I stand firm and take a more aggressive posture as I get in a *Jodan-gamae* position.

With my sword high, I immediately strike downward and cut off the arm of the first man, then I quickly crouch to avoid the blow of the pipe. While he strikes at the air with the pipe, I swing my other sword and slice his left leg off. He violently trembles on the ground in agony, until I unwillingly decide to split his skull, putting him out of his misery.

I quickly run back through the halls to make sure Gabe is okay. As I turn the corner, I'm met head-on by six angry brutes with bloodstains on their shirts, and I can only hope the blood is not Gabe's. I reach behind my back, pull out my scorpion dagger, kneel on one knee, and push the knife in one of the men's inner thighs. The man pushes his arm back, clutching the wall as he falls backward into the others. I twist the dagger out, making sure the man can't stand. With both swords in my hand, I go on the attack, slaughtering the other five men.

"Arena!" shouts Gabe from around the corner.

I jump over the bloody bodies and race into the next hall. Gabe is struggling with one of the men. I pull out my gun and shoot. The side of the guy's head splatters red on the wall and his heavy body collapses to the floor.

"Are you okay? Have you been shot?" I ask, looking at Gabe's bloody arm.

"I'm fine, this isn't my blood," he says.
"Come on, there's another open room down the hall," I hurry. I reload my gun with a full clip and we search down another hall and into an open area. There are about fifty men scattered in the open warehouse, half of whom are federal officers armed with guns. To the right is a forklift loading large crates onto a truck, and to the left is another truck filled with dog cages.

There's an officer dressed in a very unique uniform standing upon a raised platform, barking out orders to everyone down below. I tell Gabe to get ready for an ambush and gun down the armed officers first. While everyone is running around panicking, we run inside and hide behind some pallets unnoticed.

I didn't bring my bow, so I will have to take out the man on the platform with my gun at about thirty yards away. I lift the gun and rest it on the pallet, aim for his head, exhale a small breath of air, and squeeze the trigger. A direct hit on his forehead abruptly stops him from yelling orders, and he comes crashing down off the platform.

Everyone is so loud hustling back and forth that no one notices right away, until an officer nearly trips over his body and begins to shout. With both guns drawn, I take down officers one by one until all the armed men are dead—it's like shooting fish in a barrel. I put my guns away and draw my swords to finish off the remaining swine, while Gabe shoots everyone who's trying to flee off the dock. As soon as the last body falls to the floor, we hear a truck outside the open dock backing up. I'm completely exhausted, and the muscles in my arms can barely raise the sword. We both quickly hide to the side of the dock door just as the truck stops.

Two men jump out of the vehicle and are greeted with an absolutely horrific sight of bloody carnage. While they stand there in stunned silence, I grab one by the back of his hair and place a knife beneath his neck while Gabe holds the other at gunpoint.

"So, what are we delivering today?" I ask. The men say nothing, so I force the man that Gabe's holding at gunpoint to open the truck. He's so nervous, he can't find the right key to open back door of the truck, so I pull out my gun and shoot it off the lock.

"Open it now," I say. He trembles, but when the door opens, a horde of women and children tumble out of the truck, gasping for air. They've been smuggled covertly into the country for slave trade and sexual exploitation for wealthy men who have denied any respectable decency or an ounce of morality.

"Who sent you to transport these women?" I ask.

"I don't know," he says.

"Tell me now or I won't be as merciful," I demand, as I slowly cut around his ear.

"Some military gentleman, I don't know for sure," he says, stuttering and panting.

"I reserve the right to judge, and gentleman he is not."

"Iakov, they call him Iakov," admits the other man.

"How much did they pay you?" I ask.

"No money, they promise us our pick," he says, referring to the women or children they decide to choose for a sex slave.

Just then, the man held at gunpoint quickly attempts to grab Gabe's gun, but before he reaches for the trigger, I shoot him in the side of the head then slit the other man's throat. We untie all the women and children that are bound together on a continuous piece of rope.

"Run, you're free now," I yell, as they file out, nervously looking around for authorities.

"Thank, you, thank you!" a woman hysterically shouts in Russian.

"Don't thank me, thank God for your freedom," I respond in Russian. While Gabe walks back through all the rooms to make sure all women and children have been freed from their shackles, I make my rounds, killing the rest of the fallen men who are still writhing on the ground. We leave this place with the walls painted red and slaughtered bodies stacked on one another in pools of congealed maroon flowing into the rusty grates. The bloody carnage that's left will be a small sign of God's wrath for those to witness.

CHAPTER 18

People stare at my blood-soaked clothes as Gabe and I exit the premises into the main alley. Because my hands are stained red and my raven hair is dripping crimson, I'm hardly recognizable. We flee as fast as we can down one of the back streets to avoid any other officers strolling around the main areas. They will be all over the place once they see the bloodshed we created. We hide in a dark, empty alley near a fish market, and catch our breath for a few minutes.

While Gabe crouches down with his back to the wall, I fix my eyes on a shadow, dancing about just around the corner across from us. A heated argument erupts followed by a woman's scream, which I can only assume is the sound of someone struggling.

I poke my head around the corner and see a burly looking man with his pants down to his ankles fighting with what I know now is surely a prostitute. I sidle up behind the man and cock back the Colt Python that I got from inside the pawnshop. The man suddenly stops and poses like a statue when he hears the click of the hammer being pulled back on the gun.

Instead of pointing the gun directly at his head, I take an unorthodox approach and slide the cold black barrel beneath the man's groin area between his legs. I'm more disgusted when I see his wallet lying open on the ground revealing a photo of what I assume is his wife and two kids.

"If you want to keep your manhood attached, I suggest you pull your pants up, go home, and apologize to your wife for being a selfish perverted jackass, and pray she doesn't cut off that sad sorry sight for a penis," I threaten.

"It's average size, thank you very much," he says, shaking.

"Yeah, if you're a Hobbit. Hell, you're an inch away from having a gender change. Now get out of here before my conscience decides to divorce me," I order. The husky asshole scurries off, falling every few steps with his pants sliding down.

I probably should have just shot the man and done his wife a favor, but since both parties were engaged in a consensual and mutual activity, my temptation to kill retreats. I have a moment of compassion when I see the woman crying and wonder to myself how one can do that to themselves, but instead of judging her bad decisions, I simply comfort her. She just needs someone to care for her right now, and if I can be a shoulder to lean on, I will do it.

At that moment, Gabe comes around the corner. "Arena, what's going on? There's a man awkwardly staggering his way down the alley with his pants half-on, pissing himself," he says with a confused look on his face. I shake my head and gesture for him to stop, because I don't feel the need to relive the moment in front of this broken girl.

Just then, a squelching siren pierces the air, breaking up a comforting moment. I hand the girl the pistol, "here, take this, you may need it, and remember, no human being is immune to sin, He will forgive us if we ask," I say before I take off.

Gabe and I quickly leave the open area, where people are covering their ears from the hellish noise. As soon as the siren stops, everyone around us immediately notices Gabe and I covered in blood. When I draw my swords to prepare for an assault, all hell breaks loose—people scream in terror and scamper in all directions. We take off down the street back toward the hotel, hoping to find Henry and Finnegan waiting for us. Whatever is up ahead, it must be bad enough to make people desperately scramble for shelter in a panic.

We proceed with caution on the backstreets, waiting to be met by some federal assault, but not until we reach the library do we spot a small army of officers marching in from the west in a very regimented manner. About two hundred armed soldiers, who do not look like regular federal officers, are wearing gas-masks. Not sure if they are here for us or if they are waging war against the city. If we're to get out of here alive, then we're really going to need Henry and Finnegan, because I'm not going to be able to do this alone. "Gabe, tell me you got something in that backpack that will distract these neo-Nazi gorillas," I say.

"I do, but not enough to kill all of them. Here, hold this," he says.

"What is this?"

"It's called a hornet's nest."

"Let me guess, you got this idea from one of your comic books," I say.

"*Juggernaut #4*, ridiculous premise and idea, but so was your yellow-jacket nest and McKenzie incident."

"Touché, so what the hell is it supposed to do?"

"This metal nest holds about 120 explosive bees. Each bee-like round will attach itself to whatever moves within a range I decide. It's very precise, so we want to make sure we have a pretty good idea how far away those soldiers are. Once the range is set, the bees will respond to any movement within twenty feet."

Gabe sites in the weapon for fifty yards, aiming and waiting for the right moment for the soldiers to march toward the dialed-in distance. "Whatever you do, stay still," he says before he pulls the trigger.

Tiny flying metal explosives spray the sky like a swarm of bees and within seconds they swoop down with a vengeance toward the moving soldiers, just as Gabe predicted. The bees pack a punch, exploding at will, and take out most of the men. It's like firecrackers on the Fourth of July violently popping out of control. Soldiers immediately collapse when the metal bees explode on contact, while the remaining soldiers are too disoriented to stand. Before I run in closer to take advantage of the bewildered men, I take out a smoke bomb in Gabe's pack.

I pull the pin and toss it over to the staggering soldiers, making it even harder for them to engage. I draw my swords, slashing and dicing my way through the plume of smoke, killing anything that stands. I save my ammo until I desperately need it—like Henry said, I'll only become an effective killer if I trust the will of my blades. Since I can see no more than the soldiers, I can only feel my way through the haze, carving up flesh every step I take while dodging the fallen bodies around me. As soon as the smoke clears, I brace myself for any soldiers who survived the vicious attack, but I'm the only one left standing in a pile of dismembered bodies.

There was a point in my life I would have normally felt sad, depressed, or even disgusted at the sight of this carnage, but today I feel strangely comfortable. With their souls already departed from their bodies, I feel no attachment to the flesh that lays lifeless on the ground, but there is a part of me that feels pity. Whether it's the rush from the massacre or just pure exhaustion, my knees begin to buckle and I falter, but my swords hold me up. I look out at a crowd of people across the street and can't help but to think that many of those people are no better or worse than the men who have just died here. I bow my head and pray over the fallen; enemies or not, I ask God for His mercy.

As I walk over to Gabe, I'm in absolute shock as to what I'm witnessing; a few thousand people are kneeling and praying. Gabe gestures for me to put my swords away so it doesn't look like I'm posing a threat when I walk over.

The very same people who ran screaming from me when we emerged from the alley don't seem to be afraid anymore. Instead, they look upon me like a neighbor as I walk past their bewildered faces.

Moments later, the earth begins to tremble, and everyone stands to their feet, bracing themselves, but the only part of the ground that fiercely shakes is in the middle of the square where the bodies lie. Right then, the earth opens up, swallowing every dead soldier and every drop of spilled blood—just another reminder that God is in control of my fate.

While I wring out the blood from my hair, a woman carefully approaches and holds out her hand to me. I grab the old woman's hand, and she gestures me to follow her. Either she doesn't speak English, or she is too shook up to say anything; nevertheless, I fully trust her.

She takes Gabe and me down the street to one of the clothing stores, and I feel as though I've known this woman my whole life. If I never knew my grandmother, I would envision her to be like this woman—frail, meek, and kind. Inside the store, an older gentleman waves us to the back. "Come, please, back here," he says. "Sorry for the lack of communication from my wife—she's mute."

"It's okay, I understood her perfectly," I say.

"If it wasn't for those damn officers, she would be able to speak right now," says the old man.

"What happened to her?" Gabe asks.

"They came here a year ago threatening everyone who claimed Kerian," he says. Kerian is a negative term that represents disloyalty or betrayal to the government. Years ago, a man named George Kerian refused to accept a new government policy that required a twenty-percent federal merchant tax to all businesses that were not already absorbed by the federal government. This ploy was to encourage small businesses to conform, but when George Kerian was caught giving his twenty percent to a small group of non-conformists who were preparing to revolt against the government, he was extradited and sent to prison for sedition.

"They came in here accusing her of treason, because she forgot to turn in her quarterly merchant tax earnings," he continues.

"How is that reasonable for tormenting a person?" I ask.

"It isn't. They came here to make a statement, because for years we have been refusing to accept any federal assistance that may force us to become absorbed into their system. They knew exactly what they were doing when they forcefully pulled her away from me. When she resisted, they strapped a dog-like collar around her neck and pulled her on the floor, choking her.

"When she passed out from the strangling belt around her neck, they released her. They didn't feel the need to arrest a dead person, so they left her there on the ground to die and just took off. She survived the anguishing nightmare, but the damage to her vocal cords was too much, and from that moment on, she has never been able to speak.

"You know, for years, I've always said my wife talked too much, but I would give every ounce of my life to hear that pretty songbird voice again," he says with trembling lips.

The old woman comes from the back and hands Gabe and me a bag of clean clothes to wear. "Thank you so much. You are too kind," I say, holding her hand with admiration. "I'm Arena." The woman looks at me and uses sign language I can't quite make out. She points to the sky and places her hands on her shoulders, turning them out and waving them.

"We know who you are. She says you're an angel sent from God. News travels fast from the west. I've prayed every day and night that He would bring someone to deliver us from this suffering," says the old man.

As we leave, the man grabs my arm and says, "Wait." He tries to hold back tears from his red, irritated eyes. "If my granddaughter was still alive today, I know she would fight with you. You keep the course, you hear? God be with you both." I'm too heartbroken to know what may have happened to his granddaughter. I try to convince myself it wasn't anything that his wife experienced.

I can barely hold back my emotions as I leave the store, but before I cross the metal threshold, I quickly surrender those feelings when I notice a video camera in the upper corner following my every step. I ask the old man if the camera belongs to them for security measures. He tells me that the camera was placed there by the federal government just like all the other cameras in the city. He looks at me, shocked, as if I should already know this. It makes me wonder how many cameras back home were secretly watching us. The camera gives me the creeps, so we quickly leave.

There is a sudden commotion gathering outside, and I hear a young girl screaming for help over by the wall next to the library. She is lying next to a woman with her arms wrapped around her, but no one can understand what she is saying.

I quickly hand Gabe the bag of clothes and tell him to meet me back at the hotel as I run over to the young girl. The woman she is embracing has a fatal headshot wound, and just then my body freezes up, leaving me a little lightheaded. At that moment, I think back to the day I held my mother's face while she died in my arms.

I grab the girl and pull her closely to my chest; she clinches onto me, crying out in pain. After a few minutes, her hyperventilation slows down to a few bumps of breaths, and she breathes in deeper, calming down just enough to release her claws from my arms. By the time her body soothes, a few women from the crowd come over to console the young girl.

When I get up to leave, she insistently points to the back of the library, shouting, "He went that way!"

"What did he look like?" I ask.

"It was one of them," she says, pointing toward the hole in the ground where the soldiers fell.

I run toward the side of the library and around to the back, where the streets connect to the back alley. My adrenaline is pumping too much for me to even care if this man is armed, so I race down the alley, looking around every corner. I stop for a moment when I hear a scratching sound coming from my right side.

Now is the time I could use Gabe's eyes. The scratching gets louder and louder as I walk closer to the wall by the garbage bin. I pull my dagger out, ready to strike whatever is making that sound. I wait for a few seconds before moving in on the target with my knife. As I grip the blade tight, I rush over behind the bin and strike down with force into a rat the size of a cat gnawing on an apple core.

My heart slows to a normal pace and I breathe out a sigh of relief. I remove the rat from my dagger, but before I can walk away, standing before me is an officer with a loaded pistol pointing directly at my head about ten feet in front of me.

"You think you can just walk out of here alive? Killing my men like that. Well, I have a surprise for you, little girl. You are not immortal; you're just flesh and blood like the rest of us," he says, gawking at me with perverted eyes. "You're a fine specimen, I admit, but can you outrun a bullet? Oh, I'm going to have my way with you whether you like it or not, you stupid bitch," he insults, licking his lips, "and then my friends are going to take turns spoiling that young body of yours."

My heart pumps fast and my blood boils with rage, and if I can just get him to take one step closer, I will end him like the rest.

"If you want me that bad, then come take me," I goad his ego. He takes a step forward and says, "Oh, don't you worry, I'm going to . . ."

I quickly block his left arm with the gun, while I pull out my scorpion dagger and thrust it into his chest, and then into his throat. I turn the knife as he falls, breaking his elbow, and pulling the gun from his stiff fingers. As he lies there gurgling on his own blood, I leave nothing left for my emotions to cling to as I stare into his dying eyes.

I walk away, burning inside, and for a brief moment, I feel an incurable rage turning to hatred. I stare out into the darkness, shaking, and wonder whether or not if my conscience has started to wither.

I race back to the hotel as fast as I can, but when I come rushing through the room, I only see Henry and Gabe. "Where's Finnegan?" I ask in a panic.

"He said he would be back shortly. He is on the roof doing some reconnaissance," says Henry, staring aghast at my bloody clothes. "My God, Arena, you're soaked in blood."

"What the hell happened to you guys when the soldiers were deployed?" I ask.

"Finnegan and I had already left for the hotel when they were coming in. We thought you would be back here by then since it was already getting late," explains Henry. "Gabe told us about the soldiers. You better know they will bring in backup after hearing what happened."

"More than you know. Gabe and I spotted cameras monitoring all the store merchants, as well as cameras on the streets."

"Finnegan and I noticed too—that's why he's been on the roof watching out. We stumbled on the building that houses the security for this city, but it was too risky to proceed when the soldiers showed up."

"Shouldn't be a problem now."

"Show me where this building is," Gabe says.

"I can't, it's just too risky right now," Henry refuses.

"I don't care; we need a link to those cameras. It might help us shed some light on this city," Gabe insists.

"I'll go with you," Finnegan says as he stands by the door, listening.

"Let me get some things out of the car," Gabe says.

I grab Gabe's elbow and stare into his eyes for a few seconds with fear in my heart. "Don't do anything stupid. You get in and out as quick as you can. If whatever you are trying to do doesn't work, don't force it, just get the hell out. You hear me? You run."

When they leave, I quickly get in the shower one more time, knowing that this might be the last hot water I will encounter. The bottom of the shower turns red as the water runs over my body. I stare down at the murky water and think about all those who I have killed. I feel somewhat ashamed of my behavior back in the alley with the officer, knowing that person was not me. I let my hatred get in the way of God's plan and it nearly cost my life. I pray for forgiveness in the shower until the water runs cold and my toes and fingers are pruned.

After washing my clothes, I go outside onto the balcony to let them dry out, but as I'm shaking out my pants, I look up in the sky and notice a helicopter in the distance. I wonder if that helicopter is one of many backup teams deploying to this area. I suddenly feel flush when I don't see Gabe or Finnegan in the room.

Just then the door slams open and it's Finnegan rushing in yelling, "Pack up everything now, we need to get out of here."

"Where's Gabe?" I ask, panicking.

"He's right behind me," says Finnegan. "We have to go right now! They are sending in gas units to exterminate this city in response to the massacre."

CHAPTER 19

I feel absolutely wretched inside— the lives of the people in this city are now at risk, and it's all my fault. I don't think I can live with myself knowing I'm responsible for the death of thousands that innocently dwell here.

My nerves are rattled and the adrenalin has worn off leaving me in flux for a moment. I'm not sure what to do as I stand there staring through Finnegan while he speaks to me.

"Arena." I hear him, but I'm too distraught to respond.

"Arena!" he snaps more assertively. "We have to get out of here, now."

My mind suddenly resurfaces. "What?"

"They have been ordered to terminate the city immediately."

"How do you know?"

He shows me a portable wave radio set up he used on top of the roof to dial in the same frequencies as the aircraft.

"Sweetheart, it didn't take long for you to go viral." Suddenly, I'm fixed on my brother's absence.

"Gabe, where's Gabe, is he okay?".
"He's fine now, a little shook up. We had somewhat of a close call," deters Finnegan.

"Close call?"

"We encountered two armed guards in the building, one of which shot at Gabe and nicked his shoulder."

"What?"

"He's fine, more of a scratch than anything. I shot them both, but it's a sure bet they know we're here now. Your brother networked a satellite link from the security monitors in the building to his laptop. Bloody good thing too, we have a live feed of every camera in this city now."

Right then, Gabe races in the door, grabbing supplies that we may need. I stop him abruptly and tightly embrace him.

"I'm okay, Arena," he reassures me.

I look down at the floor and realize I can't be responsible for all these people's lives. No! I will not let this happen. I may be responsible for killing in the name of our Lord, but I will not let innocent people die. Not like this. I realize tens of millions will lose their lives through this bloody war, but today we make a defining statement to this administration.

"Gabe, what do you have for me to take this chopper out?" I ask.

"What the hell are you talking about? We need to get out of here. This place will be non-existent in a few minutes!" shouts Finnegan.

"We can't just let these people die," I say.

"We've got a heat-seeking rocket launcher, small, but should reach up to six hundred yards or so. And if that doesn't work, there's still plenty of explosive-tipped arrows that will scrap that beast, but ya better be damn close to it," Gabe says.

"Get the launcher and the arrows and meet me on the roof," I say.

"Are you insane?" shouts Finnegan. I pause for a moment to absorb the possibility before I answer.

"Maybe."

I wait on the roof for Gabe as the helicopter approaches closer to the main part of the city. The rocket launcher will be ideal, since I'm not sure what part of the city the chopper will fly over. We're going to need long-range weapons for this. Gabe races back up the stairs and onto the roof. I take my time to aim the heat-seeking launcher and wait until the chopper is close enough to strike. We may only get one shot at this. If we're exposed, they may prematurely release gas bombs into the city.

Just as I steady myself, Henry yells over from the other end of the roof, "Hey, we got company!" He's pointing down and over to the left.

I quickly hand the rocket launcher over to Finnegan. "Here, you take the shot, I'm going to do some duck hunting over here," I say, patting him on the shoulder.

"Thanks, no pressure," he smirks.

Over the edge, we spot two tanks and four large trucks carrying soldiers in from the south entrance. "Gabe! You got my quiver? Now would be a good time for those explosive tips," I say, waiting anxiously.

I take the first arrow out and aim for one of the trucks below. I'd rather take out the soldiers first, since they scatter like ants and are much harder to kill when spread out. The arrow grazes just beneath the truck's chassis, killing everyone on board. Fire erupts like a broken hydrant and sets ablaze a raging sheet of burning fuel to the truck behind it, sending a chain reaction of explosions from the fragile gas tanks.

I pull the next arrow, aiming for the truck in front, but Henry yells out, "Arena! No, the tank, the tank!" They must have noticed us, because the turret on the tank rotates over and up, aiming for the roof. I quickly change my position and release the arrow toward the tank. It pierces the tank's armor, taking off the turret, and sending metal flying in all directions, but not before the tank returns a shot of its own. The side of the building is struck, and half of the roof begins to collapse on our side, sending everything sliding downward off the edge. I leap up to the top corner to brace myself as Gabe holds my leg to avoid sliding off the roof.

Henry's body slides over the edge. "No!" I scream. My insides turn on me as my heart tightens up. I watched Henry die and couldn't do anything about it. I try not to cry while the strength of my grip on Gabe weakens. I look over and see that the second tank is turning its turret toward us, but if I try and take a shot I will slide down with Gabe, but if I hang on we die anyway.

I take my chances and release my hand from the metal flashing. I stretch back the arrow and release it as we slide down toward the edge. Before the tank gets off a shot, it explodes and sends shrapnel flying across toward one of the trucks, killing most of the men inside. My teeth painfully grit as my hands slide across the sandpaper roof. I desperately try to cling to anything I can, but there's nothing my hands can grip on to. I turn over and find an air vent pipe to my left. I stretch out my arm as far as I can and grab the pipe, clinging for dear life.

As we come near the edge of the roof, the pipe I'm holding breaks and sends me sliding down further. I slip down, scraping my arms across the rough shingles, but I fail to clutch onto anything except the smoky air.

"Arena!" Gabe shouts. His legs dangerously dangle off the ledge as we begin to plummet to our demise.

CHAPTER 20

Just as I reach the edge with Gabe still hanging on to my foot, I scream out for Finnegan. Suddenly, the sky lights up orange in the distance, and a fireball of metal falls from the clouds. Finnegan's successful shot destroys any chance of another nightmarish genocide, but I'm less excited about the exploding chopper now that I'm clinging ever so helplessly to the abrasive shingles for dear life. He quickly turns and scrambles toward the edge of the roof, but he is much too far away to help us, and it's only a matter of seconds before we fall to our death.

Suddenly, the top part of the building collapses and caves in to the rest of the floor below, leveling out the roof. With my knees hanging off, and Gabe still dangling below, I stop sliding, but my grip is not enough to carry the weight of Gabe hanging off me. I begin to slip, yelling for Finnegan to help.

He gets a running start and leaps over the split roof onto the other side, but he only managed to clear most of the jump, missing the other side as his feet dangle and his hands grip the asphalt shingles. I slip further, trying to grab on to anything at this point. Finnegan manages to pull himself up onto the roof and quickly sprints over to me as I slip further off the edge.

He grabs my arms just in time before I completely go over, and pulls with all the strength he has left. As my chest clears the edge, I pull my leg up and over, which gives me some leverage now to help pull Gabe up, who is still clinging to my other leg. With extreme exhaustion, I hang on to Finnegan's grip as long as I can until Gabe finally pulls himself up far enough to roll over onto the rooftop edge. We lay there for a few moments until the level of carbon dioxide decreases in our bodies as we struggle to catch our breath. The only thing that persuades us to get up and move is the creaking of the roof moving.

"You've got to be kidding me," pants an exhausted Finnegan.

The roof slightly shifts, so we quickly, but carefully, move toward the rooftop door and race down two flights of stairs.

The room trembles like an earthquake for a few seconds as we pack up our things. When it stops, we look at each other in silence, knowing what is about to happen.

"Go now!" Finnegan shouts. By the time we get to the third floor, the roof caves in and breaks through the floors above. As we race down the stairs, dust fills the air, and the debris from the crushed sheetrock falls down on us. We manage to get to the first floor and out through the lobby when the entire right side of the building collapses. We sprint out to the car, jump in, and take off right when the entire building comes crumbling down. I look back at the massive wall of dust from the wreckage and sink down into my seat, knowing that Henry is no longer with us.

"I'm so sorry, Henry," I say as I put my hands on my face and my head in my lap.

"Sorry for what?" asks Henry, popping up out of the back seat. I turn around and scream in shock to see him still alive.

"You're alive!" I shout. "Why are you all wet?"

"I fell down into the pool below when the side of the building was shot. A tree branch slowed me down a little before I plunged into the icy, cold pool. I'm just glad there was water in it," says a shivering Henry.

We travel about fifty miles outside of the city until we find an old state park that has been abandoned for some time. Maintenance has been neglected for many years, and grass and tall weeds cover the entrance and most of the inside. Before it gets too dark, we decide to drive as far as we can up to the top of the hill to set camp. It's secluded enough to make a fire without being seen, and there is enough wild game to hunt when we get hungry.

I lay my clothes out on a nice flat rock near the flames to finish drying them out while I go exploring near the tops of the tree line that overlooks the vast valleys below.

I sit upon the hill, pondering our recent escapade, and enjoy the ever-changing colors in the sky during civil twilight. It's moments like this that remind me to thank our Creator for such a glorious snapshot of His power. Many of us have become what we despise, yet in the midst of our struggles when we least deserve His Grace, we are instantly humbled and transformed by the beauty of His love. I take in every minute of His wonder illuminating above as I rest my head against a padded branch and rest.

The deep blue sky gradually turns black as the stars begin to protrude from space. I watch silently, sitting on the hill with delight as I take in the little things in life that may seem so meaningless to others. Suddenly, I hear the rustling of leaves behind me, distracting my star gazing for a moment, and turn to see that it's just Finnegan joining me on the hill.

"Mind if I sit down?" he asks.

"Have a seat," I say.

"It's a nice night to enjoy the stars," he says.

I know Finnegan has something on his mind because he doesn't usually initiate chitchat unless he's forced to, so I help ease the awkwardness. "What is it?" I ask.

"That obvious, huh. I was beginning to think it was my stench you were avoiding," he says.

"Ha, have you smelled Gabe's feet? You're a joy."

"Look, there's something I've been meaning to tell you and Gabe since we left the den. What we faced today was nothing compared to what lies ahead."

"Geez, this doesn't sound too comforting. "

"I'm not here to discourage you, but you're entitled to the truth nonetheless."

I gaze at his worn chiseled face, confused, as if he'd left out some pretty important information when we started this journey. "Whatever it is, I'm not afraid," I say, plainly

"That's what frightens me. I'm not questioning your bravery, but I certainly don't want your overconfidence to hinder you either," he says.

"I have nothing left on this earth to go to, no one to grow old with, Do you think death is my worst enemy? Sometimes I almost beg for it," I say, throwing my dagger into the dirt.

"Don't you dare say that," he scolds. "I don't doubt your valor, Arena, and I will proudly stand and fight with you till the very end, but you must learn to squelch the hatred and bitterness. You will soon know what kind of evil lurks in the darkness."

I look at him strangely, wondering what he means. Mystified by his gaze as he speaks, I ask him to continue.

"His name is Gennadi Olezka Gorshkov, the new Russian leader, who has been closely monitoring this country with the help of our own government. This international relationship our administration has shaped has destroyed this nation. And when this mutual bond ceases to exist, it will be the day this country dies . . . forever." A reasonable man, crippled by his own words.

"During my time as the special ops leader in Iraq, before I was sent to prison for treason, I had full security access to all governmental projects—short term and long term—but I was never authorized to go any deeper than the second level without security code clearance.

"Two days before my team was terminated in a reconnaissance mission, Captain Aldine, my superior, revealed information to me that was highly classified. I was the only person he trusted, and he knew he needed someone who shared the same values to expose this administration. He gave me his security clearance to the third-level classified files, and I couldn't believe what I saw," he says, now becoming a little more irritated.

"Our government has been secretly planning an invasion on its own soil. They have had long-term plans for the Russian government to mingle with our own to create a new political party that would garner absolute control over the people without being demonized for their efforts.

"You see, if the people witness an invasion coming from another country, they will cling to the new administra- tion as their savior, and yet they will never know that they are ultimately being dictated through inter politics. Sympa- thy for the government is what they implore now."

"So this is what it has come to?" I say.

"This is their solution to become a world power again," he says in disgust.

I pick up my scorpion dagger and look at myself in its shiny surface. "Then we alter their solution," I say, as I throw the dagger toward a tree stump, splitting a beetle in half. "So what happened to the captain?"

"Under extreme scrutiny from the beginning, the captain was never in a position to progress without conformity. I always admired Aldine for what he believed; unfortunately, with what he knew, he just wanted a way out, and his conscience got him killed. A few days later we were questioned and kept under strict supervision, until I was sent to prison while my fellow soldiers were executed."

"Do you ever regret working for the government?" I ask.

"It wasn't always like this, but just like the people here, I guess most of us had the wool pulled over our eyes too," Finnegan admits.

He sits down and puts his arm around me like a father would. I can't help but notice the Celtic cross that is tattooed on his left forearm. "Finnegan, I've known you for fifteen years, and I have yet to ask you what that cross tattoo on your arm means."

"It's a family tattoo. My father wore the same cross on his arm, just as his brother did. Your grandfather was much like you when he was young. I see so much of him in you today," he says.

"Yeah, and what's that?" I ask.

"The will to stand and fight for truth regardless of the outcome," he says. "You better get some rest, we leave first thing in the morning."

CHAPTER 21

I always loved dawn in the fall, just right before the sun begins to break the edge of the horizon, with a thin line of orange peeking through. It reminds me of those days I would get up early to go fishing with Finnegan, anxiously waiting for that first bite.

While everyone else is still asleep, I take all my blades down to the river and wash away the dried blood and flesh still stuck on the steel. As the red water washes out into river, I gaze through the ripples until they slow down where I can see a mirror of my face. An image of Jacob stands next to my reflection in the glassy water, and I can't help but cry; The pain of his death has yet to leave me.

The clear water begins to vibrate, and the image of Jacob quickly disappears. I look up and see a brown bear splashing in the water across from me on the other side. I stand with my sword drawn, ready to defend myself. The bear just stares at me, confused for a moment, so I lower my sword and stare back into his eyes. With my attention still on him, I notice a few fish swimming just below me. I haven't had fish for quite some time, but by the looks of that old bear, he probably hasn't either.

I carefully crouch, hovering over the water and scan the scurrying trout below. I study the hungry-looking bear once more before I spear straight down into the water with my dagger, and gig one on the fish. My stomach gurgles like an old bullfrog just looking at the trout, floundering on the end of the knife.

The hungry bear ogles my every move, jaws slobbering. I can only hope he is admiring the sight of the fish and not me, but for some strange reason, that old bear never took a step toward me the whole time I was in the water. Before I throw the fish on the bank, I stop to look at him one more time, wondering if he will charge at me, but he doesn't. He just stares at me with those same cold, black eyes, licking his chops.

I'm so hungry for fish right now, but because the bear does nothing, I feel compelled to befriend the beast, so I throw him the trout. It's amazing how two completely different species can have mutual respect for each other. As he devours the fish, I smile, intrigued, and gig another one for him. We don't see each other as enemies as much as we respect each other's company as hunters. We are so different, but God has managed to show me how much we are the same. If I had a choice right now, I think I would choose to have that bear's life rather than my own.

I walk back to camp and throw a couple of logs into the dying fire. The glowing embers beneath the charred wood hiding in the ash are hot enough to keep the fire from dying and just warm enough to dry out the cold water clinging to the tiny hairs on my legs.

While the fire gradually grows, I prepare a nice breakfast for the others, skewering fresh-caught trout on some twigs. I lay them carefully over the fire, high enough for them to cook evenly, but not too close where they might burn. The smoky aroma of the trout fills the air, waking everyone up one by one.

"Where did you get the fish?" Gabe asks, rubbing his sleepy eyes as he walks over by the fire.

"The supermarket in the seafood section," I sarcastically respond. Gabe rolls his eyes as he sits down, while Henry and Finnegan wake up to join us.

"There's food all around us, you know—you just have to go out and get it," I say to Gabe. Finnegan pulls out a couple of dented cans of peaches still left in the car that we brought with us from the den.

"Fruit and fish, now that's the kind of breakfast I've been craving. Thanks, Arena, you couldn't ask for anything more," says Finnegan.

"Sure you could. How about some nice, crispy bacon? Everything is better with bacon," says Gabe, licking his lips.

"Well, I don't see a pig scurrying around anywhere, so this will have to do," says Finnegan.

"How far are we from the prison?" I ask as I sharpen my sword.

"We're about fifty miles, but let's not get too anxious now. This won't be like the other cities. This facility can hold up to ten thousand prisoners, which means there may be a thousand armed guards," says Finnegan.

"I'll be ready," I say with confidence.

"Yes, and so will they," Henry chimes in.

"You say that car is equipped with heavy weapons?" I ask.

"Theoretically, yes. Haven't ever used them, though," answers Finnegan.

"Well, you might want to start testing them. I've got a plan." I test the sharpness of my sword and swing across the top of one of the peach cans, slicing the top of the lid off.

"I'm not sure I like where you are going with this."

"Trust me."

"Isn't that what the French always say?"

"It's a bloody good thing I'm Irish then."

"Yeah, well, I didn't bring enough whiskey on this trip to drink those bastards to death."

Finnegan walks back from the car with the laptop and sets it next to Gabe. "For what we went through, this better work," he says.

"We'll need to set up an uplink on that hill over there. It's much too dense here to get a clear signal," Gabe says while stuffing his mouth with trout.

While Finnegan sets up the portable satellite on the hill, the grainy picture on the screen clears up, and within an instant, a live feed of the city is displayed. Gabe can control any number of camera feeds we want to see. It's as if we are behind the console of the security building. Technology is amazing, but it's only as good as the person who can manipulate it.

"Great work, Gabe," Finnegan says.

"Thanks."

Gabe pans over to where smoke rises from the rubble of the hotel that collapsed. He focuses closer so we can see heat from the wreckage still burning bright, with embers intermittently flaring up underneath the melted steel. Most of the cameras have audio, but this one seems to be inaudible. Some kind of obnoxious humming distorts the sound, and then all of a sudden, dust and debris chaotically flies past the camera. Gabe chooses another camera and pans back to reveal two heavily armed choppers landing.

Six men jump out of the choppers and survey the surroundings. They notice the large, gaping opening in the middle of town, where the earth enveloped the dead soldiers.

The men walk over to observe the remaining dead soldiers scattered around the south side of the hotel where the two tanks were destroyed. Burned bodies filled with shrapnel lie on top of one of the tanks, with their flesh melted to the heated steel. Gabe follows their every move, tracking them from camera to camera. The men enter the security building and quickly notice two dead officers on the ground, the ones Finnegan shot.

"Can you turn up the sound? I want to know what they are saying," I say to Gabe.

A man dressed in a black uniform throws his hands in the air and is outraged. He picks up a radio on the console and violently throws it across the room. By the posture of the other men standing far behind, it's apparent who the leader is now. A small, beady-eyed man with glasses enters the building nervously.

"General Iakov, we have been waiting patiently for your arrival. Let me catch you up to speed of what we know so far," says the man.

"Yesterday, we deployed two hundred soldiers in response to a violent act of rebellion in the—"

" Lieutenant John, all of my men are dead, or have you forgotten to notice?" asks the general in a thick Russian accent.

"Sir, our soldiers are missing."

"Missing? What do you mean missing?"

"We lost contact thirty minutes after they arrived. They haven't been heard from since. It's like they just vanished."

"And why am I just now hearing of this?"

"Sir?"

"I assume you've contacted them many times, but at which you were given no response, you decided to wait several hours to inform me."

"Yes sir, it's just—"

"Just what? And let me remind you, lieutenant, it's much easier to say nothing at all than to say something stupid you can't afford to take back."

"There have been rumors floating across the cities about who is killing our men."

"Please enlighten me, Lieutenant, who are these rumored mongrels?"

The lieutenant nervously swallows. "A young boy and a very menacing girl, sir."

"Silence!" says Iakov, slamming his fists down on the table. "Lieutenant, I'm not sure what motivates you to climb the ranks in this régime, but if it's your will to survive, then your motives are becoming more and more expendable. So, now we have kids killing my men, how sweet. Why don't you go buy them some lollipops and have a tea party? That should distract them," he says sarcastically.

"Sir, this no joke."

"And I'm not laughing! It's your lack of control I find displeasing. Lieutenant, we control product, information, and people. One girl does not make an army."

"With all due respect, sir—"

"Respect! It's becoming abundantly clear what you fail to earn."

"My men were obliterated this morning by that poisonous demon."

"Your behavior is unbecoming. If they were all obliterated as you say, then how do you know it was this girl?"

"Corporal, bring him in," says the lieutenant, nodding.

"You better get to the point quickly, John. My patience with you is wearing thin."

A man dressed in a torn uniform, with cuts on his face and bandages on his arm, enters the room. "This is one of my men who survived the ambush on the loading dock," says the lieutenant.

"Private, surely you can tell me something of importance that doesn't have anything to do with Hansel and Gretel," states Iakov.

"Sir," says the private, saluting.

"Please, speak freely and indulge me."

"It was a massacre. No one knew what was happening. You couldn't see them. They were like ghosts taking us out in all directions, and before you knew it, she appeared. Like Black Death slashing and dicing with those swords, cutting the men up into pieces. It all happened so fast. We were completely caught off guard," he says, shaking as he recalls the nightmare.

"Thank you, private. You're dismissed," the lieutenant says to the young man.

"This is preposterous. You're telling me a hundred well-trained soldiers were taken apart by Little Bo Peep and Little Boy Blue?"

"Sir, you heard his account. This is enough proof," says the lieutenant.

"I hope you're not here to postulate these irrational statements as truth, Lieutenant," Iakov so callously questions, "because this conversation is begging for your competence to be re-evaluated. Look at him for God's sake, he's in total shock."

"Which is why I believe him."

"Are we to assume then that his testimony is the one all soldiers are expected to converge on, Lieutenant? Many soldiers experience this kind of delusion during battle. They are trained to kill and nothing else, and it's people like you and me who make sure they have no conscience to decide otherwise. Of all the people, John, I expected you to have a modicum of discernment. It's discomforting to know your intelligence is slipping."

"Sir, if I may speak?" asks another gentleman standing in the back.

"Go ahead."

"Let's just assume what the private said was true, as irrational as it may seem. If there is even a shred of evidence that supports the private's report, then it will surely benefit us to question the people who were there to witness it. I think our only option right now is for us to go to the people to find out the truth."

"And just how do you suppose we do that without conjuring up some erratic sympathy for this rebellion? Rumors can be just as dangerous as the truth itself," says the lieutenant.

"Persuade them, whatever is necessary. The last thing we need in this country is another revolution," says Iakov.

"You do remember, this nation was still standing before you came here. The people still have some social free- doms left."

"Yes, well, we're not here to practice the idea, we are only here to preserve it. Shall I remind you that it was you who called on us to resurrect your weakened nation," argues Iakov.

*   *   *

Finnegan was right about the Russian government. This is becoming all too overwhelming for my emotions to handle. This well-orchestrated plan our government has been scheming up all these years has fooled us all.

Switching from camera to camera, Gabe follows General Iakov, Lieutenant John, and two other men as they walk into town. In the corner of the screen, Gabe sifts through all the store cameras and finds every shop to be empty. There's not one patron to be seen until he finds a woman running inside a store about two blocks from where the men are walking.

Three men enter the store, while strangely General Iakov stands outside. Two women and a man try desperately to not look like they are hiding. One of the women is standing next to a stroller with a baby, while the other woman stands like a statue against the wall. The men begin to question the civilians about the dead soldiers and the giant hole in the ground. They reveal what they witnessed after the explosions, but nothing about Gabe or me.

"Did you see anyone attacking those soldiers or anyone firing upon the tanks outside the courtyard?" Lieutenant John asks.

"No, nobody, sir. We saw nothing until it was over," says one woman.

Right then, Iakov comes bursting through the doors, overhearing the woman's response. "If you saw nothing, then why are you hiding in here? You are obviously lying."

"Sir," Lieutenant John says.

Iakov points his finger in the lieutenant's face, "Don't undermine my authority, Lieutenant. You have much to learn."

The woman with the baby glances over at the man to her left. He tries to avoid her eyes and shakes his head nonchalantly. The general readily notices the awkward exchange between the two and walks closer to the woman.

"My patience grows weary, so why don't you just tell me who did this so we can all leave here in peace," he says, pulling out his gun and pointing it to her head. Terrified, she shakes and cries.

"I'm going to count to three. One," he says, staring directly into her eyes. "Two." He cocks back the hammer on his gun. The woman realizes he isn't bluffing, but before she can say a word, the man to her left leaps forward, attempting to disarm the general. Iakov, anticipating this move, quickly turns the gun and shoots the man dead. He returns the gun back at the woman's head. "Shall we start again, or do we need an alternative persuasion?"

"I don't know anything, please, I don't know," she says, crying hysterically.

"Sir, she knows nothing!" shouts Lieutenant John.

"I'll decide who knows what, Lieutenant! Now stand down." Iakov just notices the baby behind her and asks her to move over to the side.

"I understand the truth can be complicated for those who wish to hide it," he says, as he lowers his gun down to his side. Her face relaxes and her tears stop flowing. The lieutenant takes a deep breath and sighs in relief. "But in your case, the truth is all you have and nothing more." Iakov points the gun toward the baby stroller and fires into it.

"No! God no!" the woman screams, throwing herself down to the floor, reaching into the stroller for her dead baby.

The other woman falls to her knees without any expression, accepting her death and knowing she has no chance to live. The woman with the baby digs into the stroller hysterically and finds that the baby is not in there. Everyone turns to see the baby crawling on the floor behind some shelves. The woman's screaming stops momentarily as she picks up the baby and embraces him tightly on the floor, crying.

"I guess miracles do exist," General Iakov says with a menacing smirk. He turns to the other woman on her knees. "Is there a miracle bullet left in my chamber for you?" He points the gun at the woman on her knees. He cocks back the hammer and just like before, he counts. "One, two . . ."

"There were two of them! A girl and a boy, about fifteen or sixteen years old. They did this! They killed your soldiers," she shouts.

"Thank you for your cooperation." Iakov pulls the trigger, shooting her in the head.

"Is this really necessary, sir? Lieutenant John shouts.

Iakov pulls John to the side. "I am beginning to question why I appointed you. We are the makers, we are the leaders, we decide what, how, and when. Yes, Lieutenant, it's necessary to remind these people who is still in control. Perhaps you need reminding. Now take me to the loading dock."

I almost can't bear to watch any more of this. I want this man dead. Gabe sets up the feed from inside the loading dock. The men walk in and immediately cover their mouths and noses. From their reaction, the stench from the rotting flesh must be overwhelming. The pungent odor forces two of the men to put on masks to keep from vomiting.

General Iakov's face grows increasingly worried as he observes the blood bath of dismembered bodies. His jaw clenches, and he loses it. "These are my men, this is my regime. I will not stand for this! She mocks me in my own domain. You have a new mission, Lieutenant, and I will not expect anything less than success, or you too will be one of these headless men. I want this girl, and I want her alive and unspoiled. I will break-in her body myself for every man that lies dead."

"Turn it off!" I shout at Gabe. I pace back and forth, with my stomach tied in knots, and anger fanning my emotions.

"Calm down, Arena," says Finnegan.
"Calm down? What part of that did you find comforting? I don't care how much blood is shed, I'm gonna kill that son of a bitch!"

"Look, we're all pissed, but we will be better served if we keep our minds clear here. Emotions aside, we still have a mission."

"Then what the hell are we standing here for?"

CHAPTER 22

The Louisiana State Prison can be seen a mile away as we travel down a back road, and shockingly, it's much bigger than we anticipated. Judging by all the construction trucks outside the fence and the newly welded steel girders on the side of the prison, it appears they have been adding onto the compound to accommodate for more prisoners.

As we get closer, Finnegan stops the car and pauses for a moment. "Are you sure you're ready for this?" he asks, looking in the rearview mirror.

I say nothing as I look out the window toward the compound, wondering if Myra, Daniel, and Juliana are still alive in there. How will I feel if we have come this far to see our parents die again? I still can't get Jacob out of my mind. I fear his memory will haunt me until I'm dead. I reach in my shirt and pull out his necklace he gave me on our first date. I nervously rub the corners of the cross until my fingers blister and wonder how things would be different if he was still alive. I turn my head just enough so no one can see the tears running down my cheeks.

"Arena," says Finnegan, trying to get my attention, "are you okay?"

I turn to him, breaking my silence. "Let's go retrieve our lost sheep."

Finnegan climbs up a sprawling beech tree to get a closer viewpoint through his scope, but when he climbs back down, his face draws long and defeated. Confidence isn't something Finnegan lacks, but it appears to be empty.

"So what's your plan," he asks, "because there is only one way in down there. The compound is completely encircled with twenty-foot fencing, and there are guards everywhere on top of each corner of the facility. Standing in the middle of the compound is tall watchtower."

"There is always more than one way into anything. I have a backdoor," I say, pointing toward Gabe, who's holding up a mini plasma cutter.

"I do not like this already," says Finnegan.

"Gabe and I will go through the fence while you and Henry distract the guards and pull them in your direction."

"Distract them?" Henry questions.

"It's time to put that classic car to real use. Hope you're ready for this, because you're going through the front door . . . uninvited," I direct "give us about thirty minutes to get set into position before you raise hell."

"You sure about this?" Finnegan questions.

"No, but there's no turning back now, this is it. We find Juliana, Myra, and Daniel and free who we can. And if we're lucky enough to get out alive, then we burn this place."

Gabe and I set out on foot while Henry and Finnegan stay back, waiting for their move. We trek along the rocky slope down into the ravine below until we reach a flat grassy meadow. I hear Gabe panting a little as we walk closer to our destination, and by the time we get to the midpoint, he is sweating profusely.

I stop underneath a tree on the way to give him a little breather, since we are slightly ahead of schedule.

"Are you okay? You must be carrying a heavy load," I say.

"It's not too bad. I think I just ate too much fish this morning." He holds his side, cramping. He turns a little pale and starts to lean over as if he is about to faint. I quickly hold him up to keep him from falling down.

"I'm okay; I just need to . . . need to . . ." Gabe says, swaying. I feel absolutely awful right now knowing he can't possibly go on like this and that I will have to deal with this all alone. He pushes my arm away and stumbles behind a tree and vomits. Now I know he can't possibly go on, and I promptly think of the alternative, but before I can come up with a solution, he walks back from behind the tree, wipes his mouth off, and grins.

"I'm good. I knew I shouldn't have had that fourth piece of fish," he says. The blood slowly starts to pump back into his pale face.

"Are you sure you're okay?" I ask again.

"I feel just fine now, but I could use some mouthwash," he says.

"I concur."

We come as close as we can before moving any further past the tree line because the open area between here and the prison fence will easily expose our position. The positive is that the open area is only about fifty yards from where we stand, and all we can do now is wait for the signal.

I know something is up in the tower, because the guards on the roof, who have stood in the same place for the last five minutes, begin to move from their designated positions. I reach into my quiver of arrows and set a razor-tipped one resting on the bow shelf, waiting for the right time to take out the closest guard to us.

Finnegan and Henry move closer to the closed gates, and several guards run outside the fenced entrance with their guns drawn toward the car racing at them. Two fifty-caliber, electric-powered Gatling guns pop out on both sides of the car, and within seconds, the classic muscle car has instantly transformed into a killing machine.

I pull back on the tight strings of the bow, aiming directly at the guard on the roof, while I wait patiently for the sound of gunfire. "When I release this arrow, you better be ready to sprint your ass as fast as you can to the fence," I say.

The car comes speeding furiously through the last turn directly in front of the entrance, and just before Finnegan barrels through the gate, he makes a hard right turn with the brakes applied and sends the car spinning a hundred and eighty degrees. With the car stopped, and the rear facing the front of the gates, about twenty armed guards pour out a side door, shouting for them to get out.

And then it happens—the rocket launcher releases, plunging through the heavy gate, and all hell breaks loose, sending pieces of steel slicing through the air, penetrating the flesh of the guards who are running back into the compound. The car spins around and blasts through the opening with both Gatling guns violently spinning.

With my eyes fixed on the guard atop the compound, I quickly release the arrow deep into his skull, sending him plummeting four stories to the ground. Gabe and I sprint across the grassy meadow and onto a paved section where the fence is buried deep into the concrete. I grab the plasma cutter and cut a small opening in the links.

Just as we knock out the opening and enter the premises, about twenty guards come rushing out of a side door, moving toward the area of the explosion, but because of Finnegan's successful distraction tactic, we go unnoticed.

With all the doors locked from the inside, we take advantage of the one open door in front of us, where the guards came running out. Making sure no other guards might exit the door, I draw my guns carefully, dissecting every possible area and anticipating where guards may appear.

There are stairs to the right of us leading up to the next floor, and a long corridor to the left, where two doors open to an enormous open area. I start down through the left corridor when Gabe suddenly stops me. "Wait," he says.

"What is it?" I ask.

He pauses for a few seconds, then says, "Upstairs. We need to go upstairs."

"Are you sure?" I ask.

"Trust me, that's where the operations room is located. We should be able to find cell room information there."

When Gabe is specific about something, I completely trust him, so I turn around and head up the stairwell. I don't know how he knows, but I'm not about to question his instincts now. We climb three flights of stairs until we reach the fourth floor, where a set of doors lead down a long hallway. There are so many corridors that feed off the main hall and it's confusing; everything looks the same. I feel like a rat trapped in a steel cage and the only comforting thought is that I have Gabe with me to help guide us through this prison maze.

With my back against the wall, I quietly step to my left and peer around the corner to make sure the hall is clear of guards. I tug on Gabe's arm, indicating it's clear for us to move, when out of nowhere, a rush of about a fifty men come running down the corridor, firing at us. Without hesitation, I pull out both guns, squeezing the triggers until both magazines empty within seconds. The first several guards in front pile up on the floor, slowing down the rest just long enough for me to reload, but before I turn around the corner to fire again, Gabe moves in front of me with his backpack humming.

He bursts around the corner, firing flying jagged metal discs that look like saw blades. The spinning discs slice through the guards, knocking them down like blades of grass, killing everyone in their path. I quickly glance around the corner and find a hall covered in blood and tangled bodies. Gabe disappears down the left corridor, and all I can hear is the shrill scream of death from the metal scrapping the sides of the walls.

In shock, I wait for him to finish before he comes racing back around the corner. He jumps over the pile of bodies, landing awkwardly in a pool of coagulated blood, and slipping on his backside in pain.

I quickly rush over to him to see if he's okay. "Who would have thought that out of all the weapons, flying debris, and spraying of bullets, I would injure myself from a puddle of blood," he says, wincing, then picks himself up.

"Humbling, isn't it? Now get up off your ass, we haven't time to waste," I order as Gabe rolls his eyes.

We hurry down one of the other halls where Gabe believes the main operations room is located. The hall we enter is different from the others; the floor is made of steel mesh, and I can see straight down to the floors below. We walk down the hall and see a metal plaque on the wall, engraved with a map of the floor.

Gabe was right; we're about a hundred paces from the prison administrator area and the facility operations room. The halls to the left and right of the main corridor extend outward, leading to the cell-blocks.

As we get a little closer to the main room, a voice yells down from below, "I see them! Fourth floor, main corridor!"

We run down the hall, but I only notice just a handful of guards, so I stop and pull out some thin trip wire leftover from the dart guns. I have Gabe run the wire in a z-pattern across the door in front of the main corridor where we were spotted. I walk down fifty paces, draw my guns, and wait.

Five men rush around the corner, firing their guns randomly in different directions, missing everything entirely. These must be prison administrators, because they are the worst shooting guards of the bunch. When they slam into the wire, they all fall into one another, desperately grasping on to each other's uniforms, trying to get up.

I walk within five feet of the bumbling men and shoot all but one in the head. I leave the lone survivor laying there for a moment to rethink his actions. The only purpose for him now is to be our guide through the rest of this steel slave trap. I'm not sure why I chose him, maybe because he looks so different from the others. He's scrawny and young and looks like he's about to piss his pants.

I cut the wires down and force the small man over by the wall. "Where did you learn to use a gun?" I ask.

"I'm not a guard; I'm not one of them. I'm just one of the administrators. I push paper, that's all," he pleads, shaking. He is all of about five-and-a-half foot tall, probably weighing in about one hundred ten pounds.

I point my gun to his head and say, "Who is your superior?"

His brows burrow into his glassy eyes. "I don't know, I swear. I just got transferred here today. Before this, I was filing paperwork for a Chicago Psychiatric Ward, and working part-time at a burger joint." I grab his wrists and recognize soft, unlabored hands with a few paper cuts. The poor guy looks like he has never touched a gun before in his life, and the only reason he came storming with the other guards is probably because he was forced into action.

"How did these guys recruit you into coming up here with them?" I ask, pointing at the dead guards on the floor.

"Honestly, because there is no one left alive, I guess," he says. "Please, I'm nobody's enemy," he declares, sobbing like a baby.

"Stop your crying, I'm not going to kill you," I say, rolling my eyes. "If you're not an enemy, then why did you take this job?"

"I don't know. Insecurity?" he honestly admits.

"What's your name?"

"Kyle."

"Come on, Kyle, stand up, we need to move," I say. He's still trembling while Gabe makes a concerted effort not to grin. I can't help but notice the man's pants and see why. "So, is this the result of your insecurities, or do you always soil your pants?"

"This is humiliating," he says, face abashed.

"Aye, but it could always be worse."

Kyle guides us through the main corridor and to the left near the operations room. I tell Gabe to hold back a little while I carefully turn the door handle to the room. I tightly grip my guns and prepare myself for an attack inside, but right before I burst in, two guards around the corner delay my entry into the room.

As they draw their guns and force me to stand down, I also draw mine, aiming directly toward their heads, causing a stalemate.

"Put down your weapons now," demands one of the guards. They obviously are different from the other soldiers we have come in contact with, because they actually follow the simple rules of engagement by at least giving me a warn- ing. Unfortunately for them, I don't meekly surrender to the rules. I pull both triggers simultaneously, shooting both men in the head

Kyle's knees begin to buckle and he nearly faints. "Hey! You want to survive?" I ask him. He just nods and says nothing. "Then keep your head on straight. Follow me and do what I say." I have him open the operations room while Gabe and I stand back cautiously, waiting.

When he opens the door, we find the room empty. There are no operators tending the console or any signs of anyone being in here for a while. The only remnant of someone's existence is a Styrofoam cup filled halfway with ice-cold coffee.

In front of the console are ten screens monitoring the ten cellblocks in this facility. According to the maximum occupancy in the logs, each cellblock will hold up to twenty-five hundred inmates, but zooming in closer to the cells with the remote camera reveals a different number—each cell is packed beyond its legal occupancy; in fact, it's doubled. I can't believe what I'm seeing. There must be close to fifty thousand people locked up in these confined cages.

"Is there any way these cells can be automatically opened from here?" I ask Kyle.

"Yes, but it's not my area of expertise. I was briefly trained this morning, but not enough to remember the correct procedures."

"Here, let me sit down and drive," says Gabe, taking over the system. "Do you have a security code?"

Kyle puts his hand on his head, trying to remember the code he was given during orientation. "It's 116734," he says with his eyes closed, thinking hard.

"We're in," says Gabe, punching in the code.

While Gabe maneuvers around the system, checking for cellblock policies on fire drills, I stumble across some communication logs on the counter next to a dispatch radio. I open up the logbook and flip through the pages until I reach today's prison log: *Case: 136. Codename: Black Death. Prisoners 106321 and 106322 to be incarcerated under severe supervision. Female and male, approximate age: 15. Potential terrorist threat to governmental agenda. Status: unknown. Wanted:*

alive if possible. If seen, take extreme precaution and report any visual status updates immediately to General Iakov.

"Gabe, not to put you under any pressure, but please hurry," I say.

"Why?" he asks.

"Because they know we're here," I say, slamming the logbook down in front of him.

Gabe quickly browses through files after files and finally comes across an evacuation policy and procedure. "I found it. I should be able to unlock large sections at a time in each cellblock." He moves to another computer with a touch screen and follows the procedures for the evacuation of all prisoners. After he activates the locks, the only thing left is to push two buttons simultaneously to unlock the cell doors.

"Here goes nothing," he says.

"Wait!" I shout, grabbing Gabe's hand before he pushes the button. "Can you get a listing of each prisoner in each cell?" I ask.

"Sure, why?"

"I want to know where Myra and Daniel are being held."

Gabe suddenly realizes why we are here. "Juliana!" he says to himself.

He quickly drills down to the cell module file and launches the prisoner database listing of every prisoner in each cell by name and number. He looks up prisoners by last name in the search field and types in *Merryman*. The database pulls information on both Myra and Daniel: *Name: Myra Merryman. Sex: Female. Prisoner number: 65213. Cell Block: 3. Cell Number: 46. Status: Alive.* I feel a soothing comfort knowing that she is here and alive, but it soon unravels when I see the next entry on the screen. *Name: Daniel Merryman. Sex: Male. Prisoner number: 65214. Cell Block: N/A. Cell Number: N/A. Status: Deceased.* My heart sinks, and I stare completely stunned at the flashing cursor after the word *Deceased*.

Gabe leans over to comfort me, but I reject his consoling gesture, and walk toward the other side of the room. I feel dejected, as if someone has just taken a part of my soul from me. And to worsen things, a memory that I have been trying to extract from my brain painfully pops back into my head. This is the same distressing feeling when I found out about Jacob's death back at our house, and that's the last time I saw Daniel.

My old friend, despair, returns and leads me to the unknown. A tear free-falls from my eye and onto my jacket. "Juliana," is all I have to say as Gabe nervously stares at the search field. While he searches for her, anxiously awaiting the results, I close my eyes and say a prayer. When the database pulls back Juliana's information, Gabe quickly scrolls over to the status field, but it is blank. The database program has apparently crashed and is toying with Gabe's emotions. As the entry slowly loads, I brace for the worst.

CHAPTER 23

To see Gabe stressing in pain over a blank data entry field makes my stomach twist, as I can barely stand at this point. One word is all that separates Gabe from overflowing with jubilation or drowning in pool of sorrow.

"She's alive!" Gabe shouts. "She's in the same cellblock, but a different cell number. It's Cell 41."

I breathe a sigh of relief. "Kyle, you come with me; Gabe you stay here and wait for my signal to open up the cell doors. I don't want to lose Myra and Juliana during all the chaos."

"They're in the south wing on the first floor," says Kyle. Kyle and I hurry through the corridors to the right and down the stairs to the second level. We are forced to detour down another hall before descending to the next floor because of the locked stairwell doors. I draw my guns, anticipating an attack from any guards remaining that may be hiding around corners. This prison is so large I feel like we just sprinted a quarter mile. I know we're getting close, because just ahead of us is the main hub where all the cellblocks extend outward.

Heavy boots pound the pavement, trotting toward us from one of the extensions, and several guards pace back and forth on the second floor in front of the cells. I leave Kyle in the middle of the hall for the guards to see while I hide behind the corner ready to fire. The guards immediately recognize Kyle as an employee, and their pace quickly slows down.

"Have you seen the perpetrators?" one of the lead guards asks. Kyle is silent, and instead points in the opposite direction of me, which is exactly what I hoped he would do.

The guards flee down the left side, and I position myself ready to kill, but I don't shoot them right away. Whether it's cowardly or not to shoot someone in the back, I don't feel the need to justify how to kill a man in a desperate situation; I'm not here to contemplate battle ethics, after all. But in this case, I'm at an advantage, so I extend them the courtesy of my presence nonetheless, just so my guilt doesn't somehow change my motive.

"Hey, looking for me, boys?" They turn around, shocked, and after five seconds, ten bullets, and six dead men, I do believe I've made my point. I carefully sneak across the hall to get a better view of the remaining guards perched on the second floor cellblock. I have the perfect vantage point; I can't be seen, I'm protected by the metal mesh plating beneath the second floor hangover, and I have an easy open target.

I rest my arm on the side of the railing and prep my bow with a razor-tipped arrow. I wait until the guards pace back in the same direction so I can strike each one behind the other without any of them knowing. I pull back on the string and fire the first arrow dead center into the neck of the first guard. The neck seems to be the appropriate spot for this attack; I try not to give them any chance to scream, shout, or otherwise make any noise to call for help. I quickly launch the next three arrows, silently killing each guard; however, the last guard I strike falls from the second floor, causing a dramatic commotion.

The final guard abruptly notices the other dead men and runs. He darts past a row of cells where hundreds of flailing arms reach out between the bars, making my moving target even more difficult. I aim carefully, leading the arrow slightly in front of him, but I soon run out of room from my view, so I'm forced to release the arrow. It sails right into his ribs, stopping him from running any further, but it doesn't kill him. I don't have another clear shot from my position, so I draw my gun instead, but before I can squeeze the trigger, the wounded guard tumbles over the small prison railing and into the concrete basin below, killing him instantly. "Come on," I say to Kyle, as I run down the stairs to the first floor. Before I go darting out in the open cellblock area, I observe my surroundings carefully.

This place reminds me of those prisons I've seen in movies, except it's much filthier. The first two floors appear to be much older than the others, which leads me to believe this prison has been recently added on in the last few years. Since this institution hasn't been utilized in over a decade, it's apparent that these newly renovated additions were purposefully built to enslave and nothing else. And with Russian leaders at the helm of our administration, it's no wonder the conditions are so bleak. This architecturally sound structure truly is the beginning of an international upheaval.

I pace out in the open area of the third cellblock, looking for numbers above the cells. Each block has two hundred fifty individual cells, and they are in numerical order, running from one end to the other in a horseshoe pattern. I intently search for cell numbers 41 and 46 to my left where the first seventy-five cells are located.

I hear moans, coughing, and weeping as I walk out toward the cells—a result of neglect in these poor conditions. Every step I take, the noise from the floor grows into shouts for help. Hands stretch out in-between the bars of the cell doors, reaching out of desperation for freedom. I try hard not to let my emotions overcome me when I look at their faces.

Time isn't exactly on our side, and I have to hurry before any more guards decide to appear. I get closer to Cell 41, and yell out Juliana's name, hoping to hear a response.

"Arena! Arena!" someone shouts in my vicinity. Undernourished and covered in grime, Juliana pops her hand out of the cell door with her face pressed against the bars, crying out of sheer shock to see me.

I wave for Kyle to come over as I hold Juliana's hand and try to ease her pain. "I'm getting you out of here. All of you will be free to go, but when these doors open, you must hurry far away from this place and into the woods where it is safer," I say, as my voice grows louder and louder.

"Kyle, if you want to redeem yourself, this is the time." He nods. "Take Juliana with you to the courtyard and wait for me there. No matter what happens, if you are approached by any guards, tell them you have her in your custody and that she is not to be touched—special orders. If you see a black Camaro, put her in it. You got it?"

A look of confusion covers his face and keeps his tongue hidden behind pursed lips; his nerves have taken over his body, momentarily paralyzing his speech, so I ask him again more firmly, "Do you understand, Kyle?"

"Yes, yes. I got it," he says, stuttering. It's very unlike me to trust a person like Kyle, but in a situation like this sometimes the risk outweighs the worries, and behind his brown scared eyes, I know he's not about to betray me.

While Kyle stays with Juliana at the cell, I quickly run down to Cell 46 to look for Myra, but I don't see her. The cell is packed to the gills, and it's hard to determine if she is hiding behind anyone because every face covered in filth looks the same.

I yell out Myra's name, but I get no response. I'm becoming increasingly stressed and saddened, but I don't give up. I yell out again and again over the crowd of people in the cell until they stop and realize what I'm saying. They slowly back up to the sides of the cell and part the middle to reveal a broken woman with torn clothes and covered in dirt, sitting and leaning against the wall, facing the corner.

"Myra," I say softly, "it's me, Arena." Withdrawn from her surroundings and unresponsive to my voice, she barely moves her head as she mumbles to herself. Her body is shaking. One of her arms is bandaged up, but the other reveals self-mutilation—bloody scabs and claw marks up and down her arm—the result of a torn woman trying to take away the pain of being without Daniel. I can only imagine the terror swimming inside her head, and the last memories she must have witnessed when he was killed.

I call out to her again, trying to break her inert position and catatonic state when suddenly she stops chattering and turns to me with those green, glassy eyes, the ones I have been most familiar with since I was twelve years old. She slowly gets up and walks over to me. When she truly realizes it's me, her subconscious surrenders to reality, and she runs to the cell door and holds out her hand to my face. The frightened look in her eyes soon submits to weeping as she calls out my name.

"I love you," I say, trying to hold back tears, "we're getting everyone out of here. You stay close to me no matter what." I walk over to one of the cameras on the walls to give Gabe the signal, as I brace myself for a massive exodus. There's no time for any kind of organized evacuation plan; this is freedom to all who wish to accept it. I know many will not survive, but that's in God's hands now.

When the cell doors open, many people don't hesitate to run out toward the courtyard, but some stumble from lack of strength due to malnutrition. While I take Myra's hand, I turn to make sure Kyle and Juliana are together. I see them ahead of us until the chaotic mass of people scatter, blocking my view. It's much like the false alarm we experienced during that first week of school when students were scurrying around, panicking.

As we get closer to the doors, I look up and see the same chaos on the floors above, and I think to myself how many families have been torn apart by this government's gutless and savage enslavement. It's a mad house outside, and the few guards who remain in the courtyard are overcome by the wave of fleeing refugees and trampled.

I don't see the car anywhere, but Myra's legs begin to weaken, so I take her to the side of the courtyard wall to rest a bit until the chaos dies down a little. After a few moments, I start to worry about the status of Finnegan and Henry. I desperately try to help Myra to her feet while intently looking around for guards, but I see none except for the scattered wreckage of bodies that lie on the ground from Finnegan and Henry's demolition.

At this point, all I want is the strength to keep Myra from collapsing. I manage to keep her upright with her arm around my neck as a brace. After about twenty steps, the weight of her weakness becomes burdensome, and the little strength I have left begins to fail.

We finally reach the corner of the courtyard near the side entrance to the prison when my muscles give in. I stop and nearly collapse to the ground, and the only thing that keeps me from dropping Myra is the will of God. I gently set her down and lean her against the base of a lamp pole to rest. My vision grows weary and dims from the sudden rush of blood flowing back into my muscles, and everything in front of me becomes a blur for a few seconds.

I can see a figure charging at me, but I can't quite make out who it is, so I exhaustively draw my gun for defense. Just as I struggle to aim, my vision clears up and I recognize Henry. I quickly withdraw my gun and a gleam of hope suddenly flourishes throughout my body.

"Arena, you made it. We have Juliana in the car."

"Thank you," I gasp for a breath of air. "Can you please help Myra?"

"We'll take care of her," he says just as Finnegan walks up. I slowly rise back to my feet.

"Everybody okay? Where's Gabe?" Finnegan asks. Right then I realize Gabe is still inside, and my heartbeat races.

"Take care of Myra and Juliana, both of you. I will get him and meet you back here. Just don't go anywhere," I demand.

A sudden burst of energy recharges my will to fight as I rush back into the prison to find Gabe. There are still a few people scampering out as I dart back in through the cell-block entrance. I find the flight of stairs that Kyle and I used to get to cellblock 3 and try to backtrack my steps. I get halfway down one of the corridors on the second floor when I run into a guard coming around the corner. He stops as do I, but I hesitate to pull my pistol because he is unarmed.

He stares me down, as if he's about to pummel me. Standing at about six foot four, the big brute charges at me shouting, but I stand my ground and grip the scorpion dagger behind me preparing to strike. I shift to one side, dodging his rampaging fist, and thrust the blade into the side of his ribs.

He screams in anguish, but he still manages to stand and prepares for another round. He swings his fists, but I block his blows, turning my body into him, pulling down his hand, then pushing up his forearm and breaking his wrist. He shouts in pain, then swings his other arm into the side of my head, throwing me down to the floor hard, and separating me from my dagger. As he bends down to finish me off, I quickly pull two throwing knives from my jacket and jab them both into the side of his neck. I roll out of the way to dodge his falling dead weight. Like always, I waste nothing. I retrieve my knives from his neck, wipe them off on his uniform, and place them back in my jacket.

I sprint down the rest of the hall and up the stairwell to the fourth floor, but the halls all look the same and I'm confused as to which way to go. I'm hesitant to make a decision, but I realize Gabe may or may not be in here, and I'm just wasting time. I race down the first hall close to me, and look for any maps or signs.

I pass a door near an intersecting corridor, and briefly notice a sign next to it, but it's not the sign itself that catches my attention. The sign is written in Russian: Био-химическая лаборатория исследований. It says "Bio-Chemical Research Lab."

My curiosity distracts me for a few moments so I open the door. The room looks extremely clean and sanitized. Hazmat suits hang on hooks, and hundreds of vials and glass tubes are neatly labeled and stored. A contaminate chamber about the size of a refrigerator sits on a back table, and numerous charts filled with formulas hang on the walls.

On the table in front of me is a large binder labeled "log results" in Russian, with disturbing images of patients being exposed to experimental virus-inducing chemicals. Each picture represents a different stage of virus, but none of the experiments seem to go past five stages before the patient is deceased.

My curiosity is suddenly dissolved when I hear gunshots outside the door. I quickly open the door and see Gabe running around the corner. "Gabe!" I yell as I run down the hall after him. I stop briefly to hear where the footsteps are coming from and continue down the hall to the left. "Gabe!" I call out again.

"Up here, Arena."

I look up and see him running across a catwalk from an angry guard carrying a gun. I try to take out the guard, but I can't get a clear shot from where I'm standing. I look around for stairs to the catwalk, but there's only a metal ladder attached to the steel wall.

I quickly climb up the ladder, but halfway up a hand grabs my ankle. I try to reach one of my guns, but I'm stuck on a hook on the side of the ladder. My jacket is caught between the hooks and the railing, and my sleeve is stuck in a grate behind the ladder.

The load of my body gets heavier as the guard pulls on my leg. One of his arms is badly wounded, rendering it useless, but the other arm hangs onto me for dear life. All of a sudden I hear a thud dropping to the ground, then a long moan. I turn to see Gabe on top of the guard who was chasing him. The guard appears to be dead, but I can't tell if Gabe is okay. Falling on the man must have cushioned the impact, because Gabe begins to achingly move about.

The guard, still hanging onto my leg, rests his injured arm on one of the metal rungs and reaches for his gun. I'm still stuck and can't get to any of my weapons, so I scream out once more for Gabe.

He screams back at me, "Arena!"

The guard quickly turns and shoots Gabe in the chest.

Gabe falls to his knees and collapses on the floor. My body nearly falls limp, and my heart suddenly sinks into an abyss. All the guilt and pain has shifted into a place of numbness. I don't know how I can ever forgive myself for putting him in this situation. I feel a sudden urge to just give in, but my spirit won't allow it. The tears stop rolling down my face and anger replaces my despair. My baby brother is dead, and I can't help to feel responsible for his tragedy.

"Gabe!" I scream out in rage, trying to free my sleeves.

The guard turns back to me and raises his gun toward my head.

"I only need one good bullet to kill you, bitch," he jeers, pulling the trigger back to an empty chamber.

I finally free my right arm from the hook and quickly draw my sword. "I don't need bullets to kill," I say, swinging my sword downward and slicing off his arm. He falls nearly fifteen feet down onto his head, snapping his neck. I tug hard enough to free my other arm from the grate and hurry back down the ladder to Gabe.

"Gabe! Gabe!" I shout, pulling him off the floor and slapping his face. He is unresponsive and lies there limp. I try to feel where he was shot to see if it is fatal, but shockingly, his chest is heavily padded.

I rip his jacket off to see that he is wearing a bulletproof vest, and the sudden shock of him being dead quickly lifts. I squeeze my arms around him, not wanting to let him go. If there were any tears left in my ducts, it would be from pure joy. I love my brother more than anything. I vowed to protect him. I'm mad at myself for not being there with him. I'm thankful he's alive, but I've suddenly become a little irritated not knowing about his vest; I don't like surprises.

I slap him on the face once more and shake his head a few times to awaken him. He comes to with a grimace on his face and immediately feels the bruise on his chest where the bullet struck. "Are you okay?" I ask sincerely.

"Yeah, I'll be fine," he answers as he stands to his feet.

"Damn you, Gabe," I slug him on the shoulder. "Why didn't you tell me you had this vest? I thought you were dead."

"Sorry I got shot, next time I'll just dodge the bullet," he sarcastically says. His face softens. "Juliana?"

"She's a little weak, but she's fine and safe now." Though my words fill him with relief, my face reflects otherwise.

"What's wrong?" he asks.

"Myra" is all I say as I walk off.

We hurry back down the stairs out into the courtyard and fortunately do not run into any more guards along the way. We can see the Camaro peering through a broken fence and hear its engine roaring, waiting for us. Before we get any closer to the car, Henry stops to talk with us a moment.

"What's wrong?" I ask.

"Look, I just want to warn you, these ladies have been through hell, and their psyche may be a little damaged," says Henry.

"Wait, what do you mean?" Gabe asks as he tries to walk away to them. Henry holds him back. "What are you not telling me, Henry?" Gabe trembles with anger .

Henry chokes back a tear. "Many of the men who were taken captive have either been beaten or shot, but worse things have occurred among the women," he says.

Gabe looks up with glassy, red eyes, and shakes his head. He grips Henry's shoulder for support. "No . . ." Gabe rejects. His bottom lip trembles and his face quickly reddens with rage .

"Most of the women here were . . ." Henry's voice trails off.

"Were what?" I ask angrily.

"Brutally raped," Henry finishes.

Gabe loses it and collapses to his knees, crying with his head in his lap.

"Look, I know you're hurt, but right now she is all you got," says Henry. Gabe rises to his feet and screams. "Don't let this weaken your judgment," Henry wisely advises.

"Fuck judgment! I will not break until every last one of these bastards is dead," Gabe boils.

"I understand your frustration, Gabe, I do, but if you let your pain ride out like this, you will just suffer in your own misery. All this hate will burn you up. Don't let this anger drive you into passing," says Henry.

"So how the hell am I supposed to feel? How am I supposed to just forget this?" Gabe fires back.

"I don't expect you to, and there's not a damn thing I can do to stop the pain, but if you let the desire for revenge consume you, then we all suffer," Henry says. Gabe looks away. "Gabe! Look at me, look at me. You will have your time and die they will, but for now that young girl sitting in the car needs you to comfort her and nothing more," says Henry. Gabe wipes his eyes as Henry and I put our arms around him and walk to the car.

I open the car's trunk and pull back a blanket that's securely covering four large charged explosives. "Is this sufficient?" I ask Gabe.

"That's more than enough," Gabe solemnly says.

Finnegan and I take two detonators a piece and strategically set them inside of each prison wing. We are going to make damn sure this facility is to never be used again.

We quickly drive away on the other side of the hill and wait for the building to clear before departing this wretched place. Here, we can set up a temporary camp so everyone can rest.

Gabe sits next to Juliana, who leans her head against his shoulder, while I stay with Myra. Henry and Finnegan set up a radio communication dispatch and try to infiltrate a signal through military codes. After several minutes of dialing into a transmitted signal, Finnegan finds a clean frequency and a voice comes over the small speaker. Two men radio back and forth about the approximate time and coordinates of their destination. All of the sudden a third voice comes over the transmission in Russian.

"Arena, come here. I need you to translate this," Finnegan says.

While listening to the radio conversation, a sick feeling settles in my stomach and then the radio goes silent.

"What did they say?" Henry asks anxiously.

I know Gabe understood every word of the conversation, because he has that worried look on his face. "Well?" Finnegan asks.

"They're coming here with backup forces to contain what they think is a small revolt. They apparently have no idea the prison guards are all dead or that everyone has been freed."

"That's expected," says Finnegan.

"That's not what troubles me," I say, as I look in Gabe's direction.

"What is it?" Finnegan asks.

"They are searching for Gabe and me, and I'm pretty sure they will stop at nothing until they find us, but more interesting, they want me alive."

"We'll have to be more discreet. From now on, if we can, we travel by night," says Finnegan.

"Why would they want you alive?" Juliana asks. "Same reason they want her dead; she's a threat to the enemy. Question is, who is the enemy?" Henry asks.

"So what are you saying? They're going to attempt to turn me against everyone else?" I say with a smirk.

"Don't be so surprised; it's been attempted before." The manipulation of the mind has been around for centuries, but none more than the Nazi Party. They started experimenting with the exotic sciences for warfare application early on before World War II. I'm not shocked to see a revival of the occult practices today, especially with how wicked this world has become.

These are evil times we live in, and I'm convinced that a revived Nazi army will spring up from the dead to mingle with Russian blood on American soil. An unholy alliance out there awaits us, and I will fear none that attempts to poison the blood of truth.

I go back to tend to Myra, but when I kneel down to hold her, I notice blood in her mouth when she begins to cough. Her eyes are barely open, and her hands feel cold. My body goes completely numb when I look upon her pale face. "Myra! Wake up, wake up." My heart sinks, and every last ounce of pain etched into my spirit releases all at once. I can't help but to cry out. "No, don't do this . . . please God, no." Her voice is barely audible, but she can still hear me.

I hold her head up and put my hand on her face, stroking her milky skin while the others stand around me in silence. I hold her close to my chest, rejecting the idea that her death is imminent, while my body suddenly grows weary.

She looks at me one last time with her eyes half open, and I immediately think about my mother dying in my arms, whispering her last words to me as I held her bloody face.

"I love you . . . my daughter," Myra softly says with her last breath. Her body slumps down, and her head fallslimp to the side.

I cry uncontrollably, followed by violent screams of pain as I hold her lifeless body. "Why . . . why?" I cry out. Even though I already know the answer, my emotions still reject the idea, and I surrender to my natural human response with grief and anger.

Part III

Redemption

CHAPTER 24

If there is ever a time in a person's life when tragedy and suffering is rendered so frequently that emotional pain becomes numb, then that time has come for me. I'm not sure how Job felt, but I can assure you there isn't much left in me to stir. My feelings are depleted, my emotions are empty, and I have no tears left to shed. I've lost too many people I love and not enough people I loathe. If I could be in any other place, I would, and death is suddenly not such an unbearable option. I've lived too little to lose so much, but I'm committed to move on for my Father's sake.

I drop down to my knees with my face planted into the earth, begging for mercy and unconditional forgiveness. My heart stirs once again by His presence, and I'm quickly reminded about the toil and suffering my Savior endured for me. I don't deserve such grace, but I rise to my swollen feet nonetheless, staring out into the emptiness with everyone standing around me in silence.

I walk away on a small, winding trail upon a hilltop, where I'm left alone. From where I sit, I see nothing but rocky soil, dead trees, and no vegetation; it's a barren wasteland. The only thing this desolate place has to offer is loneliness; I feel right at home.

After an hour of seclusion on the hilltop, I wander back to the camp and immediately notice that Myra's body is gone. Henry and Gabe walk back from what looks like a hike by all the sweat that's pouring down their faces. Juliana lays asleep on a flat rock padded with a sleeping bag while Finnegan is sprawled out on his stomach, scoping out our surroundings.

I glance in the direction where Gabe and Henry are coming from and realize why they are sweating so profusely—a pile of rocks in the distance marks the grave where Myra's body is covered. It was wise to bury her now, as buzzards gawk about and sporadically circle above, ready to feast upon the dead.

The two give me a slight rub on the shoulder as they pass by, but say nothing. Instead of recoiling with bitterness, I welcome their sympathies, though I don't feel any better. I just stand there, struggling to leave this morose moment until every emotion I have ever experienced subsides. I feel the calm before the storm, as they say.

Moments later, Finnegan snaps his hand up to grab our attention. "Take a look," he says as he hands me the high-powered binoculars. I lie next to him, peering through the field glasses and see an unsettling sight approaching—a ten-truck convoy about a quarter-mile down the road from the prison entrance. Two helicopters can be heard in the background about a mile away, flying very low. The dispatch radio intermittently crackles for a few seconds until a voice is clearly heard.

"Sir, we are still getting no response from inside the prison. The tower has yet to send any communication back since they last contacted us two hours ago," says a voice on the radio.

"Proceed to your location and send me a status as soon as you arrive. I want to know the exact body count, Major," another voice responds.

"Yes, General Iakov."

"If there is even one soldier killed, you are clear to use any means necessary. It's time to make an example out of these people and let them know who is leading whom. For every dead soldier that lies on the ground, ten prisoners will be executed."

"And the women, sir?" the major asks.

"Do what you will with them. It matters not."

"Sir?" the major stutters.

"Major, let's get one thing clear. We are not in the business to make hospitable accommodations for the weaker sex because they are light on the eyes. We have an agenda, and I'm here to make a point. Do I make myself clear?" General Iakov snaps.

"Yes . . . yes, sir, General."

I've never wanted someone dead in all my life more than I do right now. I quickly hand the binoculars back to Finnegan and run to get my bow with a couple of explosive-tipped arrows ready. I want to be prepared in case those helicopters were purposely deployed in hopes of finding us; by their low altitude, they appear to be in a search formation.

"Gabe, how far will the remote reach the charges?" I ask.

"It should reach; we're only about three to four hundred yards away."

"Are you sure there are enough explosives down there to bring those buildings down?" I ask.

"You put enough down there to blow up four city blocks. Yeah, I'm pretty sure that will cover it."

"Then shouldn't we be further back?" I ask, looking at him with wide eyes.

"These are not ordinary explosives, like that outdated C4 or Semtex. They deliver thermo compression across the plane and down instead of up and out; however, I've modified one of the charges that you may have placed inside the prison." Gabe scratches his head for a moment and looks a bit worried.

"Yeah, and . . . ?" I say.

"And . . . we should probably be okay."

"Probably?" Finnegan says.

"What?" Gabe asks, shrugging his shoulders.

"Sorry, but you can't sell an answer with *probably*. I was looking for more of a *definitely be okay, guys*," says Finnegan.

"Were definitely going to be okay, guys!" Gabe repeats with enthusiasm. "Most likely," he adds softly. I give him a stern look with my eyebrows furrowed.

Suddenly, the car door slams, startling us, as we all turn around to see Juliana sitting in the backseat with her hands on her face. The window rolls down, and Juliana's head peers out.

"Well, I probably shouldn't be out there anyway, but I'll definitely be safer in here, and I will be most likely praying," she says as the window rolls back up. We all look at Gabe for assurance.

"She may have a point," says Gabe.

The trucks come rolling in one behind the other, stopping right outside the entrance along the torn chain-link fence. A few minutes pass before any soldiers start exiting the vehicles in a two-by-two formation.

The two helicopters circle the entire premise a couple of times before landing inside the prison walls. We wait until every soldier has been deployed inside the buildings before setting off the explosives. Finnegan puts down his scope and tries to dial into their radio frequency to make sure these are the only troops that were sent. While I look closer at the soldiers moving inside the entrance, I notice something very different about their uniforms.

These men are not dressed in the typical federal black-and-blue uniforms we are used to seeing; instead, they are draped in solid black with three buttons down the middle. The high boots really set them apart from the normal federal officers, but it is the insignia along the sleeve cuff that catches my attention—it is a black-on-white band with two red stripes that run around the band. Half the men are wearing helmets that slope in the back with decals of a red hammer and sickle like that of the Russian flag, but there are also two black lightning bolts that cross over two red stripes on a white background.

I try to find the leader of the outfit in the front of the pack near the entrance to see if he's decked out in the same garb, but he isn't. He is dressed in the standard-issued federal officer uniform, but as I turn the dials on the scope to get a closer look, I notice a skull pin on the major's collar.

Suddenly, a voice comes over the dispatch radio again: "General, my men are combing the area now, but there is no sign of her," he says.

"The casualties?" General Iakov asks.

"Yes, sir," the major responds.

"How many?"

"Sir, it's . . . it's hard to say at this time."

"Major, when I ask a direct question, I expect a direct answer. How many?"

"All of them, sir."

Either we lost transmission of the signal, or the dead silence on the radio is the result of the anger displayed on the general's face right now. "Major, call me on my private line, please."

After a few minutes pass, the remaining soldiers enter into the compound with the others searching for traces of our presence. I look at Gabe to give him the go-ahead, as Finnegan, Henry, and I start backing up toward the car. Before Gabe sets off the explosives, I quickly stop him. "Gabe, wait!" I say as the radio cracks once again.

"Bravo 129, this is the major requesting prisoner status, do you read?"

"Sir, the cells are empty."

"Which block?" the major asks.

"All of them, sir," the man says as the radio signal whistles and crackles.

Finnegan rushes over to try and fix the signal, but the frequency is being interfered by something else that is near. Right then, one of the helicopters takes off while the radio briefly comes back on with a crackling voice.

"Major, I don't care what it takes—you find her and bring her to me. I will be waiting here at the training facility in Greensville," says General Iakov.

"Greensville?" Gabe asks. Finnegan looks at me and sighs because he knows I'll do whatever it takes to see Iakov dead.

"Looks like we are taking a road trip to Virginia," Finnegan says.

As the chopper starts to ascend out of the compound, I turn and shout toward Gabe, "Now, Gabe, now!" The west wing rattles violently to the ground as windows explode from their frames, projecting shards of glass up into the air. Like a domino effect, the east wing and administrative buildings burst into a cloud of blistering flames and immediately collapses, killing anyone within a hundred and fifty yards. The last explosive charge does the most damage, exploding out and upward into the air. A bright plume of fire fills the skies, shaking the earth, spewing fragments of metal and brick toward the helicopter.

The pilot becomes blinded by the black smoke from burning diesel tanks, and the flying shards of steel cut through the air, striking the sides of the chopper cockpit. The chopper spins out of control and into the pile of burning rubble below. The massive devastation leaves no survivors, and I stand there wondering how many men have died in vain just to see another suffer in death.

We jump in the car and leave before the black cloud of smoke blowing in our direction impairs our vision from driving back down the hill. Fortunately, that's the only thing that blew in our direction. While driving away from the prison, there is stillness in the car, like the calm of a spring breeze competing against the silent flapping of a humming-bird's wings. No one says anything, but they are all thinking the same thing—that last piece of conversation on the radio before the explosions.

"You do realize we aren't just going to walk into that training facility unnoticed. It's used to train the deadliest of soldiers, and you better believe there will be cameras watching this time. Besides, our agenda is not with Iakov, so keep your hatred secluded." Finnegan says to me.

"I want him dead!" I angrily retort.

"I understand, but do you know what we'll have to sacrifice if we don't stick to the plan. You said yourself the Capitol is where we stop the enemy, to which I agree. So my concern is with our Head of State, not some general pissing in your Cheerios."

"I have to do this, it's my—"

"Vengeance is going to scar you, and get us all killed. We stick to the plan."

"Sooner or later, I'm going to face him, with or without you."

"Well, until then, the president is our target."

Gabe rubs his hands through his hair in frustration, and his confusion forces him to blurt out, "Wait!"

"What is it?" Henry asks.

"It's just . . . as if he knows we are coming."

"Of course he knows, that's why he said it, and why we need to act fast," I add.

"In time, but not now," Finnegan asserts.

"He knew we were listening to the conversation. He's just trying to throw us a bone. He's laying out the breadcrumbs for us to follow. He's tired of chasing us. He wants us to come to him," I say pleading my case.

"If he knows, then we are just setting ourselves up for a trap," says Finnegan.

"Exactly," I say.

"Well, I hope you have a good plan then," Finnegan says.

I know the Capitol is where our agenda lies, but all I can think about is Iakov now. The President is the least of my worries. I rest my head back against the seat and remain silent until we stop again. I don't want the others to know that I'm planning to go into the training facility alone. We have many miles ahead of us before we reach the Capitol, and I don't want the little time we have together to hinder our fellowship. The only way I can know for sure that General Iakov will be in the belly of that fortress is to see him face to face, and I know he would rather have me alive than dead. But it matters not; I will either see him in this life or haunt him in another.

CHAPTER 25

My eyes glaze over as I fall into a deep trance. The silence in the car has hypnotically transformed my thoughts into another vision. This one is so clear, it's like I'm in the very room, touching the walls. There is a large table sitting in an empty space of white in a location that is unfamiliar. Sitting at the table are ten world leaders discussing international diplomacy. Although every party and their constituents share the same conflict resolution strategy in creating a global support network for each other, each leader still stays grounded in their future endeavors as they continue to argue over one another. Each leader has a nameplate in front of them. Some of the names I already recognize from the news.

It appears to be a private summit that is beyond the scope of just talk. It is devised to combat immediate resolution against an international revolt created by the Israeli government. Sitting from left to right is Gennadi Gorshkov of Russia, who heads the conference, but his face eludes me. I try hard to get a glimpse of him, but my eyes can't seem to look directly at him. It's as if he's faceless. Whatever is subconsciously distracting me from seeing him, it's unnerving. It's like being in a dream where you're moving in quicksand. No matter how hard you try, you never seem to get anywhere.

Sitting around the table is Delun Yeung of China, Yasin Talbani of Iraq, Arturo Sardina of Cuba, Fedor Hoffmann of Germany, A'zam Naifeh of Saudi Arabia, Akbar Khatami of Iran, Anwar Mubarak of Egypt, Faruq Asefi of Afghanistan, and Nikolai Kriel of the United States.

These are the last of the great nations that hold absolute sovereignty, although there is nothing great these nations have offered in the last forty years. England, the last of the withering global forces, was eventually absorbed by the Federal Republic of Germany during the last decade, giving up all political rights, but still sustaining a superfluous amount of wealth, which has contributed to the political climate change over the last twenty years.

America hangs on by a thread because of foreign beneficiaries like China and Russia, who in exchange are using America's technological moxie and political arrogance to sway global relations. America will only last as long as the Russian and Chinese governments control economical trafficking. The United States is still considered a world power by its name alone, but it is becoming less and less potent.

Arguing ensues among the men sitting at the table as they discuss the true motives behind Israel's rebellious behavior. "Israel has the capabilities to destroy a nation, and we can't assume otherwise," says Kriel.

"Yes, and how do you know this?" Hoffmann asks.

"Because we supplied them with those capabilities," answers Kriel.

"But you must remember, you have dissolved that relationship with them for over ten years now," says Sardina.

"Ally or not, they still hold the technology we provided," says Kriel.

"The question is whether they have the guts to use it," chimes in Sardina.

"My American counterpart will agree that if we don't devise a plan soon, then this stalemate will only delay and hinder not only our current economic status, but also the future of a one-world government that we all seek," says Gorshkov.

"What do you intend we do, then? Sacrifice our nations for a cause that you may or may not guarantee?" Talbani spouts off.

"I'm sure Israel is in no position to dictate the outcome of this stalemate," says Hoffmann.

"Israel is transfixed by its religious culture, and there is absolutely no influence beyond that land that poses a threat to our agenda. We are the world powers, gentlemen, and we control the trade embargos," says Yeung.

"Gentlemen, gentlemen, your overconfidence in this matter will be the death of you," says Gorshkov.

"I'm not so sure my country can sustain another war," says Talbani.

"We may be in the midst of a global uprising, but we cannot afford to make assumptions based on past political mistakes," says Kriel.

Hoffman scoffs. "I don't see any real reason we should continue with this debate. This is not our main objective. The issue is—"

"The real issue at hand is right in front of you, President Hoffman, but you cowardly reject even the idea that your nation could fall," Gorshkov declares.

"As head of this international council, I extend to you all with great respect your audacious speculations, but I'm becoming frequently displeased with your political malcontent. This is the time, my fellow privileged comrades," Gorshkov says, pacing around the table with his hands behind his back. "We decide here and now, and if anyone wishes to decline their invitation, then be advised that your country will no longer be under international immunity. I have a great vision for our nations to come together with the ideals that this world was meant to be ruled under," Gorshkov says.

"I don't think it's in the best interest for my country to have to suffer through another political regime just so we can establish a stable economy," says Sardina.

"This isn't about a global economy. This is about the power to control a race of men and women who share a common ideology, and our Head of State seems to be in over his head trying to bring together ten nations to agree upon this philosophy," says Hoffmann.

"Oh, the irony coming from a nation that once failed to breed a perfect race. Perhaps you would rather join Israel and receive the same suffering?" says Gorshkov.

"My country is not afraid of your pompous threats. My devotion is to my country, and I pledge no alliance to anyone who believes differently. Your arrogance cannot force me to make a hasty decision based on a vision and precarious assumptions," Hoffman confidently says.

Gorshkov plants his cold, sober face at him. "So be it," He pulls out a gun and shoots President Hoffman in the back of the head, spraying blood and bits of brain onto the white table. "Any other objections?" Gorshkov says to the others as they stare back in shock.

He briefly turns from the men as they all look at each other, wondering what the consequences may be if they wish not to decide.

"Israel will either join us or they will be destroyed!" shouts Naifeh.

Gorshkov slowly turns back toward the men, smiling, and pounds his fists on the table. "What say you, men? Do you have the heart of a lion or the blood of a fowl?"

Just when things become interesting, I'm quickly interrupted from this vision by Finnegan's erratic driving skills. We nearly hit a deer, but he manages to swerve and miss it.

We've been driving for hours, and my jaw is sore from resting on the side of the car door. I look out the window and see nothing but darkness. The night has come upon us, and I suddenly feel a sense of urgency to get out of the car to recirculate the blood in my numb legs.

Everyone else appears to be asleep except Finnegan, thank God, because he's behind the wheel. A line of brightness outlines the curvature of the earth just slightly above the steep hill in front of us, and as we drive closer to the top, the light gradually bends upward, revealing a slight glow. Just below the other side of the hill, lights burn bright, illuminating a small city that looks to still be awake.

Instead of driving directly into the city, Finnegan finds a rundown inn off a side road about ten blocks from town. An old wooden sign swings back and forth hanging onto its rusty chains with the word, *Occupancy*, carved into it. You wouldn't know it by first glance, but the old worn cottage looks as if it was bright white in its earlier days. Although the scars from the peeling paint and termite-eaten planks tell a different story, I feel strangely comfortable staying here rather than in the city. I just hope the inside is more inviting than the outside.

Before Henry can knock, the door creeks open just enough for two wide eyes to peer through the open crevice. "Excuse me, ma'am, we are in need of a place to stay the night," says Henry.

"Possibly more than one night," adds Finnegan.

The door swings open, and an older woman appears through the rusty screen. Her frightened face is filled with a sudden shock of surprise when she sees us standing outside the door, but none of us are carrying any weapons that would imply any kind of threat. I'm a little perplexed by her reaction, but more so when she opens the door and hurriedly leads us inside.

"Please, hurry. Come in, come in," she ushers. She quickly closes the door behind us and locks it tightly with three deadbolts.

We all curiously stare at the woman rushing around and peeping through the dingy blinds by the front windows. I turn and look at Henry, who shrugs his shoulders in confusion.

While the woman intently spies out the window, she yells something out in Spanish, and a little girl about eight years old comes out from the kitchen. "Come with me, please," the little girl says. She begins to take us upstairs to our rooms, but the woman quickly stops her and tells her to take us down the long hallway.

"Wait, *por favor*," I say to the little girl as I turn to talk to the old woman "*Señora, ¿hay algo mal*" I ask. She realizes she can't hide the truth any longer when I ask her what is wrong.

"Evil men have been looking for you. They have come to ask about you," she says.

"What men?" I ask.

"Soldiers, officers, even the citizens around the city."

"Citizens?"

It's begun; the first wave of sheep straying into the darkness without a shepherd. Many will follow where they feel safe and begin to choose sides that will immediately benefit them or destroy them. Their eyes will always be fixed on what they can see, and be blind to what they cannot. They have no God to find hope in, and they will soon perish like the others.

"How do you know they are looking for us?" I ask.

She picks up her Bible, then points toward Gabe and me. "You and him have come to deliver us, no? We have been feverishly praying day after day for years, and then yesterday, we hear rumors floating in from the west about you. You are just as they described. We have heard the things you have done, the blood you have spilled. Many people have been praying for your protection," she says, holding my hand.

An older gentleman walks down the stairs and trembles with fright, hiding behind a chair when he sees Gabe and me. "*Hay muerte entre nosotros,*" the old man says.

"Why is he so scared?" asks Juliana.

"Because I have invited the angel of death into my home." She gestures for the old man to leave.

"So I have been hearing," I say.

"We thank you for opening up your home for our stay. We will try not to wear out our welcome," I say.

"You are in a holy house on unholy land. You are welcome to seek refuge here as long as you need. It's just me and the girl, and we have plenty of food, supplies, and warm water for your comfort."

"Thank you kindly," I say.

"If you need anything, you can call on me. My name is Maria, and that little girl hiding behind you is Isabel," she says.

"Please forgive me for not introducing myself. I'm Arena, this is my brother, Gabriel, and this is Juliana, Henry, and Finnegan," I say.

"It's a pleasure to meet you all. Please come and I will show you to your rooms," Maria says.

Our rooms are small, but adequate, and if there was ever a time that warm water was as essential as food, it is right now; it's all I can think about. Each room is accompanied with a mirror, a nightstand, which holds a Bible, and nicely folded towels sitting on a rather tightly tucked quilt. Grime collects on the ends of the bed skirting, and cobwebs latch onto the corners of the room. Either this house breathes dust, or this room has been unoccupied for a very long time.

I slap the center of the quilted bed and dust particles explode into the air and float around until they cascade back down. I once read that seventy-five to ninety percent of the dust in your home is actually dead skin cells. I can't wait to lie down among the dead skin of several hundred other people who have lain here before me.

The yellowing of the wallpaper and the cracked plastered ceiling gives the room . . . a sense of character, as they say. Yeah, right, the character of an old haggard and gnarled woman slowly dying. Time has transposed this once newly decorated room into a worn-out, withering story. I try to imagine how many travelers who have passed through these doors and slept in this very bed may have played an influential role in changing someone's life. People and things come and go, live and die, stand or wither, but time will always stay the same until the end comes and nothing or no one is left to see it exist.

There is an adjoining building, the bar, that sits behind and to the right of the inn that brings in the smells of cheap cigars and musky oils. I can hear two old men arguing about who bought who drinks the night before. I wouldn't have known what day it is if I was not listening to the crotchety, old geezers spatting back and forth. The days have no meaning to me anymore—just the time of day at sunrise and sunset.

While my better judgment tells me to go to sleep, I rebelliously ignore it instead. I decide to take a peek at the city with Gabe while the others stay back to get some rest. Just in case we run into some unnecessary entanglements, I take a few weapons with me. Gabe throws me my black cloak to conceal them. "No, you don't look suspicious at all," Gabe sarcastically says.

Downtown is only ten blocks away, but where we stand, darkness dominates our surroundings, and the only light illuminating the sky is coming from the moon and the dimly lit lantern outside the bar entrance. Once we cross over the hill, we see the sleepless city below as its lights glow embers in the night sky.

It doesn't take us too long to reach the outer part of the city before we are greeted by an unsightly group of strangers. The black garb draping down over their bodies dominates their wardrobe, and their faces are so pale, they almost glow in the dark.

Gabe consciously tries not to stare, and finds it hard not to laugh at the group of gothic teens. It's not until we get closer when one of the girls smiles at Gabe, revealing her sharp canines, that I suddenly realize we are passing by a ridiculously attention-seeking vampire mob. I honestly didn't know that this cultural underground following still existed until tonight.

We are hissed at as we pass except for one guy who stares intently at me. One of the older pretentiously devoted vampire leaders approaches Gabe and asks if he has any blood to share with the others. "No, but my sister has spilled enough blood to supply you for a lifetime," says Gabe. He chuckles a bit, but graciously holds back any harsh laughter that would otherwise insult these poor forgotten teens who have probably been picked on their whole lives. I almost sympathize with them until one of them tries to grope me from behind.

I quickly grab his hand, turning it behind his back, and slam him into the ground. Suddenly, about a dozen other vampire followers appear from behind the dark alley. "Release him now!" yells a voice from the pack. The only thing that keeps me from breaking this kid's arm and sling-ing a knife into the other's throat is the innocence of their imagination, even if it is completely absurd. What is mostly sad is that they have been pretending to be this mythological immortal creature for so long that they really believe they are vampires.

I'm actually in a playful mood, so I let the kid go and politely go along with their role playing just to humor them. "May we take passage through your territory, my lord?" I ask, as if that is how one talks to a vampire. Gabe rolls his eyes and looks away to discreetly conceal his smirking face.

"Who is asking?" the older one says.

The hood of my cloak hides most of my face, but I'm reluctant to remove it and possibly expose who we are. "Just a stranger," I say.

A group of boys moves in front of us and block our path. "No strangers shall pass through here unless they give something in return or if we deem you worthy enough to pass," the boy says.

Gabe looks at me and shakes his head. "Seriously, who the hell talks like that?"

"Reveal yourself now or else," the boy demands. Okay, I was willing to play along with this ridiculous charade, but now I'm becoming a little irritated. The quaint smile on my face has turned serious, and the tone has drastically changed from playful to aggravating. I'm suddenly having distaste for vampire geeks, and the only cure for this unexpected displeasure is to silence their bark, which is unequivocally louder than their bite, no pun intended.

As I pull back my hood, one of the girls asks me who I am. "I'm called by many names, but tonight, I'm a stranger who's passing through," I say.

An abrasive-looking young man, which I can only assume is the leader, walks closer to me, breathing down the back of my neck. His face is pale like the others, and the closer he gets, it's plainly obvious he's caked on too much white makeup because it is cracked along his jawline. His eyes have an animal-like appearance, probably from fake lenses. His hair is stringy, greasy, and black, as one would expect from a Goth. He's tall and lanky, but perceptibly dominant among the others. "Unless you somehow pass through this line, you're going to have to turn back," he says in my ear.

"Uh, yeah, you really don't want to do that," Gabe cautions to him.

I've been tolerant up to this point, but now my patience has grown thin. "If you even attempt to bite me with those absurd prosthetic teeth, I'll gut you like a fish."

"I don't think so," he says. I glance at Gabe, and he surprisingly nods, giving me the green light to end this small, ridiculous standoff to a bunch of *Twilight*-obsessed imbeciles.

I elbow the boy in the nose and pinch the back of his neck until he is rendered unconscious. I pull off the cloak and draw my swords toward the others standing in front of our path and swing with precision across the waist of one of the boys standing there. The sword grazes the black fabric, cutting through the tightly woven belt, and leaving the poor, scared boy standing there with his pants wrapped around his ankles.

The two boys on each side of him scram before they are met with the tip of my blade, while the pantless one tries desperately to scurry, without a trace of dignity. One of the young girls who refrained from hissing at us earlier can't take her eyes off Gabe and me, while the others trip over one another trying to escape.

"It's her! It's her!" she shouts.

"Her who?" asks one of the other girls, who grabs her shirt, trying to lead her away.

"The one everyone has been talking about in the city," she says, as they run off and out of sight.

Before I withdraw my weapons and redress my cloak, I make sure everyone has left the scene. When the earth is wiped clean by the wrath of God, I swear I'm convinced that the only things left standing will be cockroaches, mesquite trees, and vampire fanatics. The world can't end soon enough.

We decide to continue on into the city just to poke around, but we keep our distance and sustain our calm.

There's no need to stir up any more trouble than we already have. We may need to stay here for a few days, and I don't want to detract from our agenda or cause any unfortunate mishaps that may alter our plan.

The streets seem almost empty except for a few vagrants rustling around some garbage cans by an old unoccupied warehouse. We must be on the side of the city that has been gated off from the others during the first separation movement the government implemented a few years ago.

I can see the large fencing that was built surrounding the inner city a few blocks up ahead, but it doesn't seem to damper the spirits of the few homeless people who are milling about with smiles on their faces. They have either accepted their place in society, which is completely tragic, or their mental disability has hindered their perception of reality and they don't know the difference. In any case, it saddens me to the point I detest my government more than I despise my own demons.

As we come closer to the fence, we notice a homeless man sitting up against the wall, nothing out of the ordinary since there are many homeless in this area, but what has caught my eye is the sign he is holding that reads: *Please don't ignore me, I need love too.*

I tell Gabe to hold up so I can talk to the man, but before I can take a step, four delinquents come rushing down the street as if they are running from someone. They all are wearing the same type of jacket with torn sleeves. I look closer and can't help but notice each one sporting the same tattoo of a swastika on their arm. I grab Gabe and pull him behind the corner of a building out of sight to avoid any further altercations for the night, but what happens next forces me to quickly reconsider my strategy.

The men stop running and begin to argue with one another about something I can't quite make out. One pulls out a knife and threatens another, while the leader of the bunch breaks up the small skirmish. They immediately notice the homeless guy with the sign, and for whatever reason, they take out their anger on him, kicking and punching the man in the ribs and head. One even spits on him and urinates until I shout out behind the building, "Hey! You keep doing that to that old man, and I'll make sure you'll be pissing out of a tube for the rest of your life—if you're lucky!"

"Who the hell are you? Little Red Riding Hood?" one of the men asks.

"If she were in a Tim Burton movie, then yes," Gabe says quietly to himself.

"I'm your deliverer," I say.

"Yeah, where you gonna send me?" the man says, pulling out a switchblade.

"To Hell if you choose." I rip off my cloak and pull out my twelve-inch scorpion dagger.

The men's eyes suddenly widen as I approach, and they quickly pull out smaller similar knives, except one who has a set of ridiculously cheap nunchucks. I stop and play defense, attempting to lure them into a more accessible position of defeat.

Gabe just stands back and watches with his arms crossed. "If you need me, just call," he says.

One man comes running at me with absolutely no skill set other than trying to bull-rush me with a dull switchblade that has seen better days. I easily side step and trip the guy's legs, sending him hard to the ground while another comes slicing awkwardly. I dodge his blow and turn into the back of his shoulder, slicing downward across the muscle and tearing any ligaments that is holding his arm up.

The other bloke advances, spinning his cheap wooden nunchucks toward me. I grip tight to my dagger and block his swinging attempt. My blade catches the chain, and the whirling weapon slings violently back at his face, breaking his nose. He falls, wailing on the pavement.

The leader is the last man standing, but he doesn't seem as dumb as the rest, so I take precaution and slide my hand up to one of my throwing knives in anticipation of something he may do unexpectedly.

Gabe shouts from behind, "He's got a gun!"

My instincts have proven me right, and just before he lifts his gun, I fling the knife into his jugular, and he drops to the ground.

I grab the dagger, and when I turn it slightly into the direction of the moonlight, I just so happen to catch the reflection behind me. One of the other men aims a gun at my back. I quickly turn away and swing down behind me, slicing halfway through the man's hand. He screams in pain, shouting curses, while one of the men runs off, threatening that he will be back in greater numbers to kill me.

I'm not about to stir up another war that could possibly put our plans in jeopardy, so I do what I think is best in this situation for all of us; I shoot him in the back of the head. The injured man with his half hand desperately hanging by a thread, angrily tries to pick up the gun to shoot Gabe, but I quickly impede his attempt with a bullet to his head.

The man with a broken nose concedes, so I give him an alternative as he sits on his knees holding his bloody snout. I hold the cold steel of my gun to his head and tell him that today is the day he can choose to change his life and still be forgiven for all he has done in the past.

"No one is immune to forgiveness if they simply ask with their heart. Your friends chose the alternative, please don't make that same mistake," I say before I let him go.

When the guy runs off, I race over to the old homeless man. His face is swollen, and his lip is bloody, but his eyes are as clear as the night sky. I gingerly pull his body up against the wall and search his broken face.

"How long have you been exiled here?" I ask.

"Long enough to know I'm not wanted inside the city," his parched lips sigh. I softly grab his hand and examine the bruise on the side of his face.

"Why would someone like yourself come to my aid? I'm just an old, withering man who has nothing to offer," he says.

"And I'm a broken girl who wants nothing to take. Look into my eyes," I say, holding his torn, shredded glove. "What do you see?"

He seems a bit off guard, but plays along and glowers into the glassy reflection of my eyes. He pauses, then stutters, "Myself."

"Then what should make us any different? You and I share the same demons, we struggle with same understanding, we were both born into the same sinful world to be redeemed by the same God, yet we can't even acknowledge the same space because many have influenced us to think we have no value. Thank God He does."

"People ignore me when they have higher priorities, but they seek me when they feel lowly, and beat me when they don't even know me, yet I still forgive them, because I love them," the man says as tears run down his cheek, clearing a clean path through the grime and filth that covers his disheveled face.

"I'm not here to ignore you; I'm here to acknowledge your existence," I say as I help him up to his feet, but I'm suddenly distracted by gunfire behind us in the distance. Gabe and I quickly turn to see what is going on, but when I turn back around, I'm holding an empty tattered glove, and to my shock, I look down to see that the man has disappeared beneath his torn shrouds.

While I stare aghast at his vanishing, I try to dissect what just happened. Goosebumps spread across my body as I gaze silently down into a pile of cloth. I'm overcome with so much emotion, I feel like I'm drowning. I suddenly begin to detest my own selfish behaviors. I feel the burden of a million voices screaming out for my help, and I have nothing to offer them. I despise what many people are afraid they will become, guilt eating into their hearts with delusions of self-worth. I have so much stirring in my heart right now, I decide it's just best if we return back to the inn.

CHAPTER 26

Sunrises are a beautiful moment if you ever have the chance to get up early enough to witness them. Since I haven't slept a wink all night, I engulf myself in the splendor that God has so graciously extended. The cool morning breeze brushes against my skin, forcing me to put my jacket back on as I stand outside waiting for the warmth of the sun's rays to peek back out from behind the clouds. While the others are still asleep, I bask in the little bit of nature that surrounds me outside the city, hoping to find a little peace before the next storm.

I stare down at the blood on my dagger while I slide the tip of the blade across the dirt in a circular pattern, and think back to my simple childhood before Gabe and I were thrust into all of this. I remember playing in the dirt behind our house drawing figures with a stick, just to see it all disappear by Gabe's big feet sliding over them and laughing.

I gaze upon the circular figure in the black soil below through my dreary eyes, wondering how many men I must kill before my fate is fulfilled. I feel a smile on my face as I continue reminiscing about playing with my brother in the backyard when we were kids. The memories seem so vivid, as if they just happened yesterday. I can even see my father carrying me on his back and running through the rain, but those memories quickly fade away when Gabe's big feet brush across the dirt, erasing my drawing just like he did when we were kids.

"Got a present for you," he says as he sits down next to me.

"Isn't it a little early for presents?"

He turns his fist over, and lying in the palm of his hand is a metal cylinder. "Happy belated birthday," he says, smiling. I open up the metal container and inside is a pair of unusual glasses.

"They're thermal-viewing glasses. They will allow you to see the infrared portion of the spectrum through darkness, fog, and smoke. These are the best I've seen," he says.

"Did you steal these from Finnegan?"

"No, of course not, I stole them from the den."

"Thanks, I'm sorry I didn't get you anything for your birthday," I say as I tuck them into my pant leg pocket.

"You've done enough for me the past few years, you owe me nothing. I'm just grateful to have you as a sister." My lip quivers. "Even when you're a pain in the arse."

The engine from a loud truck struggles to start up before it roars with anger in the distance. It's the sound of a working man starting his early and long day. The sound reminds me of our father working long hours and sacrificing his time away from us just so we could have food on the table.

"Do you miss him?" Gabe asks, seemingly reading my thoughts.

"Yes, as much as he wasn't around, I still cherish those few and rare moments we had."

My father was a man of honor and loyalty. If he had the choice to spend time with us more, I know he would have, and I never faulted him for that. He was a good father, who never abused us, always loved us, and made sure we showed compassion toward those in need, regardless of their situation.

I didn't know my father well enough to know if he had the same relationship with his dad. I do know this: he absolutely loved my mother and would have kindly given up his life for her in a heartbeat. He had a servant'sheart.

The clouds move past, exposing the sunrise over the horizon, exploding with brushstrokes of orange and red across the sky. The scent of fall foliage in the trees floats through the air, as the crisp leaves shine glimmering red and gold. Captivated by the wonderful palette of colors, Gabe gazes with delight, taking advantage of the little enjoyments in life that seem to pass us by when we are not looking. I'm too exhausted to continue any semblance of a conversation, so I decide to retreat back inside and into my nice, soft bed.

Before I walk back to my room, I pass by Juliana. "He's outside," I say. She smiles, knowing she didn't even have to ask. I never try to pry in my brother's business, but I suddenly feel a sense of loneliness inside. I go into the kitchen to get some water, but somehow I find myself stalling to fill the cup as I stare through the open window at Gabe sitting alone.

Juliana cautiously approaches Gabe sitting on a rock by the trees, making sure not to disturb his moment of alone time. She quietly sits down next to him and leans her head on his shoulder, but he is hesitant to react. I don't know if it's because of the nature of her appalling and tragic encounter at the prison, but he just keeps his hands in his lap.

She lifts up his arm, slides underneath, and wraps tightly around him, but Gabe holds his arm in the air, as if he's trying not to touch any part of her body.

"I'm not made of glass," I hear her say, as she pulls his arm down around her shoulder. "It's okay, I won't break."

He must realize that there's no need to ever bring up the prison into conversation unless she is ready to talk about it, so he just smiles. Why should she have to relive such an atrocious act of cowardly violence?

Whether it's selfish or not, I really wish Jacob and I were sitting down together with my head leaning on his shoulder. I suddenly feel all alone and empty inside. While Gabe strokes her hair, she squeezes tighter, not letting him go. I let them be to enjoy each other's company while I lay my head on the soft pillow. It doesn't take long for my weary eyes to shut and wander off into a deep sleep and into a grisly nightmare.

I find myself walking up on a grassy hill under a gray sky, and not a soul is in sight. It's not until I reach the top of the hill, wandering through the thick mist of morning dew, that I come upon a battalion of soldiers on the other side. They are dressed in solid black uniforms with draping overcoats and a red skull insignia on the back of their helmets.

About twenty men are lined up in a disciplined formation ready to take orders, while others scurry around, rounding up prisoners dressed in filthy rags. There are two sets of barbed fencing that surround the prisoners, keeping them caged in like wild animals. Guards poke and prod, deliberately inflicting pain to those who refuse to conform to the strict rules under such cruel and horrifying conditions. It becomes evident that what I'm looking at is one of the first of many concentration camps.

A guard opens up the gate entrance to one of the fenced cages and orders about fifty prisoners to come out, forming a single line. They are held at gunpoint and ordered to line up in front of a solid limestone wall.

Among the prisoners are men, women, and even children as young as ten years old waiting to be brutally executed with their backs turned. While many of them pray, the children shake violently and cry out for their parents in terror. Before the firing squad is ordered to shoot, the parents are removed from the line and are pushed to the side.

They are held at gunpoint and forced to watch their poor children become part of a grisly and barbaric act of violent cruelty. I try to run and help them, but my feet will not move; I'm frozen in time, paralyzed. I helplessly cry out while my ankles are bound to the earth. I reach for my gun, hoping to kill the sinister squad, but when I squeeze the trigger, blood pours from the barrel instead, leaving the ground around me in a pool of red. The words play over and over in my head: ready, aim, fire. The children are gunned down, convulsing and wailing. Wretched screams fill the air as parents retreat to their children's limp bodies, crying out, "Wake up, wake up!"

Suddenly, the shouts seep from my nightmare and into my room. I open my cloudy eyes and see Gabe and Finnegan, standing over me and yelling, "Wake up, wake up!"

I dart out of bed and quickly glance out the window and notice that the day has passed and it's now late evening.

"Arena, hurry, they're here," says Gabe.

Here, who, what? I'm slightly confused and oblivious to what's going on.

"Come on, we've got to go now!" yells Finnegan. Have they forgotten that I have been sleeping for the last twelve hours, or do they just assume I know what's going on?

I leave my bedroom, a little disoriented, and see everyone racing around trying to pack things up, bumping into one another and running out the front door. I go back to my room to gather my things when all of a sudden I hear a thunderous explosion of heavy artillery in the distance. The lights flicker and shake as dust rains down from the ceiling.

I leave my weapons on the bed, grab a pair of binoculars, and hurry out the back to get a better view of what's going on. Because the city is just slightly over the hilltop, I'm not able to get a good vantage point from where I'm standing. I quickly look around and spot a tree that's tall enough for me to climb and see over the hill. I get to the top and perch myself between two branches that hang over a steep rocky decline below.

Fire blazes out of control from one of the buildings downtown, but I don't see any signs of military vehicles anywhere. A light flashes and blinks in the dark skies far in the distance and I realize it's most likely a helicopter.

I hear Finnegan calling my name from inside the inn, so I slowly descend the tall tree. I look over toward the bar and see a line of people hurrying to get inside. Families are standing around, holding their frightened children, waiting to find a place for safety.

I quicken my pace back down the tree, but I become suddenly distracted by the rustling of the leaves behind me, among the thicket of trees. At first I think it's just Gabe looking for me, so I try calling out to him, but before I get out the first syllable of his name, I notice it's not Gabe at all. It's a lost soldier, holding an automatic rifle, and scouring the area.

I stay still on the limb, scanning for more soldiers in the area, but I see none. This is either a rogue scout surveying the area for possible threats, or he is a very lost man with a gun. By the look of his uniform, I'm betting on the former. I reach for my gun and find nothing but the clothes on my back. I begin to panic and realize how stupid I was for leaving my weapons on the bed.

I try to get in a position where I can't be seen as he walks toward my area, but there aren't enough leaves in the tree to hide me. Fall must have come early in this region of the country, because the foliage has already started to turn, leaving some trees half bare.

My foot barely slips across the bark, creating a small scratching noise, and the man suddenly stops right below me. I'm totally exposed, and if he's a well-trained scout leader, all he has to do is look up.

Thankfully, the back door of the inn creaks open, forcing him to briefly focus his attention there. Gabe stands outside the door, calling out my name, not knowing the man is hiding by the tree and raising his gun toward Gabe's head.

I quickly drop down out of the tree and onto the soldier's back. His gun fires off a couple of rounds before he falls to the ground. The bullets just miss Gabe's head, striking above the back door frame. The soldier fights for his gun while I'm on his back, but the struggle to keep him from grabbing it is too much for me to bear. I scream out for help as I begin to lose my grip. "Gabe!"

Gabe is disoriented from the gunshots and tries to get up, but the scout is too close to his gun now. My boot is caught in-between two gnarled roots by the tree and I can't reach the soldier's arms. He stretches for the trigger and raises the gun up, targeting Gabe. I have nothing to grab onto but the man's shirt. I pull back his collar with all my strength, but it's not enough. The gun goes off and the back door springs open. Standing there ready to charge is Finnegan. The bullet just grazes Gabe, but now the scout has both hands comfortably on the gun. I free my boot from the tangled roots and lunge forward. I lock my arms around his head and twist until his neck cracks loose. Gabe grabs his gun, and Finnegan comes rushing to my side. I'm completely exhausted from the struggle and just lie there for a moment, beating myself up for not having my gun on me.

"I heard gunfire, is everyone okay?" Henry asks, racing out the back door. He sees the dead soldier on the ground and quickly scans the area for more.

"It's okay, I've checked the surroundings. He's just a rogue," I say to Henry.

"Look, we need to leave here right now. The city was attacked about two hours ago," says Finnegan.

While I hurry back inside to gather my weapons, I keep seeing images of those children being shot in my dream. Before I rush out the door to the car, I can't help but think what those families waiting to get into the bar must be feeling right now.

I'm hesitant to get into the car when I turn back to see the last person in line pack into the crowded bar. "Arena, get in," says Finnegan.

"No." I just stand there, staring back at the bar.

"What?" he asks.

"There's been a change of plans. We're staying the night."

"Are you insane?" asks Finnegan.

"Call it what you will. I'm not going to leave these poor people here alone without any hope. If these people are to be my sheep, then I need to be here to shepherd them."

Everyone begrudgingly gets out of the car and follows me inside the packed bar. The chattering among everyone in the bar almost immediately stops when we enter.

People huddle around each other, bracing for the worst in what they believe is a hopeless situation, yet their eyes stay drawn toward me. Every face shows a look of despair on it, and the only glimmer of hope these people seem to cling to is our presence. I haven't the heart to let them know that I'm not the hope they wish to put their faith in. I'm just as mortal and sinful as they are, but my hope stems from the faith I have in what I cannot see. That is what sustains me through these wicked times, that is what holds me together through tragedy; without that, I'm truly dead. How am I to shepherd a flock with no purpose?

I have Gabe check the back door to make sure it's locked while the others sit down near an empty table. I look around at all the families with children as I lower my hood and address the frightened crowd.

"I'm Arena, and I'm here to make sure we get through this horrifying night unscathed," I say as I walk past a young woman kneeling down and praying. "And whatever happens tonight, don't stop doing what she's doing," I say, pointing toward the woman.

"What hope do we have against an army with guns?" asks a man in the crowd.

"The same hope you had before they were here with guns. If you wish to survive, then I suggest you kneel down and pray. Instead of clinging onto the desperation that causes you to fall, hold onto the faith that picks you up, because nothing else will save you."

These people are so consumed by fear, their eyes seemingly become less responsive to me. If I can't encourage them to seek refuge in our Lord, then they will ultimately find themselves dying in a world without purpose or value, and life becomes pointless.

"We're all going to die, you know," says an old, haggard-looking man sitting in a chair by the door, drinking from a metal flask. "There is no hope left in here, child."

"What kind of heartless worm breeds such negative things in front of children?" I ask as I wander over to the old man, who smells of stale urine and cheap tobacco. I hover over him like a buzzard, giving him a stern look of displeasure.

"I have accepted my fate, why haven't you accepted yours?" he asks.

I lean closer to him and privately continue our conversation. "These folks may be frightened, but at least they cling to a thread of hope, huddling and praying together. They are starving, yet they have given their last bit of food to others in need, while you wallow in dejection all alone, taking what you can without a grain of gratitude. You're a cancer and a curse to these desperate people who desire to hang on until the end."

"Well, I meant no harm to the children," he says.

"Then shut your filthy trap."

Throughout the night, helicopters fly overhead and heavy artillery shells fire, but people begin to warm up to us and small chatter starts up again, but it soon ends.

Glasses clink together and tiny pieces of plaster drop from the ceiling as the bar rattles from a nearby explosion. Everyone hunkers down, waiting for the next blast to come and go, like waiting for the thunder to clap after a bolt of lightning strikes during a violent thunderstorm.

I walk over to a young pregnant woman whose face is painted in misery and a fright that won't surrender. "If you wish to fight off discouragement, then have a quiet talk with your Father. You'll quickly find that peace will overcome tragedy if you let yourself go to Him. Don't let your heart give way to a disquieted spirit. It will be through your faith and patience that you will inherit the promises," I say softly to her.

And just like that, silence fills the air and hearts begin to stir as the others encouragingly watch the young woman pray. For the first time in my life, I feel purposefully connected. Despite all the trials and suffering in my life, I finally understand the relationship Job had with God.

I check the window by the door and take a quick peek to see if there is any activity going on near us, but instead I'm mesmerized to see Isabel sitting on Juliana's lap. I can't take my eyes off that little, innocent girl, with those droopy, tired eyes leaning back against Juliana's chest. I look at Isabel and wonder what it would have been like to be a big sister.

The old man's rude and obnoxious behavior quickly shatters that moment. He's beginning to irritate me beyond what my patience can handle with his mocking laughter and crude taunts. He tries to stand from his chair, but the excessive alcohol prevents him from succeeding. Drunk or not, he's pissing me off.

"We're not going to get through this alive. Your lives are hopeless now, and there's nothing left to pray for," says the crotchety man, laughing.

I can no longer take it from this grouchy old codger, so I reach for my knife and grab his tongue while he is laughing. "I'm growing very tired of your malcontent. Spew any more venom from that acid tongue of yours and I'll fucking slice it off." I release his tongue and he quickly shuts his mouth. He's so shaken up he takes his handkerchief out of his pocket and ties it over his mouth just to assure he doesn't accidentally slip up again.

After five minutes of silence pass, I peek out the door toward the city and see smoke rising from the building tops just over the horizon. I almost feel a sense of failure that we are not ready for such an assault, but a voice in my head suddenly comforts and assures me that my presence in the bar has been more purposeful than if I were out in battle.

Our enemy can reside in our very own hearts, but it has come to pass that we were meant to be here in this bar. Those who have perished throughout the night have either been extended merciful grace or eternal damnation; either way, His wrath has been just.

*　　*　　*

The night has passed, giving way to another morning and another day to survive. The dingy, darkly colored drapes covering the bar windows block the sun from peeking through and reminding everyone that it's morning. I'm the only one awake, so I decide to sneak outside to have a look at what awaits us.

Smoke still rises in the cool air above the smoldering buildings below. Not a day goes by that I wish not to see or smell any more death, but my heart tells me that today is no different. Gabe awakens and joins me outside, having the same reservations about surveying the damage in the city, hoping to find survivors. He no more wants to see death than I do.

He returns inside to wake the rest of the group up while I take a few moments to be alone. The morning sun rises above the horizon as we drive down into the city to assess the damage. We cautiously drive through the empty streets, avoiding the debris left from the damaged buildings. Cars are still parked along the street as if they have never been moved. The size of the tracks that run across one of the intersections is a good indication an armored tank was here last night.

We drive further in, but see no bodies or any signs of death, for that matter. The only noticeable sign of wreckage so far are the few charred structures that are still smoldering. Finnegan rolls down the window, and suddenly the wind blows in a slight smell of singed flesh from the burned buildings.

It's not until we reach the outer realm of the city through a small residential area where I finally spot a sign of life. "Stop the car!" I shout, as I see a small child running in- between two houses. "Gabe, come with me now. The rest of you stay here."

I take off, running by the house where the child passed while Gabe follows closely behind me. I stop next to the corner of the house and peek to the side where the back gate is wide open. There are a few bloodstains on the concrete steps in front of the house next door, and a tattered, blood-soaked shirt hanging from the railing.

Cars are still parked in the driveway and porch lights are still on, but still no sign of anyone on the premises. There's a thermos sitting on the battered railing that's half full of cold coffee; it has been sitting there for quite some time.

An image suddenly flashes in the backyard, but I can't tell if it's a child or an adult. I tell Gabe to stay on the porch in case the person tries to escape through the front door. I sneak around back through the gate and come to an open entry. The screen door has been torn off its hinges, suggesting that someone was struggling to break in or possibly break out.

I draw my gun as I enter through the doorway, just in case I'm mistaken for a soldier and some madman decides to take a whack at me.

The house smells musty and stale, and the further I walk in, the more pungent the odor becomes. The place is a wreck, like it has been recently ransacked. Food is sitting out on the coffee table attracting flies, and the television is still on, but the channel is just blank. The kitchen is in disarray, with broken dishes scattered about, and a bloody knife lies on the floor.

I eagerly creep up toward the hallway, making small movements and observing every inch of the living room. I suddenly stop when I hear a faint sniffle come from the cor-ner of the living room. I peer over the chair that's blocking my view and notice a small child's shoe sticking out from behind the couch.

I put my gun away and quietly walk over by the couch, crouching down so as not to seem as threatening. "Hey, I'm not going to hurt you. I'm here to help you," I say.

She couldn't be more than six years old, with curly, bright red hair and a few freckles hiding behind some of the dirt on her face. I try my best to lure her out, but she is in too much shock to move. Whatever happened here last night has completely tainted her trust in adults, but more impor-tantly, it has destroyed her emotionally.

"My name is Arena. Can you tell me your name?" I softly ask. She is holding a stuffed rabbit, so I try to engage in a more playful conversation. "I like your rabbit. He's very cute. Reminds me of the rabbit I had growing up. I got him when I was five years old and I named him Honeysuckle. I so loved that rabbit. He went with me everywhere. I carried him around so much, I wore off his whiskers, and Mother had to sew new ones on him. Does your rabbit have a name?"

"Cecilia," she says in a sweet, tender voice.

"That's a beautiful name for a rabbit." She must be warming up to me because she snickers a little.

"No, I'm Cecilia, this is Mr. Buggles," she says, correcting me.

"Why don't you come out so I can get a good look at Mr. Buggles?" I say.

Her face glows with fright again and she starts to whimper. "No, no. The evil people are out there," she cries.

"I tell you what; I'm going to make a deal with you. If you and Mr. Buggles come out from behind the couch, I promise with all my heart to protect you from the evil people," I say. I extend my hand out to her, and she is reluctant to grab it, but she eventually takes my hand and slides out from behind the couch.

She clings to me for dear life as she shakes in fear. I gently rub my hand on her back, trying to calm and soothe her. "Do you have a mother or father?" I ask. She nods her head. "Do you have any brothers or sisters?" She nods her head again. "Do you know where they are?" She points toward one of the bedrooms, and cold chills creep up my spine. I quickly stop rocking her and rubbing her back. I'm hoping they are just hiding in there just like Cecilia was hiding out here.

I carefully carry her to the front door where Gabe is watching. I tell Gabe to go get Juliana, as I hold Cecilia, swaying back and forth to calm her spirit. When Juliana comes, I try to pry Cecilia from my body, but she clings to me like a monkey would to her mother.

I finally persuade her to go with Juliana back to the car where it will be safe. Juliana has a natural comforting motherly instinct that will be of much need right now. "Are you okay, Arena?" Juliana asks.

"I'm not sure yet," I say, as my heart begins to feel hardened, not knowing what lies in that bedroom. While Juliana takes Cecilia back to the car, Gabe and I go back inside the house to see if we can find the rest of the family.

I explain to Gabe the situation as we walk toward the bedroom, but I'm too frightened to open the door because I have already feared the worst. I slowly open the bedroom door, but we find it empty and untouched. The other bedroom is left the same way with no trace of anyone being in here. The only bedroom left is the master bedroom, and I can only imagine what pain lies behind the door.

My heart races faster and faster as I anticipate what that little, innocent girl had to witness. I open the withered door preparing myself, but to our surprise, this room is also empty. Gabe sighs with relief, and I can't understand where they might have run off to. I walk in a little further and thankfully see no one lying on the floor.

I turn toward a large open closet and my body completely goes numb. I stand there frozen in horrific shock and dismay, as nothing like this could ever prepare a person to see.

"What's wrong?" Gabe asks as he slowly walks toward me.

"Don't come over here." A cold sweat covers my face, my jaw clinches tight, and I grab the side of the bed, desperately holding back any emotional discomfort. I cup my hands over my mouth with unexpected fright as the hairs on the back of my neck stand at attention.

I look upon a family hanging by their necks from the ceiling of the closet. A sister and brother, no older than nine years old, dangle next to their mother, all of their eyes still open and staring lifeless into the void.

CHAPTER 27

I quickly turn away, still clenching the side of the bed as I surrender to gravity. I fall to my knees and just sit on the floor, crying in agony. There are no scars or signs of a struggle on the bodies, which makes me even more sick inside, knowing that this family possibly hung themselves to avoid whatever wretched, sadistic things those men were about to torture them with.

I can't possibly imagine why a mother would do this to her own children, but because I'm determined to exclude the idea that one would do such a horrible thing, I curiously examine the bodies closer.

I look at the little girl's hands and notice some dead skin stuck inside and hanging off her fingernails. Blood runs from her fingertips to the inside of her wrist, and the few strains of black hairs stuck to the dried-up blood is evidence enough that this little girl made an effort to fight back against her attacker.

I try to pull myself together while Gabe stands there speechless and stunned, when suddenly, a gunshot echoes outside. We quickly rush outside and see Finnegan standing over a dead soldier, the barrel of his gun smoking.

The man's leg is seriously wounded from a knife cut, and his bloody jacket reveals a puncture wound to the side of his ribs. "He came stumbling out from behind one of these houses with a gun in his hands, shouting expletives. The girl started screaming, 'It's him, it's him,' so I shot him," says Finnegan.

I tilt his head over to the side with my boot, and become filled with rage when I notice small claw marks on the side of his cheek, marks that could only have come from a child's hands. While I feel lifeless on the outside, the thoughts swimming around inside my head darken with hatred. If I had any sense of calm before, it is quickly overshadowed by the wrath brewing in my heart as I stare down into his cold, heartless eyes.

"You all right?" Finnegan asks.

I can't answer—I'm filled with too much fury, and all I can think about is General Iakov ordering such heinous acts of violence on these innocent people. I look down at the man's uniform and notice a red skull pin attached to his front lapel and strange markings on the back of his collar. The words are written across in black stitching.

"What is it?" Gabe asks.

"This is a Russian soldier, and those are Russian markings."

"What does it say?" Finnegan asks.

"I will not utter those words here," I say. I walk away from Finnegan and Gabe and stare out into the city, trying to somehow grasp a moment of clarity. I've read many books about World War II history, but I would have never thought mistakes over one hundred years ago would ever be repeated. Those words stitched into that bastard's collar bring forth a new fear on this land. It's an old phrase that comes from the German word *Schutzstaffel*, infamously known as the *SS*. It means *Protective Echelon*. Apparently, a new paramilitary organization is among us.

"Get in the car now," I say, as I stand there motionless, staring into the soldier's stony eyes.

"Arena?" Finnegan carefully asks with a slightly concerned look on his face.

"Take us back to the inn," I order.

While heading back, no one says a word. I never knew that silence could be so painful. My mind is racing with anger, and the only thing distracting my thoughts is the constant ringing in my ears.

I explain to Maria the situation with Cecilia and understandably, she agrees to take her in as one of her own. I know what it's like to be taken from your parents and thrust into another family, but I could never feel the pain this young girl must be experiencing right now. She's going to need the love and emotional support that I know Maria will provide for her. I ask Juliana to take her inside because I'm too emotionally drained to say good-bye to this little girl.

I turn my back toward the road to avoid any eye contact with Cecilia while Juliana takes her to Maria. I can't stop crying and thinking about her family hanging there in the closet; what a pointless waste of life.

Cecilia resists going inside and comes running toward me. "Arena! Please don't leave me," she cries out, hanging onto my legs.

I can't bear to look in her eyes, so I just stand there hoping she will release me and go back, but she doesn't, and my heart finally gives in. I gently touch her face with my hand as I crouch down to hug her. I can't hold back any tears, and she squeezes me tighter and tighter. I try to wipe my face clean when I look to her eyes, but it's no use.

"You're going to be safe here, I promise. Maria is a great lady. She has a bed just for you," I say.

"And Mr. Buggles?" she says.

"Yes, and Mr. Buggles too. You know who else has a bed next to yours?"

"Who?" I turn her around and point toward the door entry where Isabel is shyly peeking out.

She finally releases her fingers from my neck and watches intently as Isabel walks over to her and introduces herself. Cecilia gives me one last hug before carefully taking Isabel's hand and walking back into the house. I feel like a part of me has been ripped apart, and I have no way of knowing if it will ever be mended. When the door closes, my tears quickly change to fire, and the blood in my veins boils with rage.

While the others stock up on food that Maria has so generously offered, I take some time to vent my fuming anger alone near the trees behind the inn. After an hour passes, Gabe comes to get me, but I'm so enraged I don't even notice him there. I practice throwing knives into the gnarled trees, twisting them as if I were cutting into a soldier's neck, and slicing through bags of sand, pretending I'm splitting open General Iakov's gut. I stop and calm myself down for a few seconds. I eventually subdue my anger and walk back to the car, where everyone seems to be patiently waiting. I overhear Gabe and Finnegan conversing about me as I stand there waiting for them to finish.

"Where is she?" Finnegan asks.

"Trust me, she needs to be alone," Gabe says.

"Everything okay?" asks Finnegan.

Gabe stands there for a moment before answering. "She's pissed."

"Okay, we are all entitled to get mad every once in a while. She has every right to be."

"No, you don't understand, she's really pissed. She has a venomous look about her that I've never seen before. It's a bit sadistic, and quite frankly, I'm a little freaked out."

"I'm fine," I say, trying to ignore their conversation. "Good," Gabe says. Before he gets in the car, I attempt a feeble smile to comfort his nerves, but he knows the truth behind my lying eyes.

"I'm okay, really," I say, reaching to sway him. His tightened muscles relax, and his clenching white knuckles release from the hood of the car. He smiles back, but not convincingly.

I open the passenger door where the front seat is empty and awaiting my arrival. I pull my swords out, strap in, and try to calm myself though my hatred for General Iakov deepens.

CHAPTER 28

We drive as far as we can into the night until everyone is too exhausted to go any further. The only place on this long lonely road welcoming any accommodations is an aging Motor Inn desperately in need of renovation. As long as the thin walls keep the roof from collapsing, I'll be happy.

As evening approaches, I walk outside from the rickety structure to a few lively lights illuminating the lonely streets, and I can't help but wonder how small towns like this function through such dark times. Brooding thoughts suddenly pique my curiosity and I'm desperate to know what has been happening outside of my personal hell.

We haven't seen a national news broadcast since we had left the den, so Finnegan, Gabe, and I decide to take a stroll in town to gather any information we can. The only part of this dilapidated town that appears to be somewhat alive is the local tavern that feeds these poor people an escape from the depressing realities.

Regardless of the mild temperament of this humble-looking village, I conceal my weapons with the black cloak and pull the hood over my head. For my own security, I keep my dagger closely within reach before we walk into the tavern. Eyes gravitate toward me through the noise, but too many people are drunk to notice three strangers walking in uninvited. I lead Finnegan and Gabe toward a few empty seats at the bar, where I quickly notice a working television, but because of the commercials playing, I can't tell if this is just a looped recording.

Gabe looks around the bar, observing any unwanted trouble that may arise, while I desperately try to listen to the broadcast through all the obnoxious drunkenness around me. The commercial finally ends and a sudden elation comes over me when I see a cast of national news anchors take to the screen with a small logo nested in the right bottom corner that reads: *live.*

"What can I get ya?" the bartender asks Finnegan. "Sir, can you please turn the television up just a bit?" I ask, interrupting. Gabe stops from his observing pivot and keeps his eyes glued to a table of burly men gawking in my direction as I pull the hood back from my head.

"We don't serve kids in here," the bartender gruffly barks.

"We mean no harm, sir. They're with me. We just want to see what's going on in the world," says Finnegan. "Order something and you can watch all you want, otherwise I'll have to ask you to leave."

"Fine, I'll have a Guinness," Finnegan orders. The bartender gives Finnegan a look of displeasure as he wipes dry a dirty, used glass. He pours the beer and turns the television up, slightly cutting through the bar noise just enough where I can make out the top stories:

"All nations comprising the New World Order Organization will be reaching out to the rest of the remaining nations still teetering on joining. An Egyptian spokesperson recently aired caution on the deliberation of the Organization's future endeavors and said not to look for a final decision from them anytime soon. Pakistan has also issued a statement of concern on whether or not it would join the organization due to their recent turmoil with India."

Nothing too intriguing is being reported that I didn't already know, until a video shows President Kriel mingling with other dignitaries and international diplomats at a social function. I lean in to get a better listen of the coverage as the news anchor begins her story:

"President Kriel has vowed to partner with the Russian government to end the corruption in Syria. This political stalemate has grossly caused an international upheaval which has led to the recent oil embargos that have significantly affected European

countries. Two years ago, similar embargos devastated our nation, deterring this country from sustaining any support for the Israeli government and its military. These private talks will be addressed at a future summit in the next few days with joint leaders of the Arab nations attending, as well as the Chinese government.

"In the meantime, President Kriel will be discussing his future tax plans for the nation's newly reorganized regions at a special White House dinner party tomorrow evening. Among those attending the banquet will be some of the largest contributors and wealthy donors who have encouragingly proposed the recent changes and exercised their approval for the President's future office commitment."

A matter of concern draws from Gabe's face as I lift my eyebrow up. "What are you thinking, Arena?" he asks.

"I'm thinking we're going to crash a dinner party tomorrow night," I answer.

"We might be a little underdressed for the occasion," Finnegan sarcastically adds.

I follow Gabe's eyes, which are planted on a portly, brawny man approaching me from one of the tables. He staggers up to me before retreating his eyes back at his buddies for what I can only imagine is some kind of ego-tistical boasting. It's plainly obvious this man's inhibitions have greatly been reduced by the alcohol.

"I like 'em young," he leers, grinning back at his friends. If it's his lack of cunning wit that leaves him grounded from a successful pickup, his repellent halitosis gives him no room for improvement. He smiles at me with more teeth missing than he has to chew with, a failed attempt to charm me with his otherwise repulsive nature.

"How about I buy you a drink, pretty girl," he flirts as I try to keep myself from throwing up in my mouth.

"No, thank you, I'm fine," I say, rejecting his offer.

He slides his hand onto mine as he persistently tries to garner my attention. Finnegan rises from his seat, but Gabe quickly settles him right back down. "Don't worry, she can take care of herself."

"What do you say about you and me going back to my place? I'll go real easy on you," the man urges as he gropes my backside. While his crass remarks aren't a surprise, I will not tolerate being fondled—especially from this douchebag. Drunk or not, it's time to end his pathetic and crude advance. I pull out one of the throwing knives and slam it down in the middle of his hand through the bar top. The man's wretched scream immediately fills the bar while his bloody hand is painfully stuck to the varnished wooden top. He desperately tries to swing his other hand toward me but badly misses, most likely from the excessive amount of alcohol.

I push his throat up with my right hand, then grab my scorpion dagger behind my back and thrust it in between his legs and into the wooden bar below. I leave him hanging over the sharp blade with a barb pointing directly under- neath his scrotum. I stand back to watch him scream in pain while he dances on his toes like a ballerina trying not to puncture his testicle on the barb.

"Come on, twinkle toes, you're beginning to lose your balance," I say as I watch him squirm. His buddies rise from the table and lunge toward me, but I quickly pull my guns and halt their advance.

"Sit down," I say. They sit back down, while the rest of the bar is a dead calm except for the creep who attempted to pick up a fifteen-year-old girl.

"All you have to do is apologize and the pain will all go away," I say to him.

"You sick, twisted bitch," he responds.
"Now, that's not an apology where I come from." I begin to pull one of my swords.

"Dude, just apologize!" one of the men at the table shouts.

"Perhaps Mr. Yoshihara here can teach you some good manners," I say as I draw forth the katana against one of his kneecaps. "Did you know in some countries they cut off a man's limb for just making shrewd unsolicited advances to under-aged girls? Maybe we shall exercise that policy here."

Of course, I have absolutely no intentions of hurting this depraved man any further, but he rightly deserves to be scared shitless nonetheless.

"Okay, I'm sorry, I'm sorry," he begs.

"You see, now that wasn't so bad." I pull the dagger out from between his legs. I grab the knife still stuck in his hand with one hand, and hold onto his wrist with the other.

"This won't hurt a bit," I lie. I yank the knife from his skin. He holds his hand, then collapses to the floor, crying. "Now go put some alcohol on it, you big baby."

Finnegan just stares at me in shock while Gabe pats Finnegan's back. "I told you," he says.

"I think we should probably leave now," says Finnegan with a disturbed expression. While we leave the premises with all eyes cautiously watching our every step, all I can think about now is President Kriel, which may get me that much closer to Iakov. While debauchery continues to linger inside the bar, the rest of this simple town rests through the night.

CHAPTER 29

Though morning has come and gone, I found a rare and peaceful moment of sleep without a dream to haunt me. I feel rested, but anxious. Every day a little piece of me withers, and with every thought of Jacob, my heart hardens. I don't know how this journey is going to end, but I fear my hatred for Iakov will be the death of us all.

The afternoon grows closer and so does our uninvited dinner plans with the president. Though we've devised a compendious plan to reach the Capitol, there's hardly been any talk of what will become of President Kriel. His justice has yet to be clear. At this point, I don't care anymore. Kriel is an afterthought—Iakov is my enemy, but as long as the president is in charge, none of us have any hope to survive our broken nation.

We're fifty miles outside of Washington, and I haven't seen a single car drive by. There aren't many cities left standing since the great earthquakes, but the few that have remained intact are slowly deteriorating, and Washington DC is one of them. Most of the larger populated cities in the east and north have all been abandoned. The flu epidemic hit those the hardest. Too many people populating small areas caused the infection to spread like wildfire. There were too many bodies to bury, so they had to be burned. It was the only way to be safe, and keep the virus contained. People used to say that for two years they could still smell burning flesh in the air as the smoldering plume of smoke lingered into the atmosphere.

While the gloomy sky covers the capitol city, the unpleasant misery that awaits outside its fenced border is just as grim. We veer away from the main checkpoints as we cross the river to enter the city and concentrate on finding a less-trafficked area.

Just behind an old, derelict apartment building, the street ends, but it's as good a place as any to stop. It's deserted, but more importantly, unguarded.

"Henry, park the car on the side street in front of the north lawn of the White House and wait. We have a couple of hours before the event starts," Finnegan says.

"What about security?" Henry asks.

"The north lawn will have a few guards, but it's the south lawn that will bring more attention. I wouldn't worry too much, There hasn't been much of a need for security around here, not anymore.

"I don't like the idea of this," Juliana says.

"Don't worry, just stay in the car and lock the doors," I say.

When Henry and Juliana drive off, I catch a small glimpse of worry painted on Gabe's face. Being separated from her when we started this journey was bad enough. I don't know how this small departure will affect him now.

A city that should be thriving, considering it is the nation's capital, is riddled with more famine and homelessness than where we live. Outside the city, the streets are crippled with barricades, and the deteriorating buildings that have been abandoned can barely stand, let alone suffice as livable space.

Most of the city has fallen into a desolate state like many others around the nation. The only place left with a semblance of stately pride is the east and west mall and most of the central DC area. Everything else is in complete ruin. The towering twenty-foot fence that borders the city tells a much grimmer story. Where concrete and hopelessness dominates this side of the fence, the grass is greener on the other.

The wickedness that permeates this very area breeds a virus that can't be controlled. I look around at the disheveled faces, knowing their only means of survival is the hope that someone will save them from this destitute. They can't possibly have a sustainable life living with these conditions. If this city wasn't already a hellhole before, it's definitely a cesspool of filth now.

After a thorough view of the depressing surroundings, I can see why these people never try to access the other side of the fence; about every hundred yards, a camera sits atop, monitoring all activity below. The fence is much too tall for these poor prisoners to have the strength to scale it, and even if they did succeed, what's the point of communing in the same place where you are not wanted? Sooner or later, they would be sent back over, or worse . . . killed.

I would like to avoid any governmental entanglements at the checkpoints, so the only way for us to get in is to cut through the fence. Gabe and I hide behind one of the buildings while Finnegan concentrates on shooting the camera in front of us. We'll have to hurry through once the camera feed stops and someone notices.

After three shots, the camera finally shatters and is left dangling from the top of the fence. Without wasting time, Gabe quickly cuts a half-circle flap in the chain links large enough for us to push through.

We rush through and cross a twenty-yard gap between the fence and a federal bank. The streets seem to be hopping with happier faces on this side of the border. This is the first time we have been to a city that doesn't seem to be under attack or swarming with federal officers, which seems rather ironic, considering where we are.

We may appear to be a little out of place with our attire, but with the plethora of people walking about, we will blend in just enough not to cause a stir. At least the black cloak conceals my weapons; Finnegan and Gabe awkwardly try to hide theirs under their thick jackets.

Finnegan leads us down a few blocks, where rows of legal offices, executive buildings, and government agencies dominate the scenery. We turn down 22nd Street toward George Washington University, where he takes us to the Melvin Gelman Library to discuss our plan of action. If anybody knows this city, it's Finnegan; he used to frequent this town while he worked for the enemy, which gives us a slight advantage.

Apparently crime hasn't been a major concern in this area, because all the metal detectors have been removed from the entryways—an abnormality compared to the rest of the country. We ride the elevators to the Special Collections Center on the seventh floor, where we can get a grand view of the city below.

"We have a few options, but they are all risky, some more than others," cautions Finnegan.

"I say we just walk through the front doors; security around here is a joke," I say.

"Yes, but we want to try to avoid a massive scene that could possibly hinder us later," says Finnegan.

"What about underground? I'm sure you have walked through some of the rumored tunnels to the White House at some point in your career," says Gabe.

"There are many secret passages, but each tunnel is still heavily secured, and we would have to get through building security first before even thinking about getting down to the tunnels," Finnegan says, smiling.

"There is, however, more than one way to penetrate the underbelly of this city," he says.

Finnegan points out the importance of Pennsylvania Avenue, which runs parallel to one of many underground tunnels that connect to the White House.

"There is one way into the tunnels with no imminent security present, but we won't be able to just walk through the door," says Finnegan.

"I'm not following," says Gabe.

"Just below Pennsylvania Avenue is a sewer system that runs parallel to the street and intertwines around the secret passages, but there is one tunnel that connects to the sewer outflow section. It won't be guarded, but the connecting steel entry will be locked on both sides," he says.

"C4," Gabe responds, as he pats the side of his backpack.

"Just be careful how much you use. We just want to break the locks, not the door off its hinges," says Finnegan with a smirk. "Just remember, once we get into the tunnel, the cameras will be monitoring us all the way. Don't do anything unless we are forced to. And when that does happen, be prepared because all hell will break loose."

We leave the library and patiently wait in the University courtyard while Finnegan does some reconnaissance a few blocks away. The sun begins to hide behind the horizon and gives way to the cool night air. Finnegan finally returns to the courtyard, holding a steel rod.

"This is the result of your reconnaissance?" I ask, pointing at the bent steel bar he's holding. "You've been gone for nearly two hours."

"Unless you can pull a two-hundred-fifty pound cast iron manhole cover with your fingers, I would advise you to thank me for hunting down this hard-to-find tool. I had to walk six blocks before I could find a sewer utility truck," he says.

"So you stole that one?" Gabe says.

"I'm just borrowing it, thank you."

"Under the assumption you'll be returning it to its rightful owner?" I ask, smiling.

Night falls and the banquet has already started as we descend below the street through the sewer opening unnoticed. The smell is ferocious down here and would be well-suited for someone who appreciates the finer qualities of fuming feces.

I cover my mouth as we press against the sides of the walls, following closely behind Finnegan. Aside from the intolerable smell, this plan actually seems promising. After walking nearly four city blocks beneath the street, we come to a bend in the tunnel where a large opening stretches in another direction. Catwalks wander across the opening and meander around the tunnel next to a large overspill drainage channel. Signs punctuate the walls with the appropriate street names above, along with directions to each intersection.

Across the opening is a small concrete building with a sign that reads, *Utility Operations*, outside a steel door.

"This is it," says Finnegan.

Gabe reaches in his bag for some explosives, but I stop him and point my gun toward the keyhole and shoot. "No need to wake everyone up."

One shot and one broken lock gets us that much closer to the tunnel. We walk inside the enclosed concrete space and find nothing but an unoccupied room in disarray. An unorganized desk of papers, logs, and candy wrappers clutter most of this claustrophobic office that resembles more of a pigsty.

There are several screens above the desk, monitoring major underground intersections. There is an unlocked door in the back that leads down a small corridor to a much more secured door with a card-badge lock.

"This is it. This is the door that passes through the main tunnel," Finnegan says. Gabe digs in his bag for some plastic explosives to blast the lock, but all of a sudden, a voice rings out from the front of the room.

"Anyone in here? Dave is that you back there?" the man says.

I stand behind the door as the man cautiously approaches with his gun drawn in one hand and a bag of chips in the other. "Dave, if you're pissed about the back hair remark, I'm truly sorry. Not all of us can be as manly as you," he says, pushing the door open. "All right, stop messing around."

As the door opens far enough to shed light on Finnegan and Gabe, I quickly snatch the gun from the man's hand and throw him to the floor. I cock back his gun and point it at his head.

"Please, don't shoot, I'm just the night guard, I have nothing. I barely make a wage worthy of this bag of chips. Please, please don't shoot," he cries.

I open up the cylinder on his revolver and find it completely empty. "Why aren't there bullets in here?" I ask.

"I haven't earned them yet, hell, I'm not even supposed to have a gun," he whimpers.

"Stand up! What kind of night guard are you?" I ask.

"Apparently the kind who nearly soils his pants," he admits. He stands there with his hands up, half his shirttail untucked, mustard stains on his uniform, and his gut hanging out in front. He's obviously just trying to make ends meet with this job, but nevertheless, I still trust no one.

I make sure he's not armed with any other weapons for his sake, not ours; I don't want him hurting himself. I glance at his badge on his front pocket that reads: *Harold*. "Okay, Harold, can you get us through that door?" I ask, pointing to the badge lock.

"Yes, but what do you intend on doing?"

"You get us through that door and through the tunnel on the other side, and I can assure that you should live," I say.

"*Should*? That doesn't sound convincing," he frets.

Before Harold slides his security card across the lock, Finnegan tells us that he and Henry will meet us on the outside by the north lawn fountain. "I will set up outside and try to draw any officers guarding the perimeter away from you. Good luck," he says.

Harold slides his card through, and like magic the door opens to a stark-white hall that stretches in both directions. "Take us to the White House and remember our deal," I advise firmly. We follow the long corridor to the right, while cameras spaced out every so often look down at us from above the ceiling tiles.

As we come to the end of the hall, we are met by an officer dressed in black, holding an automatic weapon. He stands tall, guarding another door with a badge lock. "State your business," he says in a rough voice.

"I just wanted to show my girlfriend and her brother around," Harold says, as he looks back at me and winks.

"No unauthorized personnel can pass through this door without approval. You know this already," he says.

Harold whispers in the man's ear, "Dude, come on, help me out here. I'm trying to impress the girl. If I'm lucky, I might score tonight," he says, smiling.

The officer takes a closer look at me and pulls back my hood. He then radios to his coordinator. "63 to base, do you copy?" he says, eyeing me strangely. "Let me see some identification," he says as a voice calls back on the radio, "go ahead 63."

I take one look at Gabe, and the fright on his face reassures me what I'm about to do next. I abruptly push down the guard's gun and quickly thrust the back end of my gun to his nose, breaking it and sending him to the floor. I draw my gun to his head while Gabe searches for his security badge. Harold begins to have a panic attack as he places himself in the corner by the door in shock.

"Sweet Jesus, I think he just wanted to see your driver's license," Harold says, shaking. While Gabe grabs the badge to open the entry before us, the officer starts to come to and pulls his gun toward Gabe's back. I quickly draw my guns, kicking Gabe out of the way, and shooting the officer in the head.

"Oh my God, did you just shoot that man in the head? Did you see that, she just shot him! Oh God we're gonna die, we're gonna die," Harold nervously sputters.

"If you don't shut up, I'm going to shoot *you* in the head," I say.

"I'm sorry, I'm sorry. I got to get another job, this job totally sucks, but then if I do, of course my mother is just gonna stick it to me again about how Harold can't keep a job, why can't you be like your brother, Harold why don't you—"

"Shut up!" I say, knocking him in the ear.

"Ouch! What the hell? Next time just say please, there's really no need to hit me," he whines. I have no intentions of killing this guy, but if he labors any more over every minute detail about his mother, I may have to reconsider.

We race down the tunnel that takes us through a large open area of pipes, ducts, and wires dangling from the ceiling. There are catwalks that wind in every direction, and large mechanical machinery that emits noise so loud, I can't hear myself talk. As the tunnel winds around, the noise soon dissipates, but we are suddenly slowed down by loud foot-steps hurrying down the metal stairs just around the corner.

I see three officers scuffing the bottom of their boots on the slick, waxy floor, frantically running in our direction. Before they even know it, I pop off three rounds, killing them as they round the corner where we are pressed against the concrete walls.

We come to the end, where a massive freight elevator stands before us. Gabe slides the security card across the elevator sensor as we anxiously await with our guns drawn at the doors. The bell rings, the button lights up, and the doors slide open to an empty elevator, which we take to the only floor available—the ground.

The ground floor has wider halls and looks like a library basement that's going through some renovation. Scaffolding, paint cans, and plastic drop cloths line the walls down each passage. We walk through a large den, with chandeliers hanging high from the ceiling, and shelves upon shelves of literature graces the walls. Harold paces back and forth, mumbling to himself and making me unusually nervous.

"Harold, sit down and shut up!" I say.

Gabe wanders off to the right, scoping out the area, trying to look for another elevator or stairs that reach the first floor, while I stay in the den babysitting Harold.

"This way," says Gabe, gesturing for us to leave. Around the corner and through the next hall feels bleak and cold, as if this section of the building is completely separate from the rest. I can almost feel the climate change as we step across the metal plating on the floor. Voices from the distance delay us from going any further.

I crouch down and peek around the corner to see a door at the end of the hall marked "Stairs." I only see two officers, possibly unarmed, walking down the hall, but a food cart is blocking most of my view to know if there are any more behind them.

"How many?" Gabe whispers. I hold up two fingers and shrug my shoulders. I saunter on my toes, guns drawn, and advance around the corner toward the two officers. They notice me right away and reach for their guns, but I permanently distract them with two bullets to the head. Unfortunately, one of the officers prematurely pulled his trigger, and the gun goes off in the holster, causing a massive stir in the next hall.

"I think I just stirred up a hornet's nest."

CHAPTER 30

I grab one of the officer's guns and hand it to Harold as Gabe looks at me nervously. "Uh, Are you sure about that?" Gabe concernedly questions.

"He'll shoot himself before he shoots us. Besides, we could use the extra help," I say.

"I've never killed a man before," Harold says, shaking.

"Well, you have my permission to now," I say.

Harold sticks his bulbous head around the corner to get a look at what we are about to be up against. "Are you kidding me? There's like thirty officers down the hall," he says. His face has grown pale.

I load a fresh clip in my gun and hand Gabe my cloak while Harold's eyes grow wide as he stares at my swords. "Who the hell are you, the Grim Reaper?" he asks.

"Close," Gabe answers.

"I got this," I say.

"Got what? Does she have a death wish or something?" Harold says.

Before I draw forth my fury, Gabe hands me a flash bomb. I take a deep breath, then turn the corner and unleash hell. I arm the flash grenade and toss it in the middle of the carpeted floor as I wait for chaos to ensue.

The intense flash of blinding light temporarily disorients the officers long enough for me to empty round after round, killing everything in my path until the clip runs dry. I turn the corner to see more officers staggered down the next hall as I pull my second pair of guns. One by one, I take them down, but in the chaos of flying bullets, my shoulder is grazed.

I hold back behind a metal filing cabinet, and press lightly on my upper arm that's bleeding. The pain is agonizing, but I must press on. About a minute later, six more men carefully walk through the mass of bodies lying on the floor. I hold my breath as they pass by me, while I take out two of the black widow throwing knives.

As they look around, I stand behind them, ready to toss the blades in their necks. These are obviously not the best-trained officers, or they would have sensed I was hiding and never turned their backs.

I quickly look behind me before I move forward. I clasp the two blades together to get their attention. When they turn around, I fling the black steel knives into their chests. I immediately grimace at the stinging pain in my left shoulder. The men stagger backwards, struggling to grab their guns, and giving me no other option but to finish them. I rush forward and leap onto the end of the couch arm and eject the two blades from my boots. Gravity quickly sends me and my heavy-bladed boots falling down onto the men with the tips of the sharpened steel piercing their eye sockets. As the two men fall back, I fall hard with them. I quickly retract the knives from their eyes and tumble over to the side before I'm left standing to face the lone officer left.

He has no gun, but is armed with a long, shiny, serrated stiletto. He's a strong brute, towering at least a foot over me, and he doesn't seem to be intimidated at all. I drop back in my stance far enough to draw one of my swords. I tilt the polished blade slightly to the left, and I get a glimpse of why this man is so confidently arrogant. Right behind me stands another officer with his gun drawn toward my back.

I inch my hand down and grip the handle of the dagger hanging on my left thigh.

"I do not fear you. You'll have to strike me down with your sword before I move," the officer brags with confidence.

I quickly crouch down and sling the dagger at the man behind me, directly into the upper part of his chest. He drops his gun and holds his chest, before falling to his knees in excruciating pain. I twist the blade twice back and forth before I pull straight up to his neck and out.

When I turn back around to the tall overconfident officer, his eyes grow wide with fear and his brows feverishly crinkle. "So be it," I say. I aggressively move forward and strike across the man's gut, sending him in misery to his knees. For whatever twisted impulse that has stained my heart, it has now grown with hatred. I pull my other sword from my back, and scissor-cut his neck, decapitating him.

Gabe passes from the corner of the hall as he watches the man's head roll in front of him. Harold follows at a distance behind Gabe as he lurches over in disgust when he enters the hall into a sea of red. "Oh my God, what have you done? You . . . you did this, these bodies, this blood. I can't believe what you did," Harold says, stuttering in absolute shock. "I think I'm gonna be sick." He bends over and vomits in the potted plant beside him.

"Come on, this way," I say, walking toward the next hall where the elevators are. One lone man at the corner of the intersecting hall raises his hand up and moans for help as he writhes on the floor, suffering in pain. His wounds are too fatal for help, so I shoot him in the head as we pass by, which prompts another episode of vomiting from Harold.

I'm not sure what awaits us when we exit to the second floor, but it can't be any worse than what we just witnessed. The elevator doors open to an empty but luxurious hall, and the only thing that awaits us is the high ringing sound of champagne glasses clinking together and the chattering ambiance of a soiree.

I tell Gabe to watch from a distance near the west side of the winding stairs for any unwanted officers that may be left overlooking the party. From the balcony, I carefully peruse the guests below, but I see no other officers in sight; in fact, it's strangely unsecured for such a prestigious dinner party—at the White House, no less.

It's hard to believe all these well-dressed guests back such a wicked government, knowing they will inherit the rewards from their support. Forget that this country is dying if not already dead, as long as they are taken care of, nothing else matters to them. Wealthy constituents seem to breed a common façade when interacting on behalf of their monetary endeavors. I look over to Gabe as he nods the okay, while Harold stands behind me, trembling.

As President Kriel mingles with his guests, a couple of waiters roll out a food cart with an exquisite, marble-frosted cake that reads: *New World*. President Kriel taps a table knife against the top portion of his champagne glass to get everyone's attention.

"To the future of our hopes and dreams. Tonight we rebirth a new nation, a new law, and a new hope," he says, holding his glass toward the guests. "Now who is going to cut the cake?"

I pull out one of my daggers and sling it down into the middle of the gorgeous cake. "Shall I save you a corner piece?" I say, standing next to the second floor balcony.

The President's brows fuse together above his wretched scowl. "Who the hell do you think you are coming in—"

"Shhhhh," I interrupt him. "I think you already know. I'm the person you want on your side," I say, walking down the curved steps to the first floor.

Everyone stops drinking their champagne and quickly becomes silent.

"You think you can just walk in here, in the White House uninvited, and threaten me without being noticed?" he asks.

"Yep," I simply say as I pull the dagger from the cake.

I pinch the back of the blade and run my two fingers down the edge, wiping clean the blood from the last victim. I sling the blood onto the cake along with whatever other blood is dripping from my sleeve. "You seem to have very clumsy officers and untrained guards employed by you. You might want to reconsider hiring someone else. It appears you have a bunch of openings now," I say with extreme sarcasm.

The fire in his eyes glows with hatred, as he rolls his fists tight and grits his teeth.

"Arena, look out!" Gabe shouts from the stairs. I turn to my left as a guest falls to the floor with half his head blown off, and a gun still firmly tucked in his hand. People scream and panic, but they sit still, afraid they might be the next one to fall. Gabe may have just saved my life by killing this man who failed to shoot me.

I address the crowd with anger fueling my blood. "You people disgust me. You smile and fill your glasses with delusions of grandeur, hiding behind the very evil that stands before you, and delight in this man's fallacious tongue. A veracious man he isn't. You honor a man who breathes heresy. You sing praise to the one who has scorned this nation and burned its freedoms. Murdering, starving, and even raping our own people. And for what—money, power, glorified control? You people fall no further from blame than he does. You support a man spawned from wickedness by giving him money that he so graciously accepts. He has bled the country dry, and too many of us are too broken to stand against such devilish greed."

Right then, three officers barrel through the front doors with guns drawn as a last rush of defense. I kneel down beside President Kriel and shoot two in the head while Gabe takes out the third. Everyone lays down on the floor in massive panic, screaming.

"I want you all to remember this moment when you wake from your nightmares sweating and screaming. The law of man will not stand alone, but the law of the Lord will last forever. He made you and He will destroy you, but if it's redemption you seek, I suggest you take this rare opportunity and run home, pray to your Maker, and hope He shows mercy on your souls, because right now, I'm not feeling so merciful," I say.

Everyone just stares at each other in confusion, so I try to make it easier for them when I shout. "Now!" I say, pointing my gun at the man standing to the left of me. Everyone quickly stands up and runs out the front door, screaming.

I place my gun back in my jacket and draw my swords toward President Kriel. I eagerly pace behind him and kick the back of his legs until he is on his knees.

"It doesn't matter what you do with me, you can't stop the future of this nation," he says.

"This nation has no future, but death. Planning an invasion won't solve your problems," I say.

"It matters not, the invasion will happen with or without me. War is imminent in this world—it's what sustains fear, and that fear is what breeds cultural indifference, which is why this nation was once powerful in its own glory and will be again," he promises.

"War brings death to all who do not respect it; there is no victor in conflict until all have succumbed to the truth."

"And what is that?"

"The only victor in war is the one who doesn't wage it," I say.

"I've led this nation with great honor and dignity, and you come here to degrade my integrity with your threats. I am your President, and I head this country, not you. Killing me will not solve the world's problems."

"No, but it's a start." I slide both swords from his neck, leaving his body headless.

Harold walks down the staircase in bewilderment, while Gabe checks the front door for more officers.

"Come on, Harold," I say, grabbing his arm, "you're not done yet, I need one more favor. Do you have a car?" He just stares into space. "Do you have a car?" I ask again, trying to shake him back into coherence.

"Y–yes . . . it's around the corner," he says, stuttering.

"Go get it and meet us out by the fence in front of the fountain," I say.

"What?"

"Just do it!"

We carefully go outside on the north lawn toward the fountain where Finnegan is supposed to meet us. As we thoroughly observe our surroundings, we notice a number of dead officers spread out on the well-manicured grass. One hangs from a tree on the west side, and several decorate the steps we just passed, their blood painting the white columns red.

As we come to front of the fountain, I see Finnegan on the other side, but no trace of Henry except for his jacket that is resting over the side and into the water. I glance over to the right and see a trail of blood that leads around the fountain, so I carefully follow it. Lying against the white stones is Henry—unconscious.

CHAPTER 31

I clasp my chest as my stomach sinks. Finnegan kneels down and carefully puts his ear above Henry's mouth and nose. "He's still breathing," says Finnegan.

I quickly kneel down beside Finnegan looking for exit wounds on Henry's body, and while tearing his shirt back, we discover a bullet wound in his right shoulder. It's nothing too serious, but enough to have knocked him off his feet and slam the back of his head against the stone wall of the fountain.

Blood dribbles out the backside of his head, rendering him unconscious, but the cut isn't deep enough to have cracked his skull.

Suddenly, Harold's car comes screeching toward the front of the lawn. We carefully, but quickly pick Henry up, and carry him over the small fence and into Harold's car.

I race over to the Camaro parked on the other side of the street, and swing open the door. Crouched down in the back seat is Juliana.

"We need your help, Henry's been shot," I say panting.

I quickly reach in the back of the trunk and grab the first aid kit.

"You and Gabe stay with Henry while I go with Finnegan," I say to Juliana.

"What do you want me to do?" asks Harold.

"Follow us. We need to get as far away as we can from the city. This place will soon be swarming with soldiers."

Finnegan pulls out a syringe from the first aid kit and sucks in one mg of Epinephrine into it. He stabs the needle into Henry's upper thigh and pumps the adrenal medication into his bloodstream. Soon after, Henry wakes up in shock, mumbling Julian's name over and over as he looks around, disoriented.

Finnegan snaps his fingers repeatedly in front of Henry's face until he resurfaces to reality. "We need to get some fluids in him as quickly as possible; this adrenaline won't last long," says Finnegan.

Henry's eyes begin to refocus, and a grin grows from the corners of his mouth. "Arena," he says as he tries to sit up, but quickly wobbles back.

"I'm here, you're going to be okay, just sit back. You've lost some blood, but you're alive."

"And Juliana?" he asks.

"I'm right here, Henry," Juliana says, holding his hand.

"We need to get the hell out of here." I urge.

"I need to dress these wounds now. Blood is still trickling from the bullet hole and infection is likely," she warns.

"Just make it quick." Watching Juliana nurse Henry's wounds is just another reason why Gabe is so blessed to have her around.

We leave the Capitol broken and abandoned, yet another scar hanging from the government's ego. Though the administration lives on, its weakened armor is now stained with blood. Night begins to fall as we drive into the twilight, and I sit back, wondering if I have changed my fate, because the only ambition I have left in me is to kill or be killed.

The skies draw back, and blackness covers over us like a blanket. The only glimmer of light are the few various pinholes in space shining brightly upon the world below, reminding us how small we really are and how great our God is. It's not until we reach a small remote town in the middle of nowhere that I begin to wonder how Niki and Father Joseph are holding up. I don't think I've missed two people more in my life than them right now, but I fear having to go back and share the unfortunate news about Myra to Niki.

Before I fall back into a deep slumber, we find an old, uninviting motel just off the road to take refuge in for the night. There's nothing appealing about this place except the warm water it brings and the semi-soft mattresses for our tired bodies to lie on. It's a measurable step up from the den's less-than-desirable sleeping quarters, but I'd rather camp out on the dusty floor and risk being bitten by a spider then lay in one of these lice-infested beds. Of course, the televisions in both rooms do not work, but I wouldn't have expected anything different.

Henry's wounds are redressed and a dose of antibiotics from Finnegan's survival kit is given to him. With every drop of liquid and morsel of food Henry takes in, his body strengthens and recoups. While everyone takes rest for the night, I keep myself awake, afraid I may drift back into some dark realm that haunts my soul.

Whatever malevolence lurks among us, it knows my fears, and it will waste no opportunity to tempt my spirit. I can bear no more pain from my past, and if it is hope that this evil seeks to devour, then I will seek refuge in my Lord, for only He has the power to protect my heart from turning against me now. With the death of President Kriel, my burdens have lightened, but my anxieties have not lifted. Iakov still haunts me, and until he is dead, I will not be satisfied. As much as I want to believe the end is nearing, the president is only but a small taste of evil that has left us. Though Kriel is dead, it's Iakov that stands in my way from caring.

I leave the others at peace while I wander outside into the deep thicket of green to gather my own serenity. Even with all the creatures of the night surrounding me in the dark woods, I still feel tranquility and the calm I can rest in as I pray out to my Lord. I find a small clearing just beyond a wall of mighty oaks that stand with old age, courage, and a history of stories untold.

Their gnarled cracks, and knotting, twisted roots run deep beneath the earth, keeping them steady and wise. They seem like giants hovering over and shading the young saplings that surround them below. It reminds me of young children sitting around in the night air, listening to stories of the past from the wise elders who brought them into the world. These woods are aged, mysterious, and have an obscurity about them that I cannot unfold. I can feel the rising dark breathe within my space of stillness as the shadows beyond the oaks dance with hellish delight, attempting to disengage me from my Father.

I cry out, asking Him to ease my burdens that I can no longer bear. My tired, worn body has emerged from the brokenness most can't endure, but the pain has still been unforgiving—yet I cringe at even the thought of complaining about my own sufferings. Christ suffered more for me than I could ever imagine. Why my malcontent should be justified is purely nonsensical at best.

"Father, forgive me, I give you all I have to offer. I give you my heart, my mind, and my soul. Please, Father, I beg of you, to give me the strength to carry on this fight. I feel weary and broken, yet you have still given me the comfort to find rest in. I shall not give in nor turn from your favor. Protect me, dear Father. As long as my able body is willing to, I will stand firm by my convictions and praise your holy name, but I don't know how much more of this I can take. I fear this fight will endure to the bloody end until I break and I take my last dying breath. I beg you, Father . . . take me from this. Please take me from this now . . ."

I bury my head into my hands, sobbing, and into the night I kneel for hours, seeking refuge until I'm oblivious to my surroundings. I soon fall asleep with the light of the moon shining down on me while the rest of the darkness that surrounds me anxiously waits for me to give in to temptation.

*　　*　　*

The morning light shines through the small, tangled branches and its golden leaves reflect onto my eyelids, but before the rays shine in my eyes, I remove my shivering body from the grassy earth, realizing I have fallen asleep in the woods.

The cool fall breeze brushes through my hair and against my skin, persuading me to find warmth indoors. By the time my eyes fully open, I'm paralyzed by what is set before me—encircling the small clearing is the smell of decaying carrion of all kinds. Beasts large and small lie dead before me outside where I have lain for the night. I hold my heart in shock while vultures tear into the rotting meat, and yet I find not one scratch from these creatures on my body. Even the wound on my arm has shockingly disappeared.

Before I nervously retreat back to the others, a crow proudly perched on a small branch of one of the oak trees stares into my eyes as if to intimidate me. The bird looks at me as if it knows my thoughts. While he caws an unpleasant tune from his perch, I pick up a small stone and throw it toward the feathered creature. He dodges the rock and flies onto another branch, still staring at me, as if to mock my actions.

I look deep into those black, emotionless eyes while maggots slither beneath its wings. As my body draws closer to his cackling taunts, my spine shivers with fright, and the trees begin to moan around me. The breeze rustling through the leaves suddenly comes to a dead calm, a stillness of which only death knows. My eyes are in a trance now, fixed upon this feathered demon, as it whispers my name through the dead silence, convincing me to taste its blood.

I draw my gun toward the wretched fowl, but then I remember what Finnegan always told me—never shoot a bird unless food was scarce enough that it was needed. And that God created these singing creatures for our delight, but that any one of the black, devilish birds without a song to sing was fair game. This one seems to have gotten my attention and intentionally rustled a nerve, but instead I withdraw my weapon and ignore the mischievous fowl. Before I walk away, I'm tempted to get one last look into those stale, black eyes, but the crow disappears and I leave, almost having foolishly fallen for his deceit.

While everyone else is still asleep back at the motel, I take advantage of the warm amenities and let my bruised body take healing under a hot shower. I nearly fall asleep standing up under the inviting water, reflecting back on the paths I've chosen and the decisions I've made. I realize the plans set before me will not change unless I choose to reject my own fate.

Without warning, I begin to weep, and my thoughts cry out to my mother, hoping she will hear my silent voice through all the cluttering noise that plagues my mind. Just the small touch of her hand always comforted my ailing heart.

Though I'm tempted to move on and end these haunted thoughts of Iakov, we decide to extend our stay at the motel at least another day, long enough for Henry to recoup from his small head injury and wounded shoulder before trekking any further.

I realize this journey has taken a toll on everyone, but I have no intentions of returning to the den until I know Iakov is dead. Even if I have to go in alone, I will not stop. My hatred for him I fear has consumed me, and I'm not sure I can live another moment knowing he's alive. Tomorrow I must reveal my plan, and I can only hope they will understand.

CHAPTER 32

What would seem like another sleepless night turns out to be the only night I can remember where I fell asleep before everyone else. I quickly fall into a deep rest beyond my normal dreams and into a world of sedated suspense.

I find myself lying in an empty field, my stomach bulging, and my hands stained red. Speared into the black soil next to me my dagger drips with blood. I'm slightly disoriented until the cry from an infant screams from my womb as my loins begin to burn.

I struggle to reach over my swollen belly to examine my nightmare, while the excruciating labor lingers. The pain feels so real, I'm almost reluctant to dismiss it as a dream.

When I hear the shrill cry from my loins once more, I force myself over and grab the bloody infant hanging from its cord. Suddenly the empty field is swallowed up by darkness and a faceless man stands before me dressed in black with an ax at hand. I grab the dagger next to me, and attempt to swing at him, but I find myself swinging at the air in my bed as I awaken from this hellish night terror.

I escape the stuffy motel room and take a walk outside in the brisk morning air to clear my mind. I retreat to the back of the building where I find Gabe sitting in the car. I'm still slightly disturbed by the nightmare, but I'm too puzzled by his seclusion from the others, so I join him.

He doesn't say a word while I'm in the car until I speak to him in Gaelic. It's the only time Gabe and I can connect with each other without the intrusion of the outside world distracting us—it has become our secret language that binds our spirits.

"You know I trust in you, my dear brother. No matter what happens, remember that our fate led us here," I say in Irish.

"What then? Would you have chosen a different path if you were not called?" Gabe asks.

"I choose to believe. That's what sets us apart from those who have nothing to live for."

"You're going to kill him aren't you?"

"You know I have to."

"When will it end? Why can't you just let it go?"

"And let Iakov continue to kill innocent people?"

"And what about the others, how are they going to feel about it?"

"I will not have Juliana suffer through this. She doesn't deserve to be a part of war we started. I'll have Henry take her back to the den where she will be safe. Finnegan will understand."

"And Harold?"

"This fight is not with him. He can choose his own path."

"We're not going to survive this, are we?" Gabe asks with tears running down his cheek. Right then, I realize the true sacrifice that separates us from our souls.

"Look what we've made of this world. Do we really deserve to live?"

"I just can't understand all of this madness."

"I know it's hard, but we were never meant to comprehend everything. Sometimes you just have to leave it for Him."

"I don't know how I can."

"If you don't, you'll just end up doubting your convictions."

"I think I'd rather be dead."

"Remember when Mom would tell us that people fear what they don't understand?"

"Yeah."

"Well, it's that fear that makes us vulnerable to our sins."

"Then I fear it has consumed me."

"We worry too much about the things we can't explain, and when it's time to live life, it has become too late."

"And now?"

"And now . . . I believe it will only rob us the tomorrow we could have had today. It serves no purpose; it is but a separation between our spirit and our flesh." Gabe leans back in the seat with his eyes closed. Whether or not he wants to hear the truth, there's something deeper that troubles him. When I search his face, all I see is unrest. I feel the pain in his heart as I hold his limp shivering hand.

"I may never see Juliana again, will I?" Gabe asks.

I'm buried too deep in my own personal conflictions that I just simply don't know how to answer his question. I want him to feel better, but I don't want to give him a false sense of hope either, so I'm just honest with him.

"I don't know."

CHAPTER 33

The morning fades away into the cool afternoon and our departure has come to pass. Though my plan is to go alone inside the training facility, I tell no one—even Gabe. Very few times have I kept a secret from him, but this time I must. Though he may understand, I know no one else will. All they need to know is that we're going into that facility with guns a-blazing. I will fill them on the details later.

I sit everyone down in the motel room and explain our course of action. Henry understands and accepts his duty to take Juliana back to the den to recoup and wait for our return. It takes more convincing for Juliana to accept our decision, so I give her and Gabe some time alone to say their good-byes.

"I don't understand why this has to continue. I thought this was over," Juliana says, weeping.

"Until Iakov is dead, I will not find peace," I say. "Your obsession over this man will be the death of you."

"Our Journey has just begun, and it's only over when we are called to finish it," I say.

"And when is that? When you die?" asks Juliana.

I stand there in silence, because she may have already answered her own question. I watch painfully as she hangs onto Gabe with uncertainty. I give her some comforting but promising words to temporarily soothe her as I strap up my gear. "You will see him again, I promise."

"And as for you," I say to Finnegan.

"You know you can't keep me from coming with you," he says.

"I had no intention to. I need you for this."

"I'll fight with you until the end," he says as he loads his gun. Unfortunately, there is more truth to the words he speaks than the idea behind them, but now is not the time to start worrying about Finnegan. I just try to keep my focus solely on Iakov.

"Harold, you're free to make your own decisions. This fight is not with you."

He racks his gun back and smiles, "I'm with you."

Before we leave the motel, I gaze upon the faces around me, and wonder how much longer we can survive. I feel slightly disconnected from their fellowship because I know I may not come out of this alive.

We're only about forty miles from the outer realm of the training facility where we're headed, which makes the thirty-minute drive excruciating for Gabe and Juliana. The closer in we get, the tighter Juliana hangs on to Gabe. The anxiety of waiting in silence is excruciating.

When we are about a mile outside the training compound, I decide it's time to introduce my plan. "Stop the car here," I say.

"What is it, Arena?" asks Finnegan.
"The time has come," I say as I turn to address every- one. "This is where we part our ways. From here, I go in alone."

Everyone looks at me like I'm crazy, except for Gabe. I don't want to be responsible for their deaths if I can help it, especially Juliana, who doesn't deserve to suffer the anguish Gabe and I have been chosen for. My conscience just can't bear any more.

"She's right," agrees Gabe, "no one will be looking for us. Their attention is solely on Arena now."

"I need to go in alone. General Iakov wants me alive, and it's the only way I will be able to face him."

"This is suicide," says Finnegan.

"So what do you want from us?" Harold asks.

"I find Iakov. You find me," I say, as I hold up a small, pill-sized device.

"Brilliant," says Gabe.

"What is it?" Juliana asks.

"It's a tracking device," says Gabe.

We get out of the car, and Gabe pulls me to the side far enough away where no one can hear us. "Arena, you can't attach that to your clothes, you're going to have to swallow it. What if it falls off your jacket, or . . ." He pauses a second. "Look, Iakov is an evil man—you've seen the things he is capable of doing. What if he tries to . . ."

I understand what my brother is alluding to; the thought of my clothes being stripped off my body so I can be sexually tortured by that man shakes my confidence.

"I won't allow it to come to that," I assure Gabe. "You just better be ready when I need you." I swallow the tiny device and embrace him one last time before I say good-bye.

"Wait," says Finnegan, "take this with you."

"What is this for?" I ask, holding the pill.

"Just in case."

"In case what?"

"Should you get yourself in a compromising situation, don't hesitate to take it." I'm a bit confused. "This pill will bide you some time and delay any sedatives that may be forced on you. There may be some hallucinogenic side effects, but it will at least numb the pain if you need it." he says as he hugs me.

"Thanks, Finnegan, for everything you've taught me." I put the pill in my front jacket pocket and walk over to Henry.

"You promise me you will take Juliana back to the den, okay?" I ask Henry. He nods, looking at me like he's wondering if he will ever see me again.

I stand there for a moment, staring at the people I love. When I see Juliana, I think back to the very first day Gabe and I met her in the cafeteria. She was sitting there all alone, quiet, and not knowing the instant crush Gabe had for her. Seems like many moons ago I was starting my first day of high school, trying to avoid making enemies for the year—I guess nothing has changed.

I watch Juliana hold Gabe, delaying the inevitable, as it has come time that we sever our fellowship.

As Henry and Juliana drive away in Harold's car, Gabe stands there with a guarded heart, trying to keep his composure. I walk over and put my arm around him. "I'll get you back home to her . . . that's a promise."

Instead of taking the front road, I find a rocky but quick passage through the woods that will be less conspicuous. This will be the shortest path that will lead me through this thicket to the front gates. It seems a bit of an obstacle, but I've traversed terrain much worse.

Just across the ditch into the thick woods, a steep ravine with rocky soil leads to the somewhat-level ground below. I gracelessly scale down the side of the stony cliff with boots not made for hiking. Step by step, gripping jagged rocks, the soil breaks beneath my me, making an otherwise easy climb a difficult descent.

I finally make it down the side of the hill and onto flatter ground, where I'm greeted by a field of prickly thistles and thorny briar patches. If this is fertile soil, it's a hot breeding bed of everything that's completely opposite of beauty and purpose. The only things worth seeing are the tall eastern white pines and the few sporadic sycamore trees that make up most of the dense forest.

Behind a twisted thicket of brush, a commercial fence stands tall enough to keep out unwanted predators, which in this case includes me. I'm not much for sightseeing when I'm on the hunt, but I can't help to take in the beauty of a rare bald eagle stately perched on the rugged fence.

The irony of this majestic bird that once represented freedom for this country balances on a barrier created by the same government who has destroyed the will to be free. This marvelous creature before me teeters on the brink of the unholy on one side and the freedom to believe on the other. The near extinction of this magnificent bird has been dying along with this nation, and it would only be fitting to just go ahead and kill him. This country is already dead.

It's the persecution and horrendous affliction by the government on its own people that's so besetting.

I try not to disturb the conflicted eagle, so I walk down a little further and choose a different spot to climb over the fence. By the time I get to the next open field, I'm already within a hundred yards of the training compound. I can see the front entrance from here, and only two guards seem to be tending the gates, but by the looks of the four cameras resting atop the gated entrance, there really is no need for any more guards. This compound is tightly monitored and probably filled with teams of killing machines inside.

A lone camera attached to a tree rotates near ninety degrees back and forth, panning the outside area where I'm standing. They are going to know I'm here soon enough, but I try to make it a little harder for them to see me right away. I'm not sure I can squeeze off a round this far away to take out the panning camera, so I decide to take a shot with my bow.

I pull back an arrow and wait patiently until the camera pans back away from me before firing. I release the arrow, but it only knocks the camera off its hanger, and it dangles toward the ground. I shoot one more arrow into the side of the camera, cutting it loose from its wires and from the tree.

I wait under abated breath for a response. By now the picture on one of their screens is lost. They may or may not send someone to check it out, but I'm willing to wait anyhow. Just as I turn my head, one of the guards heads in my direction where the camera has fallen on the ground.

He examines the damage, then suddenly looks up in the tree, where he spots the first arrow I shot. He quickly pulls his gun and carefully moves forward. I try not to waste any bullets, so I draw another arrow from my quiver as quietly as possible and rest it on the bow shelf, pulled back and ready to release it into the air.

The guard calls on a radio about the arrow, but before he can get out a full sentence, I swing around and fire the arrow directly into his neck. It fails to pierce his artery, so I finish him off with my dagger. I grab his earpiece and hear someone trying to contact him. I take the radio receiver and creep up toward the gate, expecting the other guard to abandon his post to see what's taking so long.

"Ellis, what is your status?" asks a voice on the radio.

"It's probably just a bad signal where he is, sir. That area can be spotty sometimes," answers another man in the background. Apparently, the transmitter from their side is left on, because I can hear their whole conversation.

"Sir, should I call for maintenance?" asks the operator.

"We'll have it checked out later; it's probably just a squirrel chewing on the wires again. We're about to start the training exercise," another man says.

"That's no damn squirrel, Lieutenant," says a voice I now recognize as General Iakov.

"Sir, I assure you, we have had squirrel issues before with the outside cameras," reaffirms the lieutenant.

"Have the other guard go check it out," orders Iakov. I load another arrow, then creep up closer to the entrance, avoiding the four cameras on the front gate walls. Heavy footsteps trudge around the corner, dragging across the dirt. My palms sweating, I eagerly fire into the guard's chest about twenty yards away. Not my best shot, but damaging nevertheless.

He staggers back and hangs onto the front gate bars. I sling another arrow into him, this time to the heart.

His body clings wearily against the gate just below the cameras, exposing his limp body to whoever is watching.

"Jesus Christ!" the operator yells out. "Lieutenant, since when do squirrels carry bow and arrows?" Iakov angrily belittles.

"Sir, I had no idea . . ." says the lieutenant.

"You rarely do, but I know this squirrel, and she's not getting away today."

"Call the exercise off now!" the lieutenant shouts.

"Hold that order, Corporal. Let's just see how finely tuned your men are, Lieutenant. Commence with the exercise as planned," Iakov demands.

Well, they know I'm here now. I guess I didn't come in here alone for nothing.

I pick up the guard's gun and aim for the front cameras, taking out each one and hoping Finnegan and the others won't be exposed when they come to get me.

"Sir, we have lost all visual on the front entrance," a voice says.

I search around the guards' post to see if there is anything useful I might need. The gate booth is pristine and in order, but there's nothing I see that can be of help. I hear static on the radio, so I switch the channels on the receiver until I pick up a clear signal. I turn around and notice a computer screen light up when I back up into it. Nothing of interest catches my eye except the instant messaging chat log at the bottom of the screen. I scroll up to see nothing but a mindless log chat between the guard and the tower operator when suddenly I hear a voice over one of the channels giving orders:

"Sergeant, we are in position ready to proceed. Private, flank your men to the west barracks two-by-two and wait for my signal, it's going to be dark in here."

With the training exercise started, I'm anxious to get the hell out of here, but this may just be my ticket inside the complex. Before I leave the post, I type in a message in the chat log: *your guards took an early retirement*. That should rustle some feathers.

To the east side of the compound are brick walls about ten feet high staggered throughout a large open area. To the west of me is a large group of clay and brick buildings clustered together like small bungalows in a village. Some are uncovered, exposed to the hot sun, while most have roofs.

I look up and around for any cameras before I go running toward the west side of the compound. I suddenly see a shadow appear behind the far side of the cluster of bungalows, so I quickly hide in one of the small covered buildings. The floors are made of compact desert sand, and the walls are almost thin enough to punch my fist through.

There's an exposed corner of the shack that has been damaged, revealing wire mesh and cheap plaster. I'm guessing they were trying to reconstruct a small village resembling that in some Middle Eastern country. Glass jars and rags are spread out on a table near one of the walls, and straw baskets with stickers that say "Made in China" decorate the corners of the room. Yeah, I feel just like I'm in an Iraqi village.

I hear a boot grazing against the sand just behind the open door, but there is nowhere to hide and I'm completely uncovered in the open room. I haven't time to think because I was so engaged in the stupid décor of the room and left myself exposed. I tense up as I see the barrel of a gun protruding from the side of the entry ready to strike me down. I can shoot through the wall, killing the soldier, but I don't know how many more are around the corner waiting to run in and gash me. For once, I feel vulnerable.

CHAPTER 34

I aimlessly look around for a way out of this situation, but I can't think straight, so I just draw my guns and try to shoot anything that moves in front of the doorway. Before I pull the triggers, I glance down at the table and it suddenly comes to me as I withdraw my guns. I quickly grab one of the rags on the table and sit down on a worn wooden chair near the middle of the room. I tie the rag around my head, sticking the rag in my mouth, and place my hands behind the chair just as two men come in the room, pointing their guns at me.

"What is this?" one of the soldiers asks.

"S1 to squad leader, we have a civilian in custody," the lead soldier says as he radios back.

"Is this part of the exercise?" another soldier asks.

"Bring the survivor back to base," orders a voice on the radio.

The two men withdraw their guns, hang them on their shoulders, and give me a limited but otherwise manageable option. The leader closes in on me, and I quietly grab my dagger behind my back. The darkness of the room is the only thing saving me from the men noticing my weapons.

"Hey, wait! She's armed," the man shouts. I jump up from the chair with full force and thrust my dagger into the soldier's neck. He falls to the ground while the other soldier pulls his rifle toward me. His gun immediately locks up, giving me a brief, but timely moment to draw my gun and shoot. He falls dead, but not before the bolt catch unjams and fires off a couple of rounds.

Soldier's boots, beating the floor, race down the left passage in response to the gunfire. Just as the soldiers rush in through the entrance, I turn the injured man around, grabbing his arm, and pulling his finger back that is still firmly attached to the trigger on his gun. Round after round, I empty the magazine as six men drop dead in front of me, not expecting live fire return on them.

I stand there feeling a little more confident now, knowing that these men are fully unaware of a live enemy in this makeshift maze of tunnels. Static on the radio buzzes again, so I quickly change the channel until I find another signal. I can just barely make out the general's voice in the background.

I pick up one of the soldier's guns and proceed out the door, but as I look over the entryway, I notice a very small camera staring right at me. I realize I'm now at a disadvantage, that there are probably hundreds of cameras positioned in hidden areas throughout this training field.

"Is this what you had in mind?" I provoke to the camera before I destroy it. I'm sure to stoke a fire now, brewing inside the general's head.

I move down to one of the left tunnels as fast as I can to the outer part on the far west side before any more soldiers show up. I come up to a small opening where light is visible from the outside. I slowly approach the end of the passage when I recognize another shadow on the wall parallel to the window outside.

I crouch down underneath the window and pull my dagger close to my side. As the soldier peers through the window, I quickly jab the dagger in the side of his jaw and pull him inside, throwing him to the floor. Right then, two more soldiers round the corner. I pull my guns and swiftly shoot both at the same time in the head. I can hear voices bickering back and forth on the static radio signal. I carefully move down the hall and the signal becomes clearer every step.

"Now at what point do your men take out the enemy?" Iakov says.

"Sir, I assure you, this is the most highly trained military group we have put together. They are trained to do one thing and one thing only—kill," the lieutenant says.

"Yes, well Lieutenant, your highly trained men appear to be distracted by a fifteen-year-old girl killing them," says the irate general.

I move against the wall where the sunlight isn't shining through and try to hide in the shadow. I find a dark corner that's hidden in obscurity next to an open window that leads into another room. I stay buried in the shadow for a while, leaving myself an option to bolt into the other room if I'm forced to.

A lone soldier deep down the south corridor carefully shuffles from side to side, shifting his bobbled head back and forth, anticipating an attack. My back clings to the tattered wall, hiding in the dark crevice unseen. I quietly retract my bow and carefully rest an arrow against it. As I draw back the strings, the tip of the arrow just sticks out far enough into a small beam of light shining through the cracks of the roof, but the soldier is too far away to notice. I release the arrow, and it sails deep into his chest, piercing his heart. He falls dead to the ground.

I steadily hold my position a little longer and rest another arrow on the shelf of the bow. I keenly wait in anticipation to strike again.

A damp cool breeze swoops past and the patter of a chattering soldier flutters through the dark. My heartbeat races and my fingers cramp. I pull back, anxiously waiting for the next victim to expose themselves, when suddenly a voice muttering on another radio comes from the right of me. I withdraw the string and rethink my position, but another soldier down the long corridor has already spotted the arrow sticking out from the man's chest.

I now have two men to think about—one in my sight ready to kill with the bow, and one to my right who is too close for comfort.

Without any hesitation, I aim for the soldier who is kneeling by the dead man and release the arrow directly into his skull. I drop my bow, draw my guns, and pop off two rounds into the soldier to my right. Just then, two more soldiers at the end of the long passage spot me out in the open light and begin to shoot. I pick up my bow and lunge through the opening in the next room while gunshots fly past me, grazing the upper part of my jacket. The gunfire is too heavy for me to fire back through the window without getting hit, so I scramble around, looking for a way out of this room.

I suddenly feel a tingle in my arm. I look over and see a bloodstain growing wide. I guess the shock of being hit has worn off, because I begin to feel the throbbing discomfort now. I hold my arm up, resting it against my side as I grimace in pain.

I quickly look around and notice this room has a window but strangely, no door. I race around, desperately trying to kick in the walls, hoping to find a weak spot in the hardened clay, but I'm trapped. I search frantically around the room when I suddenly spot another camera protruding out from one of the corners.

The wires are exposed, hanging down and through the top of the wall where it meets the ceiling. A tiny bead of light shines where the wires have been installed, and a small ledge along the wall where the roof isn't attached. I step back a few paces and rush forward, jumping onto the ledge. I pull myself up and kick open the partial straw roof by the camera wires, then roll over to the other side of the adjoined room. My arm throbs a raging pulse of pain.

These rooms are really beginning to look the same, except this one has two entries: one leading to another long corridor, and the other that leads into a hall with a window accessing the outside of this tunnel of hell. I make a mental note of this room and the outside window before I head down the long corridor that leads to the north, closer to the main complex.

About halfway down the passage, I find a large crack in the wall. I lean against the side of the wall to catch my breath as I hear footsteps approaching in the distance in front of me and behind me.

The only spot left to hide is to my left in a small, dark crevice where the wall is split into an area large enough for me to squeeze my body through. I quickly conceal myself in the shaded corner, crouching down where the sun can't shine on me.

I impatiently wait for the men to pass, and the sound of their boots pressing against the hardened sand floor begins to diminish. Another group of soldiers is coming. I draw my guns, preparing to fire in both directions when the soldiers pass by. I try to calm myself to keep my breathing from being audible as the men get uncomfortably closer. Suddenly, the soldiers to my right stop in their tracks, and my heart races. My fingers firmly grip the triggers.

"Sir, should I call in reinforcements from zone three?" a voice on the radio asks.

"No, let them be. This is what we trained them for," says the lieutenant.

"Yes, and I train my dog not to shit on the carpet, but I don't see the need to have it repeated if I do nothing to correct him," Iakov so eloquently says.

"She's just a girl, sir. I'm sure my men can handle this one," says the lieutenant.

"Are you familiar with *The Mourning Bride* by William Congreve?" the general asks.

"No, sir," answers the lieutenant.

"Too bad, or you would have known that Hell hath no fury like a woman scorned."

Beads of sweat crawl down the sides of my temples as I brace myself for an all-out attack. A sudden burst of adrenaline surges through my veins. I cling to the darkness as long as I can, hoping I go unnoticed. I close my strained eyes tight and pray to my Father for protection before I'm forced to sacrifice my position and storm the hall with guns a-blazing.

The soldiers creep closer, and the tension increases in my muscles. It's not until I look down at the side of my pant leg that I notice a bulge protruding in the shape of a cylinder. I had completely forgotten about the thermal viewers Gabe gave me for my birthday back at the inn.

I quietly put my guns away, pull out the glasses from my pant leg, and reach to the side of my jacket to grab a smoke bomb hanging from a clip.

The silence finally breaks when the sound of the squad leader belligerently voices his concerns over the radio. "What the hell's going on in here, Sergeant? I've got three dead men back there, two of which have been pierced by arrows, ready to be stuffed and hung on a wall," he says.

"I guess we got a hunter among us, boys," the sergeant replies.

"No shit, and we're down here scurrying around like lab rats for our fearless leader while some rouge menace has decided to start playing cowboys and Indians," a man says.

"Get a grip, Private! Hold your position so I can keep you in view. We're coming toward you now," says the sergeant.

Before the pandemonium ensues, I unexpectedly find a serene moment to cling to while I firmly hold the smoke bomb and wait. When the sergeant's team closes in at about twenty feet, I pull the pin and release the smoke bomb out in the corridor. A sudden roar of voices scatters, and a ruckus of movement stirs about. Men are shouting back and forth while the tunnels quickly fill with plumes of gray. When I put the glasses on, I can now detect clear images of the soldiers through the smoke. I draw my swords, take a deep breath, and prepare for unmerciful carnage.

I leap out from the crevice and sweep to the left, cutting down the sergeant first. One by one, I slice into flesh as men blindly stagger around, trying to find a sense of direction. I dodge and duck, swinging violently and efficiently, taking out the sergeant's team within minutes. I trek back to the right, stepping over bodies still convulsing on the ground in shock until enough blood spills out, leaving them motionless.

With this small maze of buildings being almost completely covered, the smoke in the tunnel has clouded almost every passage within two hundred feet. Many of the soldiers to the right of me have already bolted, but most are still left trying to find their way in the thick plume of fog.

I rush through, swinging and gashing my way through the crowd of men, killing the last of the soldiers still standing in this corridor. As the smoke begins to dissipate, the cameras in the hall reveal a terrifying image of human butchery.

"This is what you have to offer me!" Iakov angrily shouts over the radio.

"Call 'em off now, Lieutenant! Have them route back to the northeast section out into the opening. If she wants them dead, she'll have to follow them. It's time to lure this snake out of its den. I want this bitch where I can see her!" yells the general.

I pick up the orders from the general on the earpiece and make the jaunt back toward the northeast corner. I'm fully aware of their intentions, and if it's the only way to see Iakov face to face, then so be it.

"Corporal, order the men to hold steady in flanking positions, and do not engage in any fire. Do you understand? Do not engage. I want this bitch alive before I break her," General Iakov says.

I race back on the outer corridors to make up time lost chasing them in the middle of these connected huts. As I pass the last connected building next to a lit uncovered opening, I get a small glimpse of the soldiers running parallel to me from a distance. I know I won't catch them from here, but I can at least keep them from escaping into the opening, which will piss Iakov off even more.

I draw an explosive-tipped arrow from my quiver and tuck it snug against the strings, while I sprint toward the southeast corner. About every ten steps I see a glimpse of the soldiers in-between the buildings, running. They start to pull away from me the closer I get to the eastern wall. I race past the final corner of the village with my bow pulled back, but when I try to stop, my momentum carries me forward, sliding on the loose dirt. Before I slam into the wall, I turn and fire the arrow toward the last of the soldiers exiting the premises. The entire northeast corner abruptly explodes in a cloud of red dust, and shattering limbs spread afar with explosive force.

My shoulder gives in with unforgiving agony, as I lie exhausted against the eastern wall. The right side of my ribs is tender from the collision, and my arm is badly scraped from the coarse ground. I'm not sure I have anything left, so I rest until the smoke clears.

"Jesus, who the hell is this girl?" says the operator.

"Sir, what makes you think she's going to come out?" the lieutenant asks.

"There's no one left to kill, John," Iakov answers. "Your elite force of killers have all been executed by a hormonal fifteen year old."

When the dust settles, I slowly exit the makeshift village with the last explosive-tipped arrow settled between my knuckles and nestled tightly in the strings. I walk out in the middle of the large open area, slightly wincing from my wounds. With whatever strength I have left, I raise my bow upward toward the tower, ready to fire, but a helicopter suddenly distracts my concentration. It hovers over the prison walls with guns loaded, pointing toward me.

I quickly switch my target from the tower to the chopper and let the arrow go free. The reaction time is a split second, and the helicopter has no time to react when the arrow explodes on contact, sending blasts of fire rising into the sky and pieces of steel falling to the ground. The back end of the chopper clips the high wall, knocking half of it to the ground, and the props spin out of control, knocking into the bottom half of the wall and the ground below. The spinning blades shatter into pieces, just grazing past my head as I fall to my knees with sheer fatigue. A dark plume of black fills the air above as fuel burns with intense heat; the fuselage begins to melt within minutes.

I rise to my feet and draw my swords one last time. I look toward the tower and stare deep into the dark glass that shades a rather irate General Iakov. Right then, hundreds of soldiers come rushing in front and to the sides of me, forming a line of attack.

The adrenaline pumping through my tired body has finally surrendered, and my fate has taken a toll through weathered emotions and calloused hands. Iakov and I stare at each other through the tower window, and we have a brief emotional standoff until I lower my arms, drop my swords to the ground, and fall to my knees.

"Nice to see we have some viable means to an end," General Iakov says. "Bring her in, and Lieutenant, I want her bound. Do you think your men can handle that simple task?"

"Yes, sir."

I take the earpiece off and realize I'm about to finally meet the man I desperately want dead.

About a half-dozen soldiers cautiously approach me, not sure of my intentions nor trusting my position. While still at gunpoint, two men forcefully pull back my arms and cuff me.

Lieutenant John walks toward me and looks upon my face with fear in his eyes, but he's still disgustedly angry. With a cold, stony stare piercing deep into my eyes, he removes his leather gloves and slaps me with unforgiving antipathy across the face. The sting of the leather numbs my jaw momentarily, but is shortly replaced by the backside of the lieutenant's hand punching my face and splitting my lip. He smiles while blood drips from my mouth.

"You're mortal after all," he says, rubbing the blood off his knuckles. "He's waiting for you."

I turn my head up and spit whatever blood has filled up in my mouth at the lieutenant's face. He heatedly wipes his cheek and draws back his fists, possessed with anger.

"Lieutenant! Stand down your place!" shouts General Iakov from a distance.

Lieutenant John firmly stays in his pose, guarded with reverential hatred. "That's an order!" Iakov yells. The lieutenant retreats back to the line, while General Iakov stands there with his silver eyes gleaming from the shadows toward me. He takes a step forward, revealing his long, jagged face and menacing scowl that can only be drawn by a man of incomprehensible hatred. His eyes glow like that of a wolf in the night. His physique is of a soldier bred for battle. Only the gray in his hair and scars on his face hint at his age.

"Take her to my chambers and prepare the infirmary."

CHAPTER 35

I'm taken through the main complex to an elevator that shuttles us down two floors beneath the ground. I'm then thrown into a small glass chamber the size of a closet that quickly fills with gas, most likely a sedative. I guess theydon't trust me enough to use the traditional needle method.

I drop to the floor, my face painfully stings, and my bruised body agonizingly aches. I hold my breath as long as I can while I desperately try to shake out the pill from the pocket on the top of my jacket. After struggling for what seems to be an eternity, the small pill falls to the floor. I quickly grab it with my teeth and swallow, hoping at least to mask the pain that may soon follow.

I'm immediately affected by the gas when I take in a deep breath, falling limp into a state of hypnotic slumber. I briefly experience a moment of sleep psychosis and surrender my mind to a string of nightmares as I'm pulled into a dark, deep torment.

It's not until the drug begins to kick in that I struggle to combat the riddling terrors, and if they do not stop soon, I'm afraid I'm going to die. Gradually, the tormenting images of demonized beasts feeding on dead children and wingless angels falling to the earth dissolve and fade to a black canvas of emptiness.

What seems like an eternity has only been minutes of subdued pain as I'm taken to a new state of unconsciousness. Thoughts and memories that have been kept tucked away in my brain resurface, but the images before me are only just that—memories that haven't been forgotten.

I tilt my head up and peer through the tiny slit of my eyes as bright lights instantly blur my vision. *Have I met my*

Maker? I ask myself, as I see my mother reach out to me through my warped hallucination. I cry out to her, but she does not respond—she just reaches for my hand, grasping into thin air. Out from my body a little girl appears and grabs her and walks away. I see myself emerge from my own body as a young child, walking out in a field of flowers alongside my mother, a memory I've kept with me to com- fort my pain on the dreariest of days.

The image fades and another materializes before me, but this time it's too recent a memory that I wish not to remember, yet the drugs are forcing me to anyway. I see Jacob and Myra sitting down at the table during our first dinner date, smiling and laughing. My hands and feet begin to tingle as the drug slowly wears off. There's a growing reassurance that my spirit is still connected to my body, as blood rushes back into my veins untainted with those sedating toxins.

Reality begins to emerge and my mind resurfaces to the world I know. I wake up to find myself in another room, in a real nightmare, and all alone. Everything in this space is in pristine order, and no trace of neglect exists but that of a person with OCD.

I see my weapons sitting on a bar top to the left and a large leather couch to my right. I search the walls, ceiling, and corners, but I see no cameras, which leads me to believe that whatever goes on in this room is strictly private.

My hands and feet are bound to a metal chair, and there is no way of sliding the cuffs from the legs or back brace of the chair. I look down to see my jacket undone, and I shudder at the thought of my virtuous body being spoiled by any man who should violate my innocence and take advantage of my helpless state under such heavy sedation.

I try to stretch forward and slide my petite hands out of the cuffs, but the steel rings are closed too tight. I lean over to the side just enough to get a glimpse of my cuffed ankles. The braced bars on the chair leg keeps me from sliding the cuffs off the bottom, so I slam down the cuffs hard against the braces, trying to break through. After several attempts, my ankles painfully weaken, but I do have success in breaking through most of the welds from the metal bar.

I can still feel a slight snag where the cuffs are hanging on a small barb of welded steel. Although my ankles are badly bruised, and my boots are probably filling up with blood, I continue to try to free my legs from the chair. I raise my knees once more, slamming down as hard as I can through the steel supports. The sheer force of the cuffs crashing against the metal finally breaks the support bars from the legs, but the cuffs are now stuck between them. Suddenly, the door flings open and standing there with an ominous grin is General Iakov.

I quickly pull my head back against the chair and return his menacing smirk with dead calm and a cold dreadful stare.

My stomach churns with every step he takes toward me. The natural scowl on his haggard face keeps his permanent wrinkles from flexing, giving him one emotion—anger. And the thought of this repulsive man smiling would only deform his stretched skin, creating a face of a goblin.

"So, this is our Black Death they speak of," he says while he fixes himself a drink at the bar. "A vixen of venom spreading terror among my men."

Avoiding eye contact, I look toward the door while he slings back a shot of vodka. He walks over to the table where my weapons sit and picks up my scorpion dagger. "Such crude weapons for a talented marksman," he says.

"I thought you would be much taller," I say in Russian. He immediately drops the dagger with extreme prejudice, as I have purposefully emasculated his stature.

"Yes, and I thought you would be much smarter, especially a fine specimen like yourself who seems to have abandoned her comrades," he says while pouring another drink.

"The only thing I've abandoned is the will to die."

"Hard to survive when you're bound to a chair and surrounded by men who want nothing better than to see you bleed to death," he cackles. His laughter makes me shudder with disgust as the vile shrill crawls up my skin.

"I've seen enough blood from your men; some of it is on my boots," I retort.

"Enough!" he shouts, throwing his glass toward my chair and breaking it. "Your reverence for my men may be lacking, but you will show respect in here."

"Don't you talk to me about respect. It's the lack of it that got your men killed."

"I admire your confidence, but your pride will be the death of you. Alluring or not, it's your skills that I seek. Soon, you will succumb to our program and be one of us," he says.

"Then you'll have to kill me."

He strokes the back of my hair with his cracked hand. "If I wanted you dead, I would have done it already, but why waste death on such a fine killing machine," he says, sliding his hand down my chest and over my breasts. "There are always medical persuasions, and the alternative would just be pointless."

All I can think about is what form of psychosurgical terror awaits me. The vile stench of his warm breath on the back of my neck reeks of wretched evil, and even the darkest of demons that scurry along the Earth are not as revolting as this man. As he licks my cheek, I recoil in disgust. "The taste of honey spoils my tongue," he foully says.

"Shouldn't you be reporting to your . . . *Head* of State, or has he *lost his mind* too?" Iakov smiles with disgust, but it's the crude laughter beneath his breath that shares a disposition of equal respect.

"You did us a favor. Kriel was weak, and had no business leading this regime. Only a fool would follow."

"He led you," I simply say. I think I've just reaped the attention I was looking for now, because the permanent wrinkles on his already gnarled face has suddenly multiplied.

"Nations are not built at the front to which a leader is given. They are won behind the lines where a leader is born."

If the killing of his men didn't question his abilities, I'm sure to have emasculated his leadership now.

"Kriel was the least of your worries," he continues.

"You're no better than him—"

"He was careless! And it got him killed. I don't suspect we'll make that same mistake here."

"What makes you so confident?"

"I'm not an American."

"Yet he's still dead, and I—"

"You didn't do anything that would have soon been done."

"Yes, but by a fifteen year old girl?"

"Oh, I applaud your effort, but it won't garner you any favor here."

He walks back over to the bar, pulls out two shot glasses, and pours vodka in both. I quickly tuck my knees back and try to push down on the support bars one more time with the heels of my boots, but the cuffs only move slightly; they are still wedged when he turns back around.

"The least you can do is have a drink with me. It will make the pain tolerable," he says, unzipping his pants.

"Pain, I can tolerate. It's your uninviting nature that I will take wrath with."

He shoves the glass to my pressed lips, but I resist, so he pinches my nose until I open my jaw. I can hold my breath no longer, and I surrender as the liquor slides in down my throat.

I sit there struggling to hold the vodka burning in my mouth while he shoots his down. I wait until he's finished swallowing before I vehemently spit the mouthful of liquor in his face. He reacts with extreme rage, pulling back his hand, and violently sweeping it across my face, bloodying my nose.

He grabs the sides of my jaw with his gnarled hand. "I'm going to break that virgin body of yours whether you like it or not." He leans into me, puts both hands on the sides of the chair, and looks into my eyes while I stare back at him, laughing.

"Is it laughter that rejects the truth?" he irately asks, slapping me across the face again.

My laughter quickly turns to silence. "No, but you're going to die today."

He gently grabs my throat and leans me back, as I'm balanced on two chair legs now. "I'm going to thoroughly enjoy your young body ravished, spoiled, and bled."

I push down my boots as hard as I can, trying to free my cuffs, but they are still stuck. He grabs my breasts and fondles my skin with his course, gnarled hands as I try once more pushing down using all the energy I have left in me.

A snap of the chain whips toward my ankles, releasing me from the chair legs. The anxiously awaited freedom releases a surge of anger as I furiously thrust my boot into his crotch with unforgiving rage.

He quickly grabs my leg and looks down to see my broken cuffs. "You tricky little bitch. Unfortunate for you, I've got balls of steel," he says, pointing to his padded uniform. I stretch my right hand and extend my fingers toward the left cuff where the remote is attached for the retracting blade in my boot.

"We Russians are full of surprises," he says, smiling.

I stretch out, almost pulling my arm out of its socket, and press the remote under the cuff. Out pushes the blade from my boot and into his tender skin. "Surprise," I say, as his smile quickly flattens.

I slowly pull the blade out from his testicles, as blood pours from his crotch and onto my boot. He immediately falls to the floor, screaming expletives while trying to grab my other leg. I swing the side of my boot into his face, striking him down with a hard blow as I jump my free legs onto the chair. I pull my legs over the back of the chair and over my cuffed hands where I now stand behind the chair, swinging it toward him, knocking him out cold.

I grab the keys hanging from his belt, and race to find the right one to unlock the cuffs. A small scuffle breaches just outside the room and the door handle slowly turns. I quickly find the key and un-cuff my hands just as two men with guns walk through.

"What the hell . . ."

I throw the chair in their direction, knocking the first man in the face and tripping the soldier behind him. I race toward the table for my weapons, and just as the other soldier gets up off the floor with his gun raised at me, I sling a dagger into his eye. I pull the dagger out and plunge the point into the skull of the man I hit with the chair, and like a coconut, it cracks and splits open.

I quickly gather my weapons when out of nowhere sirens scream down the halls. I recognize that hellish shrill from that day when students were sent running the halls at school in a panic. I shove the last knife in my jacket. I look over and see Iakov trying to slowly get up. I push him back to his knees and his head tilts back. I press the dagger firmly against his prickly throat, deciding whether or not to let his pain linger.

"Some men are reborn or remade while others are redeemed, but you have left nothing to offer that would convince me otherwise. Only the Creator can decide your mercy," I say into his ear as his neck bleeds from the sharp blade.

"But I'm not your Maker," I say, sliding the knife across his ragged neck, spilling his blood onto the floor.

Suddenly, a large blast shakes the building, nearly knocking me to the ground. I race out the door and down the hall, searching for the elevator that I came down on, but this place is so large and every corridor looks the same, just as it did in the prison. I continue down the same passage until I pass a large open room encased in glass. There is a sign near the door the reads: *Special Medical Research.* I press my face against the glass wall and see medieval machines waiting to indoctrinate the next helpless victim; I stand there wondering if the next experiment would have been on me.

Through the glass, I notice a blur moving in its reflection. Screaming soldiers are running down the hallway toward me, but I realize they're running from something. I hide around the corner and hear gunfire rapidly popping off round after round. I draw my guns waiting for the soldiers to go through, but not one passes by; in fact, the screaming has stopped and silence has replaced the running pace of the men's boots stomping in rhythm.

I hear the faint sound of shoes scraping the glossy floors and heavy breathing getting louder and louder as the soldier gets closer. I crouch down and prepare to lunge for- ward, but the steps slow to a slothful stagger. Just as a large gun protrudes from the side of the wall, I leap out and swing my elbow across the man's head.

"Gabe! I'm so sorry. I didn't know it was you. Are you okay?" I ask, trying to pull him up off the floor.

"I'm okay, but I have a headache now." He stands up with bended knees, panting and holding his chest.

"Are you sure you're okay? Why are you breathing so hard?"

"Besides being attacked by my sister, I'm a little out of shape. That gun is heavy—the damn pack weighs nearly thirty pounds."

"Where's Finnegan and Harold?"

"They're not far back cleaning up my mess." He dumps the heavy ammo pack on the floor. "Come on, this way. We're not in the clear just yet."

Running through these hospital-like hallways, we twist and turn around corners, jumping over dead bodies until we reach the stairs. We climb to the first floor, and hear gunfire right outside the stairway door, followed by a high-pitched scream.

"Juliana!" shouts Gabe.

"It can't be."

"I know that voice." He rushes out the door, and just around of the corner, a man is pulling Juliana, her legs dragging on the floor through the cylindrical hall.

Gabe races toward her, but he is quickly stalled by gun- fire. Before he takes off around the curved corridor again, I hold him back. "No, don't do it, you have no weapons," I say, persuading him to hold back. Just then, Henry comes racing around the hall behind us panting.

"What the hell are you doing here? I told you to leave," I say angrily.

"Juliana didn't want to leave Gabe behind, and I sure the hell wasn't going to let you do this by yourself." Juliana screams louder.

"Quick, follow Gabe around the corner toward Juliana. I'll cut them off at the other end. Just distract him for me, and let him know you are coming, but don't get too close."

I cut through a common area where another open hallway connects to the other side. I hear them getting closer because Juliana's scream grows louder. I take a quick peek around the corner and recognize the man as the lieutenant who slapped me across the face and split my lip.

I pull my gun up to the side of the wall, anxiously waiting and pray, "please make me accurate." I have only one shot at this without Juliana being harmed. I take one last peek around the corner before pulling the trigger, and just then the man yells out.

Juliana has bitten the lieutenant's arm, and he belligerently strikes her across the face, sending her crashing to the floor. He raises his gun and points toward her limp body when I turn the corner with my gun aiming directly at the side of his skull.

Just before he pulls the trigger, the bullet has already left the chamber of my gun and into the left side of his temple. He stands still for a second before he falls, leaving the clean white walls beside him stained red. By the time I race over to help Juliana, Gabe is already there to meet her.

He pulls her up, and she seems a little dazed. She struggles to stand to her feet and cries, hugging Gabe. "Are you okay?" Gabe asks as he kisses her on the head.

"Finnegan!" she cries out.

"What about Finnegan?" I ask.

She struggles to answer, trying to control her sobbing when she blurts out, "They shot him."

CHAPTER 36

I feel completely detached from the fellowship now as everything seems to be spinning out of control. My heart sinks, and my face pales almost instantly. "Where is he?" I ask.

"We got separated back toward the right wing of the complex. It's my fault, Arena," Henry admits.

"No, it's mine. He was trying to protect me," Juliana says.

"Get her in the Camaro, and get out of here now!" I tell Henry assertively. "And don't stop. You just get her back to the den safely, you hear me?"

Henry carefully helps Juliana to her feet, but she's too emotionally attached to Gabe to let go of him.

"Sweetie, you need to go now," I reiterate.

"What about you?" she asks.

"I'm not leaving here without Finnegan.

Suddenly, Harold bursts through front complex doors shouting, "We need to get out of now! There's still a few troops left on the south side looking for you.

My stomach tightens, and the worry on Juliana's face worsens.

"Go now!" Juliana holds onto to Gabe's hand, refusing to let go.

"I'll bring him back to you . . . I promise," I say trying to reassure her. She finally releases him and walks off with Henry, sobbing.

"What are we going to do?" asks Harold, panicking. "Go get your car, and have it ready at the front gates. We'll meet you there," I press.

I grab Gabe and rush out the side door toward the right wing of the complex. I look around and see absolute devastation; the tower that stood before me earlier has collapsed to the side, breaking through the outer east wall. Dead soldiers are peppered throughout the training grounds while the front gates have been completely blown from their hinges.

Gabe abruptly stops, turns, and stares hopelessly toward the entrance. The Knight rumbles loudly, and races out of the complex. Gabe just stands there, stricken with sadness. I can only hope he will forgive me for my decision, but I know it was the right thing to do.

"Come on, Gabe!"

We sprint to the right side, where the walls are charred and the ground is covered with dead soldiers. There are so many men lying dead, I can't tell if one of them is Finnegan. I call out his name while I desperately search through the tangled bodies, but there's no answer. It's not until we reach the corner of the complex that my hope has finally vanished. Buried behind two large men against the wall protrudes Finnegan's head, but he's not moving.

I rush over and pull the men off while Gabe gingerly holds his head up. Finnegan moans, and the sinking feeling in my stomach excitedly releases. His eyes open wide and he smiles as I caress his f ace.

"Are you okay?" I ask. His leg is bleeding, but he's alive.

"I'll manage."

He holds his wounded leg with a slight wince on his face. Gabe and I help pick him up to his feet, as Harold's car races through the front gates.

"Are you sure you're going to be okay?" Gabe asks.

"I'm fine, just hit in the leg," Finnegan says as he walks delicately.

"Let's go!" Harold yells from the car.

"Wait, my gun," Finnegan says, searching his side.

"I'll get it, just go." I reach back down to pick up his gun next to the wall, but as I turn back around, Finnegan yells out at me. "Arena, watch out!" Finnegan leaps toward me and holds me down as the sound of gunfire rings in the air. I fall to the ground and see blood pouring out of Finnegan's left side. Another gunshot goes off. I turn my head and see Gabe with his gun drawn, hovering over a dead soldier on the ground.

"Finnegan!" I cry out, knowing his wound is bad. I press hard against the opening by his ribs, but the hole is too big for me to stop the rush of blood from pouring out. Gabe rushes over and picks him up while I keep my hand pressed on his wound. Finnegan grimaces and moans and it's all I can do to keep him from stumbling to the ground.

Harold jumps out of the car shouting. "They're coming!"

With all the strength I have left, Gabe and I quickly put him in the back seat of the car.

"Go!" I yell at Harold. The car violently spins around, shoveling sand with the back wheels, while several soldiers barrel around the left wing firing at us. We barely make it through the front gates with a shower of bullets grazing the sides of the car.

"Take us as far as you can and out of sight!" I yell at Harold.

Finnegan's eyes begin to shudder, and his face turns milky white. I grab his cold hands as his head falls limp to the side. I scream out, cursing my own mistake in anguish. "Damn you, damn you! I yell, holding Finnegan's shirt and pressing my cheek against his bloody chest. Though he leans lifeless against the seat, I'm still glued to Finnegan's body, crying uncontrollably with the delusion that he may still be alive.

After we're miles outside the complex, the dark paved road in front of us suddenly brightens and the brim of the horizon flashes with red lights. To evade any more unnecessary entanglements, we immediately detour. My tears finally dry up and we pull off the main road, down into a small, rocky canyon. We sit in the car silently for a moment, and wait until the flashing lights disappear. But all it does is further the agony inside of me while I hold onto my dead uncle.

Time has elapsed, but it feels like it has stopped, along with my will to move. I'm too broken inside to leave him, but I know I must let go. He's dead and there is nothing I can do to change it.

We carry Finnegan down into a small ravine, and lay him beside a small cluster of bushes near some softer ground. There we bury his body in a shallow hole, covered in stones. Harold and Gabe walk back to the car while I stay by the grave, reflecting on my poor choices. I lean my head against the rocks, begging for a merciful end to all of this, but I'm left with a comforting peace in my heart instead. I rub my bloody hand across the white stones and think back to the first time Finnegan taught me about death.

I was eight years old when my dog, Jasper, was hit by a car. I watched him whimper and bleed out until he stopped breathing. I remember standing next to Finnegan while he buried him. The soil was too rocky to dig deep, so we piled up stones like the ones I'm leaning on now. I hovered over Jasper's grave while Finnegan comforted me. He told me that life was temporary, and that it's to be respected and enjoyed. He said to make the best of the gift that was given to me, because none of us really deserved life. It's our thankfulness that sustains us. Never forget your Father. It's by His grace you are here. Those words and that moment have stuck with me forever. I know now that the only thing guaranteed in life is our death. I struggle to lift my body up from the gravestone before I walk back up the rocky incline toward the car.

I grab all my gear from the trunk and walk toward the woods.

"Where are you going?" asks Harold.

"The roads will not be safe anymore. We'll have to travel on foot for now until time permits us the alternative," I say.

"She's right, we'll have to go into hiding for a while," Gabe agrees.

"What about me? What am I supposed to do now?" Harold asks.

"Go live what life you have left in this world," I say.

"That's it? Just like that?"

"I'm sorry."

"No! I'm coming with you," he demands.

"Stop! Look, I have nothing against you; in fact, I thank you for what you have done for us, but if you come with us, we will just bring death upon you. I don't have thestrength to see another innocent friend die. Now go," I say.

"I'm not trying to be a burden, but—"

"Then don't be," I say, interrupting him. "Maybe our paths will cross again someday, but for now, it's just better this way." Gabe runs back toward the car and says something to Harold that I wish not to know. All I can do is just stare into the stony grave where Finnegan lays to rest before I walk away from a moment of discontent.

CHAPTER 37

Soon the cool fall breeze turns to an unforgiving winter frost as the months pass by. We have been well hidden from the world and know nothing of what the nation has gone through since the death of President Kriel and General Iakov. I'm oblivious to what is going on, and I feel strangely comfortable with it.

We've traveled a weary journey into treacherous canyons, around rocky mountain ridges, and through intolerant fields of barrenness while eating on wild game and consuming nature's vast expanse. We've seen no sign of life since we left Harold by the road, until we come upon a flicker of light glowing in the distance.

Down an unmarked road we see an old, weathered pub that stands awkwardly in the middle of nowhere, but it's probably more warm and inviting than the bone-chilling cold air and creatures that wait for us out here. After a dithering conversation with Gabe about whether or not we should take the road, winter's chill decides for us, persuading us to take comfort in the old tavern. We trust no one, but it takes less convincing when traveling in these frigid temperatures.

The building looks like it has seen better days, but the smoke from the chimney quickly dissolves any prejudgment I have and reminds me of the warmth waiting for us inside.

"The Drunken Duck," says Gabe, reading the sign above the door. "Well, this should be a familiarity to a couple of Irish kids."

I push open the door and a reaction of cold silence stretches out toward us—the stares from what looks like mostly working men and a handful of poverty-stricken families huddling next to a fire.

The heat of the flame warms the silence for a moment. "Would you mind if a couple of strangers take refuge in your fine establishment?" I say.

The bartender just smiles and says, "You are welcome to stay, but you are no strangers here."

By some of the awkward stares we receive, I can only imagine the kind of viral rumors that may have been spreading across the nation about Gabe and me, but I'm not convinced they know. It's not until I hear an old woman shouting from the corner of the room that I realize now that some of these people recognize our less than encouraging presence. "*Es el ángel de la muerte!*" she shouts.

"Shhh, hush," the bartender says to her. "You are welcome to stay here as long as you need. Come," he says, gesturing us over by the bar. "Don't listen to that old woman; she's a bit crazy . . . one of our regulars. Come. I have beds upstairs you can take rest in," he says.

"We thank you kindly, sir, and by the way, she's not crazy," I say as I remove the cloak, exposing my weapons and climbing upstairs behind Gabe. Just one glance at the swords attached to my back and the bartender backs up, nearly tripping on himself as he realizes who we are.

"*Te lo dije,*" says the old lady, smiling.

After hours pass during the frigid night, I abruptly awake in a cold sweat, as does Gabe. We both look at each other and know the time has come. We gather our things and head down the stairs to a crowd of people gathered around the television.

People are dancing and cheering as if happy hour never ended. "What's going on?" asks Gabe.

"Come, look. It's over, it's over," the bartender says, smiling. Gabe and I look at the television and see a scrolling ticker at the bottom that says "Breaking News." The news anchor begins another replay of the report:

"If you just tuned in, this morning congressional leaders issued a statement earlier that President Kriel has been hospital-

ized, and is in critical condition from an unfortunate stroke. The status of his mental health is uncertain, but it has been reported by some doctors that he may never be able to function normally again. As the President's health deteriorates, administrators scramble to advise a new strategy for future plans regarding the countries new reorganization policy. As the government struggles to find new leadership to take over the new order, the nation's current policies and federal legal battles with military controlled regions seems to be in limbo and at a standstill. There has been no further word on the country's direction at this time."

These people haven't a clue that this artificial story has been conjured up by this administration in an attempt to gain sympathy for the government. But why would they play it now—or even at all? It's been two months since his death, and this is the first we are to hear about it? What purpose does this serve to benefit the administration now?

"These people are all going to die!" Gabe shouts to me over the crowd's exuberance. Everybody hushes over Gabe's statement and immediately stops what they are doing.

"Why in the hell would you say that?" asks the bartender, dropping his stein on the floor.

"Because it's true. This war isn't over and it never will be. These lies they feed you on the screen only delay the inevitable. Evil will deceive those who let them."

"How do we know you're not lying?" asks an angry man in the back. I search for his voice until the crowd suddenly parts for this irate man, who comes dangerously close to me. He hastily raises his hand toward me as if he's about to swing, but I quickly point my gun to his face, halting his disconcerted overreaction.

"Don't be fooled by the sting of his tongue lest he smite you with it," I say.

"That snake of a president is dying; it's the only joy we have left," says the bartender.

"That snake is already dead," I say, putting on my cloak.

"And what do you know of this to be true?" asks the gentleman in front of me.

"Because two months ago I took that serpent's head with this very blade," I say, pulling it from its sheath.

Gasps fill the stuffy air inside the tavern as the smiles and laughter quickly disappear. "You have not seen what evil can do. The world you live in now will change forever, and the only thing that will keep you from surrendering to its lies is your faith; nothing else will matter."

"But it's over now, this administration will soon die," says the bartender.

"Over?" I ask. "Nothing will ever be over until history ceases to exist. What is it that you seek in life? Does it have purpose, or is it merely a mirage that ignores the truth? Most of us think we control our own destiny, when in fact our fate has already been chosen for us. The question remains—are you willing to accept a life of eternal salvation, or eternal damnation? It's your choice, not theirs, because in the end, death becomes us all. Over? This is far from over."

I pull the shaded black hood over my head, and I look at them in pity as I walk out the door. I may not fully comprehend the choices people make, but I must leave them to decide for themselves. Some days, I feel my own convictions being threatened, but today they have not strayed. I don't know what will happen to these poor people, but I'm convinced the grimmest days will soon be upon them. My heart is broken for them, and it weighs on me to address these poor souls one last time before I leave. "May God have mercy on you all."

We leave this place like many others across the nation that will fall into deceit and wither away, but Gabe and I know the truth—this is just the beginning.

331

THE END